TRUE
TRUE

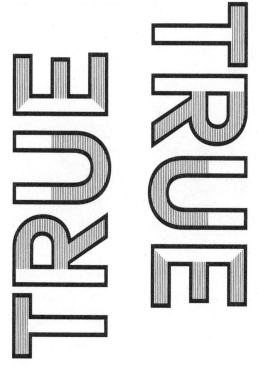

DON P. HOOPER

Nancy Paulsen Books

Nancy Paulsen Books
An imprint of Penguin Random House LLC, New York

First published in the United States of America by Nancy Paulsen Books,
an imprint of Penguin Random House LLC, 2023

Visit us online at PenguinRandomHouse.com.

Library of Congress Cataloging-in-Publication Data
Names: Hooper, Don P., author.
Title: True true / Don P. Hooper.
Description: New York: Nancy Paulsen Books, [2023] | Summary: When Gil, a Black
teen from Brooklyn, struggles to fit in at his primarily white Manhattan prep school,
he wages a clandestine war against the racist administration, parents, and students,
while working with other Black students to ensure their voices are finally heard.
Identifiers: LCCN 2022052481 (print) | LCCN 2022052482 (ebook) |
ISBN 9780593462102 (hardcover) | ISBN 9780593462119 (ebook)
Subjects: CYAC: Preparatory schools—Fiction. | Schools—Fiction. |
Racism—Fiction. | Jamaican Americans—Fiction. | African Americans—Fiction. |
New York (N.Y.)—Fiction.
Classification: LCC PZ7.1.H6554 Tr 2023 (print) | LCC PZ7.1.H6554 (ebook) |
DDC [Fic]—dc23
LC record available at https://lccn.loc.gov/2022052481
LC ebook record available at https://lccn.loc.gov/2022052482

Printed in the United States of America

ISBN 9780593462102
1st Printing

LSCH

Edited by Stacey Barney | Design by Eileen Savage
Text set in Adobe Caslon Pro

For those who have been pushed under a lens and been made to think your stories weren't worth sharing. Your voice matters.

TRUE
TRUE

PART I
Laying Plans

War is a matter of vital importance . . .
The province of life or death; the road to
survival or ruin.

SUN TZU: *THE ART OF WAR*

1

I'm leaving Brooklyn.

I'm not moving or anything. Just going away. *Stop. Don't think about that.* This is my last night out with my friends. Summer is over. And there's one last party every Caribbean in Brooklyn is at. J'ouvert.

Well, maybe *every* Caribbean is an exaggeration. But everyone wanting to party from nighttime straight through sunrise.

The night sky is a mix of powdery smoke and mist. The freshly paved asphalt reflects the light rain like a field of diamonds. Silhouettes move to the rhythm of steel drums. Shoulders bounce and hips sway in harmony with the beat, while paint and powder fly. I can't make out faces. All I see are horned crowns, braids, flowing locks, and every Caribbean flag waving in unity. The Fourth of July has nothing on this. This is a celebration. Right now, here, we are truly free.

A few people wear heavy steel chains, some of which drag on the street. Two shirtless men, who must've done a million pull-ups, are covered in molasses from head to toe. Others push carts with barrels full of paint up the street, splashing the crowd, a reminder of the freed slaves in the Caribbean who mocked the slave owners after emancipation. This is the Jab Jab.

I dodge the spatter, but then a hand reaches out and grabs my shoulder, holding me in place while someone else pours paint over my head from a repurposed water bottle.

"Gotcha!"

I don't have to open my eyes to know the culprits. Rej grabbed. Stretch poured.

Rej has always been the initiator in our trio, friends since meeting each other in third grade at the Always Persevere Dojo. He's the shortest of us, has dreads still trying to reach his neck, and an undercut fade. The Haitian flag is draped around his shoulders and a painting of Dessalines is on his chest like a Superman *S*. But anybody spotting Rej sees the way he carries himself before anything else. He walks with an air of regality. When my dad was home, every time Rej came by, Dad would jokingly ask, "Prince Akeem, weh di rose bearers at?" Dad loves his movie references; *Coming to America* was a top-ten Friday-night fav.

"Woy mezanmi," Rej says, throwing his hands up like I'm being a fool for wanting to stay clean. He was born in Haiti and knows Creole even though he moved to Brooklyn before he could speak. His dad was taken by ICE last year, then lumped into a mass deportation in March. Home of the free? Yeah, right. They're undocumented immigrants like my dad, except

Rej didn't have a choice at his age. "Dis man was really tryin to stay clean at J'ouvert." It's good to see him laughing, even if my clothes paid the price.

"Rockin the polo too," Stretch says. He's got the evil smirk on, dripping disdain. The streetlamp catches his tilted head, bronze skin, slightly darker from spending the last two weeks with his folks in Trinidad. His high fade highlights the textured curls with the bleached tips rising inches above his head. "Gotta. Loosen. Up." Loose is Stretch all day. Some people have zero chill, Stretch is chill twenty-four seven.

I look down. My crisp white polo shirt is covered in blue paint. Dammit. "My granma got me this shirt," I say with the straightest face I can hold.

She didn't.

I needed to upgrade my wardrobe before senior year, so I got a summer job at the supermarket. But I want my friends to feel bad, so I drop the guilt-trip lie 'cause nothing commands respect like Granma's name. All my friends grew up eating her cooking: oxtail, curry goat, stew peas. Somebody caught a whiff of food when Granma was throwing down, there'd be a line up the block and past the corner store for a plate.

"Aww, did we mess up Granma's shirt?" Stretch mocks, flashing a fraction of teeth surrounded by a pencil-thin goatee that's barely connected.

I should've known. Give Stretch two Heinekens and a Shandy Carib and he transforms into the most patronizing clown on the block.

"My fault, man," Rej tags in without cracking a hint of a

smile, locked in this wrestling match of sarcasm. "I shoulda told Granma not to let you come out dressin up in your Sundays for Carnival. That's my fault." He slams his hand on his chest twice to emphasize it, dragging out his words. "Myyy fault."

Before I can come up with a clever reply, a girl jumps in front of me, pushes her back up against my chest, wraps her hand around my thigh, and starts to wine to the music. It's Nakia. She's wearing a bikini top designed like a Bajan flag and khaki shorts that are covered in molasses and paint. I feel her round hips pressed against me, urging me forward. *I love Carnival.* She's blowing her whistle as we dance. In less than a minute she hops off my body, waving her flag, whirling with one leg in the air.

"You gonna miss me when you go away, city boy?" Nakia asks, her eyes locked on me.

When I worked at the Associated on Church Ave, she would pop in every Thursday and spark conversation. We'd hang outside during my break. She liked the Flamin Hot cheese puffs. I did too. We both dug getting to the bottom of the bag and scooping out the last bit of seasoning with our fingers. It turned to mild flirting. She'd run her hand against the nape of my neck; I'd gently touch her twists. Then she got a job at Associated too.

Nothing ever came of it. Too much on my mind with Granma's health and Dad's status. This year hasn't been easy.

"I'm not going anywhere," I say, failing at speaking up, like every time I didn't ask her out during the summer. If this were Rej, he'd just go for it, perpetually in boss mode. He wanted to produce music, so he made it happen. Stretch vibes like he's floating on a hoverboard across a beach, drink in hand, wherever he goes. Can't tell him nothing.

Nakia leans in. "Oh no, you fancy now," she says, her hand on my cheek, sending a warm shiver through every point in my body. The muscles in my face twist and distort, wanting to conceal the bright smile trying to bust out. "Leaving Brooklyn 'cause you big-time."

"Yup." Stretch slams his arm over my shoulder, his tall wiry frame casting a shadow like one of the streetlamps. "Our boy super fancy. You seen this fresh white polo his granma got him?" He flicks my collar. "And the shorts. Ooh, he's gonna be upset you got paint all over—"

I elbow Stretch in his gut. He has terrible timing. "Ima still be in Brooklyn. We can hang."

Before Nakia can respond, a young girl about seven years my junior with two neck-length French braids and the skin tone of a Caribbean beach cuts between us.

"Big bro!" she says, extending her hand with a glittering smile. It's Kenya from our dojo. I still remember when she first signed up—small, stocky, and unsure of herself. Her parents hoped that martial arts would give her confidence. Now she's like lil sis and I'm big bro. We exchange Always Persevere's trademark handshake, ending with a salute, before she gives me the warmest hug. Then she greets Rej and Stretch.

"What're you doing out here?" I ask.

"I'm with my sister," Kenya says, pointing. I look over and see Nakia off to the side, chatting it up with her friends, giggling. And it dawns on me. The girl I been failing at flirting with is Kenya's actual big sister.

Nakia walks over and wraps her arms around Kenya. "Gimme a call," Nakia says to me.

"I don't have your number," I reply.

"Next time ask. Don't wait till you moving to the city."

"Wait, you're moving?" Kenya asks, confused. "You're gonna be at my belt test on Wednesday, right?" Her expression could break me down with guilt if I didn't.

"Course I am," I say, but Nakia is already dragging her off. "And I'm not moving," I mutter, defeated, as they disappear.

"Daaamn, you don't have the number." Stretch lets out a gusty sigh. "That's an *L*."

Rej shakes his head. "What I tell you, man?" he says. Rej's got a deep voice with a lingering rasp that's twenty years and a few cigarette cartons older than his age, even though he's never smoked a cigarette before. Weed, yes. Cigarettes, a big no.

"I dunno." I roll my eyes, humoring him, knowing what he'll say. "What'd you tell me?"

"My guy! I told you she was into you."

"You think everybody into me or you or somebody."

"I mean, that's reality." Rej presses his hands together like he's praying and conducts class, street professor extraordinaire. Here it goes.

"Somebody is gonna be into you or me or somebody," he says. "This particular gem was into you. I mean, who goes to the supermarket to wait in line to buy one soda? You go to the corner store for that. Supermarket is for groceries. You're leaving with bags, a cart, you know, mad stuff. The corner store, bodega, dem's for single-item purchases. One soda, bag a chips, maybe two sticky buns or a sandwich. Not one a dem gentrified sandwiches either. A real one."

"I ain't hear nothin but facts," Stretch cosigns. "Plus she went and got a job there too. So yeah, you dropped the bag on that." Then he starts laughing before snapping again. "And if y'all get married, Kenya will be your literal little sister."

I got nothing. That's my boy, but I hate when he's right.

"Hol up, man," Rej says as we pass by a corner store on Nostrand. It's just before dawn, so the door is locked. But you can still buy things through the walk-up window made of bulletproof glass. "Lemme grab some waters." A sly smile coats his face as he pulls out his phone. "But first, one time for the people. Need to capture my boy before he goes off to college."

"You a fool, yo." I say. "We both seniors." And it's the worst time to transfer into a new school, like pressing reset after finishing 75 percent of a test you didn't wanna take. And this school, Augustin Prep, it's a reset fareal. Not only have I always gone to school with Rej and Stretch, but the students, the teachers, they've always primarily been Black and Latinx.

This new school. It's anything but that.

"Except you goin private on us," Rej says.

I didn't want to. Not initially at least. But I spent three years fighting with my school's administration, and my middle school before that. Arguing for more resources for the science department. Freaking working lights and enough seats in all classes. Emailing the district, writing letters to the DOE, going with Dad to school council meetings. Everyone knows New York got money. Where the resources going? *Not to us.* Occasionally, a nonprofit would kick in to do some after-school program. Then they'd disappear. Education should be free. *It's not.*

Augustin's pitch is that it molds the future business leaders, lawyers, and politicians of America. And now, with their expanded robotics program—the future engineers too. So no more arguing with the public school admins trying to get resources.

That's why I transferred.

But the photo of Augustin. Phew. They're as white as they get. Like horror-movie. Small-town. White. Finding a Black or Brown person in their brochures or on their website is a straight-up game of Where's Waldo. But I gotta do this. My family needs a win. *I need to win.*

Rej hands the phone off to Stretch, who's got the longest arms. It makes Stretch annoying to spar with, but the best at taking group selfies. Rej reviews the pics as if he's a teacher red-lining a paper. "Nah, nah." He shakes his head. "They good, but I need something for the story."

Producing music isn't just a hobby for Rej. It's his life. Converted his closet into a booth to start working with artists. As an independent producer he's looking for that one shot. Going to Augustin will set me up to make connections that'll help his dream too.

He presses record and goes into action. "Yo, this is your boy Rej, aka TheR1, King a Flatbush. Out here at J'ouvert with my man Stretch and Gil." He grabs me into frame, hugging my neck close enough to choke, embarrassment creeping through my dark brown skin. "He got a little paint on his white shirt, but that's how it be. Learned a lesson." He lets me go. "You come to J'ouvert, you come to party. The sun ain't rise yet and we not goin home. N'AP BOULE." A few quick taps on his phone and the story's out to his ten thousand plus followers. He tucks his phone away and knocks on the walk-up window.

"You betta introduce me to some of them international women, son," Stretch says.

My eyes roll. "Look around you. We Caribbean. We are international, fool."

"You know what I mean," he says, sucking his teeth.

Augustin Prep is on the Upper West Side. It's an hour away by train, but a world away from BK and my crew. But I keep telling myself no more fighting for resources. I toured their lab. Everything is right there. Enough for multiple schools. So after taking their special test and interviews, off I go.

"Jokes aside, it's dope what you doin," Stretch says. "Robotics competitions. Phew. That's some next level."

"Different borough though," Rej adds solemnly. He scrunches his face as if he's swallowed his own bile. "City ain't Brooklyn, man. Won't know anybody." His eyebrows hang like this is a funeral fareal. "Who gonna have ya back if shit go sideways?" The laughter has faded, leaving only concern. Rej has always had my back. That's what we do. He and Stretch are more than friends, they're brothers. Another reminder. This transfer isn't just about me.

"Y'all actin like I'm leavin the country," I snap. This whole idea of me leaving like I'm moving off planet got me aggy as hell. "It's a new school. That's it." At least it's what I keep telling myself. Trying not to envision myself becoming a Waldo buried in the prep crowd. "And yo, what Stretch said is the truth. Gonna be nice to actually have a STEM department."

A group of police walk by, two white cops, one Black. One of the white cops has his baton out, looking ready to make use of it. Whenever cops are on patrol, you know the deal. Slavery never really ended. The one with the baton says, "Let's keep it moving, fellas."

"Just buying water, sir," Rej replies.

"What'd you say, boy?" the cop asks. "Turn around and address me."

My lungs stutter. The word *boy* used by a cop is as historically loaded as his sidearm. We all do martial arts, but none of that means a damn thing against a cop with a gun. Mom is always worried about me going out for J'ouvert because of the cops. Always gives me a list of things I shouldn't do or shouldn't wear, comparing life here to Jamaica, because *here* police kill unarmed Black people systemically. You need a manual just to stay alive.

When the cops see us, they don't see humans. They don't see people who have lived in and built this community. When I walk down Flatbush by the roti shops, the boutique fashion dealers, and the Caribbean grocers, I know the parents, the kids, the aunts, the uncles. I know the butcher who cuts up our oxtail by his first name: Michael. The streets may have changed with all the gentrification. But this is my home. Nobody's ever gonna make me feel like an outsider.

Rej turns around giving the smile that says *I know you're messing with me and I'll play this game if I have to.* He moves deliberately so nobody can say he was holding a weapon he doesn't have. "Just getting water, Officer," Rej reiterates. "It's hot. Don't want my friends passing out from dehydration." I can't tell if he's trying to be patronizing or polite. That's Rej's style. I prepare myself. Anything can happen. "Y'all should get water too, y'all lookin real thirsty." That answers that. Black cop looks down and away, getting Rej's not-too-subtle knock.

"Okay," the officer replies, "no loitering." He points his baton at each of us. "You don't want to get into trouble—or pass out."

I know a threat when one is waved with a baton. We nod, mouths shut, waiting for them to leave. They do. My chest finally releases the clamped air that was ready to burst out.

"Freakin cops," Stretch says. "You see how they try to instigate, right?"

I nod. "They really getting paid overtime to be assholes."

"Fareal, man," Rej cosigns. "Anything we do or say they gonna switch up like we were resisting arrest or pullin a weapon."

"That's how they got Byrd."

His real name was Marvin, but to the streets he was always Byrd. He was fourteen. If you heard a clarinet that could bring sunshine to a storm, that was Byrd. Night or day, he could be walking up Foster Ave by the projects, playing some beautiful melody, bringing joy to everyone he touched. The cops killed Byrd right over on Foster Ave by Vanderveer. They call it Flatbush Gardens now. Never got picked up by the news. But if you from the neighborhood, you know the deal. He was never armed with anything more than his love for music. My dad brought me along to the protest. It was my first one.

"True," I say. "Took him out for loving music."

Our nerves relax like we dodged a speeding truck. Another cop, another day, another time, and that small encounter could've gone much different.

Rej turns back to the store and passes money through the

revolving window. Three waters and a pack of rolling papers come back. Rej hands out the bottles and we post up in front of the corner store taking in the sounds of J'ouvert. Floats with steel drums and massive sound systems explode through the streets ready for sunrise.

Rej shows us his phone. "Already over a hun'ed views. People are UP. I love J'ouvert."

"Hell yeah," I say, happy for the change of subject. "Let's get back into the Jab Jab."

Rej laughs. "C'mon."

We fill up our empty water bottles with paint from a nearby cart. I'm already soaked. Might as well go all the way.

We spend the next hour parading through the streets. Throwing paint, dancing, having fun. The air horns grow all around us. Soca and reggae vibes everywhere, fetes converging onto Empire Boulevard to mash up the parkway and play mas.

The sun is rising over Brooklyn. This isn't a going-away party—this is a *who-I-am* party. I may be switching schools. But this is my home, my world. I ain't *leaving*.

2

A scream startles me out of a restless sleep. The wailing cry through the thin postwar apartment wall louder than any alarm.

"No! No! No!"

I jump out of bed, toppling over my sheets to stand. I pull at the door, which fights back. I'm still barely awake. But I know that voice. In agony.

Granma.

The doorknob finally does me the kindness of opening. Granma's room is right next to mine. I don't knock. I nearly bust down the door to get in. Adrenaline threatens to blast my heart right from its chamber. And then I see her. Sitting up in her bed, watching the morning news, ready to throw the remote control at the TV.

"Cyaan believe dis idiot," she says. She turns to me, loose strands of untwisted gray hair waving as if a wind caught it. Seeing her narrow eyelids widen like that—it's like looking into Dad's eyes. "Yuh all right, GC?" she asks me as if I was the one crying out.

"I heard you . . . I was just checking that you were . . . Morning, Granma," I say, finally settling on a response, putting on a makeshift smile. Ever since she was first diagnosed with dementia, when me and my parents were still trying to make sense of it all, Granma told us to never make her feel like she was any less than the person we love. She's in a between stage, the doctor said. Got control of her thoughts for the most part. But certain things are complicated. Numbers. Dates. Memories. Locations.

"Dis fool right here." Granma sucks her teeth, slamming the bed. "Killian really out fi mash up di schools. Him wann cut all a di budget. Talkin bout infrastructure. And now dem sayin him ahead in di polls. Tankful dis a yuh last year a high school, 'cause if him take office . . . Lawd Jesus save us."

Every day it feels like I'm losing a little more of her. Sometimes I listen at the wall to her morning prayers. Gives me a sense of how she's doing—if she's coherent. It sucks. When I close my eyes, I picture Granma moving, dancing, living life to the fullest. But that vision is fading.

"Breakfast, bighead!"

My cousin Renee stomps in, fit from a lifetime of martial arts. She's wearing a BLACK GIRL MAGIC tee her girlfriend designed and lounge shorts. The tiny curls on her head dyed red complement her beige skin. She's in her second year at NYU, didn't have classes today, so she stayed the night. Renee's been around more since Granma got diagnosed, always dropping off something new for me to read: Maya Angelou, Toni Morrison, some philosophy books. If she reads it in college, it's ending up here next. I think she wants to keep me busy so I don't get too caught up in my head thinking about Granma or Dad.

"C'mon, cuz, Auntie got a feast for you." She claps me to attention like a military bugle. Wednesday mornings shouldn't feel this urgent.

"Oh word," I say. My head's pounding from springing out of bed. I tend to get migraines from lack of sleep or just stressin. Gonna have to drink some tea so my first day at Augustin doesn't start with a headache. "I'll be out in a minute."

I head into my room, take a sip of water from the cup next to my bed. Then wipe the sleep from my eyes. Nobody in the history of the world has ever looked forward to the first day of classes. Me included. And my day is starting over an hour earlier 'cause I gotta go into the city. *Relax. It's a new beginning.*

Staring at me is a futuristic view of the Brooklyn Bridge with my favorite martial artists, Bruce Lee and Jim Kelly, on one side and B.I.G. and Audre Lorde on the other. Next to them is a Jamaican flag. I'm second generation, but I rep hard. They all remind me of the perseverance needed to succeed in martial arts and in life. Renee's girlfriend painted it for me almost two years ago, a gift on my sixteenth birthday. Life was simpler, not filled with so many fading memories.

Doctors can't help Granma's condition. But the disease can't take away her defiance. She told the doctors she wouldn't give in to the disease. She doesn't take nothing from nobody. I got art of heroes on my wall. I got a real-life hero on the other side of it. So I'm doubling down on STEM as if this commitment is a contract that helps her live long enough for me to help find a cure. 'Cause the scientists today ain't cutting it.

It's crazy. But I need hope.

Directly below the painting is a yellowing flyer for a robotics competition. Next to that is the first robot I ever built. It's assembled like LEGOs, and looks like a Transformer with tank wheels. Maybe it's bootleg compared to Augustin's robotics lab, but I still love it. A gift from Granma on my eighth birthday. Me and Dad put it together. I was so little then. His broad shoulders would hug me close to his belly that rolled with every laugh, before dropping some random movie reference from *The Matrix* or *Black Belt Jones*.

Today should be a milestone like this robot, but all I feel is the distance between us.

Dad chose to go back to Jamaica to get his immigration papers shortly after Rej's dad was deported. ICE been going hard at Black and Brown families. He could've waited till after I went to college, been here with me today. But no. He had to get it sorted ASAP 'cause if he gets deported, then there's no way he can come back into the country for five to ten years. So I get it. *I don't.*

I walk down the hallway, past my parents' room, then the living room. Scents of ackee and salt fish, sweet plantain, mannish water, and escovitch fish guide me to the kitchen.

"Morning, Gil," Mom greets me. Her full face and pearl eyes are tucked behind stylish glasses. She has an expectant smile, her cheeks a deeper brown than Dad's and mine. There was a time when I always gave her a hug and kiss in the morning. I don't know when it stopped. Maybe it was after last summer's growth spurt. I tower over her now like Stretch looms above Rej. Instead of giving her a kiss, I adjust the purple bonnet rising halfway off the back of her head as if it were trying to escape in the night. I could hear her fitful sleep through the walls. Rest hasn't been easy in this house.

Mom lights a paper towel from the fire under the plantain and draws it over to the other range so that it catches, then immediately puts it out, the remnants of sulfuric ash dwindling in the air. The stove is just one of the things that didn't get fixed or replaced when the bills started piling up. Can't rely on the landlord to do it. Not in this building.

"Morning," I say to a room that feels empty without Dad's boisterous laugh and corny jokes. He'd probably be singing some song right now about the plantain, and we'd have to wonder if it was real or if he made it up on the spot.

I look at my phone. My last one was a relic, the free cell that came on the family plan. Renee may give me a hard time, but cuz is deshi at the dojo and big sis outside, always looking out. She gifted me her old phone since she got an upgrade. Now it's like I've stepped forward in time. The pic of me, Rej, and Stretch at J'ouvert with our flag colors is set as the background, beaming like a Caribbean Justice League. Superpowered friends that I'm leaving behind for engineering opportunities at this private school. *This white school.*

No missed calls. *Figures.* Only a reminder I got testing at the dojo at 5:00 p.m.

"Did anyone call?" Mom and Renee look at each other, shaking their heads in unison.

"Eh, cuz, cheer up," Renee sings, trying to invigorate the morning. "You become a prep student today," she says mockingly.

I roll my eyes. She's getting some sadistic pleasure out of seeing me attend a prep school like she did. "Don't you got somewhere to be?" I ask. "You know, like your dorm, your folks' place, anywhere but here—"

An elbow buries itself deep in my stomach reminding me who's big cuz and who actually enjoys doing burpees. "Aww, Auntie, I think Gil is choking up with excitement to be an Augustin Tiger," she says, fakin like she all nice. Meanwhile, I'm massaging my stomach from her strike when I hear the toilet flush. "Oh, before I forget," she says, sarcasm dancing on each syllable, "you got a visitor." I know it couldn't be Dad, but for a moment there's a glimmer in my heart, that feeling of expectation before opening a gift, the culmination of weeks of hints leading up to the holiday.

"Hey, Gil!" The squeaky voice crushes hope. Coming out of the bathroom is Mr. Neckles, the only person I know who can still look dusty in a suit, despite perfect posture. Maybe that's his whole wardrobe—a row of navy and gray suits with pastel button-downs. He's got a wide guffaw grin that could make a chipmunk jealous. It's befitting his acorn-complexioned face, speckled with tiny pockets that never quite recovered from pimple-popping puberty. He fixes his pants, which he should've done in the bathroom. Acting like he live here.

I suck my teeth. Only Renee notices.

I hate when Mr. Neckles shows up. He's Dad's friend. They met when they were teenagers and have been friends since. I don't see how. Dad is unapologetic about his Jamaican heritage. Mr.

Neckles makes nothing but apologies for his heritage. Starting with his first name, which is really Shareef. But he goes by Allen.

"Seeing as some of my co-workers are Augustin alum and have kids there," Allen says, "figured I'd pick you up a gift for your first day." He reaches into his Tumi bag and hands me a box. I already know what's in it by the rectangular shape. The gift every kid hates, right up there with socks. I open it and see a striped gray tie. "Clothes make the man." There's an eager sparkle in his eye that's probably never seen a down moment.

Stop tryin to make me into you. "Thanks," I say, barely masking a groan.

"Oh, it looks lovely," Mom says. "My son, the biochemist."

I went to one career day, mentioned biochemistry, and I've already got my PhD in Mom's mind. But if that's what I need to make a difference, I'll get it.

"Well, I better be taking off," Mr. Neckles says. He picks up a cup of mannish water he'd been working on and finishes it with a loud gulp. "I always like to get in a solid hour before my managers. Once they arrive, all the conversations change to the stock market, elections, and how elections will affect the market." His head bobs side to side as if these are conversations we relate to. They're not. You got to have money you're willing to lose to invest. That's not us. And as for elections, my mom votes for whichever candidate wants us dead the least.

"Do you think that independent will win?" Mom asks. "The fintech or whatever CEO?"

"Hugh Killian? He's really conservative," Mr. Neckles says. "He just calls himself independent because the city is blue and a conservative candidate can't win."

Mr. Neckles leaves and I go to snatch a piece of fried plantain off a plate on the counter.

"Ow." A spoon knocks my hand.

Granma. She's like a wizard who pops up when you least expect it. I didn't even hear her come out of the bedroom. "Ya haffi wait fi everyone else to eat, Ahmad."

"Ahmad?" I ask, puzzled.

"Sorry. Sorry, GC," she says, shaking away the fog. My parents call me Gil. Granma calls me GC. "Haven't had mi morning tea yet. Yuh juss remind me so much of your uncle."

She's referring to Dad's older brother and her eldest son, Uncle Ahmad. I've seen pictures and sort of see the resemblance. He was a tall, dark-complexioned, lean figure with dreads. He passed before I was born.

"Oh, you did get one message," Mom says brightly, strategically changing the subject. "Vicki texted, wishing you good luck today."

"Vicki?" I ask.

"Oh, sorry, Ms. Rowe." They texting now? "I ran into her when I was out with your aunt," Mom says, referring to Renee's mom. "We had a drink and hit it off."

Wow. Leave it to Mom to befriend my teacher. Ms. Rowe tried to support me and Rej's interest in robotics as best she could at Union, which meant getting us out of Union. Said it also would be a good way to boost our college applications. She talked to Mom, then some connect on Augustin Prep's board of trustees.

During the interviews, the Augustin reps talked about the robotics competition with schools from around the world. Competitions that would never be on Union's radar.

Honestly, I thought that would be the end of it. Private school tuition is up there with college, which is why Rej skipped it altogether. Even with a partial ride from Augustin, Mom had to take out some hefty loans. As if Granma's medical bills weren't enough, here I come adding more debt. But I'm gonna make it count. Ms. Rowe showed me all the grant money that's out there for people in tech. I'll make my family proud so this transfer pays dividends.

"So what kind of robot are you going to build?" Mom asks.

"Won't know till next week," I say, setting the table for breakfast, forcing a smile because my mom wants it to be a celebration. "That's when the robotics team has its first meeting."

"Just stay away from that artificial intelligence stuff," Mom says. "Your dad playing *The Matrix* once a year is enough for me."

I laugh. It's real. "Probably won't be on *Matrix* level yet," I say. I know I should be more hyped, but me and Dad were always a team. But I guess even in *Fellowship of the Ring*, another Dad favorite, the fellowship gets broken. "I just hope everyone else isn't too far ahead of me." Me and Rej did a lot of self-learning, picking up coding, getting kits whichever way we could. Playing catch-up to schools like Augustin is the worst. "I dunno. Testing in math is one thing—"

"Yuh needed a challenge," Granma says. It was rough enough downloading pirated software onto Union's computers so me and Rej could get a taste of CAD. Another reason Ms. Rowe thought it was time we took our *ambition* elsewhere. Granma rests her hand on my shoulder, using me for balance as she eases toward the table. "And one ting I know is dat my grandson is a fighta." She stops to pound her foot on the floor a couple times, circling her ankle as if it fell asleep. "Him can run anyting him put his mind to. He nuh back down from nothing. School, martial arts, anyting. So yuh gonna waltz right inna dat school and crush any test dem trow at yuh. All a Jamaica gon big yuh up!"

Leave it to Granma to lift my spirits.

"Lord," Granma starts a prayer over the food, "thank you for the food that we are about to receive. Bless the hands that prepared it. And please bless GC as he begins this new journey."

That's what this is. A new journey. A chance to grow, persevere. I wanna leave my mark. Be remembered. And robotics, Augustin, is the way.

3

I'm looking over my back every two seconds, wondering if I'm being followed, on my way to change the world.

The green Augustin blazer I got on is a giant target that says *jack me*. And these khakis Mom picked up from a back-to-school sale are so stiff they got me looking like I'm constantly pulling out a wedgie. She was glowing as I stepped out the door. Chasing me down the stairs. Taking pictures with her phone as if I were dressed for prom.

Augustin sent home a letter about dress code last week. In bold letters it read, ***All clothes must be ironed, and no sagging pants.*** Straight-up coded message. At Union, I knew who I was. We were every shade of Black and Brown but still different. I could wear a shirt celebrating Jamaica, Black culture, Black joy. I've already sacrificed a piece of myself.

The streets are littered with boarded-up construction sites.

Residential homes bulldozed to make room for *upscale* apartment buildings. Lining the walls are campaign signs interspersed with ads for parties and building permits. Dollar-van drivers, that charge more than a dollar, honk horns, yelling, "Flatbush! Flatbush!"

"Walk of shame." It's Rej, popping up behind me like a stalker at the Newkirk Avenue–Little Haiti station.

"Damn shame." Joined by none other than Stretch, in his torn jeans and TRINI 2 DE BONE shirt. "You gotta hold ya head up high, son," he says coolly. "Walkin around so serious." Easy for him to say. Both his parents are home and their pockets way deeper than me and Rej's. But that's him. Always relaxed, sure of himself, gliding through life. Never worried about what's next, he just lets whatever happens happen.

That's my brother. But that's not my life.

"You know we had to see you off, man," Rej says. We dap each other up.

"Big tings." Stretch nods in agreement, giving me the one-armed hug. I have to shuffle my bags to not tip over. I gotta get used to carrying both. When I was at Union, I had time to go home after school, drop my books off, and grab my gi and equipment before heading to the dojo. With the commute, I gotta haul everything with me to school. "You gonna be like that Maya Angelou poem. 'The dream of the slave' or something." He starts snapping his fingers, looking to Rej for an answer. "You know what I'm talking 'bout. What was the name?"

"'Still I Rise,'" Rej says, grabbing a palmful of dreads to shake his head.

"That's the one," Stretch says. "The hope and dream of Brooklyn right here."

"Sup with this material." Rej pulls at the cardboard tube I'm wearing called pants. Meanwhile, he's comfortable in black cut jeans with a custom TheR1 patch, and a Basquiat-like design on his long-sleeve shirt. He could be going to the club or a music video shoot, but it's just a regular Wednesday being Rej off to Union. "Mezanmi! Can you even do a side kick in those pants?" The look of disgust on his face mirrors how I feel. "Definitely can't run."

"Leave that man alone," Stretch says, always the peacemaker. His pinched brow cringes speaking his truth. "Not many people get these opportunities." *Man. This fool. Why'd Stretch have to say that?* 'Cause "not many people" includes Rej. It's hard to be happy when I know I'm getting to do something he can't. I love Stretch but he don't be thinking sometimes. "Couple months, Gil gonna be all the news. Scientist extraordinaire. Robotics champ. Nah. Like the Notorious B.I.G. of robotics to BK." His exuberance pumps me up. Forget the fashion. I'm gonna give Mom, Granma, a reason to smile. Know they didn't throw money away on me.

"I better hop this train," I say.

"Let me get your phone first," Rej says. "Want to make sure you got this new mix I put online." I hand him the phone and he downloads the playlist. He grabs my shoulder, leans in to my ear, talking low so that only I can hear. Between us, there are no secrets. "Me and you, we understand each other's situation in a way others won't." He's talking about our dads. Rej was on vacation with his family in Florida when they were pulled over during a traffic stop. The cops ended up taking his dad into custody and later sharing that information with ICE. From there he was taken to a detention facility for being an undocumented immigrant. Every week, me and Dad were helping them, making calls, trying to get legal counsel to speak to Rej's father. But less than a year later, he was still lumped into a mass deportation. "Now you got something to vibe to . . . remind you where you from. And that you can always come back."

It's Rej's going-away gift. He got jokes, but he shows up. "Thanks, yo," I say. Now I got something to nod to on the way into the city—my fam is with me. "And, yo, anything I do in robotics, I'm recording." He produces music, but it's always been a dream of ours to form our own robotics company, something to help build better housing in the hood. Probably came from being around Dad and all his ideas to use science to make socioeconomic changes.

"Aight, man"—Rej laughs, giving me a pound—"we'll see you at the dojo. I know lil sis'll be looking for you too." *Wouldn't miss it.* I'm excited to see Kenya spar through the gauntlet. Root for her the way my seniors at the time, Joshu Smith and Joshu Wong, did. I probably would've quit if they weren't there championing me on. Now I'm a black belt too.

"You got this," Stretch says brightly, encouraging as ever.

"True, true," I reply. Rolling my shoulders, adjusting my bags, the weight of Brooklyn on my back.

THE 2 TRAIN screeches underground, stinging my ears. The MTA has tried to spruce up the subway stations as deep into BK as Newkirk. Redo the wall tiles. Add mosaic art. The platforms may be power washed at night, but the concrete clings to a stain of yellow grime laden with chewed-up, spit-out, and fossilized gum. On the tracks, a parade of rats scramble through discarded sports drink bottles, fighting for tossed food scraps—a constant reminder of New York's true self. Try as you might, it's the one thing this city can't bury. *Truth.*

Since it's still early, there's enough room to get a seat. By the time the train hits Franklin Avenue, not only are the seats gone, but the train is also packed. At each stop the business suits, New York's *professionals*, who work in those skyscraper offices, battle their way inside, cramming into the slightest opening—so much tension it might pop. Pretty sure they're sucking the air out of the train and every dollar out of our community. This is the future Augustin's selling. In five years, these will be my class-mates doing the same thing to my hood. *Is this who I'll turn into? Just a suit reporting to an office?* I spot maybe two or three Black people in corporate attire lost among their peers. One makes eye contact, like he's accusing me of something. *But what?* Trying to be something I'm not. Leaving BK behind. Abandoning my friends. Like Dad abandoned us. *Stop it, Gil. He left temporarily. He'll be back soon.*

"You okay, honey?" the woman next to me says, clutching my arm. My chest is heaving. Each breath stumbles out. My fore-head is dripping with sweat. I wipe it with my hand and then onto my blazer. She offers me a tissue and water bottle. I wave it away. She insists. "Uh-uh, baby. Take the water. You need it."

I take a big gulp. She's right. It soothes me, my heart rate steadies.

"You look handsome," she says. But I feel like a fool in these clothes. "What kind of school you going to?"

She reminds me of Granma, except this woman has a tan com-plexion and no accent. I don't like sharing personal information about myself on the street, but people like Granma—like her—have a way of making you share. "Augustin Prep," I say.

"Oh, that's a good school," she says. "You must be smart."

"Nah," I reply, my cheeks warm.

"Don't be bashful, baby. You're a Black man in America. Don't hide your intelligence." She smiles and I'm certain that she must be Granma's personality doppelgänger. With a few words, she calms me down, changing my whole mood. "Well, this is my stop," she says, getting up. "Remember, when you go to that prep school, you let people know who you are." She's right. Focus on the positives. The robotics club. Augustin's resources. They're all springboards. While Rej makes a name for himself in music, I'll make a name for myself so colleges have no choice but to see me.

Five stops later, I'm on the Upper West Side. Traffic lights flash and yellow cabs whiz down wide avenues. There are rows of restaurants and boutique clothing stores huddled below brick and limestone buildings. Gothic architecture soars above furniture shops that can only be afforded by the city's wealthy residents. A coffee shop is at every other corner, giving commuters their daily highs, while trees lining the streets flounder to soak up the carbon dioxide. I'd say this ain't Brooklyn, but downtown BK looks just like this with all the new construction and overpriced apartment complexes. Escalating rents from Bed-Stuy, East Flatbush, Gowanus, everywhere make it abundantly clear the colonizers have returned.

The 8:00 a.m. sun hits Augustin Prep's remodeled exterior. Light shimmers over glossy marble and stone like a beacon. The architecture, dating back to the 1800s, may have seen its fair share of change, but it hasn't hit the student body. White kids swarm from all directions, converging on these massive solid glass double doors with steel handles. It's like the entrance to a Midtown office building and not a high school.

I take the biggest gulp of Manhattan air and brace myself to enter, reflexively checking my phone. There's an alert. A message from Dad:

DAD

Gil sorry I couldn't be there for your first day. But know that me and all your family in Jamaica are cheering for you. When I was your age, I could only dream of the feats you'll accomplish. Big tings a gwaan fi yuh, mi son ✊🏾

ME

Thanks dad.

It's not the same as him being here. But I feel myself relax, ready to take on the day.

Students pile through the entrance, bumping each other like it's rush hour in Times Square. A group of boys push into my back as I enter. I'm not sure if they were trying to get past me or what, but I do what any New Yorker would do during a morning commute: I make a slight turn with my arm bent and extended so it looks like an accident when I elbow the closest in the chest. Renee would be proud of that move. The group of matching blond-haired students look like they are on the way to a Future Republicans of America photo shoot.

Blue eyes and burgundy cheeks give me a confused look and

I respond with the *oh, I didn't see you there* look. Then keep it moving.

Dean Bradley, the dean of students, welcomes everyone as we walk past the school's reception desk. He's got on loafers, gray corduroy pants, a pastel-yellow dress shirt, a green sweater-vest to match the school colors, and a striped tie that may be uglier than mine. I'm not a fashion guru. But if I were to give a name to his style, it'd be: busted.

He says something, pointing to my head. I turn down Rej's mix to hear him repeat it. "Take those earphones off, son." *Did this dude just call me son?* "No earphones or caps on in the building or I'll take them. You're inside. This isn't the ghetto."

Ghetto? Who says that? Shoot. Grabbin someone's belongings when you didn't pay for them sounds ghetto to me. He being extra for no reason. I remove the earbuds, then trace my tapered fro, drop fade, with my palms, thankful for the fresh cut. Ain't no way a hat going over this.

"Morning, Mr. Powell," Ms. Willis greets me, adding the subtle nod that says, *I see you.* She looks like she's older than my mom, probably above forty. But Black don't crack, so who knows. Her twists are pulled back in a bun, so her squat neck can be seen above the collarless gray pantsuit with the white blouse. She's the only Black teacher I met during my interviews. So I remembered her name. And she made it a point to know mine.

"Morning, Ms. Willis," I say before joining the pre-class locker rush.

Everyone is fixing their ties, some putting on athletic letter sweaters they can wear instead of the blazer. The first floor is filled with glass trophy cases highlighting Augustin's varsity athletics program and its accomplishments. Looks like almost every other year the football team's got a championship. The antique wood adds to the stuffy atmosphere that feels like a mausoleum. I don't spot one Black student in the wave of white faces.

Everywhere I turn, there are pockets of people catching up with each other, chatting about all their shared experiences. I shouldn't care. But it's another reminder it's just me here. In martial arts competitions, we may fight alone, but my team, the dojo is there, cheering me on. At least I'll have robotics next week. A group of people competing together in science. We do good, Mom will prob tell everyone I'm up for a Nobel Prize.

I jam my gym bag inside my locker, sighing at the gang of textbooks I gotta haul. I notice the clock on the wall. Ten minutes until my first class. *Wait . . . what do I have first period?* Is it AP Physics? Nah, maybe it's AP Lit. Ah man, I can't remember.

I dive through my book bag, folders, locker, then my pants and blazer for my schedule, but it's gone. I reach for my phone to try and pull up the doc.

Of course. It's dead. I slam my locker closed and swing my book bag over my shoulder to head to the dean's office for a new schedule. And then I crash into a wall. It's the chest of someone twice my size with a neck made of muscle. He's got wavy black hair long enough to tuck behind his ears, dark brown eyes, and a chiseled jaw. His arm, clothed in a varsity sweater, hangs around a slender girl with a styled lob and highlights, holding a luxury handbag that's too small to carry a laptop or notebook. They cling to each other, not a single pimple between their white faces. It's like they've practiced this pose nonstop and are ready to be on the cover of a magazine.

"My fault," I say reflexively. I actually don't know who bumped who, but his expression says it doesn't matter and it's definitely my fault.

I move around him and he steps into my space. "That's right, it is your fault," he says as if it were a matter of scientific fact.

"Hey, Terry, Jill." A girl slides between us, wafting the gentle scent of coconut oil from the curls puffing out from rubber band twists. Her skin is like the moon touching the trees at night. She's the first Black student I've seen all morning, and here she is flying in to save me. "You better hurry or you'll be late for class," she says to the dude. "Even football players get detention." She grabs my hand assertively, sure-footed, pulling me away. "You must be new."

"Yeah." The lone word flutters out, my hand warm in hers, as she pulls me down the hall to the staircase. She may be five six, and glasses with a blueish tint hover below strong eyebrows. Her back moves like a swimmer's as I follow. I pull my hand from hers and it slips easily away from the heat and damp anxiety. "I forgot my schedule," I say, as if she needed further information on my newness.

"You don't got a phone?" she asks.

"Forgot to charge it," I reply.

She smirks. "You look a little old to be making freshman mistakes."

"Just had a lot on my mind, transferring to a new school and all," I say.

"Oh," she says, tilting her head in. "You got them transfer-student blues. Gonna write a poem about it?"

"Nah, nothing like that," I say, channeling Stretch, trying not to laugh and play it cool.

"I'll show you the dean's office," she says with a turn. "Not the place you want to go on your first day. Dean Bradley loves giving out detention more than he likes cigarettes." She gives me the quick tour, highlighting different places of interest as we go up the stairs. The school's Legacy Wing. Business offices. But all I see are her curls leading me on, now giving me hints of peaches drifting off each movement. I keep my eyes up, not tracking the skirt as it moves rhythmically with her hips, and the charcoal leggings beneath.

"So, what's your name?"

"Gil." My eyes shoot to the ceiling.

"You a sophomore? You look too old to be a freshman."

"Nah." I add bass to my voice. "Senior."

"Don't lie. Augustin doesn't admit senior transfers. Against policy."

"Well, they made an exception."

"You rich?"

She's got jokes. "Pssht. Yeah, right. You think I'm one of these white kids bouncing from country to country during the summer?"

"Well, we're here." She gestures inside an open door. "I got Calc on the fourth floor, so I better get going. By the way, since you were rude enough not to ask, my name is Tammy."

Damn. It's like not getting Nakia's number all over again. "Sorry. Was about to ask." I've been looking for other Black students since orientation. Finally find one and I don't ask her name.

"You should come out to the Black Culture Club."

"Oh, we got a club?" I ask. She nods. "Yeah, maybe I'll come through."

"Chill with the maybe and do that," she says with authority. "Today. After school." I dip my head to say yes, even though I know I can't make it. "It's cool," she adds, spotting my hesitation. "New school. You a little shook. I get it."

"Whoa. Ain't nobody shook." Rej and Stretch would like her. No opening missed.

"Getting defensive," her voice sings. "Anyway, you owe me for your rude introduction." Her lip curls to one side and I feel the blood rush to my face.

"Somebody being rude to Tammy?" This Asian cat with a sleek rasp to his voice like he's always in chill mode limps over on crutches. His hand brushes the black hair with brown highlights from his eyes, then he and Tammy exchange a friendly hug.

"What happened, CJ?" she asks.

"That influencer life." He chuckles without smiling. "Perils of me being me." He uses his crutch as an extension of his arm to motion to the door. "Had to pick up the elevator key 'cause, you know. Anyway, got Calc with Abato. I better go."

"Hey, I'll go with you." Tammy turns to me to say, "Don't forget, after school, fifth floor." I watch her as she fades down the hall and out of sight.

The dean's office is broken up into two rooms. The waiting area has a bench, bookshelves, and a desk on the right for the dean's assistant. To the left is a door leading to the dean's private office.

The dean enters, the more prominent side of his receding

hairline poking out first. His short brown hair has turned gray at the sides. Up close, he's got a funny smell. He's clean-shaven, so it might be aftershave, but it's like inhaling coffee and air-fried gym socks. I get the feeling this guy rarely smiles.

"Let me guess," he says, eyebrows raised in judgment. "No schedule." I nod apologetically. "I get it. First day. But you're not a freshman. You're a senior." Never had a conversation with this guy before, if I can call it that, and he knows I'm a senior. Guess it makes sense since there aren't that many Black people here. They made a point to know the transfer. "There's no excuse for tardiness. This is the real world you're in now."

Sup with this? He Morpheus? Have I been living in the dream world? "The bell hasn't rung yet." I try not to clench my teeth too hard. *If you give me my schedule, I'll get to class.*

"We don't use bells at AP," he says as if it's a crowning achievement. But checking the office clock, yeah, I'm late. One strike against me in his book. "This is preparation for college. We trust our students to be adult enough to keep track of time. Don't you have a phone?" That's the second time this morning. Literally just got the cell last night, one that can actually use Google Docs without blowing up. Phones weren't even allowed in class at Union. "Now I have to print out a new schedule," he says. "Which wastes paper. And we're eco-friendly here."

But not Gil-friendly. Instead of giving me a lecture, he could press the button, print the schedule. Not everything has to be a teachable moment. But no, some part of him is enjoying this. Like he took the job to flex authority over people half his age.

My old school never had a dean, only a principal, and he wasn't much better. He got some twisted pleasure out of telling us that college wasn't necessary or that we would never achieve the successes of private school kids. We butted heads more than once.

The dean finally prints my schedule and I head through the empty hallways to AP Gov. I can still feel his gaze on me as he shakes his head.

I let it go . . . as much as I can. First days of school are forever trash. Next week, robotics team starts. Things can only get better.

4

This ain't the start I needed. I swear I'm getting glances, and it's not ones that simply say *transfer student.* Been late to almost every class. Can't keep up with all the names, faces. Even the room numbering is weird, a mix of letters and numbers—not sequential.

Finally. Last period is over. Gotta say a quick hello to Mr. Abato. Then make a run for my locker. Outside of Ms. Willis, Mr. Abato is the only person I remember from my interviews. Not my AP Physics teacher, but he runs the after-school STEM activities, including New York State Science Honors Society and the robotics team. I was hoping to have at least one teacher who was Black or any person of color, but in the classes I had, they all turned up white. Just like Mr. Abato.

"Mr. Powell," he says, exiting his classroom. He's proudly rocking a lab coat like he's been conducting some ill experiment. He's got a young face, he may be in his thirties. His hair is a premature matte silver, based on the budding lumberjack beard that's only starting to turn from its original brown. "How are you enjoying your first day at AP?"

AP. That's what the teachers here call the school. Brooklyn is BK. Augustin Prep is just Augustin Prep. Don't think an acronym is gonna make the school sound less white.

"It's nice," I say, like complimenting a haircut when the barber jacked up your hairline. "The mix of new and vintage design. The architecture definitely stands out from the city." It's like I'm in the middle of another interview, manufacturing a voice and smile that isn't me. But this guy holds the keys to the kingdom if you're STEM focused. So I do what I got to.

I got my guard up—a little cautious after the two encounters with the dean, plus muscle-neck dude. But the day wasn't all bad. I can still see those blue frames and curls. Almost taste the scents that dripped off her like an island breeze. My day-one hero. Tammy.

"We're celebrating a big anniversary this year," Mr. Abato says. He adjusts his lab coat, which fits a size too big for his lanky frame. "Our sesquicentennial. One hundred fifty years. Lots of history here." He rattles on, sometimes too fast for me to keep up. The time is ticking, but his energy and love for science have me hyped like when I first met him. "Distinguished alum."

"Anybody I'd know?" I ask.

He starts name-dropping people who don't ring any bells.

CEOs. Athletes. TV personalities. Conservative politicians that I always see getting dragged on social media. Nobody that really hits. Another reminder that everybody he's into—probably ain't Black. "Alum at Boston Dynamics. Then there's Dr. Gunther, whose latest patent on robot-assisted neurosurgery has been utilized by Intuitive. Haru Nakamura, who just left a position at FANUC, doing some amazing things with automation in manufacturing."

"Wait, go back to the person working with medical robots," I say, the last bit of information grabbing me. "You said you got someone in neuroscience?"

"Oh, Dr. Gunther," Mr. Abato says. "Truly a brilliant scientist. One of the donors who helped fund our new STEM Lab and Fabrication Center."

"Is there a chance to meet them or something?" I ask. I think about the possibility of helping people with dementia using robots and nanotechnology. This is what Augustin's about.

"Well, she's pretty busy," he says. "But who knows, I'll talk to the alumni office, maybe we can set up some kind of virtual meet with the team."

"That'd be cool," I say, noting it on today's brighter-side list right under Tammy.

"There's going to be a lot of opportunities for internships and to meet industry professionals as we expand our corporate sponsorship," Mr. Abato says. He taps his head, an idea popping up. "Since you're already here, I'd love for you to meet the RoboAugs' founding members," he says. I reach for my phone to check the time, thankful Ms. Willis let me charge it in her class during lunch. She didn't give me any judgment like the dean, just said no problem. Mr. Abato sees my hesitation, adding,

"They got the school interested in making Augustin competitive in robotics, which is a big reason you're here. It will only take a few minutes."

"Sure thing," I say, swallowing a sigh as he walks me inside.

"This is Heath and Lydia," he says. I do a double take at the matching hair that looks like a phoenix touched their scalps. They must be related. Freckles dot their noses and across their cheeks.

"Yes, we're twins," Heath says, curtly answering a question I didn't ask, but that must come up regularly. He's the shorter of the two, stocky with a hint of arrogance in his crossed arms, judging me out of the corner of his eye, wondering if I belong. His hair is pressed down as flat as possible to his scalp.

I ignore him 'cause his sister obviously took all the civility in their genetic split. She extends her hand with a welcoming smile, her cheeks flushing as red as her eyebrows.

"You're going to love it here," Lydia says, spiraling atomic energy as if she's on the verge of exploding. They may be twins, but they couldn't be more opposite. And the only thing wilder than her enthusiasm is her hair, which is as jumpy as she is. "When the season starts, it gets kind of bonkers, but brainstorming together is the absolute best. The STEM Lab down the hall and the Fabrication Center downstairs are like toy rooms for us." Her eyes widen, closing in on my personal space, expecting me to respond. I've never seen someone my age so hyped for science. Me and Rej are geeks for it, but not like this. She's got no reservations. "Seriously, anything you need, Augustin has it."

"That sounds great," I say, sneaking back, reclaiming my

breathing room. "I can't wait to get my hands into it." There's no matching this excitement; it's almost overwhelming. But I force a smile with every muscle I can muster because robotics is what I love and I can't get freaked out by every new person I meet.

"You build before?" Heath asks like a gunslinger throwing down a challenge.

"Here and there," I say cautiously. He nods, maybe my answer pleased him. "Nothing on the tournament level."

"Well, don't worry," Lydia says. "We're just happy to expand the team. The more brains in the mix the better."

"That includes me." That Asian dude Tammy knows glides in on his crutches.

"CJ, you made it, perfect timing," Mr. Abato says. "CJ will be working on CAD this year."

"Always looking for more content for the following," CJ says, effortlessly joining the group. There's barely a smile on his face, but the confidence is undeniable. He could probably battle Stretch for the "most chill" award.

"We're all learning together," Mr. Abato adds. "And, some other news." Mr. Abato grins. "Freedom Academy will be hosting an off-season competition in late October. That means we'll have a chance to fix our robot from last year and really show the other schools what we can do." He takes out his phone and motions for us to stand together. "Let's take a picture," he says. "Headmaster DeSantis wants to add it to the alumni newsletter."

This moment feels right. They talk about the goals for the year, fixing the drivetrain from last year's robot, a new fabrication machine, recruitment. It's all pretty cool, especially some of the programming applications. Then I look at my phone.

It's 3:39.

A few minutes turned into thirty plus.

Flying through the double doors at the entrance, I stuff my blazer in my bag and rip off my tie without breaking stride. My cousin once told me that the school crest on your chest is the perfect place to hit you. I take the comment seriously. When I get to the corner, I find a bench and swap out my shoes for the sneakers I have in my gym bag.

The Jordan IV retros with the black cement. I'm not a full sneakerhead. My money's just not right. And with things the way they been at home, I can't really spend like that. But this is something I gifted myself over the summer. Despite the khaki pants and my shoulders lugging two bags, I'm feeling comfortable, more like myself as I swipe into the subway.

I lean on the train doors and put my earbuds in to listen to Rej's mix, bumping my head. He's got so much talent. Not just local DJ talent, but someone the world needs to know. My family's not the only one that could use a win. Sucks that his time is split now. Trying to meet with nonprofit lawyers, get his dad back in the country.

The 2 train is running smoothly—fingers crossed. I should still make martial arts by 4:45. I'll miss the kids' class but I'll catch Kenya and the other kōhai test for belt promotion. Always Persevere is a second family. If they're struggling, Ima be there to push them, cheer them on. Big bro got you. And I'll prove to Rej and Stretch that this school isn't gonna affect who I am.

Three heads get on the train at Hoyt Street. They're at the far end of the car, but for some reason my senses tell me to pay attention. Martial arts taught me mindfulness, trained me to constantly be aware of my surroundings. One of them makes a gesture and I'm 90 percent sure that motion was toward me. Normally, I wouldn't think anything of it. They ain't dressed any different from my people at Union. But something doesn't feel right. They're quiet, not talking, only looking over in my direction. When the train passes Atlantic and more people get off, they move to the middle of the train and my chest tightens.

These damn khakis. Rej was right. I can't kick in these. The blazer may be in my bag, but the rest of the dress code is screaming *rob me*. The closest dude cases me like a bank vault. I act like I don't notice, nonchalantly making a move to the next car. It's a little more crowded. I should be okay.

When I first took the bus by myself, Dad told me there's one thing heads like this love to do—jump you as a group. He said it's fear.

I keep my pace steady, but quick. I don't want them to think I'm scared, and I need to keep a good distance between us. I'm missing Dad even more right now. That encouraging nod he'd give me before a martial arts competition always hyped me up like I could take on the world. My gut tells me I could defend myself against one, maybe two, but not three, and if they have a weapon, I'm done. Too many heads wanna be shooters. And a black belt doesn't protect you from getting jumped.

They follow me.

I can almost feel them at my back as the train leaves Bergen.

I'm in the last car. Nowhere to run. They come closer and I can't help but shrink into the steel doors.

"Yo, wussup, kid," the tall one says, barely opening his mouth. He's wearing a black vest over a charcoal hoodie and it's over seventy degrees out. His facial hair with connected sides makes me think he's got a couple years on me. "Where you goin, like a job intaview or suttin? We tryna talk to you and you runnin."

"Ain't nobody was running," I reply, showing them I'm not intimidated. *Maybe they'll move on.* They get closer. Dude with the vest gives me the smirk of someone not afraid of lockup. He measures me, sees a prep school kid that stepped into the wrong borough, an easy target for a beatdown. I raise my voice a few decibels hoping someone will hear me and step in. "What, you need something?" People willfully look away as if I don't exist. I might as well be on an empty train, but I'm not. Everybody just wants to continue on with their day, avoiding drama even when they could help. Maybe they think I was asking for this.

He puts his hand on my shoulder and says, "Yo, I need a dolla. Tryna git one adem mail room jobs like you. So wussup?" He pats my chest.

I push his hand off and say, "Nah, man. I'm broke."

"Fancy kid sayin he broke," he says, turning to look at his minions, pointing at my sneakers, my pants. He taps my pockets with the back of his hand, feeling the cell phone, wallet. My skin crawls. Nobody's ever rolled on me like this before. But things are different now.

It's these damn clothes.

One day and people already looking at me like I ain't from my own hood.

He presses his forearm into my neck as the train enters Grand Army Plaza. I'm trapped between the train door and his arm.

"Run the pockets, and doze sneakers."

I can feel the steam coming out of his nostrils. My chin tucks into my neck. My heart races. My back, pressed against steel and plexiglass, wants to burrow its way out.

Can you even do a side kick in those pants?

The train door opens. I pull my knee up to my chest, launching a stomp kick with the sole of my foot into the center of his vest with every fiber in my body. He tumbles into his friends, the momentum sending me down to the stained concrete, littered with a day's worth of garbage and spit. I don't waste time. I scramble up and run. I don't know if they're behind me. I need to get outta here. Escape this train. Escape this day.

I charge up the stairs. Through the turnstile. Out the subway exit. And I keep running. I look from side to side, not sure where to go, barely registering where I am. It's rush hour. Cars and people swirl around. Truck drivers hurl curses. Pedestrians scream back. They all combine into a whirlwind attacking my senses. Then I see it, the Soldiers' and Sailors' Memorial Arch standing like a stone mountain above the roundabout. I turn toward it and keep running. A car screeches by. I leap back, toppling under the weight of my bags.

"Hey, get out the road," the driver yells at me.

I wait at the intersection for the light to change, catching my breath, looking over my shoulder. I think I lost them, but I'm not sure. One intersection between me and safety. The light changes to a saving green. I rush across the street to the Central Library. I fly up the concrete stairs, taking them two, three at a time.

Fifty-foot pillars that touch the sky and windows adorned with gold etchings ripped from literature mark the entrance like a roadway to the Roman Colosseum. I always come here when I want to just enjoy quiet time alone. Now, here it is, a real sanctuary. I press through the revolving door, flatten my back against the wall, trying to catch my breath.

I look outside. Nothing. I know I can't leave yet, they could still be lurking out there. *What time is it?* If Mr. Abato hadn't stopped me, I would've got to the dojo on time. If it wasn't for this uniform, I wouldn't have been marked on the train.

If I didn't choose this school, I wouldn't be in this situation.

I WAIT A good fifteen minutes before heading to the B41 stop, constantly checking behind me. The bus is a longer ride but I don't want to risk getting back on the 2. Of course, it doesn't come for twenty minutes and rush-hour traffic isn't forgiving either. I cross the street just in time to see Kenya exiting the dojo.

Her cheeks and eyes droop sadly. "Hey, Joshu Powell," she says with attitude that I can't fault. "You promised you'd be here."

I instantly feel like crap. "I'm sorry, lil sis," I say. This is on me. I messed up. I gotta do better. "How'd it go?"

"I passed," she says, even though it sounds more like defeat. She flashes her new belt tip.

"That's dope!" I say. "You deserve it. All that work you've put in."

"It was rough," she says. "I had to spar against sooo many

people. I felt like I was gonna pass out." *And I wasn't there to cheer you on, pick you up.* The worst big brother. "You'll be here Saturday for demo practice, right?" she asks hopefully.

"You know it," I say. At least I don't gotta worry about the subway or school on weekends. "And you been showing a lot of improvement. I think we can add on an extra movement to your nunchuck routine."

"Really?" she says, with a spark. I can still make this up to her.

"You have your chucks on you?" She nods anxiously, pulling them out of her bag. It's one of the best parts about getting onto our demo team, learning new techniques before other students of your same age and rank. "Check it," I say. "You've done your figure eights and shoulder passes. Now I'm going to work with you on rip rolls and throws." I take the nunchucks from her hand. There are two people passing by on the sidewalk who have stopped to watch what I'm about to do. Once they step back and give me room, I start to demonstrate basic figure eights. Then I transition into a wrist roll, spinning the chucks, the chain connecting the sticks sliding smoothly through my thumbs, across the back of my hands in endless cartwheels. Finally, I end with a shoulder-to-shoulder throw, my gaze locked forward, not once blinking.

"Whoa," she says, her jaw open. "I get to do that?"

"You're a quick learner," I say. "We don't have any demos until next year, but with steady practice, you'll be able to do a few wrist rolls and maybe some throws by then." The smile on her face fills me. Maybe I'm even forgiven. "Which means I gotta step up my routine too. 'Cause me and Stretch come out right after you."

Nakia crosses the street. She's never come to the dojo before. She's like five three. Never really noticed what a mean walk she got. Like she's commanding the earth with each step, fully comfortable in her body and who she is. "We gotta run," she says to Kenya.

"What're you doing here?" I blurt out the words, which sounds like attitude, forgetting any sense of the good manners my mom would expect of me or the swag Rej and Stretch would mock me for not having.

"Um, rude," she says assertively, a one-eighty from the vibe she was giving at J'ouvert.

"Nah, I'm sorry," I say, trying to clean it up, tripping over each syllable. This whole day is messing with my head. "Usually your mom comes, I was surprised that's all."

"Mm-hmm," she says. "Well, we gotta go." It's like something's on her mind but I got too much going on right now to do a deep dive. "Give me your phone." When she returns it, I've got a new contact. She looks at me with such certainty. It's different from the summer hangs at the job. Not that *I wanna get to know you* look, but the look of knowing who I am and where I'm from, nudging us to go further. Her hand wraps around the back of my neck, gently rising along my fade. My face heats up. "No excuses now."

Kenya giggles. Then turns with her sister to walk away. For a moment, lil sis looks back at me with hesitation but then merely waves. "Bye, big bro," she says, taking off with Nakia.

Stretch throws up his hand, flashing a wussup grin as he walks out of the dojo. "Where you been, son?" He sees Nakia walk off.

And turns to me with the devilish smirk. "Hope you got that number." I nod my head, showing him my phone. "Okaaay." Stretch beams. He taps me with the back of his hand on my chest. "Let me find out private school life got you stepping up."

"What's up with that rip in your crotch, man?" Rej asks, studying me.

I look down and realize that the stomp kick ripped open a hole in my pants.

My cheeks gets hot. Oh no. Did Nakia notice?

I tighten my lips, the part of me that wants to tell my friends what happened on the subway. But I can't. First day of being out of BK and I get jumped. What's that say about me? That I can't be out on my own? Like I'm a little kid. The whole hood will be laughing at me. Trying to break me. So I lie.

"Cheap material. I slipped."

"Pfft. Any pants you can't kick in—" Stretch shakes his head. His mood light, accepting my answer.

Rej though . . . After things went down with his dad, me and him got closer, promised we'd always tell each other the truth. Neither of us knew that our dads were undocumented. Not formally at least. They did the grind. Things was always harder and we just thought that was another part of life. Our parents didn't want to burden us with the concern.

He has one hand crossed at his waist, the other up by his chin, deciding whether he wants to believe me. But I don't think he does. He only says, "We did warn you."

As we walk to the bus stop, they tell me about the test. How grateful the kōhai were to have them there. All of the younger students passed, putting their hearts into earning their promotion. That's Rej and Stretch's memory. One that I'm not a part of. Whenever they or the kōhai recall this day, I won't be able to share in the conversation. My memory will be of Augustin Prep, the 2 train, and letting lil sis down.

And this is only day one.

5

I just gotta make it to the weekend. It's Thursday. Augustin's renovated cafeteria reminds me I'm the new fish in a tank full of social rules, hierarchies, and a routine I'm not used to.

Bright LEDs from a range of geometric fixtures spotlight me as I walk along a mix of emerald and cream checkerboard tiles through a field of white faces in green blazers. The lingering scent of bleach doesn't quite mask several decades of processed-meat lunches.

If I were at Union, I'd head straight for the table in the far corner. Fifth period would be leaving and we'd dap each other up as our sixth-period lunch crew took its place. Stretch would be talking about sports—all of them. Football. Basketball. Soccer. It gets bad come hockey season when he talks about the one or two Black players we need to be following. Rej would bring it back to hip-hop or some new artist he's producing. But by last September, instead of hip-hop, it was immigration law. Talking about deportation cases, trying to reach out to lawyers, anyone who could help him get in contact with his dad as he was bounced around from detention center to detention center. I hoped helping Rej would help my dad's situation. But it only made Dad realize that the clock was ticking on him too.

After yesterday, I kinda feel like that. As if I don't belong here. Not only not in Augustin, but not in Brooklyn either. I haven't even texted Nakia. After the train . . . I don't feel like myself. Like I've been holding on to some fake image of who Gil Powell is and it's just been shredded. *Aight, you gotta chill. It was only a day.* By next week this time, I'll have my hands in machine parts and code.

"Hey. Gil, right?"

I turn toward a melodic familiar voice. Blue frames, bright eyes, and those vibrant curls call to me like a tractor beam in one of Dad's sci-fi movies.

"Oh, wussup, Tammy," I say. Not sure if I should give her a dap or hug her, so I stuff my hands in my pockets as we approach the lunch counter. I pick up a chicken sandwich and fries. It looks more like a church wafer of dehydrated chicken on wet bread with a side of soggy potato wedges that need to be cooked another ten minutes. For a prep school, the food is as wack as public school, except here I gotta pay. Ms. Rowe would break down all the reasons Union couldn't afford basic educational tools; subsidized meals was one of them. "You, uh, sitting with anybody?"

"Only me," she replies, grabbing a salad. Her eyebrows rise and her lip angles up to one side. "Welcome to join." I nod, following her to the soda machine, which is as gentrified as downtown Brooklyn. It's got teas, coffees, every flavor of sparkling water, and that boxed coconut water that don't hit right if you been raised on the *real* real. Not even a ginger ale. Honestly, I could really go for a Kola Champagne or Ting, but they don't got that in the city. Harlem, yes. Manhattan, no. It may be on the same island, but it's not the same. I tap the button on the 7UP and regret it instantly.

Tammy leads me over to a stage area off to the side. We climb up. There are four long tables, each with only a few students. It's a little odd because the rest of the cafeteria is packed and people are scrambling for seats.

She sits in a chair opposite one of those varsity sweaters with the big green *A* for Augustin stamped on the chest. "Move it to the table behind you," Tammy says. "It's the senior section. Somebody probably left it last period." So I move the sweater and sit down—

And get caught up in those dark eyes that glow like gemstone pools. I want to lean in. Something's igniting my senses again. Hair conditioner? Lotion? Some body spray? Maybe she just naturally smells good.

"Um, hello." She waves a hand, shaking me from my dream world.

Sometimes people think I'm zoning out when I'm taking it all in. And there's a lot to take in with Tammy, especially her inquisitive lips that only lift to one side, as if locked in a debate between whether to smile or question you. "Sorry, AP English Lit. Ms. Column gave us some work yesterday. So going over it in my head."

"Oh no . . . not homework." She gets melodramatic like she's in a daytime soap. But all I see is her confident posture. Shoulders back. Chest out. It's like she's not afraid of anything and can run the world. "You have it so bad." She's good. Mocking me with a straight face. "Hey. If you want to leave and work on your essay so you don't have to be rude to me *again*, by all means, the stairs are right there." There's that word again. *Rude.* That's what Nakia said. I wonder if she'll pick up Kenya next time she's at the dojo or will her mom be there like usual?

"Nah, I meant, I had some things on my mind." For the first time, I'm glad Rej and Stretch aren't here. 'Cause they'd be clowning me hard.

"Re-lax," she says, taking a sip of sparkling water with a label that says *Hints of Lychee* on it. I never understood how people get upsold on water that ain't even fully flavored. But I guess when on the Upper West Side, you do what you do. "I was playin."

"All good yo. I shoulda known." I dish some sarcasm back her way. "I mean, day one desperate to get me to join your club? Obviously you don't have friends."

"Oh, new kid has jokes now, does he?" She gives me a chuckle with that half smile still trapped in thought. "Seniors get to go out to eat, or they eat in different lounge areas around the school, 'cause the food here . . ." She cringes, but it looks cute as hell. I take a bite of a damp fry so I don't look too fixated. Gotta keep it chill. "Anyway. I got friends. But I work a lot. So usually I'd be in my office or hanging with my girl Janeil." Whoa, she got her own office. Let me find out we got people in power places here. "But being around everybody gives me a chance to clear my head." She makes a sweeping motion to the cafeteria. "Observe. Find the story."

"What kind of stories you looking for? And what's this office?"

"Well, I'm the editor in chief of the newspaper, so . . ." She shrugs, letting me work out the obvious, while sending scents of cucumber my way, transporting me from the surroundings of subpar processed meats.

"That's dope yo," I say. Black people in media. After the cops killed Byrd a couple blocks from where I live, Dad started sending me articles from *The Root* to read, help me process it and all the history behind police violence, not just in New York, but nationwide. I wish I could plug out like Stretch. But me and Rej see life differently. Each time we see an unarmed Black person get killed, it's like losing family, and we relive it, over and over. "We need that."

"It's hard," she says. "Getting that position. I was doing more than twice as much work as the other staff. Not just articles. Layouts. Photos. While trying to get more Black students to write, share their perspective. Have a voice." She sighs out the strain of years of hustling. "Did get an artist, which was something. But the previous editor . . ." It's brief, but I catch her shoulders slumping like she was carrying a book bag full of bricks and dropped it for a moment to breathe. The sarcasm has faded along with the half smile. She's giving me a glimpse of her truth. Her bright eyes dimming from the melancholy of her own struggles. "Don't get me wrong, Augustin is great. I'm doing Early Decision to Yale."

I was thinking Stanford, but it's too far and too costly to regularly come back and see Granma. MIT is closer. But Boston? I don't know if I can do it. I really need to land a corporate grant for any school, especially if financial aid isn't right. Then there's Howard, it's an HBCU, and Dad got me really excited about what they been doing in robotics.

"I got a great shot, and Augustin is a big part of that," she says. She cuts herself off. Resets. Rises back into that proud posture. "Anyway, what's your story? Who is Gil?" She changes the subject, leaning in like Oprah doing an interview. Her half smile returns and a part of me melts. "First senior transfer in a school that doesn't accept senior transfers. You said you weren't rich. What's the deal?"

"Definitely not rich." My stomach clenches. "It's just my mom and granma at home." My gaze falls on my tray, realizing I left Dad out. But he isn't home, so why do I feel crappy for not mentioning him? I don't really know Tammy and there's no reason for me to tell her about Dad. Even when I'm with Rej, we just kinda focus on his dad's situation. Feels silly for me to take time away from him anyway. "I know Moms is stretching the credit and loans to help cover this. She finally got a job at the MTA. Owe 'em a lot." Stretch joked about me becoming a local celebrity, but that's what I need. Not just college. Something to show that their sacrifice counted. That I wasn't a waste.

I dunno what success is, ten years out of here or out of college. But I always pictured buying my parents a house. Taking care of them so they don't have to keep worrying about the bills. Give them a chance to travel without dwelling on the financial strain. Immigration. Granma. Me. Then never stop doing. Bring technology to schools like Union and the hood. Use

Augustin. *Every mikkle mek a muckle,* my dad would say, quoting the Jamaican proverb.

"Don't I know it. I actually work in the library and switchboard as part of my financial aid package. Like indentured servitude."

"Yeah, they got me for their robotics competitions," I say. "Got a partial ride from that. Kinda wanted to prove that I can compete with any of these privileged kids."

"Got it. Science savant. Has something to prove." She starts counting off on her fingers. "And no sense of humor." She smirks. I shake my head. "So what music do you like?"

"Same as everyone," I reply. "Dancehall, hip-hop, soca." And thanks to Dad's movie collection, I'm also a fan of pretty much any song from an eighties action or sci-fi movie.

"You know, you should really come to the next BCC meeting."

"I will," I say with the half-hearted conviction of anyone who says maybe. I really do want to meet some of the other Black students. Part of me also wants to check out Mock Trial and Debate. All the activities Union lacked. But I already missed testing at the dojo. And I need to be on the train at a different time, to avoid the heads who tried to jump me yesterday.

"I am the president," she says. Impressive. Tammy don't got just one title here. She got two. Maybe more. She like running this joint. That's what I have to do in robotics. Really push it. Get on her level. Make people pay attention. "I'm saying, you kind of already disrespected me. You really want to another time?"

"C'mon. I'm the new kid. That's gotta negate the botched intro." I find a word that Stretch uses 'cause he also manages to watch golf. I don't know where he gets the time. "Like a mulligan."

"Okay, you got that." She takes a sip of her lychee water. "Come through."

"Aight, bet." Dip in for ten minutes, say hi, then be out.

"Cool," she says. "I'll be right back. I want to get some fries."

When she heads to the lunch counter, I begin thinking about my route home. If I sit on a different train car, I'll be good. No, what am I thinking. I'll switch to the 5 train at Fulton Street, completely avoid the 2 in Brooklyn, but stay on the opposite end of the train just to be sure. Damn. They really got me on the run.

I feel a tap on my shoulder.

"Hey, new kid." It's the muscle-neck guy from yesterday by my locker, towering over me like a fortress. "You moved my sweater?" His words are slow, measured, eerily polite like a politician.

"There was nobody here," I say, looking over at the evidence in question. *Why does everyone feel compelled to put their hands on me?* First the heads on the train, now this fool.

He hocks up some unnecessary gravel into his voice. "If I put my sweater on a chair, there must be a reason, right?" Muscle-neck lets the question hang even though I thought it was rhetorical. But I'm not taking the bait. The calm demeanor doesn't fool me. "So do me a favor, don't ever touch my sweater again." *Seriously?* He cracks his neck from side to side like a boxer loosening up before the bell rings, facing down his opponent. And that opponent is named Gil.

But this ain't like the train and we ain't predator and prey in a nature documentary. *He's one guy. And this is a damn prep school.*

"Calm down, aight," I say, standing up. Maybe he thinks I'm a mark 'cause I'm new. But I ain't the one. I summon the gentlest, most deliberate voice I can manage. "It's a sweater. There are seats everywhere. No need to make a big deal about it."

"So you think I'm making a big deal about someone touching something that's not theirs?" He doesn't talk like those old movie bullies picking on the skinny kid, like Biff in *Back to the Future*, another of Dad's top picks. This guy's a different breed.

I'm tall. But he's weight-lifting big. He may actually be my height or a little shorter, but when he tilts his head I swear he's casting a shadow. Two of his friends appear, one on each side of him, wearing letter sweaters. The one on the left's got a quick and dirty military buzz cut and is wide as a train. The movies where Bruce Lee takes down an army, they fight one at a time.

This ain't that. I'm alone here. No such thing as a one-on-one anymore. These guys will tackle me like I'm the football and then it's over.

The stage turns into a sports arena and the hushed audience is waiting for someone to throw the first punch. *Why are people tryna fight me? In a DAMN prep school.* I'd get it if this were Union. But if this happened there . . . Somebody try to step to me like this? Nah. Stretch and Rej woulda popped up behind each of my shoulders—my back covered.

Academics. Science. That's what I'm here for—that's what everyone here's supposed to be here for—not this bullshit. Instead this is like walking down the street and taking threats from the cops just 'cause we hittin the corner store for some snacks.

"Terry," Tammy jumps in. Her fries drop to the table. That was his name. Terry. "Our mistake. We thought someone left it there last period."

"That's two times," Terry says pointedly, as if I broke some rule.

He walks to the table opposite mine, sits down with his friends, and bites into an apple. I can feel him staring at me while he eats. I try not to stare back. I just wanna leave right now, but if I do, it's like I'm admitting defeat. Can't do that. Not two days in a row. I think of Granma's promise to not give in to the dementia. Rej fighting to get in contact with his dad after ICE took him. Dad making the plan to go back to Jamaica to avoid getting deported, get a temp visa, then work out a permanent green card. So I definitely ain't letting these fools beat me.

Tammy places her hand on mine. "You okay?" she asks.

I'm not. I'm counting seconds and minutes again. The cafeteria has gone back to normal as if nothing has happened. Well, if there is one thing that's like my old school—not a teacher in sight when something pops off.

Maybe three minutes pass by, maybe ten. Whatever it is, I've hit my limit. "Yo, I'm out," I tell Tammy. "I should get to my next class."

"I'll head up too," she says, exiting with me.

I can feel Terry sizing me up as we leave the cafeteria.

6

He's still staring at me.

Same day. Last period. And I have to suffer through AP English Lit with Terry ice-grilling me across the room with those Frankenstein eyes.

Instead of the standard classroom aisles, the desks are positioned in a giant U shape, with the opening facing the teacher's desk. It's supposed to promote discussion while we're interpreting some outdated, long-dead white author to prepare for the AP exam. They had this class at Union, but the fail rate was higher than 50 percent. Maybe the class didn't give students the tools, maybe the material was just boring and irrelevant to a school that's mostly Black and Latinx, but either way, we weren't set up to win.

As for the desk positioning, all I know is it's definitely had

Terry eyeballin me from the moment I entered class. Doesn't matter if I'm looking at my book or the teacher. His gaze is right there, fixated on me and no one else. *Would he be glaring so hard if I were a white transfer?* I think about the cops at J'ouvert. The scowl that one cop gave us. If something pops off again, I know ain't nobody here got my back.

A loud beep on the PA system interrupts the lesson on Keats versus Frost. All eyes dart to the recessed wall speaker waiting for the voice to come through.

"This Saturday, the AP Tigers, led by last year's MVP quarterback Terry Parker, will be taking on the Cardinals." It's Dean Bradley, voice booming. *Terrific.* I'm being stalked by a guy who gets mid-class shout-outs from the dean. "It's the first home game of the season, so let's all cheer him and the team on in the Augustin way! Go Tigers!"

Everyone in class starts clapping and doing these creepy tiger sounds that make my skin crawl like I got caught up in some cult ritual. But there are two people who aren't clapping: Terry, who hasn't abandoned his one focal point, and me, the outsider. It's like the class has drifted away and we're the only life-forms left. Dad would compare it to a Western movie, call it a showdown at high noon. I keep thinking about Dad in the past tense. I feel hollow, coming home, not being able to talk to him every day. Mom says to stay focused on school. Things'll work out.

So . . . I clap. It's forced, and awkward as hell, uncomfortable like the clothes I'm wearing. I'm down to only one pair of pants after the other one got ruined.

The Tigers homage dies down. Ms. Column sighs back into the lesson. Unlike the students flooded with chat from the brief outburst, she's barely moved. Her participation a formality. She's a tenured teacher and seems over it, ready to retire from academic life.

I actually enjoy poetry. A lot. The Keats and Frost poems she gave us to read last night were cool. But poetry covered in the classroom isn't fun. It's like a teacher can suck the life out of it for the sake of proving to everyone that these poets, or Shakespeare, or some other white dudes are the prototypes for poetry gods, when there were probably ten other Shakespeares who lived down the road who were too poor or too Black to get a chance to have their voices heard.

Makes me think back on them times Dad and Granma would put me on to poems from Miss Lou, Phillis Wheatley, and Gil Scott-Heron. They would debate their favorite writers like so many other things. Granma would always win, but it was fun to see Dad squirm under her wisdom. I miss those debates.

"Mr. Parker," Ms. Column says, calling on Terry. The teachers here always call us by our last names to recognize us as adults. "What are some of the similarities and differences in the two poems?"

"What?"

Ms. Column clasps her hands behind her back, teeth clenched and flashing like the Cheshire cat, reeling her mouse in. "Mr. Parker, you were given a reading yesterday, correct?" she says, dripping condescension. "'Choose Something Like a Star' by Robert Frost and 'Bright Star' by John Keats. Now, what are some of the similarities and differences in the two poems?"

He scours the poems on his desk. Without a word he's admitted to the entire class that he hasn't read them yet. I honestly don't know why he chose this class. "Iambic pentameter," he finally replies.

"You didn't specify if they were both iambic pentameter or not, but fine. Anything else?" Ms. Column offers him a second chance, letting the pause hang long enough to be uncomfortable. "Anything at all."

He riffles through his papers like the work he didn't do is hiding on one of the sheets. "I think love and longing are themes in each." His voice is arrogant, like he knows he's nailed it.

"You 'think' they are? You read the poems, did you not?" Part of me wants to laugh. But this is grueling, like watching a guy catch a low blow in a Mixed Martial Arts match—even if you don't like him, you feel the pain.

"Practice went late last night and we had the Joyce chapters." He offers up the argument, basically complaining that she gave us too much homework.

But Ms. I'm Enjoying the Squirm isn't having any of it. "Oh, so no one else has other activities?" This seems personal for her.

"That's not what I said." Then he comes with, "It's football. Ask Coach. Practice wears us out."

"Football is an extracurricular activity," she says. "Do you need me to ask your coach to explain to you the meaning of 'extracurricular'?" I swallow a chuckle, crushing my lips together. And I can tell I'm not the only one as others look down and away. For a school acclaimed for academics, I'm starting to realize the administration caters to the athletes. But not Ms. Column.

"No." Terry flushes red.

"You read the syllabus before you signed up for this class," Ms. Column says. "You're in an AP class. Please act like it."

"It's the second day of school!" Terry blurts out.

"This is your senior year, Mr. Parker." Terry's shoulders heave. The daggers he shoots at the teacher are the same ones he gave me in the cafeteria.

"Okay, anyone else?" Everyone is silent. To answer now would be like throwing yourself on a social grenade, gloating over Terry's failure.

All hands stay down.

"Fine. I'll have to call on someone." She scours the room. Everyone is doing a silent prayer hoping they aren't picked.

"Mr. Powell." Seriously? There's gotta be like twenty other students. "Similarities and differences between the Keats and Frost poems."

"Well . . ." I stall. Terry's over there licking his lips like the grim reaper wanting a reason to be more pissed. I'm not trying to play teacher's pet, but I'm not here just for robotics. Class participation is part of my grade. I'll take a college recommendation or scholarship any way and in any subject I can get it.

"We don't have all day, Mr. Powell," Ms. Column prompts as if I'm the last straw.

Whatever yo. This is AP Lit. Can't be in this class unless you're a nerd on some level.

"Both poems are personifying the moon," I begin, my voice screeching from baritone to tenor as I search for the right phrasing, "as this grand symbol of stability." My vocab is extra proper, more of an imitation of how I speak. It's not the same way I talk to my friends, my parents, or even the teachers back at Union. It's like I've shifted into Mr. Neckles. I can picture him fixing his tie, giving me a wink of approval. It's gross.

"Go on," the teacher says.

"Frost seems inspired by Keats." I look down at my hand-outs and find the section I highlighted. "He actually says 'Keats's Eremite,' directly referring to a line from 'Bright Star.' But I think Keats is more describing the moon and why he can't be as isolated, especially from the woman in the poem's second half, while Frost is not necessarily talking about the moon, just something like it . . . Maybe God? 'Cause the moon says 'I burn' and in the Moses story, the burning bush said 'I am.' But yeah, they're both looking for guidance. Keats for himself and Frost probably for his country." I'm pretty sure I nailed it.

But Ms. Column is looking at me like I said the dumbest thing ever.

"Wow, that was really articulate," she says, obviously surprised I can string two words together that make sense. She's not the first teacher in the past twenty-four hours who's called me articulate. "You spotted the allusion and mentioned several strong points." I think that's about the pinnacle of saying "well done" for her. She opens up the discussion. Now that I've gone, everyone else is joining in, speaking up on love, loneliness, and isolation.

Everyone except Terry, that is. He's withdrawn into a tunnel with me on the opposite end.

And I'm sure he wants me dead.

7

Terry's hunting me.

I broke outta class the minute Ms. Column dismissed us yesterday. That glower Terry was giving me was intimidation, nothing less. It's not that I'm scared—

Well, maybe I am. Not necessarily of him. I ain't a stranger to fighting. As a black belt, I spar and grapple every week at the dojo, then in tournaments. But it wasn't just him in the cafeteria. There were three. How many more football players will pop up like that? If I get into a fight here, I'll get expelled. Deported from Augustin like Rej's dad was taken from his family, his future. This country is always finding more ways to target people of color. What kinda fresh start is this?

My head cramps like it's being squeezed between two walls. I'm overthinking it. I massage the bridge of my nose, taking a moment to let this nervous headache subside. I remind myself—there are good things about Augustin. I just gotta make it to Monday. And he's just one guy.

Fifth period ends and the flurry to lunch begins. It's a stampede of footsteps mixed with thunderous chatter. Laughter. Everyone's going about their day. Three hours and Friday is over. I'm nobody here. My fears not even an afterthought. I'm scanning the swarm of students like a parent looking for a lost kid, except this kid's a senior and I don't wanna find him.

The crowd goes right. No sign of Terry or any letter sweaters. I go left. I peep the bathroom before I use it, make sure Terry isn't lurking in the cut, trying to catch me at the urinal. I thought of letting Rej and Stretch know the situation. And each time I deleted the text. They'd either laugh or come to the city and wait outside. Can't have them go down for me.

I head over to the Augustin Lounge for lunch. It's a quiet area off to the side of the main cafeteria, next to the freshman lockers. The lounge has a computer students can use, gray carpet, a round table, and two wood-framed couches with green cushions. The door gives a creaking sound as if it's the same door that's been here since the building was constructed. There's only one student inside at the computer writing an essay. He doesn't seem like one of Terry's crew, no letter sweater, no smug expression.

As the door closes, my reflection glares at me from one of the trophy cases. I swear he's shaking his head.

I need a pick-me-up. Reset my mood. I pull out a plastic container. Inside is Granma's oxtail with rice and peas, lots of gravy. It's not the same microwaved, but it'll still be good. She loaded it up too. Nuff oxtail. Not like when you go to some spots and they give you all rice and peas with three pieces of oxtail that are mostly bone, and mad cabbage to fill the foil container.

I got one eye on the food, one eye on the door. I'm listening out, Biggie's "Warning" can come in at any moment. I look up at the college pendants pinned to where the wall meets the ceiling, surrounding me. The Ivy Leagues dead in the center and not an HBCU in sight. I chew. Not able to enjoy my food because my foot is pounding against the floor waiting for the moment to jump. I pop an ibuprofen, hoping this stabbing sensation above my eyes doesn't turn into a full-blown migraine. Then take a gulp from my water bottle that lasts forever.

The door gives a whining screech. My heart skips. The bottle drops.

"Has anyone seen Mr. Tasilo?" A short girl with blond hair flounders in, looking confused like she didn't want to be here. Not Terry. I exhale.

"No," the student at the computer replies.

When she leaves, I look down at the table. My oxtail is swimming in water, and the rest is on the floor. Well, there goes lunch. RIP. I grab some paper towels near the microwave and begin blotting up the spillage on the table, then the floor.

"Hmph. Now this makes sense." I shouldn't know that voice so well, but I do. Terry. "On the floor. Cleaning." That matter-of-fact tone, so bland and precise, is more condescending than the words, like he's on the verge of epiphany. "You're not a student. You're part of the custodial staff."

My stomach grinds, my body rigid. *Get out of here. Make it to the weekend.*

"Ew, who made this?" He stares at the food Granma cooked

with disgust. He has no right to critique anything she does. I stand up. He grabs a piece of meat and flings it at me. I shift just in time, the shrapnel barely catching my blazer. "You think you're funny, sucking up to the teacher like that?"

My fist clenches and loosens. I'm staring at the door, my book bag a couple feet over, the dude by the computer, Terry, taking it all in, thinking five moves ahead. I know where this is going if I don't escape. And so does the student at the computer. He logs off and bolts out the door.

I can't get expelled. Not after all the money my folks put into me. Not with people like Stretch believing I can succeed here. Me believing. I back up slightly, enough to tighten the distance between myself and my book bag.

"You going somewhere?" he says, stepping into my space, close enough that I can smell the greasy lunch he recently devoured.

"Oh yeah, I think I saw Ms. Willis walk by." He turns around. Bait taken. I dive right, grab my book bag, then springboard over the couch like I'm on the Jamaican track team, an Olympic hurdler going for gold. I cross the threshold to the door and tumble into two letter sweaters.

"Where you going, Powell?"

They know my name. This isn't the kind of popularity I need. The one that spoke is the same truck with the buzz cut from the cafeteria.

Terry comes out of the lounge. And then there were three. Just like the subway. Just like those cops. All gangs.

"Back away from him," he orders them.

My biggest challenge was supposed to be catching up to the other robotics members in engineering. Not this—

I'm fully boxed in, trapped in a hallway lined with trophy cases proclaiming Augustin's greatness. The walls covered with conference plaques, some probably earned by these assholes. My heart thumps like a banging door. My breathing stressed. *Come on, GC. You've been through worse.* But no. This isn't like some heads on the street interested in my Jordans. These guys aren't out for money. They just want to hurt me. And I been trying to avoid the reason why. But I think I know.

"Hey." Terry walks closer, sizing me up like a meal. "You never apologized."

"For what?" I ask.

"For bumping into me," he replies. His voice is slow, methodical, malice seething from the pseudo-polite voice. The fibers press out of his neck like he's charging up, before splintering out of his eyes. I've seen that look before from white people, like when the cops attacked me and Dad at my first protest.

I hear Granma calling me a fighter. But I don't think she pictured this. I've never been the aggressor in a fight outside of martial arts tournaments. But I'll defend myself.

Sixth period's gotta be ending soon. Half the school should be walking outta the cafeteria. But it's just me and them. And nobody to save me.

"You moved my sweater," he says, circling me. "Embarrassed me in class."

"Ms. Column asked a question. I answered it." Why am I pleading for my life?

"Did I say you could talk?" He gets closer. "This is our school. I didn't give you permission." *Our school?*

"Probably got some government handout to come here," says

one of Terry's friends, shuffling his hand through his brown hair while he talks. "That's what always happens."

Terry starts posturing. "We need more laws for these people." It's like he's talking to me and not me at the same time. "You don't know what it means to work. To be American."

There it is. *Be American. These people.*

The dress code, the tie, none of it matters. This is about my skin. Emboldened racists turning me into a target like so many Black people. I left Brooklyn thinking these clothes made me less cool. Made me into some garden-variety prep kid. But the world doesn't see any of that. They just see a Black kid. And every hope, every goal, every want for the future I had fades like those fleeting seconds after waking from a dream that I could barely hold on to.

"What am I saying. Daddy's probably already in jail." Terry flashes teeth, forming a repulsive smirk, talking as confidently as someone giving a TED Talk, wholeheartedly believing the trash he's spewing. *You know what?* I don't even care anymore. Throw a punch and we can do this. Three-on-one. Whatever happens, you'll remember me. I didn't come here to be afraid. I came here to win. "Baby daddy, right?" Two more periods and I would've been out. At the dojo with my friends. Home with Granma. "Is that what your whore mom calls him? Or is he dead?"

I drop my bag. "If you gonna do sumptin, do it." I shift into a ready posture, knees slightly bent, my arms loose, toes flexing in my shoes ready to move if he throws a punch.

This isn't my school. This isn't my life. This rage I'm feeling, I can't hold back. They want to test me. *Then test me.* I'll show you who I am.

"Sit your ass down, nigger," Terry says. I get pushed from behind. Blindsided by one of his friends. I fly, off-balance, right into Terry's fist.

I taste blood as my teeth clamp my tongue.

I barely brace my fall. This gang is huddling over me, filled with scorn. But I'm not going to sit down for these fools. Instinct kicks in from training. This ain't a tournament. Real fights are messy. There are no rules. I hurl my fist right into the crotch of the dirty-blond. He keels. I use him as a projectile, shoving him into the guy to his right. I shuffle away, create enough distance to regain my balance. And launch a spinning back kick to knock them down.

Terry charges at me like a bull, plunging me into one of the trophy cases lining the wall. Glass explodes like a car through a store window. My neck is hot. I'm sure I'm bleeding. I don't care. He's given me the perfect angle to grapple. My arm wraps around his, interlocking his elbow, turning it like a crank. His friend attacks and I use Terry as a shield. He takes the blow to the face that was meant for me. But I've lost track of the other. *Wait, are there four of them now?* My vision's blurry, a haze of red washes over my eye. It's another attacker, lurking in the far corner by the stairs, holding something up in his hand.

Stop! Focus!

I choke. An arm grabs my neck from behind, strangling the life out of me. His weight presses against my body. I get punched in the stomach. Twice. Three times. I don't know who's punching me or who's choking me. I'm gasping for air, a mix of salt, sweat, and blood. If I try to hit him, I'll only sink deeper into the choke hold. I hunch my shoulders up, keep my strikes contained, slapping viciously at the rear of my head, hitting both of us so he can't finish the lock. I gotta break free. I sink my center of gravity and throw all my weight back, hoping to ram him into the wall. We topple to the ground.

"MR. POWELL!"

I turn and see the dean.

"Fighting? Damaging school property? To my office."

I try to hold back the tension, but it's a levee that bursts. "What about the rest of them?" They're standing like a unified front. The home team. And me, the visitor. Not a friend. Not a witness. Not an ally in sight. "They attacked me!"

"What I saw is you very clearly attacking Mr. Parker and the others. Now go."

He points toward the door. I've been indicted before there was even a trial.

"And I thought you were one of the good ones," Dean Bradley remarks as I head upstairs to his office.

8

'm about to get kicked out.

It's the start of last period. Students who have a future here are counting the minutes until their weekend begins. No care in the world. *Not me*. I've been sitting in the waiting area in the dean's office, massaging my jaw where I got sucker punched. The nurse gave me a cold pack for the swelling and put a gauze bandage on my neck where the glass got me the worst. She said I might need a tetanus shot. Three days at Augustin and I've got battle wounds that'll probably be with me my whole life. What have I done? Failed my family. Myself.

Rej predicted this. *Who gonna have ya back if shit go sideways?* he asked me.

No one. That's the real.

I'm staring at a rustic bookcase in a room with even older

antique wood moldings like the inside of an unchanged brownstone from the 1920s. It's lined from top to bottom with yearbooks that span several decades. The faded bindings look like the decaying flowers in a cemetery. The history of Augustin lies in these books. How many Black people are in those pages? What year did they even *allow* the first Black kid into this school? Did they survive?

"Would you like a cup of water?" the dean's assistant asks me. It's the same question I've been asked every ten minutes for the last hour or so. The dean is in a meeting, so his assistant is the warden.

I look at my phone. I was texting with Granma while waiting, needed somebody to talk to who would listen without adding on any "you shoulda done" this or thats. But she hasn't replied to my last message. *Did she drift off.* Damn. I shouldn't have texted her. She doesn't need the stress.

"I'm fine," I reply, on edge. My fingers tap violently at my knee, so I put my other hand on top. I wanna close my eyes, do a breathing exercise to bring myself back to the present. But I got one eye looking out to the hallway, wondering if Terry and his friends are gonna stroll by, and the other waiting for the dean's private office to open. The way the dean looked at me . . . what he said. I can already feel it. When that door opens, it'll be official. I've killed whatever future I had here.

Terry barely spent five minutes in this office. Everyone was worried about him. Asking if he'll be okay for tomorrow's game. He left with an ice pack, his eye already a puff of deep violet. Meanwhile, I'm waiting for my mom to come get me. *This is such bullshit.* No repercussions for their prize quarterback. *Their prize white quarterback.* Terry skated. Whatever story he told the dean was the truth no matter what I said.

Mr. Bradley steps out of his private room sipping coffee, standing between me and the bookcase. "Your grandmother should be here to get you soon."

What the hell?

"Granma?" The thought shakes me as if from a daze. My mouth dries up, I'm crumbling, trying to make sense of it. "I thought you said my mom was coming?" I force myself not to jump outta the chair. *Granma can't travel alone.*

"Well, no one else was available and that trophy case you broke was an antique," the dean says, the condescending tone falling like an axe. "We're going to have to figure out how much it's going to cost to fix the damage."

Nothing he says matters. I take out my phone and text: Granma, you ok? You taking a cab? It's gotta be over a hundred to take a cab. She wouldn't—

"Mr. Powell," the dean says, brushing his jacket back to put a fist on his hip. "We're having a conversation, it's churlish to take out your phone and text. You should be thinking about your actions."

"You don't understand," I say.

"I think you don't," he says. "Being here at AP, it was a gift."

There's only one word I hear.

Was.

Past tense. So it's over. My shot gone. How do I face my family?

"Not just our academics," the dean continues. My fate was sealed the moment the fight started. "Also being a part of our legacy." Or maybe when I first stepped through those doors. That woman on the train said it: *You're a Black man in America.* This was always what was in store for me. "You're in a school that's been around for one hundred and fifty years. This is our sesquicentennial," he says, dragging it out like I brought shame to them. "Your classmates understand what it means to be an alum. It's not something to toss away lightly."

Just like that, no robotics competitions. No access to all the technology and fabrication equipment that weren't at Union. Meeting with the alum Mr. Abato mentioned. Talking about robotics in neuroscience. All gone. And college? Expulsion will be on my permanent record. Who'll want me? All for a fight I didn't start.

"You're a smart fellow," he says. "I've seen your scores. Not everyone like you gets this kind of opportunity."

There he goes again. The subtle phrasing. Not everyone *like you*. Another backhanded compliment that I'm supposed to accept. You. The Black kid from the *ghetto*. So articulate. You. The Black kid that was *given* a scholarship even though I earned it with my score. You. *The good one* that stands up for himself. That's how he looks at me. Like a charity case.

And where's Terry? Tomorrow he'll be cheered onto the football field like nothing happened. They jumped me. Called me a nigger. And all the consequences fall on me.

Granma enters the office. She's an imposing woman in spite of being only five foot five. She wears a royal-blue suit jacket over a pink dress, metal belt buckle, pearls around her neck, and her thinning twists hang resiliently to the right side of her head.

Her glasses call attention to her eyes that have seen so much. She could be going out to a formal dinner or a club. But it's her swollen ankles in flats that make me notice her age.

"Welcome, Ms. Powell," Dean Bradley greets her.

"Ms. Bailey," she declares. "I hope you haff a good explanation fi calling me all di way out 'ere."

My heart rises. Her statement was directed solely at the dean. For the first time today, I'm not suffocating. Someone has my back. Someone's always had my back.

She looks at me—neck and jaw swollen despite the ice. Her eyes droop, echoing the pain inside. I catch her fingers digging into her palms as she turns back to the dean.

"Hol' on, so you wan punish my granson and not di person who call him a nigger? What kind a fool ting is dat?"

"Ma'am," the dean says, "I'll ask you not to use that language here."

"When my granson texted me, im tell me dat *dat* is what di bwoy call im. Wheh im deh?"

"I'm sorry," the dean responds. "I didn't really understand all of that."

She takes a deep breath. I know when she's doing one of her silent *Lord, give me the strength* prayers. She repeats each of her words, slowly, overenunciating every syllable. "When I talked to my grandson, he told me that the other bwoy called him *that* disgusting word. Why is he allowed to speak like that? Why is he not here?" She usually drops her *h*'s. When she doesn't, she's holding back the wrath of God.

"Well, we have no evidence of that," the dean responds.

"I'm sorry," Granma says. "They teach mathematics here?"

"Of course," the dean responds, oblivious. "It's one of the reasons we recruited your grandson."

"Right. And from my understanding of arithmetic, a fight involves multiple people, no?" She shakes her finger with force, her voice loud enough for the whole school to hear. She hurls the rhetorical questions like weapons. "At *least* two. One plus one. Is dat not basic addition, correct?"

True. True. Granma always been my hero. Today is no different. She took an hour-long train ride straight up here, stormed into the dean's office like she owned the place, and is going to war for me. People in the hallway are watching. The dean closes the door. I don't think he's ever had someone rise up to him before. The vibrant maroon on his face is exposing his embarrassment.

"Technically—"

"Well, technically there were three of them." She cuts him off. Terry and his two boys, but in the melee I swear I saw someone in the cut—watching. "*Right?* That is what mi granson text me. Are you callin im a liar?" The floodgates are open. "Now, yuh accusin me of raising im to tell lie. Dat about sum it up?" Before he has a chance to respond, she turns to me and says, "Let's go."

Those are the last words Granma says to me as we walk out of the dean's office. All I can think of is how much I've let her down as we take the train home.

The subway is emptier than usual. The after-school rush hasn't started yet. No gossiping students. No screaming passengers. Only the lingering smell of piss and garbage.

She reads her Bible. The silence between us is louder than the metal-on-metal roar of the 2 train barreling downtown. I just want to hug her. She put her life in danger to speak up for me. Who knows what could've happened. Granma could've got lost. Hurt. I can't even think about anything worse. And it would've all been on me. *But what could I have done differently?* No apology makes this right. So I read every ad on the train. Ads for TV shows. Lawyers. Plastic surgery. Once I'm done, I read them again.

Sometimes I feel I have more memories of Granma being around than my parents. She was home when my parents were at work. She can hang with me and my friends and everything is cool.

An hour later we get off the train at Newkirk. Kids are in the streets laughing, eating a slice or a beef patty, clowning each other like life is all good, chatting about clothes or some new song. We turn the corner to head home. It's one of those big brick-box apartment buildings that are interspersed between houses. Not quite the projects, but run by slumlords who don't care about the tenants. Sometimes the elevator is down for weeks. Sometimes there's no hot water. This week, it's a little of both. Sounds of jackhammers and construction vehicles remind me of our recent rent hikes. Higher bills like the tuition they wasted on me. More stress.

The walk up to the fifth floor is like a death march. Granma stumbles on the second flight and I reach out to steady her. It's an odd feeling to offer her support when she's the one who's always supported me.

"Bwoy, me neva noticed ow many stairs dem aff in ere, Ahmad," she says, calling me by my uncle's name again.

"Gil," I say. She looks through me like she's looking into the distance at a mountain range too far to touch. Her breathing is sputtered, skin pasty, weathered from the trip. "Let's get you upstairs so you can rest."

She returns to the present, taking a long breath. "Sorry, GC, so many stairs, felt a likkle dizzy. Me juss gon haff some tea an relax."

"They need to fix the damn elevator. It's been a week now."

"Eh, watch ya tongue." She smiles.

"Sorry, Granma."

My apartment opens up into a small foyer with wood-tile floors. I hear the TV on in the living room. We take off our shoes and Granma hangs her coat in the closet. Directly ahead is the kitchen. Usually, the first thing that hits you is the smell of confections. Granma is always baking cakes and cookies in case a random visitor, which is usually Mr. Neckles, decides to stop by for a chat. She says you always have to have cake on hand for guests, but I've always thought that was an excuse to satisfy her sweet tooth.

I gag when I enter the kitchen. It smells like rancid eggs. The table is littered with the makings of cakes that could've been. Flour, sugar, nutmeg, mixing bowls are all out on the table. The eggs that were meant to be whisked into the flour batter have been out baking into a flour paste in the heat. A trail of spilled milk goes from the bowl to the floor.

"Lawd," Granma moans. "Let me go an clean dis up."

"I got it, Granma," I say hurriedly. I grab her hand and lead her over the disaster area, past Dad's wall of Friday-night DVDs. There are hundreds of movies, each with a memory of how things used to be, in the living room. I'm glad he's not here for this. His disappointment would crush me. I sit her on the couch in the living room.

"No, no," she says defiantly. "Let mi juss wash mi hands an clean up."

"Just chill," I say, trying to convince her. "Let me get you something to drink." I turn on the kettle. Then grab her a glass of water that she chugs thirstily. She gets up, makes a move to go to her room, and I help her to lie down.

When she's settled, I get a damp cloth and begin wiping up the chaos. The eggs already started to cake into the floor, so I dig into it with my fingernails. More evidence of my screwup.

Maybe an hour or so goes by before I'm done.

"Gilbert Clifford Powell!"

My mom's voice rings through the apartment, alerting the neighbors to listen in for what's next. I turn to the front door and there she is. Her arms crossed, one leg forward, her head angled, her face a scowl.

"You just started at this new school and you're fighting?" Mom kicks off round one. Ever since I was young I've been doing exactly what I'm supposed to do. Sure, I've stayed out late a few times and forgot to call home, and occasionally I get an attitude about washing dishes when neighbors come over that I didn't invite. But I get good grades, don't do drugs, and have never broken any arrest-worthy law.

"That's not what happened," I explain. But that's how it feels. "They came at me. I didn't have a choice."

"And breaking school property. Yuh know how much dem seh it cost?"

"There were three guys who jumped me," I plead my case.

"It's a private school. What'd you do to provoke them?"

My chest heaves. "I dunno what the dean told you but it ain't true." *You. Dad. You always encouraged me to stand up to bullies. That's what I did.*

"Gilbert, we're investing so much in you," she says. Choosing to go to Augustin made me just that. An investment. Another bill. But it's the heartbreak in her tone that hurts the most. I was on a pedestal. The anguish in her eyes—all the expectations she had for me bulldozed and demolished like the buildings in my neighborhood. I had one simple mission: Stay in school, get good grades, go to college on time. Have the chance they didn't. "And to get suspended."

"Suspended?" The word leaks out of my mouth like a foreign language. "They didn't expel me?"

"Is that what you want?"

"No, of course not," I say, still letting the information register. *I'm still a student there.*

But do I belong? How do I survive a school ready to fight me because I'm Black. Look what I'm doing to Mom. Granma. I couldn't even be there for Kenya. I'm letting everyone down.

She sucks her teeth. "And your dad. He wants you to have the opportunities he didn't."

But he's not here, is he?

"And you have yuh granmudda goin all di way into di city to deal with it." Mom barely has an accent anymore. Her mom had her in the States but she was raised in Jamaica. When the patois comes out like this—"Because yuh wann pick fight."

"Now 'ol on, daughta." Granma bursts out of her room. She

looks at Mom as her daughter and not just one by marriage. "Yuh haffi hear his story."

"Picking fights?" I can't hold back. The room starts to sway, everything inside boiling over. "You think I wanted this? That I woke up this morning and said, 'Oh, let me try and take on a bunch of football players'?" The rage explodes. And I hate myself for it. "Somebody knocks me on the ground, calls me a nigger, and you think I caused it?"

I've never used that word in my mom's presence before, much less any curse word. She knows I curse with my friends, but I don't let those words come out of my mouth in front of her. Until now.

Mom's jaw drops.

"Some white boys attacked me. And I defended myself, the way I was taught, the way you taught me. And I'm wrong?"

I don't wait for what's next. I storm into my room and slam the door.

9

My bedroom fits a bed, some shelves, a dresser, and a desk. Never really wanted more. I sleep here, but this apartment, this building, this block, this whole neighborhood are all home.

But mentally I'm not here. I'm back in school. Replaying every moment. A vinyl record that keeps skipping back to *that word*. Playing out the scene. Over and over and over again.

I'm not expelled. But this room is my cage for however long this suspension lasts. I was supposed to start robotics on Monday. See the robot they used in last year's competition. Show the team what I can do, or at least learn everything I could.

Scrolling through my phone, I land on the group chat with Rej and Stretch. I start typing.

ME

You wouldn't believe the

I delete the words with a wince. They'd give me advice. That's not what I need. I want someone to actually listen. Hear me. There's a message to Nakia. She must've texted herself from my phone so that she'd have my number. I think of her wrapped in Bajan colors, those thick hips moving against me, the touch of her hand on my skin as we danced before sunup. It feels distant. Someone else's memory. I try to put together a message for her, but all I've got is this jumble of emotions that I can't connect. Then I see that crooked smile Tammy has. The way she knew to pull me away when I had my first run-in with Terry. The feel of my hand in hers like together we could be untouchable. But there was nothing there. Only her doing a good deed. *Right?* Seeing a Black person she didn't know in danger and rushing in to help.

The flyer from the robotics competition Dad took me to when I was in fifth grade calls me over from my dresser. The paper is dog-eared with age, but I can't seem to throw it out. The tournament was in Stamford, Connecticut. I could barely keep my eyes open as we took the 5 train to Grand Central to get the Metro-North. But once we were there, it was heaven. I'd look up at his beard every second as we watched the robots compete. His arm, heavy and chiseled from years of manual-labor jobs, wrapped around my shoulder, shaking me: *Yuh see dat?!*

Don't think I slept for the next week.

I grab the robot from my dresser. I still remember when I first opened it up. The kit had hundreds of tiny parts, more than I'd seen in my life. I remember thinking it'd take a billion years to assemble. But Dad was next to me. Always encouraging. His narrow eyelids would widen. Shining black pupils drew me in like a constellation to the broad nose and rich smile of teeth that had gnawed a little too much sugarcane as a kid in Jamaica.

Where's that encouragement now?

I set the robot down on the floor. Power it on. It doesn't do much. Forward and back. Left and right. Back then it filled me with so many dreams. Visions for what the future could be. Dad next to me, telling me about some new business idea he had. There was one game that would teach kids how to code. He tested out the prototype on me—my gateway into programming. He wanted to make it free for everyone in the hood, but could never get the funding to finish it.

I put my earbuds in, cue up one of Rej's mixes, and lie back on my bed, holding the robot in my hands, trying not to think about Terry or the dean.

Knock. Knock.

I turn over in my bed to face a small window. My phone reads 9:21 p.m. I musta dozed off for a few hours. One missed message alert on WhatsApp, how every Caribbean communicates.

DAD

Gil. Give me a call.

Getting another talking-to or advice from someone who isn't here—I just can't right now. The argument with Mom is still fresh in my head. I'm not even sure who I'm more pissed at: Terry or myself. Then there's the dean. Blood rushes to my head, a migraine taking up space. This whole situation is jacked. Augustin was supposed to be a beginning. But it's just the beginning of more fighting. Not for resources, but just to exist. Will Howard or MIT even look at me with a suspension on my record?

Knock. Knock.

The migraine amplifies the sound like a hammer. I know it's not Granma at the door because she uses a special knock. Parents are tryna double-team me, but I wanna be left alone.

"Gil," Mom says through the door. At least she's not spelling out my whole name like earlier.

"Come in," I reply, my voice hollow.

She enters, closing the door behind her. "May I sit down?" I shrug my shoulders, and she sits. I lean up against the wall.

"How you feeling, Gil?" she asks.

"I'm good," I reply, while my belly groans a different response. I stare at her braids, tied up and back, to avoid her eyes. Then back to the wood-tiled floor.

"I'm sorry I didn't take time to hear your side of the story." She hesitates. "I know if your dad were here he'd . . ." She has that look on her face when she's about to drop something on me. "There's a lot on my mind right now, the new job, bills." She was on the wait list for years at the MTA. Then Dad left, I got into the school. The bump of the city job drained immediately. "I'm just trying to keep it all together. And the way the dean made it out, you were the only one who was suspended." Figures. No repercussions for Terry. He's home right now sitting comfortable. "But then your granma told me the whole story. I called the dean up about this suspension. If they're not going to suspend the other student, then they shouldn't suspend you. And for a week . . ." She groans, sucking her teeth. "It's disgusting."

"Granma didn't have to hear any side," I say, my thoughts reflexively slipping out. "She knew I wouldn't have fought unless I was forced to." I draw a line between us. I've never done that before. All I see is the worry on her face. And I don't want to take the hurt away because it's the truth. *What's wrong with me?*

A few years ago, everything seemed so simple. Did well in school. Had plans for college. Going to Jamaica was a summer vacation with my mom. On the weekend, my aunt on my mom's side would DJ at night in Port Antonio. Plug her system into some giant speakers in the street for a dance party. Dad never flew down with us 'cause he had to work, or said the flight was too expensive. But the real reason was that he couldn't leave without finding a way to get back in.

"I know I'm costing everyone," I say. "I'll do better." It's not an apology. It's a promise to myself. Tammy said she had to do double the work of the other students to get her position at the newspaper. So I gotta go harder. I'll drown myself in class work and double down on the robotics team. I won't fail anyone again. I have to succeed. There's no other option.

The migraine hits so hard my eyes tighten from the tungsten light overhead.

"Hush," she says. "It's not the money." It's always the money. "We want you to have opportunities 'cause you deserve them. I shouldn't have made it out like it's your school's tuition that's a burden. Anyway, I'm sorry. I trust you to make the right decisions. You've always done that. There's just a lot . . ." She trails off. Does she think about Dad the way I do? Wondering if his application for a visa will be rejected again. If his interviewer will have a heart this time. As if being apart from your family wasn't enough. "I better get some sleep. I left dinner on the stove if you're hungry. If not, just leave it and I'll take care of it later."

She exits. I want to ask her how she's managing everything. But the question doesn't come. It never does. I should've hugged her. Years ago I would've. But I tell myself not letting this school break me, going back to Augustin and getting every win I can, however I can, is the way to show I'm grateful for every sacrifice. And that I love her.

I sit alone, staring at my walls. Granma's prayers are bleeding through them. For Jamaica, Dad, Mom . . . me. She gives so much, and all I'm giving is grief. I close my eyes until sleep finally takes me.

10

It's Saturday morning and I'm unloading on the pads like it's fight night and I'm the main ticket.

The Always Persevere Dojo is a second-floor walk-up in Midwood. Blue padded mats line the training floor. Six-foot-high gray mats surround us, blanketing the wall should a student have an unfortunate case of flying into it while sparring. Otherwise the walls are painted bare white to highlight our school's logo. There's a cloud of perspiration from the humidity. A commercial fan in the corner blows around the stench of controlled battle. As the deshi in charge today, my cousin Renee walks around surveying the field, correcting the kōhai on their form.

Saturday-morning class is for mixed ranks and ages. We focus on strength and conditioning, plus it's one of those random September days where summer says it hasn't left yet, so every-where feels like the 34th Street–Herald Square station, where even the rats sweat. So no full uniforms. I have my lightweight blue jiujitsu pants on and a black T-shirt. Sensei is out of town. Today, Stretch, Rej, and me are the only black belts other than Renee. The other students look to us for guidance in how we carry ourselves. But I can't help the gnawing inside me.

Every time my roundhouse connects with the kick shield, my foot slams down to the mat before snapping back up. I don't hear the sounds of the other students going through their drills. I don't see their faces.

I see Terry. The curve in the kick shield Stretch holds is the letter on each of those varsity sweaters that protected his team-mates from blame. A badge of whiteness. I kick harder. The dean who said I failed to be *one of the good ones*. This is the culture that attacks us for protesting the killing of unarmed Black people.

"Combinations," Renee calls out, and the class pivots to attention. "Roundhouse, back kick, cross punch, stomp kick."

We step to the wall so we have enough room to execute the combo.

"You good, fam?" Stretch asks me in his usual carefree way. He's holding the kick shield in one hand while stroking his almost-a-goatee with the other, as if by constantly touching it he can coax it to grow in. Outside of the obligatory whatup, I haven't said much to him all morning.

"I'm aight," I say, hoping he gets the message to leave me be. If I just keep punching and kicking, my mind won't have a chance to go back to the replay. It won't have a chance to remind me that I'm breaking my mom's heart. Will I look back on this moment and realize what I did put more stress on Granma, advanced her disease?

"You seem . . . I dunno . . . a little off," Stretch says, not taking the hint from my silence. "I mean, we're going for technical, not power, but you fitna barrel through the pad like I did you somethin." I can feel his eyes on the bandage on my neck. But he gives a jovial chuckle as if life's the same as it was two weeks ago. For him it is. It's not like I'm gonna pour my heart out so he can tell me I'm making too much of it. He'll tell me that Augustin will get better. That I'm meant to do big things. *I can't live in those dreams.* All I have is the pain of right now. Not the bright side he sees. He makes a point to turn off the news and wave off conversations about racism 'cause it brings him down. He wouldn't get it.

"Yo, if you need someone else to hold the pad, you can switch." I growl more than say it. Other students look over. Kenya's expression asks, *Why's big bro gettin loud?* Rej has an eyebrow raised, almost judging, saying, *Your dad is gonna get to come back into the country, not mine, what you got to be angry 'bout?*

"I gotchu," he says, bouncing on his toes, flexing his wiry frame, ready to spar. "Just wanted to make sure you was good."

"Excuse me," Renee interjects. Her scowl lets us know we're disrupting class. "You see everyone else? They're doing their combinations. Let's go, black belts."

I do the combo once, twice. My strikes get less contained, more savage. Stretch deepens his stance after each pass to maintain balance, shuffling backward with every hit. If Rej transferred with me, maybe things woulda went down differently. Maybe it'd make me feel like everything wasn't changing so fast, firing out of control like each kick, each punch. Maybe I want to make the pad explode. On the third reset, I drive my last kick forward with all the distress, all the agony, all the tears of being less than the person everyone thought I was. The person I thought I could be.

"Oof," Stretch wheezes, slow to secure the pad, the force propelling him into the wall. He holds his chest, crumpling to the floor, snapping me out of my funk. "What's your problem?" Stretch says, the bleached tips on his high curled fade soaring up like a phoenix as he jumps in my face. The always-cool expression gone. We've been friends since we were kids, he doesn't want to fight. Maybe he wants to know my pain, but we never talk about things like this. Not on the level I need to. "Sparring was yesterday, you missed that."

"Black belts!" Renee bellows, signaling us. "Sensei's office. Now." She motions to Rej. "Joshu, you have the floor."

We bow off the mats and head out the door and into Sensei's office. The room is a cramped space with bland floor tiles that are probably decades old. The hundred-dollar do-it-yourself desk is littered with envelopes. The wall has pictures of top students and instructors as well as Sensei's teacher. In the corner are some of Sensei's most recent trophies. On the left, a bookshelf and a mini-fridge.

"What's the deal?" Renee asks, closing the door. "Y'all looking real bad in front of the underbelts." Stretch simply looks away, the chill smile returning, waving his arms up 'cause he has no answer. He's known my cousin almost as long as he's known me. But he's not giving me up. "If there's something going on between you two, I need it squared away, 'cause we got demo practice after this. And I need people on point for routines, synchronizations." She's right. The only thing worse than being out of focus in a fight is losing focus in a demo. No matter how much training you have, fights always turn to chaos. But demos are choreographed. Mess up and the audience is left staring, snickering, knowing that the fault is all on you. "Y'all two gotta be in sync, don't need one of your nunchucks flying at the audience mid-demo."

"It's my fault, cuz," I say. "Lot on my mind."

She sighs and motions for Stretch to leave. He bows and heads back to the mat, making sure to close the door behind him.

"So wussup?" Renee asks. She's dyed her hair a dark green since the last time I saw her. Her arms are crossed and her mouth is a straight line, channeling Granma's assertiveness, letting me know that telling her the truth is the only way out this room.

My chest heaves, me not knowing where to start.

"Been dealing with some drama at school," I say. She returns an expression that's not anger, but something she's given me since I was a kid. Why she's not just big cuz but big sis. Empathy. Her eyes sink with the sadness shaking me inside. I should've known. In my family news travels fast. Renee knows. And everyone from Church Ave straight down to Newkirk and back in the Caribbean will know before the weekend is over. The Jamaican Word-of-Mouth News Network has been around long before social media. So I unload everything that has happened since I started school at Augustin, from the moment I bumped into Terry until the suspension. Then Mom's reaction. She listens. No opinion. No judgment. Reminding me that what I say matters.

She sits down on Sensei's desk, shaking her head. "Well, that's jacked."

"Ain't it though," I reply, distracting myself with the letters on Sensei's desk, some end-of-season tournament invites, and then the bookshelf. He's got his own set of philosophy and essay books: *Go Rin No Sho, Letters to a Young Poet, The Unfettered Mind* . . .

"Can't say my time in private school was flawless," she says. "Well, any Black person's really. I can tell you stories. Hell, when I entered there were fifteen in my class, by the time I graduated, we were only six. Probably not much different at Augustin."

Only six. That's it right there. Augustin. Union. All these schools. Both sides are set up for failure if you're Black. Either your school doesn't have the resources or they try to make you into something less than you are for partaking of the same resources everyone should have. I'm supposed to be glad I wasn't expelled. Take suspension as some kinda gift. A reminder to make sure I know my place, stay *one of the good ones* or it can all go away.

"I feel like I'm trapped." My thoughts leak out. "Like any way I turn, there's no win, and I keep reliving it."

"That's trauma," Renee says. "Ain't no slur you can call a white person that has the history of the N-word," she says. "They made sure of that. Truth be told, using that word, attacking you, that's a hate crime."

"They dangling my future like the keys to a cell," I say. "But how can I fight? I'm just one person. Ain't nobody gonna listen to me." My voice rises, the acid in my chest pouring out. "And when I come off suspension, I gotta go back there looking over my shoulder." I'm sure the kōhai can hear me through the particle-board door. I try to breathe out the frustration, but the knot strangling me is so tight.

"There's nobody else you can go to?" Renee asks.

"I can't even keep up with all the layers of bureaucracy there," I say. I still remember orientation. The dean gave the opening speech, but there's also a headmaster, president, Board of Trustees. But that route just feels like some bizarre level of snitching. "The dean was okay with this happening. Prob gonna be the same with the headmaster or president."

"I hear you, cuz," she replies. "Whether it's Augustin or the rest of the country, you gonna be in these white spaces. You was talking about being a scientist or lawyer. You wanted to fight those battles. Gonna be racists there too. You never hear stories about mass deportations of Europeans." She rests her hand on my shoulder, probably realizing there's no win for me in this situation either. She looks me straight in the eye, her face a coupling of calm and stern truth. "But you can't just go knocking Stretch into the wall every time something comes up." She grins. "Then the kōhai gonna wanna do it. Then I'm gonna wanna do it."

I smile for the first time since I had lunch with Tammy on Thursday.

"But seriously, cuz," she says. "You see that book on Sensei's shelf?" I glance over.

It's Sun Tzu's *The Art of War*.

"Do me a favor. Read it. I want you to be a teen, but you gonna have fights." She shakes her head with the certainty of wisdom. "Most of them not physical. Managing the stuff with Granma alone. I can't imagine how that's affecting you."

"So this book's gonna give me the answer?"

"Not about answers," Renee says. "If you tryna find an answer, you gon be searching forever. Read the book. Take a breath.

Then figure out how to move." I grab the book off the shelf and start flipping the pages as if something might call out to me. "Just make sure to return it when you're done or else Sensei gonna come for you. That's a war you don't want."

We head back out onto the training mat. I dap up Stretch, and say, "My fault, man."

"Say less," Stretch says. We get back to training.

The dojo's name calls out to me. *Always Persevere.* Maybe this is like a martial arts tournament. I'm a point down. But it's not over. With everything that's going on with family, health, and immigration, I've felt like I've been in nonstop battles. I got a lot more to do at Augustin. And I can't let anybody shut me outta doing it.

Augustin Prep is war. And I'm ready to fight. I just need a new playbook.

PART II
Ground & Strategy

Know the enemy and know yourself; in a
hundred battles you will never be in peril.

SUN TZU: *THE ART OF WAR*

11

Wars are either fought in secret or they're right in your face. A week has passed since I was suspended. I can't tell what war I'm in here. There's no school district, no community board, no DOE. No tangible protest. Just 150 years of history—

It's second period in Ms. Willis's Philosophy class. The air is different. It's an elective that I only have twice a week. The students here chose to have a Black woman as their teacher. She's one of only two Black faculty members. There aren't posters of philosophers on the walls, but signs for BLACK LIVES MATTER, PROTECT ASIAN LIVES, LGBTQIAP+, STOP AAPI HATE, MY BODY, MY CHOICE, DEFUND THE POLICE, STOP BULLYING.

Somebody like Terry would never sign up to be in this class. Surrounded by humanity. It should be a safe space.

But my brain is stuck. Calling me the N-word is one thing. Fighting another. But how the dean . . . No. How the school handled it . . . Who's the real enemy? Every time I think about it, my jaw tightens, each vein in my head squeezes, and the migraine forces its way back. Maybe if Dad was here to help me reason it out, but a phone conversation don't cut it. So I turn to the book.

Sun Tzu says in "Offensive Strategy" that the height of skill is to *subdue an enemy without fighting*. Sounds like play nice. Get your victories where you can. But Sun Tzu also says to attack the enemy's strategy. Divide them. And to learn how to use small forces when you're outnumbered. If only I had a force.

The class is broken up into five tables, each with four to six people sitting around it. It's still mostly white, but CJ from robotics is here. Plus there's a mix of Asian, Black, and Latinx students, which makes it feel a little more like Union. But not by much.

Each student has a notebook and their copy of Plato's *Five Dialogues* open to the "Apology." Socrates's testimony before death.

"Is Socrates deliberately corrupting the youth with his ideas?" Ms. Willis asks the class while they diligently write down notes from the last question. This is one of the few classes students are allowed to have their laptop or phone out to take notes or look up references on the internet. I have my phone out with the voice memo app open on record so I can just listen back at home.

I'm in my quiet space. Forget Socrates, Sun Tzu's given me a decision to make—to channel the anger or bury it.

He wrote a chapter called "The Nine Varieties of Ground." Each space is a different terrain to maneuver on: classes, the cafeteria and lounges, after-school activities. Each interaction a new campaign and each conversation a chance to change the course of a battle: meetings with faculty, administration, alumni. Any group can be an enemy, an ally, an army. I already know where the football team stands—enemy and army. And me without a single ally.

Well, not fully true. There's Tammy. My face warms thinking about those glasses, the midnight tint that makes her eyes sparkle like the moon. The half smirk that always seems to have a secret. The tension in my head begins to ease up, releasing the pressure, giving me a moment to breathe. Tammy runs two clubs. And I need people, call 'em allies or whateva. Anything to make me feel like I'm not alone here or at least get me through this week and each week after.

Then dominate in robotics. Walk around with a win on my chest.

"Gil." Ms. Willis says my name as if for the second time. It's the only class where a teacher doesn't refer to us by our last name.

I got no idea what Ms. Willis asked, but she doesn't need to know that. And if there's also one thing I learned from my parents, it's never ask to repeat a question—that unleashes all types of *you weren't listening* hell. "The conversation is a little confusing," I say, playing it off like I was deep in thought. "Everyone contradicts themselves, especially Meletus. Like on page 30. Is the claim really that everyone from the Council to the jury improves the young, while Socrates alone corrupts them? It's like politicians and the rich forgetting to point the finger at themselves." Teachers only care that you read something. Show effort and they'll usually hand the answer to you.

"That's a fair comparison," Ms. Willis responds. "Though it brings us back to my original question, what's Socrates's assertion? The crux of his defense?"

There it is. The question I missed. I skim through my book, and find the line I marked off. "That the unexamined life is not worth living," I say with a mic drop. The line called out to me over the last week. All this reading I've been doing on the art of war. It's been an examination of the past few years, negotiations with doctors over Granma's medical bills, helping Rej figure out where ICE had taken his dad. Them moving his father from place to place made it harder for us to try and stop him from getting lumped into a mass deportation. I tried to help Dad find legal counsel to figure out how to fix his own immigration status. But he didn't trust waiting for the legal system. He weighed the cost of lawyers versus me coming to Augustin. *Am I the reason he's gone?*

"And the unexamined fist is not worth giving," CJ quips, referring to Terry's injury. The class bursts out in laughter. "Terry's still examining his eye." Great. Even the Asian dude from robotics is getting on me. I wonder if he'd say that joke if Terry was here. Whose side is he on?

"CJ! Class!" Everyone falls silent. Ms. Willis looms over us like a general surveying her troops. The calm wrath is almost frightening. What's worse is the disappointment she casts over us. Like we let her down, the one teacher who makes no qualms about proclaiming she's got everyone's back. "This is not the room for gossip and side conversations," she says. CJ can barely meet Ms. Willis's eyes. "That's the end of class. I expect everyone to bring back their decorum next time."

As the class clears out, CJ grabs his crutches from the wall and hops toward me with another student.

"Hey, sorry about that," he says, his voice laid-back like a fall breeze. He brushes a light curtain of hair from his face. The jet-black strands fall back to the same mark. He flashes a practiced smile, almost posing on his crutches.

"Janeil." A Black girl introduces herself. She has thick curls parted down the middle and thin eyebrows. She's always raising her hand in this class and AP Lit. "Don't mind CJ, he's cool. Just has terrible timing."

"Yeah, I guess," he says with a sheepish eye roll. "That's what Zan keeps telling me at least. They're my partner."

"Oh, so it's official now," Janeil says.

"It is." CJ grins. "You could take yourself off the market too."

"Let's keep my love life out of it," Janeil says.

CJ shrugs and turns back to me. "Anyway, Terry's a known bully. And if you're a person of color"—he lets out a long sigh—"I don't even want to get started." So he's not boys with Terry. That's good. And it sounds like CJ's got his own history with him.

"We wanted to say hi and welcome." Janeil grins. She's one of those people who can't help but smile. And that proper voice—probably grew up around money in the suburbs. She touches her hair, grooming it like she's getting ready in the mirror. "Have to get to next class."

"I'll see you in robotics," CJ says to me. "Trying to get Janeil to join. Do some CAD. She's a great artist." She tugs at CJ's blazer. They say their goodbyes and turn.

I hesitate. The pages of Sun Tzu urging me to speak up. "Hey."

I chase them down. "You going to the BCC meeting after school?" I ask Janeil, gulping my words.

"Oh indeed," she says, tapping me on my blazer crest. "I guess that means you're coming too. Tammy will be glad to have more people show up." The way she talks throws me off. I need friends, but if they're all a bunch of rich people sold on Augustin's Kool-Aid, I don't know if I'll relate—or if I can stomach it.

At least Tammy will be there.

DAD

Stay focused and keep your head down

It's recess. Students are heading to their lockers to swap out books, catching up on the weekend, and getting ready for their next period.

Not me.

I'm still outside Ms. Willis's classroom, reading over this message. The hallway might as well be empty because it's just me and this one line. I try to picture him saying it to me in person. The narrow jaw with the freshly shaped-up chin beard. The slim frame with the belly from one too many Red Stripes. But that confident smile that always eased my nerves doesn't quite form in the haze of memory.

"Mr. Powell."

I jump to find Ms. Willis standing behind me. She lets out a hefty sigh, squeezing her lips. Her eyes look up, the way Granma's do when she doesn't know how to find the words and says a prayer for strength.

"You have a meeting with the Disciplinary Board during your lunch period," she says.

"About what?" I ask. The muscles in my face grind. I feel my eyes flare because there is no keeping my head down in this school. "I just got back."

"It's a formality." She sighs, frustrated by the task of being the messenger. "One to make sure there's no . . . retaliation for what happened." It's like she's being forced to speak, but I can tell she's making sure I hear the exact words that were told to her. So I can remember them.

"You serious?" The Brooklyn in me lashes out unchecked. "Am I the only one?"

She shakes her head, powerless. "As you'll come to learn, this school is very much driven by money and politics." Her eyes are locked on me, unwavering, like she's holding back some truth that could break the reality Augustin is selling. "When the number of Black students falls, it's personal, and it hurts. Enrollment of people of color in general hasn't been going up. It's easy to feel alone here."

This isn't a pep talk. Just reality. And if they still think they need to discipline me, then I'm not going down easy.

12

I just gotta make it through the next ten minutes.

I'm sitting in a swivel chair with a high mesh back, at the end of a long rectangular table in a conference room with gray carpet and glass walls. Occasionally a person or two walks by, dressed in a suit, wondering what's going on. Outside of a star-shaped speakerphone on the table and a pitcher of water, the room is barren—

Except for the four people staring across the table at me.

It's sixth-period lunch. I'm in Augustin's business wing on the second floor. It's basically a row of offices totally sequestered from student life. Across from me are Ms. Willis, Headmaster DeSantis, Ms. Column, and Dean Bradley. Two faculty members. Two administrators. And me. I wish the water was closer, or that they'd at least offer me a cup, because my throat's dry and my chest feels like a hole is about to open up from my heart kicking so hard.

"Let's not dip too much into your lunch break," the dean remarks. The folds in his brow are stiff, his lips refusing to form even a glimpse of welcome. There's cool air being pumped into the room, but I'm suffocating. "Your probation will be a month. During which time—"

"Probation?" My eyes pop. This isn't real. It can't be.

"Yes," the dean says. The matter-of-fact tone is more condescending than a smack to the face. "You have no idea what your outburst has led to." *What about how you let Terry skate? How you blamed me—the victim. Where's the consequences for that?* My jaw tightens so hard my teeth might turn to dust. It's the only thing stopping me from screaming. Sun Tzu says to subdue the enemy without fighting, but that's what they're doing to me. My arms are trembling against my ribs like I'm being attacked and I don't know where the next strike will come from. "The calls from parents and alumni that we received." So it's not just students. The hate for me has gone beyond the school's walls. "We have to do what's best for our students." *Am I not one of them?*

"But I served my suspension," I plead. They've turned me into a convict and are now strapping the ankle bracelets on me 'cause of some calls. Ms. Column has a straight poker face on. And Ms. Willis, I almost can see her bottom lip change color as she bites in.

"Mr. Powell, this has been a very difficult time for all of us," Headmaster DeSantis says. He has a box-shaped face, cheeks hang over an empty smile, almost mocking, when this moment is anything but good for me. The headmaster is the oldest one in here and looks like he's never failed to enjoy every moment life brought him. Does he even get what he's doing? "But the probation will give you a chance to ease into Augustin life. Instead of being burdened by activities and other social events, you can focus on your academics."

"No activities? What about robotics?" The pain claws its way up, ripping through me. Robotics was one of the bright spots of my first day. Talking to Mr. Abato. Being around that infectious energy Lydia had toward science. Sure, her brother, Heath, was a little standoffish, maybe even territorial. But being there, with the twins, CJ, it all felt right.

"You'll be able to return to robotics mid-October," the headmaster says as if he's doing me a favor.

"But we have a competition next month," I say. "That doesn't give me any time to help the team. I won't do any other activity, just let me have that." I'm begging. Asking for some understanding. I snap so hard on my tongue that I taste blood.

"I'm afraid it's already been decided," the headmaster says.

"That's the reason I came here," I say. My voice cracks into a whimper. I feel myself falling through the mesh chair. This is all what Sun Tzu called enemy ground. There are no highs for me here. No victory in this terrain. I can't even do the one activity I wanted more than anything. "The reason you recruited me."

The dean mumbles something under his breath that sounds like "not the only reason." But I can't tell. All I see is the side-eye Ms. Willis shoots him.

"And Black Culture Club?" I ask.

"All clubs." The dean drops the definitive hammer, shutting me out of not only my passion, but also a community of people who look like me. They've divided me from my allies before I had a chance to even make them. "Break your probation and that will be another strike against you. Three strikes, and you'll be removed from all clubs for the duration of your senior year." Three strikes, like Bill Clinton's push for mass incarceration. Determined crow marks form on Ms. Willis's face, as if she's studying me. No. She's urging me. *To fight?* Maybe I'm reading too much into it. Granma reminded me on day one I was a fighter. So that's what I'll do.

The next battle—I'll be the one to start it.

13

I'm not walking up to the Black Culture Club meeting so much as I'm being pulled. I'm on autopilot in a hall of quiet marble. All I know is: *I'm not supposed to be here.*

Sun Tzu said, "Nothing is more difficult than the art of the maneuver." Try being Black in America.

The club uses the lecture hall on the fifth floor for its meeting space. The room can probably fit a good seventy people comfortably in the tiered seating. The front of the class has freshly buffed hardwood floors, a two-level dry-erase board, a teacher's desk off to the side, and a podium in the center. The wall opposite the entrance is one large window to the city and a bright afternoon sky. A projector hangs from the ceiling and speakers dot the corners, making this a great spot to screen a movie . . . or to plant the seeds of war.

"How you say you like hip-hop but you don't know Outkast?" Janeil asks, sucking her teeth, her foot up on the adjacent desk.

Some students have ties and blazers off, looking relaxed, while others have fully transformed into their street wear. But what really stands out is the level of Blackness in this room. There are only ten students inside, eleven if I enter, but the energy feels like a basement party about to jump off.

"Calm down with all that," Tammy says. She's sitting on the tier below Janeil. Unlike everyone else, Tammy's still in full dress code, not even a top button undone. The green blazer, the white shirt, the pants all feel tailor-made the way they accent her body—especially her hips. "I didn't say I didn't know who Outkast was. I know who they are, I just don't know all their songs. Most of their albums came out before we were born."

"You wildin," Janeil says, sounding like a whole different person from in Philosophy class and AP Lit. She's not just giving off a different vibe. *Janeil grew up on the block.* She's got confident in-your-face swag. Gotta be from the Bronx. "That's hip-hop history. We talkin change-the-game quality." Janeil throws up her hands. It's like a Union lunchroom debate. Rej would love being in on this. And I can't even enjoy it because I'm on a mission. "Have you even listened to *ATLiens*, or *Aquemini*?"

I wanna smile. Enter the room like everything's good. But my face is still twitching from that meeting, and Sun Tzu says I have to play the role of the calm and good general if I'm gonna reclaim my senior year. Let the administration know Gil doesn't back down easy. So I break probation. Cross the threshold. Nobody gonna stop me from talking with my Black people. And if I'm diggin in the crates, and it's not the Notorious B.I.G. . . . "I hear y'all on that Southern rap," I jump in, the lingering anger making it sound like I'm anti-Outkast. "But what y'all know about

Liquid Swords or *The Infamous*?" That's what I am to Augustin. Infamous.

"Come on, Gil." Tammy groans. She brushes her fingers against her brow, those blue frames pressed against a nose that's looking even cuter smooshed. "Please don't turn this into the old-school hip-hop club. Janeil will start criticizing 'Rapper's Delight' again."

"I got things to say." Janeil stands up.

I lean in to Tammy, trying to keep my voice to a whisper even though there's no privacy here. "Can I talk to you for a sec?" I motion my head to the door and she gives me a quizzical look. We walk over while Janeil continues her discussion on the finer points of old-school hip-hop, starting with DJ Kool Herc.

My arms are crossed, one arm raised, my knuckle pressed against my lip. My feet are doing a two-step, pacing in place, as I try to gather my thoughts. Maybe it was the conversation in the cafeteria, about her struggle with the newspaper, that makes me think she can understand some of what I'm going through. But I can't say everything. Not until I know for sure. Tammy locks her hand on my shoulder, grounding me, the grip firm and comforting. Her eyes steady, asking me what's going on. "They put me on probation," I say.

"You were just suspended?" Her head snaps back and the puzzled expression lets me know everything. I'm an outlier. She goes into it. Suspensions are rare here. And there's only academic probation for students whose grades drop to failing at the end of the quarter.

"They're making an example of me." But why? My brain's stuck on the obvious. It's because of my skin. But it still seems excessive.

"You have to talk to Ms. Willis."

"She was there." I shrug. "She didn't really speak up for me." I saw the anger in her face, but where were the words. Granma doesn't hesitate. Dad wouldn't, but he's not here, is he? I don't need a text. I need someone to be on my side. By my side.

"Uh-oh! Uh-oh!" A student dressed in his football jersey, pants, and shoulder pads bursts through the entrance. He's got one hand up to his mouth and the other holds a wave brush pointed at me. "Look at the champ richea!" His voice is more smooth jazz than teenager. He's about Rej's height, but Rej is built more like a football player than him. This dude seem more sprinter than linebacker.

Members of the football team generally get dismissed ten minutes before the end of last period so they can change for practice. But he obviously likes making an appearance. "Let me stay out of arm's reach," he says. He hops back while throwing a stiff arm. "I know you like to knock out football players." He starts brushing his waves. "And I'm too pretty to get punched in the face."

"I dunno what people are saying happened," I say. I try to stay calm 'cause it's just him teasing, but my voice kicks up. "But whatever you think happened ain't the full story." That's what I want to yell at the dean, the headmaster, even Ms. Willis and Ms. Column.

"Then you should tell it," Tammy says, her voice resolute. The sun catches her frames, accentuating the jeweled undertones in her skin. "This is what we need to be doing." The way she talks— it's empowering. "Sharing Black stories." Her voice hardens as she urges each person in the room to join her cause. "It's what

I couldn't do under the previous editor. People need to know that Gil's side of the story matters. The biases here are real and destructive. We can't let the same problems we faced be passed on to the next class and the class after that without pushing for change. It's not right that the administration—"

I grab hold of her hand, letting her know silently that I don't want to discuss the probation, not with the group. Not yet. Her lips flatten. She draws in a strong breath through her nose, her shoulders squaring. Then gives me the ghost of a nod. Not just saying she understands, but that she's been there and gets me.

"Aww. Here we go," the football player moans. "Tammy gonna try and recruit you now so she can get her Pulitzer."

"Boy, if you don't shut up," Janeil says to the athlete. He gives Janeil puppy dog eyes while spinning his hair with the wave brush. "You don't even got to explain," she says to me. I wish she'd explain this total Jekyll and Hyde one-eighty. 'Cause it's disturbing. "That's the problem. This school's first reaction is to punish the Black student. When everybody knows that Terry and his people always on one. They get away with everything 'cause sports is the bread and butter of the endowment. I mean, how many of the trustees were on the football team here?"

"You know I'm only playin," the athlete says, putting his arm on Janeil's shoulder, which she promptly shrugs off. He shakes his head and turns to me. "Aye, I'm Saleem." He gives me the one-hand dap and chest hug. "Hope you didn't take it any way. Just having a little fun."

"It's good." I nod. Soaking in the Blackness slightly calms my nerves.

"I gotta get back to the team, but let's chop it up more." Saleem dips his head, giving me a goodbye pound. "Janeil, you're gonna come see me at practice, right." It's not a question.

"Uhh, byeee," she replies, throwing up her hand.

Is this the only place Janeil is her true self? Where we can all be ourselves?

When Saleem walks out the door, Tammy leans toward me and says, "They're dating, trying to play it off like they didn't hook up over the summer."

"You can mind your business," Janeil snaps. She walks out after Saleem, and Tammy gives me the *see what I'm sayin* look.

"I better go too," I say to Tammy.

"Stay," she says. Her eyes are thoughtful and commanding. "Ms. Willis said she wasn't stopping by, and nobody here's snitching." Something about the way she says it compels me not only to stay, but also to feel at home.

I unbutton my collar and take off my tie, then rest my blazer down on a seat to say what's up to some of the other Black students here. There are five freshmen and three sophomores. Two juniors show up while we're getting acquainted. They're all here to hang out and make friends. In another timestream, like one of Dad's sci-fi films with a multiverse of possibilities, I would be too. But thinking about the Disciplinary Board has a million questions popping in my head. And I realize one thing: I need the BCC to have my back . . . so I can pick a fight—

THERE ARE TWO things Sun Tzu said in the "Nine Varieties of Ground."

One: I have to be "serene" and "self-controlled." Whether it's the students or the administration, I can't let them see my anger. Smile. Let them think everything is good.

Two: I have to "be capable of keeping officers in ignorance" of my plans, change my methods, and alter them so people have no knowledge of what I'm doing.

Now I just need an army. And I gotta give them a reason to fight. Because I'm not enough.

Tammy takes position at the podium. The movement alone brings the room to order. We take our seats in the front two rows. Janeil is back at her spot in the second row.

They start discussing activities for the year, potential partnerships with the Student Events Committee. The conversation runs on while I remain on the sidelines, useless. They're thinking about social activities, but if they were to host one, I couldn't even show my face at it before my probation is over without getting another strike. I should be thinking about college essays, winning my last martial arts tournaments before the end of the season, dating.

"Real quick, why y'all keep bringing up the Student Events Committee?" I ask. "You gotta partner with them on everything?"

"Well, they kinda do everything," Janeil says. "Harvest Dance. Winter Dance. Golf outings . . ."

"Trips to Italy. The Ivy school tour," Tammy adds.

"What's the Ivy tour?" I ask.

"Student Events works with the Parents' Committee to host a weeklong trip to a few Ivy League schools. Select students get to go."

"Like our girl here." Janeil motions to Tammy.

"Got it," I say. Hearing her mention parents takes me back a few hours to that meeting. The dean mentioned calls from parents and alumni about me. Did any of those calls come from the Parents' Committee? "And why do you need Student Events to plan our activities?" I ask.

"Funds," Tammy replies. "That club's been around forever, so they have a pretty big budget. Ours doesn't cover much."

"So students don't pay?" I ask. "For things like the Ivy tour?"

"It's all drawn from tuition and endowments," Tammy says. "In a way you've already paid for it. Each activity has its own budget approved from the prior year. Anything above that budget requires a proposal, or partnership with another organization, fundraising, or out-of-pocket costs from the students."

"That'd be dope," I think out loud. A tour. The school already does it. But the Student Events Committee is definitely not doing this kind. In a perfect world, where I wasn't on probation, I'd get a feel for the commute to DC. See how easy it is to travel there and then back to check in on Granma. And it would give me time to get to know everyone here. That's the objective everyone needs to know.

"Um, what?" Janeil asks.

"An HBCU tour," I say, focused on Howard. "I think there are eleven universities in the DC-Maryland-Virginia area."

"That's a great idea," Tammy says to nods of agreement from the other members. "I'll talk to Ms. Willis." If the budget is limited, we'll need to partner with somebody. Enter Sun Tzu's hostile territory. See how the school responds to that. Based on how the administration's treated me, they won't go for it. And that'll give me an army. Each person in this room. This battle has to be bigger than me.

"We shouldn't let budget be an issue," I say. "If anything, we can partner with Student Events, right?" Then another idea escapes my mouth before I have a chance to second-guess it. "I'd be down to work with you on the proposal." I try to cover up the thirsty look forming on my face.

"That could work," Tammy replies. Her eyes sparkle with excitement. "It would really give other Black students more reason to show up. Let them know what these years here are about, put them inside the college atmosphere, make real what they're striving for."

That's what Augustin was supposed to be for me. A college atmosphere. But how can you strive for anything when this school takes away so much?

14

ROBOAUGS

LEARN MORE ABOUT OUR GROWING TEAM
EVERYONE WELCOME
MEETING IN FABRICATION CENTER 3:15
LOWER LEVEL AUGUSTIN
THERE WILL BE PIZZA

It's Thursday, 2:47 p.m. I'm staring at the announcement board on the third floor. It's been stalking me all week. If I'm not hearing Mr. Abato pump up the team over the PA system, it's this bold-lettered poster on the wall among signs for parent-teacher night and school play auditions. Mr. Abato is recruiting heavy, but he's not going to find programmers like me who aren't already on the team.

The team I can't be a part of.

As the school empties, I head up to the fourth floor, checking my text messages.

REJ

> Think I got a lead on an immigration lawyer that'll talk to me about my dad's situation, might be able to talk to you too. Gonna meet with him end of month.

I also got around to texting Nakia last night, but didn't know what to say. So I responded:

ME

> Hey, how goes it?

And she just replied—nineteen hours later.

NAKIA

> It goes . . . 🙄

> Sorry I haven't called yet. School been crazy after the suspension. Tryna figure things out. Ima give you a call Friday night.

The animated ellipsis appears. She's reading, responding. Then it stops. I wait for the three dots to return. They don't.

Conversation used to flow so freely between us. She kept me smiling over the summer, we could talk about life or just joke and kick it in silence. But over text message, and while I'm in the city . . . I dunno. Truth is I been thinking about Tammy. The way she held my shoulder Monday made me feel like I wasn't alone. Like she'd have my back—and maybe I could have hers. She talked to Ms. Willis on Tuesday, who verified the BCC's budget couldn't cover the trip. Then she wrote the proposal by herself during a free period and submitted it to Ms. Flemming, a French teacher and moderator of the Student Events Committee. I just grinned and said "dope."

The way she moves—no hesitation. But I'm bummed she didn't take me up on my offer to help. Sure, I wanted to be involved. But I also just wanted to hang out with her outside the club. Get to know her one-on-one.

When I get to the fourth floor, I do one last message check. There's one from Dad.

DAD

> I know yuh busy with the team, but WHY YUH HAVEN'T SENT PICTURES OF THE LAB YET?! ☺ C'mon mi dyin to see it.

Haven't even told my family about the probation. I can just see the looks on their faces. Mom trying to hide the disappointment, saying something like, *Well, it's only a month.* Granma would try to keep my spirits up with a pep talk, and it would remind me that each moment I'm failing is one of the last memories she'll have. And Dad—

Fifteen hundred miles away, I see his bright smile fall. So I keep the truth tucked away for now. Give my family some sunshine to cling to. The RoboAugs meeting is about to start in the Fabrication Center. That means no one will be in the STEM Lab.

Setting foot in the STEM center is like walking into Disney World for the first time as a five-year-old and seeing all the cartoon characters come to life. Magic is real on the Upper West Side.

For some people . . .

Each room is glass-walled so you can see everything inside. Formulas, diagrams, and lines of code are scrawled everywhere, graffiti to the untrained eye. One room is an armory of mechanical engineering wonder. There are all sizes of brackets, gears, wheels on one side. Plastic drawers are filled with sprockets, spacers, chains, sensors, wires, and motor pinions. Opposite is a computer lab lined with thirty-two-inch XDR monitors and 3D printers.

This, right here, was Augustin to me. It called to me the moment Ms. Rowe showed me pics and suggested I transfer. But a barren space in the middle of an otherwise cluttered design table reminds me of what I'm missing out on. The team probably took the drivetrain, the base of the robot, downstairs to the Fabrication Center to show potential recruits, get them excited to join the team. Can't dwell on that. Got my family to worry about. Give them a reason to believe in me again.

I take out my phone and do a video call to link Granma, Dad, and Rej.

Granma got me into science when I was three. She took a battery, some wires, and a light bulb from a broken toy and showed me my first circuit. It's my oldest memory. From something as simple as a marble falling to the sound a car makes screeching to a halt, she'd find a lesson to teach on gravity, acceleration, friction. Those cold nights when the heat wasn't working, she'd discuss the architectural design of houses in Sweden that didn't need heat because the insulation was designed to withstand the climate. The world was a playground of experiments she opened up for me that always came with an economic lesson. I wish her first steps into Augustin were to see me in the STEM Lab, not the dean's office.

"Yuh all right, GC?" Granma says, answering my call, her face way too close to the screen, so I can only see her eyes and forehead.

"Yeah, I'm cool," I say, putting on a bouncy smile like Janeil does in front of white students.

"Dem nuh try bex yuh again?" she asks.

"Nah, nah. Nothing like that, just got something to show you."

"Sa kap fêt piti?!" Rej says, entering the call. "You got my text, right? Caught me in the middle of some work. Trying to hustle up some extra DJ'ing bread to cover legal fees." He notices Granma on the call. "Ehh, wussup, Granma!" While Rej and Granma chat, I see the avatar for Dad's call drop off. It's like he knows I'm about to lie and is ignoring me. I know it's not the case. But after these months apart—

"Want y'all to check out this lab," I say to Rej and Granma, trying to maintain the smile. I flip the camera, walk around, giving them the tour. Their eyes light up. Woulda been cool for Dad to be on for this. His reaction would've meant something.

"What kinda apps y'all got up in there?" Rej asks. He pulls

back his dreads, wrapping them with a band. I log in. The computers have just about every software package you can think of. "Whoaaa," Rej squeals when he sees the music production software and plug-ins. "You got access to all a dat and not even cracked versions either." He gives me a knowing wink. Downloading illegal copies always came with unwanted porn or malware. "Fiya."

"And the computers can prob run them without crashing," I say.

"Right!" Rej agrees, laughing.

"Di lab is impressive," Granma says, her teeth filling the screen. "Yuh know we all lookin forward to seein yuh compete. Show dis school what a Jamaican cyan do."

I hear voices down the hall and bobble my phone, nearly dropping it.

"Hey, I gotta go." I give a wave.

"Love yuh, GC," Granma says as I end the call.

I don't know how long they been out there, but down the hall, CJ is saying goodbye to his partner, Zan, giving them a long kiss. The two hold for a second, locked in a hug that doesn't want to end. I picture holding Tammy like that.

Then Zan leaves, and CJ makes his way over to the door. He limps toward me on his crutches, still managing to strut like he's posing on a runway despite balancing a book bag that's pretty loaded up. I open the door for him.

"Thanks, bro," he says, angling sideways, nearly toppling into me to shake my hand. I brace his momentum so he regains balance. "Sorry about that."

"No problem. I was just—checking my email before heading out." It's a good enough excuse.

"Why not use the lab in the library or your phone?" he asks with an ear-to-ear smirk like he knows I'm lying and is dying to expose me. He lays his crutches down, taking a seat at one of the raised desks. He wants me to squirm. Act nervous that he's gonna rat me out. As if it matters. What else can the administration do to me? "And I kind of saw you taking video." He motions around the lab. "Walls here are all glass."

"You milkin this, you got something to say or what?" I don't mean to sound stressed, but outside the BCC, everyone here's got me marked.

"Chill," he says. "I asked about you after school Monday and Mr. Abato told us about the probation." He bobs his head to each side, debating if he should say the next thing. "Although I kinda already heard. You know, 'cause Zan is on Student Events with Jill, who's Terry's girlfriend. And between Jill and Terry, they kinda know everything, so the gossip chain moves quick." He shrugs it off like it's nothing, even though he's talking about my life.

"Shouldn't you be in the Fabrication Center?" I say.

"I got no time for all that. Eighty percent of the people who show up won't be back. They just do it to say they showed up and put it on their college apps."

Must be nice. "I better go."

"Why? You're already here." He brushes his hair to the side and it lands flawlessly in the same place. I study him, trying to figure out his game. The angle. Janeil and Tammy are cool with him. That's gotta mean something, right? "They'll probably be in Fabrication all afternoon. Mr. Abato talks—a lot. Sit down, let me show you some of the stuff we're doing."

I don't know. But thinking about the gossip network here reminds me of Sun Tzu's "Employment of Secret Agents." He talks about using foreknowledge to gain victory, from people in your camp and people in the enemy's camp. Whose camp is CJ in?

"I can stay for a bit," I say. "Don't want to stop you from doing work."

"Chiiiill with that. You Black, I'm Chinese, we all have to be united." My eyebrows rise. "That Friday you got attacked . . ." He shakes his head. For the first time the coolness drops. CJ takes in a long breath. "For whatever reason, that week, those guys were looking to start something. Don't think I don't know that if it wasn't you, it could've been someone Asian, queer. White supremacy is real. So I got you."

CJ extends his hand. And after a flicker of hesitation, I nod, and I grab it into a dap hug.

"Hey, you want to see something funny," he says. He pulls up a thread on robotics competitions on Reddit. "This is a video of the team's robot from last year." I watch as the team's robot spins violently out of control, crashing into every obstacle on the event field.

"Wow, that's crazy," I laugh.

"You should check out some of the memes."

He walks me through the RoboAugs setup. Talks about the Fabrication Center downstairs and the CNC router. Apparently, they can build their own machine parts on something called a lathe. All things I'll have to turn to Rej or Google to understand. Then he shows me the code. Mr. Abato already gave me my log-in credentials, so I'm able to open it up. Which gives me an idea. Maybe I can still work on the code without them knowing. Be a part of the team behind the scenes. Might not be the same. But it'd be something. And I wouldn't be fully lying to my family.

"What're you doing in here?!" The lab door swings open. It's Heath, one of the twins who founded the team, giving me an icy glare.

15

The look in Heath's eyes below the flaming-red eyebrows says it all: *You're on probation. You don't belong in our lab.* We haven't spoken since that first day when I met him and his sister. Lydia did all the talking. She was peace, extra enthusiastic. Heath was a little curt, seemed introverted. But the way he came at me just now. That was all accusation.

"Relax," CJ says in his easygoing way. "I needed help carrying my bag upstairs. Elevator was getting claustrophobic. And Gil offered." CJ knows this terrain. His lie makes me suspect that while Heath can't be trusted, I can trust him.

Heath ignores CJ and comes over to look at my screen. His face curdles when he sees the open code. "Who said you could go into our code without anyone around?" He makes it clear that this is his territory and I should be under supervision. "You don't know our protocols."

"I was just reading through it. I didn't make any changes." Mr. Abato told me during my interview that they needed better coders. This dude might be a founder, but he can't be that good. Still, here I am defending myself—again. *Is no place safe?*

"Having a free ride here doesn't give you permission," Heath says. Free ride? It's coded language, saying I got a handout. But I'm not even tripping off that so much as his attitude. He didn't say more than two words to me when I met him. Now he's on some rampage. Lydia walks through the door next, eyeing the scene, probably waiting to double-team me. "Log off now," Heath continues. "You shouldn't be here after school. Those are the rules."

Lydia sighs, resting her arms on her brother's shoulders. She's taller than him, and her lanky build stands in sharp contrast. "Don't mind Heath," she says, radiating that exuberant smile. They may be twins, but she's obviously the big sister. "He's just protective." She stage-whispers to me, "Gets it from Mom."

"Well, I'm going to get Mr. Abato—"

"Heath!" Lydia stops him. "He's going to be on the team at some point. Don't be a rat. Jeez." Heath squirms away, logging on to a computer on the other side of the room. He's not slick, I can still see him glancing over. Wonder if he's writing up some snitching email. Can't put it past him yet.

"Soooo, how are you?" Lydia leans in, putting me under the microscope. She's close enough that I could count the freckles on her cheeks.

"Fine." I pivot, sticking my head in my book bag. *I can't retreat now.* She did get her brother to back off. Maybe she's cool like CJ. "So what got y'all into robotics?" That gets her talking about something other than me. And she's into it. The thrill of competition, working with the team, internship opportunities, meeting alum and industry professionals. But more importantly, she likes creating something out of nothing.

"Science is an equalizer," she finishes. "The results are empirical. It's all about what you can do." That's how I feel. If I design a robot, code an application, there's instant gratification. No one can doubt that it's my work. There's power in that. "Stinks about the probation. I'm an ally. School doesn't understand that 'Black Lives Matter' includes the treatment of Black students." She's saying all the right things.

"I bet he can't even design one of the kits Mr. Abato uses for freshmen," Heath mutters out the side of his lip.

He's really challenging me. It's a trap. I know it. If he sent an email to Mr. Abato, he could walk in right now and I'd be caught in the act. But if I back down, he'll think I'm not good enough. That my scholarship was a handout. I shouldn't care. I shouldn't have to prove myself.

But I do. There are a few basic robot kits off to the side. He's probably used them before. There is one way I can give myself an edge. "Me and you. A timed challenge."

"Fine," he replies. He gives a low chuckle like he's already won. "One hundred says you can't beat me in a machine challenge."

"I don't have—"

CJ pulls on my arm to shut me up. "I'll cover it," CJ says. I don't want to be anybody's charity, but I don't want to back out of the challenge either. "Let's make it two on two. After all, with these kits, two people can do it in two hours. Otherwise, you'll be here all night. I'll partner with Gil." It's like he read my mind, found a way to step inside so it wouldn't come off that I can't afford it. CJ points to the twins. "You two partner up."

"We could just not compete against each other," Lydia says, her eyes wide, hoping to offer a pragmatic solution. "We are a team."

"No, let's do it," Heath says.

"I'm in," I say with enough conviction to let him know that I'm not afraid.

CJ claps his hands and gives me a sly look. "Old versus new." I think I hear Lydia mumble out a groan. It's not lost on me that this isn't just old versus new, but also white versus people of color. Maybe she noticed too.

"Two hours," Heath says, his mouth a flat sneer. "Make a machine that can go left, right, forward, backward, pick up, and throw. The robot has to start off autonomously by sensor reaction, or auton. Afterward it's controller driven. Whoever finishes first will receive a bonus point, and the other team will lose one point every ten minutes thereafter." He motions to two tables, each with a box. "These are first-year kits, so hopefully it won't be too hard." I can't wait to knock that smug expression off his face. Adrenaline is rippling through my veins like at the start of a martial arts round, waiting for the ref to throw down the hand and say, *hajime*.

Me and CJ head over to our design table. "You prefer building or coding?" he asks. Each kit has a basic prototyping tool, so it won't take long. This is about teamwork. Communication.

"I'm good with either," I say. "As long as we don't lose."

"That's what I'm talking about," CJ says with an excited cheese smile. "If you don't mind, I'll build. Kind of something my dad and I used to do."

"Why'd you stop?" I ask.

"He's just so . . . busy with work," CJ says, grimacing through his usual chill mask. I take the hint as we get to work. I get him though. Me and Dad was a team too. When we were together, we'd bounce off each other's energy, sending sparks into everything we touched. Being apart isn't the same, always searching for that missing piece, a broken circuit that you hope comes together by going harder on your own.

CJ moves quickly, screwing in the mounts to the board and setting up the wheels, gears, and sensors. The prototype tool allows me to use my phone as a controller, thankful once again for Renee's gift. It's object-oriented-based development, so I don't have to write full Java code, which saves a lot of time, just not very nuanced.

This is my zone. Code. Engineering. That twitch in CJ's eyes with each piece he bolts in. He has something to prove too.

"So what happened to your leg?" I ask.

"Trying to make a cool gram video while snowboarding." He chuckles. "Still got the likes though. My followers dig it. Travel, art." He points to his phone. "I record when I'm doing CAD sessions."

"Um . . . Back to the snowboarding," I say, more than puzzled. "It's September."

"Oh, yeah, I was in New Zealand," he says, as if it's a regular thing. "Great time to snowboard there while school's out. Dad was going to send me to Saas-Fee in Switzerland, but I figured this way I could also check out where they filmed *Lord of the Rings*."

I give him a "Sounds cool" as if that isn't the most incredible thing that he just gets to do. "Dug those movies," I say. "Watch the trilogy once a year with my dad."

When I talked to Dad last week, he said he was going to set up a new appointment with the embassy. Hopefully, he can get back before another half year goes by.

It doesn't take us long to reach a workable model. If I hadn't used this tool before, we'd be way behind the other team. That's what Heath wanted. I add in a few additional lines of code for the sensors. We finish twelve minutes after the twins, so we start off behind by two points.

"Got your back, bro," CJ says as I pick up the controller to begin. "You got this."

We start with the autonomous movements. The robots are almost equal. Moving left, right, forward, and backward. Then we switch to controller driven, where I move the robot using the app on my phone like a game pad. Heath is their driver. These challenges require finesse. We each maneuver our mechanical hand to pick up a square block. Their robot drops it. Ours doesn't. CJ pounds me on the shoulder. The game is tied. I try to stay focused but my phone is getting slippery in my sweating palms. I can't lose. Can't have him think that I'm anything less. Because that's what's going to happen. He'll walk around thinking I was never good enough to be here.

Next is the toss activity. Lydia sets up a yellow target. Heath lines up the shot and misses the mark. I flex my neck, ready to spar. My robot arm leans back, springs forward like a pro baller, and nails the target.

We win.

"We did it." CJ hops on his good leg, holding on to the table for support. "OGs got nothing on us!" he says, taunting the twins. But his expression gives me hope. And a true ally.

"You're good." The words leave Heath's mouth like he's sick. It's about as much of a compliment as I'll get, but I take the victory. He opens his wallet and pulls out a hundred like it's nothing. I wave it off. CJ gives me a confused look because I'm turning down the money, and it's technically his because he made the bet. But he lets it slide.

"I just want to be able to program in peace," I say. "When Mr. Abato's not around, let me help y'all. And we'll call it even."

"Definitely." Lydia rushes in before Heath can talk. "We need the help. Especially based on the recruiting this week. We have some freshmen who might be promising, but they'll need a year or more to grow into it. Right now we just need a strong developer."

This isn't just a victory. I beat the veterans. Earned respect. But it's not enough.

16

So yuh beat dem!" Dad stares at me from my laptop screen, his grin bright and toothy. "Ras!" He slams his hand down on the table, excited as if he were closing out a round of dominoes. "That's how yuh show em who run ting."

It's Friday evening. One day after my robotic tussle with the twins, no fists drawn, no punches thrown. No added beef. Mr. Abato wasn't around after school today since he had an alumni function. So I got to work with the twins and CJ. I took the lead on mapping out the code for the drivetrain. The existing functions were a mess, not scalable at all. So I been figuring out a way to revamp it so it can be used for future years. Sun Tzu's tactical approach might be the move. Missed grappling at the dojo, but the time was well spent. Heath's holding to the terms of the bet. Can't trust that he won't snitch. But luckily his sister runs the show.

Feels good to see Dad, even if it's only through an app. He's wearing a gray tank top with a towel wrapped around his shoulders. His belly's slimmed down. Probably back to swimming since he's right near the sea in Port Antonio. We keep it light, no mention of the suspension or politics, focused on the thing we enjoy most. Technology. He's sitting on the patio. The sun has set but I can see the outline of trees in the background as he takes a sip of his drink, which is probably an Appleton. He's comfortable. No looking over his shoulder, worrying if ICE will randomly grab him in the middle of the street.

"It was just a friendly match." I downplay it. Maybe by the end of next month he'll be back. And I'll be off this probation, able to compete. "We got two months to redesign the robot's drivetrain, while doing other upgrades."

"Good. Good. Mi happy that things are working out fi yuh now." Dad's lips crush together in a hesitant smile. His eyes droop, thinking, wandering from the conversation. "Yuh know while I been down here I've met some engineers. Innovative programmers I've been working with." Dad's always been the family idea guy. He comes up with new concepts for apps and games. Me and Rej would watch him pitch projects to friends. It fed our interest in entrepreneurship. But the enthusiasm Dad usually has, it isn't there.

"That's great, right? You always said it was hard finding people to invest in you." And he couldn't get a proper job in tech without his immigration papers. So it was always manual labor, while trying to start something from the ground up. He'd come home sometimes, massaging his lower back or neck, and I'd know he strained something. Dad laughed it off, of course. Never wanting to bring down people's spirits. Then he'd get on the computer and start coding. Wake up at six in the a.m. to go to work, and do it again. The dark circles under his eyes constantly growing.

So what isn't he saying?

"It's good, yuh know," Dad says. "Helps me to send money home to you, your mother, and Granma." *He's been sending money up?* "I never once regretted leaving. Being in the States with your uncle before he passed. Raising a family." He draws in a deep breath. "But it has been nice to actually get paid what I'm worth. Never could do that up there. Di work also gives me something to keep my mind busy, while I'm not in the States with yuh." His shoulders draw up with a long breath that takes several seconds to release.

"How's the visa going?" It's the question I always ask on these calls. Each time I bring it up a little sooner, cutting the conversation shorter, leaving less time for us to talk like we did, Dad and son.

"Well, it's a process." He gives an uncertain wave, like he wants to avoid the topic. "If I want to go back to Brooklyn, I had to get the Jamaican passport first. That required some paperwork. And di visa take sixty days just to get going, and dem want all medical examination and interview." We know he's not the best at filling out paperwork. Put him in front of some tech and he goes into autopilot, give him a pen and a few pages with fill-in-the-blanks and that's not gonna be done for days if not weeks. But I can't help but wonder if the security of working down there has him delaying his return. Is the process of getting his passport and visa real or an excuse to finally do what he loves? What wouldn't I do for that freedom?

"Do whatever you can to get it done," I say. "Granma needs you."

And so do I.

17

Hanging in the stairwell of my building with Stretch is like old times. But those days feel long gone.

I got off the phone with Dad about a half hour ago. Just about when Mr. Neckles stopped in to check on Granma. Can't shake the feeling that Dad's procrastinating, prioritizing work over coming home. It's got to be hurting Mom too. I can see it in her mood, the smiles she flashes that she can barely maintain. Maybe it's only been a few months over the course of a lifetime, but I'm so used to seeing the way they'd be together. Mom rolling her eyes at Dad's corny jokes. The way they'd hug each other, turn on the music and start dancing. I loved seeing that affection every day. Well, except those times they were doing they thing in the bedroom when I was trying to read or do homework. I shiver. Walls shouldn't be so thin.

"I can almost smell the stew peas," Stretch says, his nose

pointed up the stairs, referring to Granma's cooking. I miss being around that relaxed energy Stretch puts into the world. Never stressed 'bout school or home. "Taste it too."

We're two floors down from my apartment. Sometimes it's the only place to find privacy. I'd post up here when I didn't want to put music on to tune out my parents' bedroom performance. As awkward as that made me feel, I miss it.

"I don't think that's stew peas you're smelling, dude." Years ago you might smell dog piss or something worse in the stairs, now it's just generic Clorox that can't erase years of don't-give-a-fuck management.

"Wonder if Rej comin through," he says, grabbing his cell to text.

While Stretch checks on Rej, I get back to journaling. Dad used to give me these mini-notebooks to collect my thoughts. I dug it because writing was another introduction to coding. He taught me how to break down problems—reverse engineering them. Then he'd dissect a poem by my namesake Gil Scott-Heron or another writer he loved. Using the notebook to map out the landscape of Augustin makes me feel as though he's here.

"Lewis!" Mr. Neckles says, coming down the stairs. No one calls Stretch by his government. Not even teachers or fam. But Mr. Neckles does. Stretch immediately puts his cell to his ear, walking away, pretending to be on a call like he can't talk.

Smart. I wanted to have a minute with Mr. Neckles anyway.

"Gil," he says. "Started helping your granma with dinner. Rolling out the dumplin is a workout." He starts rotating his arms. Can't blame him, kneading dough is rough. "Trying to pick up all that I can from her." I force a smile. His words reminding me that time with Granma is finite. "Things getting better at your school?" he asks.

"It's cool," I say. "I wanted to ask you about that. You said you had friends with kids at Augustin? What are their last names and what year?"

"Well, not friends, c-co-workers." Mr. Neckles stutters the reply. "Stevens and Todd." Not familiar with either last name. "And I want to say they're sophomores because I remember them talking about it last year. How proud they were."

"Have they said anything about the school or things happening?" The dean made it sound like the parents were upset. And if the students gossip, the parents are probably just as chatty. So I get to it. "The fight. Did they mention anything about me or a fight happening at school?"

"I don't think so. Can't say it's a topic that comes up. Well—" His eyes squish together, scanning his memory for some lost information. His pear-shaped head always reminded me of commercials for cereals or fruit snacks where the cartoon character's head would plop into a fruit once they took a bite. "They sometimes talk about this podcast they listen to. I think it's called RNY. It's kind of an NPR for conservatives. You know Killian, right?" Who doesn't? He's all the talk right now with the mayoral election coming up. The independently wealthy white guy who pulled himself up by his bootstraps in commercial real estate while starting a fintech company. The story never talks about the money he got from his parents. Or the neighborhoods he destroys. "He was a guest recently." His eyebrows jump as if he's just realized something, then hides it.

"What is it?" I ask.

"It's . . ." He sighs. The type adults give when they're not sure if I'm old enough to deal with news. As if my experiences don't count. "There was a conversation about busing. And how a private school like Augustin is trying to integrate more, similar to what public schools are doing." *Integration.* It should be an outdated word, but NYC schools are more segregated than the South. Just like America, NYC's got a public relations team focused on making it look like we're above reproach. "Look, don't pay it any mind." He gives me a look like he wants to offer some comfort like my dad would. Thankfully he doesn't. "All you have to do is focus on the work."

Easy to say from the outside.

REJ CAME BY maybe fifteen minutes later. We went to the park down the street, past the kids' playground and the jungle gyms and over to the blacktop where the benches are, so Rej can smoke his blunt outside instead of in the stairwell like he was planning to. If Granma caught a whiff of that, it'd be Rej's ass.

Plus, I needed the mental space to check in on what Mr. Neckles said.

This whole time I've got that RNY podcast with Killian playing in my ear. The episode page had the picture of me, CJ, Heath, and Lydia. I dug deeper. Turns out Augustin used the pic on their social to promote the team. *That I'm not officially on* . . . And the podcast lifted the image from there.

Part of me didn't want to listen and give them a free hit.

I don't know how they track podcast stats. But the thought of some conservatives getting extra ad revenue or my phone now recommending conservative content feels like a betrayal. I regret each second I keep listening. My stomach churns, threatening to heave.

Because every word Killian says—is about me:

> In our day you got into school off merit. We respected standardized tests. Because in life you get tested. Constantly. And this is what I'd hope to protect my children from, because the standards in public schools are always dictated by the masses. But private school should be safe. Now at Augustin, there's fighting happening in the first week of school. That's what happens when standards drop. When you eliminate intelligence in the favor of optics. And that's what my campaign is about. Redefining education. So that New York can get back to being New York.

Rej says something to me that sounds like "Take your earbuds out, man." For whatever reason he looks irritated. So I press pause. "You hear me now? I said I got the meeting with that pro bono immigration lawyer Thursday evening," Rej growls at me. "You gonna come with, right?"

"Yeah, yeah, Ima be there," I half reply.

"Put it in ya phone. This coming Thursday. Five. Aight?"

"Doin it now, yo," I say. He's pressin me. I get it. He gives me the address and details. But I'm looking at the episode's web page, skimming comments from more than one person who must be Augustin parents.

J. Doherty: My daughter told me a transfer student attacked the quarterback. They're letting thugs in the school.

kelstrug: Liberal agenda. Diversity Equity and Inclusion is just another form of affirmative action taking away seats from deserving students. Killian for Mayer all the way to the white house!

Anonymous: Thank you for stating the case so succinctly. Diversity is important but not at the cost of education. Why are we breaking over a hundred years of top tier schooling? Our ivy league matriculation rate exceeds most in the nation. I plan to bring up these issues at the next parent-teacher meeting.

"You good?" Rej says through the haze. His head's tilted so his dreads graze his shoulders, waiting for a reply. Rej can read me, probably more than Stretch. It's like Rej is my cornerman seeing me on the ropes. But in this park, surrounded by fifteen-foot wire fences with crisscross patterns, I can't help but feel like I signed myself up to be in a cage.

"It's nothing," I reply. There's so much pressure in my chest it hurts.

"Sure don't look like nothing," Rej says, his voice thick with gravel. "You been lookin chewed-up and spit-out since we left the building."

"You know that rich mug running for mayor?" I ask.

"That Killmonger dude?" Rej asks.

"Nah, son," Stretch says. He's shadow dribbling around the court, enjoying the night air in a way that I can't. "Killmonger was Black. Killian's the tech dude. He with that real estate trust that owns all them new luxury apartments downtown and been buying up half of Little Haiti."

"Yeah, that one." I turn on my phone speaker and let them listen to the part of the RNY podcast. Their reactions mimic my own.

"White people bein white." Stretch sucks his teeth, waving his hand, dusting it off like it's nothing. As if this is just the way life is and I should accept it. It's that approach to life that made it harder for me and Rej to talk to him about things last year.

"Don't mean it ain't jacked," Rej says. "All the white parents gonna listen to this and turn Gil into an enemy."

"They already have," I say. I tell them about the meeting, the probation, that I can only work on robotics when Mr. Abato isn't around. I tell them about the BCC and Tammy. I end up spending more than a minute talking about Tammy. The newspaper.

"So now you just doing work for a team that you not gonna get credit for," Rej says. "And they got you on the diversity posterboard."

"Sonnn. Y'all stay stressin," Stretch says. "Focus on the good. I heard Gil talk about that Tammy girl. Talk more about her. Be about her. And wussup with Nakia?" That reminds me, I texted her yesterday that I would give her a call tonight. She never replied. "Have you checked for her yet? I mean—" He throws his hands up, brushing back the blond tips on his high curls, letting me know that I'm the one that's out my mind. He's frustrated because me and Rej focus on the problems. *But if we don't deal with 'em now . . .* "You putting all your energy into some billionaire who gonna spit his nonsense. Some parents you got no control over. And you both got family situations. Don't put more on top of it worrying about all these politics. Date somebody that's into you. Finish the year. Go to college, be good. It ain't . . . healthy to keep dwellin on everything else."

"This man." Rej explodes up, standing on the bench, pointing his hand at Stretch, the blunt pinched between his fingers. "That's why I can't talk to you, because you always tryna find the easy solution. That ain't life. Least it ain't mine." He turns to me, the wrath still cranked. "What'd you expect? That private school was gonna be sweet 'cause you smart? They kicking us outta the buildings we live in and our parents out the country. You think school was gonna be different? You see how they be chopping up our schools into four different charter schools trying to sell some new lie or give all the resources to one section and not the other." He takes the last puff and crushes the dregs beneath his foot. "You left the fight." He gets off the bench. Stares me down like he's never done before. "I told you, you could always come back home," he says.

We head back to the apartment, not exchanging many words. Lines drawn in our friendship. But Rej made something clear. I put one fight behind me just to enter another. One that might be worse.

It's almost 8:30. We been having dinner later since Mom was switched to second shift.

As I walk upstairs, a dusty, almost smoldering scent hits me. "You smell that?" I ask.

"I can only smell the weed on Rej's clothes," Stretch says. "You better Febreze yourself before you go inside."

"Nah," I say, my senses ringing the alarm. "That's smoke."

Granma!

I bolt up the stairs, taking them two, three at a time.

I smash through the door, falling into my apartment. The smoke singes my lungs, making me choke. I try to force my eyes open, but the scorched air is too much. My arms flail, useless fans, as the hairs on my skin turn to ash.

"Gran—" I try to call out to her, but I can barely say her name as I barrel through to where the smoke is most dense. The kitchen. Horns go off, pounding against my eardrums.

Through the slightest squint, I see the fire, threatening to rage and take away everything I've known since childhood.

I can barely make out Stretch next to me. "Throw some water on it," he commands.

Stretch is wrong—using water could make it spread. I grab a hand towel and start blotting down the fire. The smoke rises with each wave, choking me more. It's not enough. The fire reaches from the stovetop for my arms.

Rej emerges with a bath towel, joining me, suffocating the fire beneath the towel's weight, robbing it of the oxygen it needed to grow.

"Open the windows," Rej yells at Stretch.

"Gotchu," Stretch says, flying the windows open and turning on the fan.

"Where's Granma?" Rej yells, choking through the smoke.

The question stabs me through the heart as I scour, blotting out the sounds of frightened neighbors emerging from their apartments.

On the living room floor, I find her. Passed out. I cradle her head. She looks through me with that glossy expression. *I'm losing her.*

"Call 911," I cry, rocking her in my arms back and forth hoping that this moment isn't her last.

18

The street is lined with fire trucks. People from the apartment building and the neighborhood have piled outside. Talking. Taking video of the spectacle. But all I see is Granma, lying flat, wheeled out by paramedics. The oxygen mask on her face. Her hand grips mine.

"You're gonna be okay," I say. "I'm sorry I left you alone." I don't know how many times I've repeated these words.

"Gil!"

Mom cries out, emerging from a cab. She rushes over, barely holding in the tears, and covers me in a hug. My body is rigid, too worried of letting go of Granma's hand to return the emotion. Still unable to process what happened. What I allowed to happen because I wasn't home.

"Mom," she says to Granma. But Granma can't speak. Either

because of the oxygen mask or she's too tired. Please don't let it be anything more.

"We can have one person in the ambulance with us," the paramedic says.

"I'll go," I quickly say.

"No, Gil, I'll go," Mom says.

"I can't leave her."

"I'll be with her. I have all her paperwork. Check on the apartment. Make sure everything's okay."

"Rej and Stretch are upstairs," I argue.

"Gil! Please," she says, letting me know this isn't a time to argue.

I watch them fold the wheels on the gurney. Granma turns her head to me as she's hoisted up. She smiles, but I think it's more for me than for her. The doors close and soon after the ambulance rolls off.

MAYBE TWO HOURS have passed. Rej and Stretch left a little while ago. It's all a blur. There was no significant fire damage. The wall behind the oven and the ceiling above it are charred. Looks worse than it actually is according to the fireman. Apparently it was all caused by a paper towel Granma used to light the pilot. She must have dropped it and it caught on something when she got distracted.

Dad looks out at me from the computer.

"Ya all right, son?" he asks. I force a nod. It doesn't matter how I am. All that matters now is Granma. "Juss got off di phone with yuh mudda. Looks like yuh granma will be coming home in a day or two. They just want to keep her to check on di smoke and run a few tests." His eyes close for a time, thinking about what to say. Some comfort to offer that won't help the situation. "Haffi be thankful everyone is safe, yuh understand," he says. "She cyaan cook anymore. Least not alone. Cyaan have that."

It's like he's accusing me when he wasn't even here. But neither was I.

"Me talk to Shareef," Dad says. "His wife, Amber, gon come over an check on Mom until yuh get home from school or your mother come in from work."

"That's good," I say. Mr. Neckles's wife has a home business, so she's got the flexible hours. But I feel the gap widening between me and Dad. Perhaps it's 'cause of the call from earlier, or maybe it's what just happened with Granma. "I got back to journaling," I say, offering up something to break the tension.

"Writing's such a good way to look at a problem," he says, trying to be positive. "Yuh know, whenever mi wann clear my mind, mi put on *The Revolution Begins*," he says. "Dat first song! Lady Day and John Coltrane. Lawd, it really juss pick me up."

"Yeah, maybe I'll put that on after I get off." His mom is in the hospital and he wants me to listen to a song. Why not tell me how he's feeling about all this. About being apart. Not just the things that are going on, but what's going on inside him.

He hesitates. And we're just staring at each other, eyes not connecting as time goes by. I want him to tell me what he's going to do to get back here as soon as possible instead of asking other people to help out. Those words never come. "Mi juss wann yuh to be strong," he says.

He wants me to be strong, but saying that just makes me feel like I'm gonna break.

19

Tammy sits behind her desk, intently listening to me. I don't know why I came here to unload on her. I'm holding back tears through each sputtered word.

It's Tuesday, sixth period. Four days since the fire. I'm sitting in one of the high-back tufted lounge chairs in the newspaper office. The school's paper is called the *PAW*, a play on its beloved mascot. The chairs, the desks made of actual wood and not the composite IKEA stuff, are stripped right out of a movie where some old white men would sit, smoke cigars, drink brandy, and discuss the fate of the world.

Meanwhile, I'm staring at a stringy turkey sandwich on hard-dough bread, where the cheese has melted into a soggy mess from perspiring in my bag, my thoughts wrestling between Granma and Killian's podcast. I wipe away the liquefied mess and take a bite. Mr. Neckles came by Saturday to help me clean the wall and repaint it. Still, the two-toned mix of old and new ivory paint is a reminder of what happened. Granma was released from the hospital on Sunday. She seems fine on the outside. But the neurologist Mom talked to yesterday ordered additional tests.

"You should've asked for a couple days off from school," Tammy says. Her hands are clasped. She's been leaning forward like a therapist studying her patient. So I switched the conversation to Killian. Played the recording. As if concentrating on a tangible enemy, one that's straight-up opposed to the Black experience at Augustin, will make dealing with the enemy I have no power over, dementia, easier.

"Imagine me asking for time off with the way this school's treated me. That'd be the subject of Killian's next education talk." I slouch back in the chair, my mouth sinking into my palm, while my heel pulses like a pile driver against the ground.

Tammy crinkles her lip. Not in that half smile she has when she's joking. But that look you get when confusion turns to realization and there is no solution. She gets up, walks past the adjustable standing desks for graphic design, the only thing that sets this space apart from a vintage Sherlock Holmes sitting room, and grabs a seat next to me. "When I was a kid, my dad would always bring home the newspaper from work," she says. "I don't know what my oldest memory is, but the one I love the most is the first time he handed me an article and said he wanted to discuss it with me after I read it. I don't know why I love that memory so much. Maybe it was the first time my dad asked me for my unfiltered thoughts on what was going on in the country. He just listened. As if my perspective helped him make sense of the division happening in America."

"That's dope," I say. "That's how it was with me and my dad."

She pulls at her curls, caught in the scene from her past. Her expression isn't joy. More gratitude. "It's what got me into journalism. Mom was next. Every magazine she had, she discussed the bias." Recalling her journey winds her up as if recharging her mission. The thunder of students walking the halls, seeping through the crack under the door, crawls to a hush, leaving just the sound of her voice and heart, thudding with excitement. "Augustin has one of the oldest school newspapers in the state."

Tammy goes over to the computer and opens up the *PAW* archive on the web. "Look at these articles from the 1980s." She starts going through a collection of bookmarks. Articles about housing, the drug epidemic, the militarized police force. "The writers were calling attention to socio-economic problems. Then it stopped. Started again around the mid-nineties. Then after that, it's been pure fluff pieces."

She slumps back down in the chair. "I was going to get my start in journalism here," she continues. "Create exposés. Deliver the type of journalism that was missing in mainstream media. And then with each editor there was a fight. Me arguing for a story to be told. And I always thought I was alone. That I was being singled out."

"You weren't?"

"Well, in the newspaper I was," she says. The half smirk returns. "But not the only Black student going through it." Tammy inches close enough that floral scents fly off her twists to touch me like the autumn air. She pins my eyes, commanding me to listen to whatever she says next. And I want her to move closer, to trap my hand under hers so I can feel the touch of her skin. "You're not alone. Don't forget that."

My mouth is open. I want to say something really cool that catches her attention and makes her remember this the way I know I will. "You should be a lawyer," I say. My whole face squints at the absurdity and I want to smack myself.

"What?" She draws back. Her eyebrows rise over her blue frames.

"I mean, you're so convincing." I hobble out the words, trying to remember how sentences are formed. "The way you talk. It could be to the BCC, or just me, but it's like you know how to make someone feel like they're the only one that matters."

Her body relaxes back into the chair. "We all need to be reminded that we do." She chews on her bottom lip with uncertainty. "That anniversary gala Augustin's having in November . . . Headmaster DeSantis asked me to speak at it. I don't know. He probably just wants me to read some script. But part of me wants to use the time to talk about our experiences as Black students." She lets out a long sigh, her shoulders heaving, burdened by whatever she's holding on to. "Saleem makes fun of me for wanting to get other Black students to write articles. But that's one of the main reasons I became editor. So we have a platform. A place to shine."

"That's why we need to assemble." She rolls her eyes with a hefty snort. The Black Avengers reference not slipping by. I try to compose my thoughts. "You can ask the other Black students to write, but not everybody's a writer. Not until they have a real reason. Something that grabs 'em in their gut. Until they have no other outlet than the page."

"What do you suggest?"

"That proposal for the HBCU trip," I say. "It's been almost a week. Has the Student Events Committee said anything?"

"Not really." She grunts. "I ran into Ms. Flemming before first period and she said it's still being discussed and we'd get an answer by end of month. Said it's not just a matter of money, but also chaperones. So she'll bring it up with the Parents' Committee on parent-teacher night."

"Can't we just have our parents?" The minute I say it, I realize I couldn't even get my mom to do it. That would leave Granma alone for the weekend. Maybe Renee could come over, but that'd still depend on school.

"Yes and no," she says. "I know a lot of the Black families. Between work and home it could just be hard to line up. Many of the parents who do the Ivy tour work nontraditional jobs. So they have more freedom."

So it's back to the parents. Possibly the ones who called about me. Maybe parent-teacher night is where I stage the battle. It could also give Tammy a chance to get more students to write. Sun Tzu said in his chapter titled "Terrain" that the person who shows up first has the advantage. That a general or sovereign must know themselves and the enemy. *How much influence do the parents have?* Are they willing to listen?

"The signs for parent-teacher night say they need volunteers,"

I say. They were plastered all over the school. My guess, volunteers are limited. Who wants to sign away their free night? "It's Thursday. Think we could get some of the BCC members to sign up?"

"What're you thinking?"

"We need the parents, right? So we take our proposal right to them."

And see what kind of battle they're ready for.

20

Two days later, it's parent-teacher night. In a couple hours the parents will enter those Augustin doors. One or more of them may have commented on that RNY page about me.

Sun Tzu said in "Weaknesses and Strengths" that "the enemy must not know where I intend to give battle." This ain't a traditional fight. Not like Sun Tzu was talking 'bout. But the parents sure as hell won't expect us to walk into their private meeting with the HBCU proposal.

I'm in the STEM Lab, trying to keep my mind clear, enjoying what I love. My fingers pulse at the keyboard with each new line of code I write. Heath, Lydia, and CJ are here as well as Janeil, who came to hang out with me and CJ before the night starts. I look up at the glass wall that has the scribblings of pseudo-code I wrote when I pitched my design plans to the group. I let out a silent laugh. Sure, nobody outside this room knows I'm still secretly working on the team. But that's *my code*. I know.

One thing Heath didn't put into the original code was a way to handle voltage adjustments. Still, his head is fully inflated, constantly reminding me that he founded the team, to which his sister clarifies *we did*. He's in his corner doing his thing. I do mine. Every once in a while I have an idea and he's mildly intrigued. Like it would hurt him to pay me a compliment. Whatever.

Mr. Abato is with the other teachers in the faculty lounge—eating, drinking, gossiping about who's dating who. At least that's what Lydia says. So I'm free to work.

"That's really cool," Janeil says to CJ. She's looking over his shoulder, watching him connect a motor to a mounting bracket in 3D space.

"You need to join up," CJ says to Janeil. "I need a partner." His tie hangs loosely around his neck and his jacket's off to the side. Even with the cast on, he manages to have his leg up on the chair, chin on his knee, looking like he's kicking it on the benches in the park while he adjusts the machine designs on-screen.

"I don't know," Janeil replies. "I'm already in Video Production Club with you. It's senior year, I'm not trying to do all the activities." She's staring at her phone, using the camera as a mirror to check her hair. It's pressed flat, straighter than her usual style. "Why doesn't Zan join?" Her voice is that higher pitch she uses when she's in white spaces. "Ain't that your partner-partner?"

"Oh, they don't do tech," he says. His cheeks barely hiding the pink. "But they'll drag me to a sports game."

"C'mon, J," I say to Janeil, "I've seen some of your drawings, you'd be great." She makes these satirical cartoons for the newspaper. Even made one of me standing over Terry that looked like Muhammad Ali after he knocked out Sonny Liston. Thankfully, Tammy never published it. I could only imagine how the school would've took that.

"We can definitely use the help." Lydia walks over, a fireball of cheerfulness. "At least try it out," she suggests. "CJ can walk you through how the CAD software works."

Janeil gets comfortable and starts following along CJ's tutorial.

Working with the team these past few days has been a good distraction. Lydia's energy, CJ's calm enthusiasm, they're like fire and ice. Reminds me how cool robotics is, helps power me through classes. Lydia has been good at keeping me off Mr. Abato's radar. If he's meeting downstairs in Fabrication, she texts me and I stay up in the STEM Lab. If he's in the lab, I'm down in Fabrication. It's like the chapter "Employment of Secret Agents": foreknowledge can only be gained by someone who knows the enemy's situation. More importantly, when I'm here, I'm not home. Looking Granma and Mom in the eye after what happened . . . It's rough. The way Mom's brow furrows when she sees me. She doesn't say it, but I feel it. Like she wants to say *Why weren't you there?* And Granma—acting like nothing's happened. But I can barely meet her eyes. 'Cause I know if I didn't take that walk to listen to Killian's interview, I would've been home.

Tonight's another day I'm missing martial arts. But it's worth it to hear what the parents say. And walk in with this pitch. I just hope it's enough to get other members of the BCC talking where I can't.

Shocking, but while I'm banned from activities, the school had no problem accepting me as a volunteer to lift boxes and get tables and chairs set up. Tammy, on the other hand, will be one of the student greeters standing at the entrance to welcome parents when they arrive.

Thinking of wasting time reminds me—I was supposed to call Nakia Friday. So I bite down and start writing.

ME

Hey Nakia, sorry I forgot to call. Had a fire at the house. Granma had to go to the hospital.

She hasn't sent a text since sending that *hmm* emoji. She must think I'm such a punk.

"Aye, yo, what're you doing?"

Janeil's street voice jars me back into my surroundings.

"I was just curious," Lydia says, startled. Her shoulders are mid-shrug. "I couldn't tell if your hair was real?"

"So you just gonna pull it." Janeil's filters are all off. She's right up in Lydia's face, her finger pressed against Lydia's shoulder. I get out of my chair, trying to register what's popping off.

"I didn't pull it," Lydia says. "Why are you so angry?" Lydia backs away, defensively waving her hands as if someone else did the deed. "I only touched it. I . . . I'm sorry doing that offended you." She stammers out a confused apology, unsure of what she did.

"Yo, you good," I say in a low voice to Janeil. I see it in her expression. She's triggered. Like me that first week. I don't want her to get got too. "Let's go outside."

168

She doesn't hear me. Her body flies, pushing past me. I almost tumble from the force. "Don't ever touch my hair," Janeil says, her voice breaking. She's up in Lydia's face, but holding back from snapping. Fuming, Janeil takes a long guttural breath, begins pacing around, knowing she's lost her cool. The suburban facade falls. She grabs her bag and storms out the door.

"I didn't mean anything," Lydia says. "Her hair is really cool. I don't know why she's so excited and sensitive about it."

CJ shrugs, biting his lip. Heath is holding his phone vertically, almost like he's recording. I grab my book bag and chase after Janeil.

THE STAIRCASE IS empty, but the sound of hurried footsteps fading below tells me to follow in that direction. When I get to the first floor, I get caught in the bustle of student volunteers grabbing tables and chairs from storage to set up reception. I lost track of time. It's half past four. Setup's already begun.

My head snaps back and forth, scanning the switchboard with the overhead LCD that says WELCOME, PARENTS, the hallway, the far staircase that leads to the cafeteria and gym, searching for Janeil.

That's when the lights go out.

Fingers with the scent of freshly picked flowers slip around the sides of my head. Textured coils sweep against my skin like the cuddle of a warm sweater in winter. "Gotcha, Brooklyn."

I know that voice. That fragrance. I want to stay in this trap, rest cozily in her palms. But I have to find Janeil.

Sinking my knees deep, stepping off center, under her arms to escape the hold, I spin around, my arms arcing around her waist. Face-to-face, I can taste the air she breathes as she leans back away from me, while her thighs, stomach, are pressed in close.

"Oh, so you a ninja now," she says. The subtle curve returns to one side of her lips. The same one that I see whenever I close my eyes since we first met. And I'm frozen. Her head tilts down to the right, her left eyebrow raises, and she looks right into me with this curious glow. My hands drop quickly from her body, still holding on to the fraction of eternity that we touched. I remember why I'm here.

"You seen Janeil?" Before she has a chance to respond, I spot Janeil outside, her body small against Augustin's towering glass entrance. I do a scuttle that's not quite a run, Tammy following.

When I meet Janeil's eyes, I see the streaks from tears that have been brushed away, across reddened cheeks.

"Nel," Tammy says. She steps in front of me, drawing her friend close. Janeil's face finding comfort, hunched under Tammy's blue glasses.

"I dunno what happened," I say. "Lydia touched her hair. It set her off." Tammy gives me a look that could be disapproving, but I'm not sure if it's of me or what I said. I didn't even catch what happened. I never really had nobody just touch my hair like that except my barber or my mom. Not without asking at least. It was just weird—asking if Janeil's hair was real. *Who does that?*

"Let's go inside," Tammy says to Janeil. I follow them, but when they go for the girls' bathroom, I back up against the wall and wait.

I don't know if five or ten minutes pass, but it's close to 5:00 and they're still in there. So I join the other volunteers.

In my head, I'm cycling through every page in Sun Tzu's "Employment of Secret Agents," while hanging up signs that will help direct parents as they tour through designated areas of the building or talk to different academic chairs or activity moderators. During lunch, I played Killian's interview for the BCC in the newspaper office. It got a few interested enough to sign on. Then me and Tammy mapped out the night for those who volunteered. They're all secret agents now. Soon they'll be listening in on conversations with parents and administration. Most importantly, I switched positions with some other students to help with setup of the studio theater.

Unlike the main theater they use for assemblies and large drama performances, the studio is more of a black box with wood paneling. There's light rigging overhead and a surrounding balcony. Great for hosting speakers or small receptions. Tonight it's being used for a special meeting with parents that's not part of the main tour or meet and greets. Instead of sandwich trays for the regular guests, there are full catering tables. One even has the heated lamps for a rib roast. Next to it, a bartender is stocking a bar, lining up glasses and liquor bottles like we're at a wedding reception. Whoever's coming to this is important.

Me and the other students are positioning twenty chairs in the middle of the room. There are high-top tables sprinkled about where parents can eat, drink, and discuss our future. I'm given a printed agenda to drop on each seat that only has three items on it:

1. Announcements
2. School trips
3. Sesquicentennial Gala

The dean comes in like an inspector who can't have one item out of place or it would tarnish his reputation, and as for the workers who messed up, it would be off with their heads. He surveys every chair, making the tiniest adjustment to ensure the rows and columns are in perfect symmetry. He's more put together than usual. Dressed in a solid sky-blue suit, green tie, and white shirt.

He makes a motion with his chin to the volunteers, then points to the door, letting us know we're no longer needed and we're not allowed back in. "Be sure to pick up all of the empty boxes before you leave," he says.

I grab what I can manage. On the way out, I notice a silver placard on the wall I hadn't seen before. I heard some of the other students mention the name of this room but it never registered in my head. Parker Hall. The same as Terry's last name.

"Mr. Powell." The dean gives me a shooing motion, snapping me out of my head, letting me know this meeting isn't for me.

I look at the balcony level, the door with the center window showing the staircase behind. My way back in.

21

They haven't noticed us yet. The door to the emergency staircase, a bland blue-gray-tile passageway with grayer walls, is open just wide enough for me and Tammy to stick our heads through and peer down at the parents meeting teachers.

But I'm thinking about the missed texts I got from Rej over the last hour.

REJ

Where u at, man?!! outside the lawyer's office. Meeting's in half hour

Hello?!

GIL!

WTF So you just gonna not respond?

Whatever man. Now I'm late. goin in

Rej also left a voice message, where he really told me how he felt.

ME

My fault yo. Got caught up at school.

It's kind of a lie. I totally forgot. And I was so focused last Friday on listening to the Killian interview I never put the lawyer meeting in my phone. So I didn't just send Granma to the hospital. I let my brother down too. How am I supposed to manage everything at home, when I gotta deal with everything here? Stretch would tell me not to stress. But that's what life is—isn't it. And there's just not enough time. How can I hold down my family when I'm struggling with my own problems? The migraines are coming more frequently. I try to avoid the ibuprofen. But damn . . .

Nakia also responded.

NAKIA

Gil so sorry to hear about ur grandma. Prayers up 🙏 Sending hugs. If you wanna talk, lmk. Or we can meet. I'll even bring the flamin hots

I'm thinking about Nakia's text while Tammy's right next to me. My thoughts constantly split between Brooklyn and the city. This is the longest our bodies have been this close. Then there was earlier when she surprised me from behind. The way the light made her eyes sparkle. I wanted to ask her out. Be that cool dude like Stretch. No pressure about school. Life. Only living in the here and now. But Tammy wasn't flirting. Was she? Still, my skin is tingling, my hormones question me, wondering if I'm gonna say something or not. While Nakia is sending hugs and Flamin Hots. It was a definite sympathy text. But she made it clear weeks ago that she was interested.

I pull back from the door, away from Tammy's smooth skin and full lips that seem to be asking me where I'm going. I give my body a chance to simmer down. Janeil is leaning against the wall. The acoustics in the room carry the voices from the bottom floor up pretty well when it's only one person speaking. So Janeil can hear fine. I can't read her expression though. She doesn't have that mask on she wears in class. Her arms are crossed in deep thought.

I hear the phrase "Ivy League." Tammy clutches my hand, sending my pulse into a frenzy, pulling me back to the door.

"The goal is to cover Yale, Brown, Harvard, and Dartmouth over the course of five days," one woman says. It's hard to see her face from where we're standing. Her voice is direct and punchy like a lawyer or my middle school principal directing a fire drill.

"That's too much," another woman replies. This one's voice is soothing and mellow, like that of the nice welcoming neighbor in a suburban movie who brings over baked goods. "Some of us are traveling directly with our children, and others will be pooling on the charter bus. To ask us to connect four times is a lot of pressure." There are a couple mm-hmms from other parents.

"I agree with Julia," a third parent says. "I'm flying with my son and we shouldn't have to rush from place to place once we arrive."

"So there we have it," the second woman says. Her calm declaration sends a cold shiver down my spine. "We'll do Harvard and Yale." No debate. No vote. Whoever Julia is, she runs the show.

"Ms. Flemming, you mentioned earlier you had a proposal you wanted to bring up." It's the dean.

"Yes." A voice that must be Ms. Flemming responds. "The Black Culture Club would like to do a trip to visit a few historically Black colleges and universities. Since their budget doesn't cover it, they'd like the Student Events Committee to sponsor it. That means we'll also need chaperones."

"I'm sorry," the lawyer voice says. "We just discussed the Ivy League trip, why are we doing another . . . one that doesn't seem to benefit most of our students." She's more uncertain now, like she doesn't know the right phrasing. "We can't visit all schools. Only the best. So that shouldn't come out of a budget for all of our children."

"Let's go," I whisper to Tammy, stepping through the door. She drags me back, keeping the door propped open with her foot.

"You're still on probation," she says, her voice hushed but assertive. Her eyes widen, beaming with concern. "You head out there, and they'll prolong it. Or worse." She folds a hand around my forearm, letting me know she's got this. She's pulled me close enough that I can nearly taste the mint drifting off her tongue. I don't want her to let go. The softest hand touches my cheek.

Sparks must be flying off my fade 'cause my whole body feels like a rocket about to blast off. "Just chill. I got this."

Tammy takes off down the stairs, and I'm left suspended in time. Thinking of the way her half smile said *I got this*. She goes around the long way so she doesn't expose our position.

"Trust her," Janeil says. "She isn't the president for nothing."

I give her a nod, and tune back in to the conversation below.

"No," Julia says. Her tone is proper, definitive, as if she's been leading meetings her whole life. "If they wanted an expanded budget, the request should have been put in last year. Let's move on."

The door to the main floor opens, and my whole stomach plunges. "Pardon me," Tammy says, entering. She's unwavering. Posture tall, shoulders back, knowing she belongs here. No wonder they chose her to speak at the gala. She's a boss. I wish I felt that way, had half her confidence. "I was told that the BCC proposal would be discussed tonight, and I wanted to make sure I could answer any questions you had and further explain why this is so important." I can't see her eyes from here, just those blue frames sitting regally on her nose.

"Ms. Washington," the dean says. "This meeting isn't for students."

"I actually mentioned it to her," Ms. Flemming interjects. "And it looks like she took the initiative to come. Why not hear her out. I'm sure she can present the proposal better than I." The dean seems to acquiesce with a grunt before conceding the floor to Tammy.

She steps to the center of the room. Looks from left to right to make sure she has everyone's attention. Then begins. "This isn't just another college tour. It's a chance for all the Black students to visit HBCUs in the DC-Maryland-Virginia area. That's 6 percent of the student population at Augustin. Whereas the Ivy League trip is only for a small percentage of the seniors. It's a great chance for the Black Culture Club to explore all the options for higher education, and put Augustin on the map of some of the top HBCUs in the country."

"Is this part of the diversity initiative?" one parent asks. "If that's the case, I don't see any problem with it. It's one of the reasons I sent my kids here, because this is a private school that embraces inclusion." There's a murmur of approval. But those words echo in my head. *Inclusion. Diversity.* Tammy broke down the numbers to me earlier. The school is 6 percent Black, 7 percent Latinx, and 11 percent Asian. That doesn't make it diverse. It makes me think of that picture Mr. Abato took of me and CJ. As if that's representative of Augustin culture. My fingertips claw into my palms.

"There's a huge problem with it," the third parent says. "This is exactly what Hugh Killian has been saying about education in New York." *There it is.* The nods of agreement are stronger. I walk by the posters every day, hear the ad campaigns, but being caught in the midst of his supporters, the people who'll vote for him, fills me with dread. Who's on our side here? Mom couldn't come out tonight because she's still at work. Would she even be allowed into this special meeting? Who decides on the membership? "You're talking about pulling funds away from paying students for a specialized activity as if this were public school."

"Paying students?!"

It takes seconds to figure out where the voice came from. All the faces turned back and up toward the mezzanine make me realize that I was the one who spoke. And my head's not poking through the door, it's with the rest of my body, right up in the balcony. Janeil groans. I'm pretty sure she just called me an idiot. There's no part of *The Art of War* that says to rush into a battle recklessly and give up your position. That's what I just did.

"It looks like Ms. Washington isn't the only student who's opted to crash our meeting," Dean Bradley says. "Since you're here, you might as well come inside and address us."

I head down the same way Tammy went, past Janeil, who is wincing from my actions. When I enter the room, I struggle to avoid Tammy's eyes, hoping she's not angry.

"This is Mr. Powell." The dean introduces me to a room of mostly white parents. His forehead is a cascade of lines rolling down on each other. "A student who served a week's suspension after transferring to Augustin." Everything inside begins to twist and curdle.

"You mean this is the thu—" The lawyer catches herself. I'm sure the word she was looking for was *thug*. She's dressed in a suit. Her chestnut hair is pulled back into a bun. She replaces what was briefly shock and outrage with a demeaning smile. Each word more deliberate than the last. "The student who attacked Terry." Even the parents believe the stories. Hanging that lie over my head like a curse. Never to end. The lawyer looks over at another parent with perfectly groomed eyebrows and a forehead that's clearly had several rounds of Botox. She's in a white dress with long sleeves. The pleasant waxed smile doesn't match the glare she's been giving me since I entered. "Aren't you on probation?"

Wait. So the parents know? Were they the ones who pushed for it?

"Technically, this isn't an activity," the dean says to her. "He's a volunteer." The dean shifts his gaze back to me. "Though that doesn't excuse barging in."

"First of all, I didn't attack Terry," I say to the lawyer. "Him and his friends attacked me. And you said 'paying students' . . . Whether we're on a partial scholarship or not, each one of us pays. We're students here and we matter just like anyone else."

"This is a financial situation," the woman in the white dress says. I recognize the voice now. Julia. The one with the final say. "It's not about race."

"Oh, it's not?" I ask. I can't stop the words from coming. "'Cause I didn't say 'race.' And Augustin has the money—"

"To budget for all of our students," she cuts me off. "I don't like what you're trying to infer." Her tone is even, not shifting for a moment. I may have tried to start a battle, but this is her terrain. She's the one in control. "The Ivy League tour is a tradition. Whereas this other trip—it's not even on the agenda. So we can table it for another time."

"Tradition is also about change," Tammy says. Unlike me, she hasn't lost her composure, it's been honed from three years at Augustin. "A trip like this shows how far this school has come. Progress in celebrating students of color, whose percentages here have been dwindling over the past decade. Leadership, by showing that Augustin doesn't just talk about diversity, but champions it."

"I think you've said your piece, Ms. Washington," the dean says. He fixes his tie with authority, sending a stern warning.

"Oh no, Dean Bradley. I'm so thankful for everything she's shared." Julia stands up, taking the spotlight. "And so eloquently. It shows how much Augustin is changing lives. This is why we all are so giving to the endowment that funds scholarships and grants. Because we want students like you to thrive."

"So what's the issue with letting the Black students check out HBCUs?" I ask. Everything I read in *The Art of War* falls apart. There's no subtlety. Just raw emotion.

"I know you're smart," Julia says. She tilts her head. Her eyebrows are raised and she gives an unwavering smile that's anything but happy. "Think about what you just said. You're making it political. That's reverse racism. Not inclusion. A Black college tour wouldn't be *inclusive* of all students. But I don't want you to think I'm shutting this down." Her head tilts to the other side, the mask stronger than before. "This definitely sounds like something the Black Club can lobby for in its budget proposal for next year."

I CAN ALMOST see the fumes from Tammy as we leave Parker Hall.

In Sun Tzu's "Marches" he writes: "When the troops are disorderly, the general has no prestige." Tammy's the president of the BCC, took point on this, and told me to fall back. And still I advanced. Rushed in. Botched it. But was there any other outcome? Everything they said was loaded. They used faux niceness and tradition to hide their advance, and push aside the Black college tour. Julia may as well have called our proposal critical race theory and banned it.

Tammy makes three lefts and heads down the staircase, away from the clamor of parent-teacher night. I don't know where she's going or where Janeil is, but I follow. She leads me to the school's Legacy Wing. The hallway is dimly lit. Chandeliers hang from high ceilings, each light like an upside-down candlestick. Paintings of Hall of Fame alumni and teachers from Augustin's past line the wall as if in a museum exhibit. It's quiet enough that Tammy's shoes echo with each stomp. When we hit the center, Tammy pounds her foot on the green and cream tiles, snapping toward me like she's coming for my throat. "Did you hear them." It's not a question. She can't believe what went down either. "The way they spat out the words 'inclusion' and 'diversity.' Called being Black 'political.'"

There's fire in her eyes. Like she's ready to go a few rounds.

"They may as well have said all clubs matter," Tammy says, ready to burst. "You're new here, but I'm tired of this nonsense." She motions to the surrounding walls, the hallowed paintings that now seem to taunt us. "Every time we try to do something, they manufacture another roadblock, anything to stop us from just existing."

Sun Tzu also said, when in enemy ground, "Speed is of the essence . . . strike where he has taken no precautions." But at Augustin, in these white spaces, is there any ground that's safe? It's like Brooklyn, all those houses getting bulldozed. Whatever ground we had keeps getting taken away. Or immigrants like my dad and Rej's dad, always worried about their safety here. No matter how much work my dad did, always coming home clutching his back, covering it up with a smile. Could he ever feel comfortable building someone else's dream?

"I'm sorry I rushed in there like that," I say. "Hearing what they said . . . They want us to think that they're elevating us, even though we're putting just as much work in or more. It's like what you said about the newspaper . . . fighting every year to get your stories told."

"Not just my stories," she says firmly. "Each of ours. It's one thing to have to deal with it on the student level. To have to fight with the prior editors . . ." She averts her gaze, stuck in an unspoken grief. I grasp her hands, staring at them. Feeling the sadness inside me rise. Not only from the last hour, but every-thing. Dad not being here. Not being there for Rej. Leaving Granma alone. And I feel a rush of regret flood through me.

My hands warm. I'm not sure if she started massaging my hands or if I did hers. But we pull each other close and look each other in the eyes. It's not that we finally see each other, it's more that we've let the walls we built up retract. Everything fades away. And our lips touch. It's quick, but they touched. And everything inside explodes. She leans back to look at me. Her forehead dips toward me and I kiss it as softly as I can. Then she pulls off her glasses, folds them up, and tucks them by the handle into the front of her shirt. And we kiss. Full-on kiss. The tears on our faces colliding, the salt touching our lips, reminding us to savor this. I don't want to let go.

I don't know how long we stay wrapped in each other's arms. It may have been seconds or minutes. But when we leave the Legacy Wing, it's in silence. We don't hold hands or mention the kiss. We just walk. Down the stairs to our lockers. And an idea begins to take shape. I lost another battle. But in losing I also gained an ally who's ready to fight. *No. More than an ally.* Now we just gotta get the others.

"You said the newspaper gives us a voice," I say. "Well, I think we got a story that needs telling." If I call out the school for racism and the Parents' Committee and administration comes after me or the BCC, all the Black students will have to speak up, fight back. They can't suspend us all.

"The parents can't go unchecked," Tammy says, resolve in her voice. "That's how these biases get passed down."

"True, true." Let's bring the war to the public.

22

Tammy's in this war now too. Officially. Me and her didn't just kiss two nights ago. We made a vow. To expose Augustin's underbelly.

TAMMY

train just pulled in. see u soon 🖤

She sent the text almost an hour ago. I don't know if this is a study date, a work date, or what. Writing an article isn't like writing an essay. And I needed a little help. I'd go up to Harlem, but I need to be home with Granma. And that heart emoji was everything.

It'll only be us three. Mom's working another double. Renee came over last night with her girlfriend to watch *Black Belt Jones*, to keep Dad's Friday movie night tradition going.

Dad loves that moment where Jim Kelly beats up the gangsters attacking his dojo. The scene makes no sense. Lights keep going on and off. Shots are in slow-motion. All of a sudden Jim Kelly has the hat of one of the gangsters on top of his fro. In the next shot, the hat's back on the gangster's head just in time for Jim Kelly to KO him. All the while, the gangsters are yelling about getting shot or their jaws getting broken. It's brilliant, mostly 'cause of Dad's energy, rooting Jim on even though he's seen the movie a hundred times. Whether it's movie night, or cheering me on at a martial arts tournament, that *energy* was infectious. It made winning possible.

I'm hustling around the house, making sure everything's clean. The dust's built up on the window ledges and tiny layers of grime creeping into the kitchen and bathroom are a reminder that I haven't been around to do my chores 'cause of robotics. Maybe I'm just looking at things a little too closely 'cause Tammy's coming. But there was also my room to clean, laundry to hide, and baby pictures to cover up.

"GC, yuh goin kill yuhself, runnin round like dat," Granma says. Phrases like this never meant much to me when I was younger, but when she uses death words now, it makes me think of that night with the fire. How I wasn't there.

"Don't worry, Granma." I hug her and give her a kiss on the cheek to make sure she didn't think I was ignoring her. "Just making sure I don't embarrass us with any dirty drawers lyin about."

"Well, yuh betta be wearing clean undawear if yuh and her do anyting special," she says. We both laugh. For some reason sex convos are never awkward around Granma. Long as I've been old enough to remember, that's just her way of talking, unfiltered, uncensored. It's different with Mom and Dad. Their protection convo still gives me shivers. "Tek a break, nuh," Granma says. "Haff a piece a cake."

The apartment is filled with the sweet scents of freshly baked grater cake and gizzada. Despite what happened, there's no stopping Granma. Baking, sharing what she's made, seeing our expressions, brings her joy. I grab one of the grater cakes, a small white shredded-coconut mountain with a pink top, been a favorite since forever. I bite in, forgetting that I just brushed my teeth. The lingering toothpaste sours the sweet confection like chasing Listerine with pineapple juice. I should've stopped myself, but I can't resist these treats. I take back a cup of water, swishing the mint out of my mouth as I drink. Then finish it off. So good.

The doorbell rings.

Damn. No warning. Guess someone let Tammy in downstairs. I glance around, everything's as good as it's gonna be. I take a meditative breath. Here goes.

Opening the door, I feel the brightness forming on my face like sunshine peeking through the blinds after a restful sleep. But it's not Tammy at the door and whatever expectation was there quickly erodes. It's Mr. Neckles with that air of exuberance that's too much for any day.

"Hey, Gil," he says, beaming. "Happy Saturday!"

"Hi, Mr. Neckles," I say with less than a third of his enthusiasm. He's dressed corporate casual on a weekend, cradling a big Dutch pot and one of those shoulder-strap coolers, which makes me nervous. I step aside so he can come in, when I want to tell him to leave 'cause I have a date. But he and his wife have a key now to help with Granma, so there's no shutting him out.

"Come in, come in." Granma welcomes him with a hug as if he's one of her children.

"Amber is away this weekend for a conference," he says, meaning his wife. "So I got a little adventurous in the kitchen. Made curry chicken like you taught me to." He walks into the kitchen to rest it on the table. "I'm sure it's not on your level," he says apologetically, "but Amber thinks it's getting there. Fried some plantain, got white rice, did rice and peas too in case anyone wanted a choice."

It's times like this where I can't tell if he's being fake or if this is his true self. Makes it doubly irritating that he's here.

"Why yuh nuh go hol a rest," Granma says, directing him to the chair. "GC, help him wit di dutchie." I grab the iron pot with the curry out of his hand. My shoulders slump toward the ground like I just grabbed a sack of bricks. How was he lifting this?

"Hey," a voice enters through the door I left open. "Ms. Powell. Mr. Powell?"

"Tammy," I say, surprised to see her head peeking around the corner. She's wearing an olive coat with a fur hood, and carrying a book bag. I hustle to rest the pot on the stove, then return to grab her coat. I help her take it off, one shoulder at a time. The coconut scents from her hair wash over me like a gentle breeze. I try not to stare too long at the unzipped hoodie, her chest modestly pushing out the T-shirt beneath that reps the cross streets of 125th and St. Nicholas. I'm not really focused on the words. Her thighs are flexin through tears in her jeans. I want to touch her skin. Feel those full lips pressed against me again. But Mr. Neckles and Granma are hovering behind me. "Sorry, that's my dad's friend, Mr. Neckles," I say.

"Show her weh di bathroom is, see if she wan wash her hands and freshen up," Granma says. "Since mi child bring ova di food, we can all sit down, an eat di food him mek."

"Okay," Tammy says agreeably. "I am kinda hungry." Was so lost in the fact that she was coming over that I didn't even think about food. Another win for Mr. Neckles.

"We gon mek sure yuh fill yuh belly," Granma says, grabbing Tammy by her shoulders, then spinning her around to give her the once-over. If it weren't Granma I'd almost feel uncomfortable. "GC doin all right. Yuh so pretty, pretty."

"You better wash your hands," I say, grinning, and sliding Tammy out of Granma's grasp. "Granma don't play with train germs." I take Tammy on a tour of the apartment, pointing out Granma's room, my parents' room, then mine.

"Wow," she says, peeking inside. "That painting is so dope." She adjusts her glasses, entering my room to study the painting.

"Yeah, my cousin's girlfriend Nicole painted it," I say. "Straight talent." I reach for the door handle—

"Oh, you tryin to close the door while your granma's outside?" Tammy says. "You not slick." Yesterday we talked about the parent-teacher meeting, about what I might include in the article, but we haven't talked about the kiss yet. Every time I feel it's about to come up, the subject changes, as if one of us is purposefully trying to avoid talking about it.

"My fault," I say. "Habit. I close the door when I'm in my room."

"Well, we can come back later to work," she says.

On cue, Granma knocks on the open door. "Yuh haff a minute?" she asks. We follow Granma into her room. "Take a look at this." She holds a sketch up for Tammy to see. Earlier today I walked Granma to Designs by Pauline after she got her hair done. It's a storefront with dresses in the window and a smaller sign that reads: Licensed CPA, Taxes and Accounting Done Here. Pauline's from Grenada. She makes Granma get at least one custom outfit done a year, for as long as I can remember. "Juss yuh wait. I gon mash up any dance floor inna dis fashion."

"It's beautiful," Tammy says. "The flowers and color will really bring out your eyes."

"Ooo, me like her," Granma says, smiling, pressing her hand to Tammy's cheek.

"Brunch is ready," Mr. Neckles calls out. I can't help but wish it was my dad here making us food and meeting Tammy.

She helps me set the table and we sit down to eat. I don't say much during the meal. The curry actually tastes mad good. Not sure if I should let Mr. Neckles know that, so I just keep eating, reaching over to the center of the table to re-up on the plantain. Could go for some more rice and peas with the curry as well. So I take my plate over to the pot on the stove.

"This is so good," Tammy says.

"Well, thank you." Mr. Neckles accepts the compliment. "Gil grabbing seconds is all the thanks I need." Why'd he have to say that? He gives me a thoughtful look, considering a question he's not sure he wants to ask. "So, things picking up at school?"

"Yes and no," I reply. The yes: She's right next to me. Tammy. It's not just how I feel about her emotionally. But she motivates me. Got me signing up to write, doubling down to make Augustin the place it could be. The no: All this drama with the administration, the parents, everything that's stopping me from living out my senior year the way I was supposed to. "We were pitching an HBCU tour. It got rejected by the school, the parents. So I'm gonna write about it." Me and Tammy give a rundown of what happened at the meeting. What we were trying to do. But she doesn't know this is kinda what I wanted. A fight that's not just against me, but the whole BCC. A reason for them to stand with me.

Mr. Neckles sighs, like staring off into a memory. "I know when you look at me, you think of me as a corporate sellout of some kind," he says, directing his words at me. I bite down too hard on my fork and wince. Did I say something? "Your dad may have told you that my first name is Shareef, but I have everyone call me by my middle name, Allen."

He looks at me like he's waiting for a reply. Tammy pinches my leg, and I pinch her thigh back, secret messages exchanged under the table. We're both confused about where Mr. Neckles is going with all this. Tammy doesn't remove her hand from my leg, so my hand stays on hers, feeling the smooth skin through the hole in her jeans. "Dad sometimes uses your first name, but never really talked about why you go by Allen. And I never called you a sellout." *Not to your face at least, and pretty sure not even behind your back.* At least not in those words.

"I'm glad you're protesting," he says. "Maybe I don't do it enough. My first job after college, they kept on me about my name, how difficult it was to pronounce, how it would hurt me trying to advance. Couldn't even spell the name right on my check." He lets out a heavy breath, frustrated at the memory. "And that's just typed into a computer," he says, his voice rumbling. "You have to intentionally get it wrong, when that's your one job as Payroll. Write what I put down on the paper. But I said nothing. Switched my name. Kept it moving."

"Why?" I ask. "That don't eat you up?"

"Every day, Gil," he says. "Sometimes I want to scream." He lets out an uneasy laugh and I feel the pain behind it. "It's like I gave in. My dad was always protesting, fighting the fight. He died of a heart attack before he turned fifty. Maybe it was nutrition. Maybe stress. Being Black in America, you're always under attack. Happens all the time in finance. They're always looking for a reason to belittle me. Something I wore or the way I said something. Use it to say that I'm not adapting to the company culture. Using my middle name, it was my way to survive." It's just like the woman on the train said about being a Black man in America. Told me not to be bashful or hide who I am.

I close my eyes. It's the first time I've ever heard Mr. Neckles talk like this. Maybe that's why Dad really went back to Jamaica. Maybe he regretted coming here. Maybe that's why he always encouraged me toward science and robotics, to live the dream he couldn't. I don't want to look back and regret that I didn't achieve everything I could while Granma was here. Sun Tzu saw that every interaction is a war. With others, with himself. That's why he broke it down, pondered every scenario, so when the opportunity came, he reacted on instinct.

Tammy's hand moves down to my knee and squeezes as if she's sensed the war raging in my head. The pressure calms me, warming each point in my body. My eyes open with an exhale.

Her cheeks rise in that way she has when she's analyzing a scenario. Not smiling, but digging for a story. I feel so exposed next to her, the way her body leans in, the almost touch of her shoulder against mine. Without a word I'm disarmed. All the walls I've built from a life growing up in the hood broken down.

"My fight is different," Mr. Neckles says. "Donating to causes, bringing Black and Brown people in for job interviews whenever I can—"

"Building an army," I say in barely a whisper.

"What was that?" Mr. Neckles asks.

I see Tammy's confused expression and try to clean it up. "Nothing," I say. "Just thinking about Augustin's alum network. Mr. Abato mentioned there may be internships for people on the robotics team. And they have an alum doing things in neuroscience."

"You know I went to Howard. I should introduce you to another alum," he says. "My friend Rashida. She writes for *The Root*, also for a few other news outlets like *The Atlantic*, the *Washington Post*. Went to Augustin too." I raise an eyebrow to Tammy. Meeting someone like Rashida could help her too.

"Would Ms. Rashida want to come to my robotics competition?" I ask. "Then she could meet Tammy . . . Us." Then I realize I didn't actually invite Tammy to the competition. "I—I mean, if you want to go." I stammer out the invite, wondering if I overstepped. "I'd want you to go. I think it'll be cool. Could be something to write about."

She holds my hand. "I'll be there," she says. Granma giggles and I feel the embarrassment hit my cheeks.

"I'll ask her," Mr. Neckles says. "I know Rashida mentioned

going to the alumni gala your school is hosting. Heard another alum at my office talk about it too."

"Oh, the anniversary?" I say. "Tammy's the student speaker. It'd be cool if they met."

"I'm sure that can be arranged," he says. Mr. Neckles is looking out. Maybe I been judging him wrong all this time.

A COUPLE HOURS pass before Mr. Neckles takes off. I didn't notice the time slip by. Listening to his stories about work hits different now. Granma went to rest while Tammy and I finished up the dishes. She also gave me a wink before closing the door.

Granma be wild.

"That was great," Tammy says, drying a plate with a towel. "Your granma is amazing."

"She is," I say, reflecting on all the good times we've had. "Glad you got to see her like this." Tammy rests a comforting hand on my back. She's next to me, my hands immersed in the soapy dish water. I wait for her to say something, fill the space. But she doesn't, so I do. "Hearing Granma joke. Talkin 'bout her dress and dancing." I get caught up in all those memories. Granma showed me what it meant to live. "She's everything to me."

"I felt that," Tammy says.

"And your family?" I ask.

"I love my parents," she says hesitantly. "I know I got it better than some. But every conversation this past year is about college. I like talking about the news, covering it, not when the news is me." I want to trace her jawline as she talks, cup her ear in my palm. But I suppress the urge because my sudsy hands might send the wrong signal. Or not. "As soon as I get home, one of them will bring up financial aid, if I leave the city, cost of living, food." She sighs. "It's a lot."

"Aye, at least if you stay in the city, you know where to get the Jamaican food now."

"I do," she says through a smile. I hand her the last dish to dry.

"Food was decent," I say, covering up my hormones. "But Mr. Neckles is kind of Jamaican adjacent. You gotta come back for something official."

"Not before you get a taste of Uptown," she says. "My parents throw down." *Wait. Is this a first date?* She's thinking about more hangs. I lead her over to the couch so we can sit. She eyeballs Dad's DVD collection. "You got as many kung fu movies as my dad's got Shaft flicks."

"That's funny, those are my dad's." We're practically at opposite ends of the couch. I'm staring at the DVDs, the TV, the coffee table. Everything but her. I'm thinking about that kiss. I don't want her to feel pressured, like that's the only reason I asked her over. "I'm trying to figure out how to start this article." I talk business, open up my laptop to show her what I've written. It gives me a chance to slide closer.

She gives it a read. Then meets me with those shimmering onyx eyes. "I always find it's best to start with an emotion, or describe the setting the article takes place in, bring the reader in," she says. "Or you can start with the title, and let the pieces fall from there."

"I'm trying to figure it out," I say. "It felt like an assault on Blackness. Maybe that's what got Janeil when Lydia touched her hair. I dunno. Whatever I write, I gotta expect the administration is going to try to extend my probation."

"And tell me no more articles like this," Tammy says. "But I've already printed several articles from our archive to show them that covering social issues in the school like this isn't new. And then we keep writing."

"True. Still gotta start the article though," I say. "Maybe I just need some Lady Day and John Coltrane."

"What does that mean?"

"Something my dad always says," I say, twisting my body to face her. "It's a song by Gil Scott-Heron on *The Revolution Begins*."

"Oh?" Her eyebrow lifts, sending a gentle shiver across my skin. "Play it." I put on the song and lean back. The strings and keys play in anticipation of Gil Scott-Heron's first line. Her head nods to the beat. She likes it. I nudge my body closer as Gil begins to sing. "What's this?" She reaches past me to the coffee table, sending a rush of heat along my spine. She grabs up *The Art of War*.

"Just a book I been reading," I say. She settles back into the couch, letting my arm wrap around her while Scott-Heron serenades us.

"In Philosophy?" she asks, referring to Ms. Willis's class.

"Nah, it actually belongs to my sensei," I say. "Reminds me I have to give it back." Her legs fold up on the couch. And I'm hoping Granma doesn't come out to say something about her feet up on the furniture.

She skims the book. "You got wars to fight?" she asks playfully. Her lips are doing that beautiful tilt they do.

It's just me, her, and my namesake giving me the nod. So I go for it. "That kiss the other day," I say in the softest pitch I've ever heard my voice reach. "I been wondering if it was real or in my head."

She examines me. "I'm still trying to figure out who Gil is," she says.

We're suspended in time for a moment. The lyrics begin to fade. The room drifts away. And it's just us. Our heads inch closer, but we're still questioning, wondering if this is right. Finally our bodies begin to melt together. Our lips collide. I pull back, taking her in. It's like seeing her for the first time. Her eyes measure me in return.

BZZT! BZZT!

The doorbell rings, breaking the moment. I jump, rushing over to the door so it doesn't wake Granma.

When I open the door, it's Rej, staring at me. No, accusing me. "So what's good, man?" he says, his voice cold.

"It's been crazy," I say, off guard. I know I owed him a text over the lawyer appointment, but why's he coming at my throat like this? "That whole podcast, the comments, remember? Well, we went to the parent-teacher night."

"We?" he asks.

As if on cue, Tammy dips her head out of the living room. "I'm gonna run to the bathroom," she says from behind me. "Oh hey," she says, spotting Rej. "I'm Tammy."

"Rej," he replies with a smile. They shake hands. "You from Augustin?" he asks. "I think Gil mentioned you." She returns the smile to both of us, then heads to the bathroom. He looks over my shoulder. When she's gone, his smile vanishes. "Got caught up at school, huh?" He says it in a hushed tone filled with resentment. But why?

"Nah, it's not like that," I try to explain.

"I think it's exactly like that," he says. "I needed you there for me. For us. But I see you. Fam ain't fam, I guess." Before I have a chance to reply, offer some reasoning, he walks out, closing the door behind him.

23

Parents Condemn Blackness as Political

It's the second Tuesday of October. I'm walking over the checkered tiles in the school's Legacy Wing, newspaper in hand, reading a headline to an article I wrote, now etched in Augustin's history. Janeil is next to me with Saleem's arm draped over her shoulder.

White students are walking by giving me the side-eye. Black students are giving me the nod. Luisa grabbed me after Philosophy to say some of the Latinx and LGBTQIAP+ students are considering writing articles about their experiences for the paper. My head's high. This is not just a victory or a challenge to the status quo. It's a definitive strike. Letting the school know it needs to change. Can't wait for Granma to read the piece. I don't need a mirror to know I got a little grin forming.

Tammy was right. There's something different about seeing words in print. Within these walls, this article means something. Some of the Hall of Famers lining the corridor will probably receive a copy of the Augustin *PAW* in the mail, a gift for being longtime donors.

"You're really trying to fight all the fights," Saleem says coolly, sipping a latte.

It's meant to be a joke, but there's truth in what he said. The past month has felt like one massive dogpile of fights. Even Rej has beef with me now. We haven't talked since that Saturday over a week ago. I basically spend five-sevenths of my time in school. It's more now that I'm coming into Augustin on the weekend to work on the robot. So this is where I have to focus.

"Only shining a light," I say. "Terry's a racist bully, yeah. But I realized it's the culture here that allows people like him to thrive." In "Weaknesses and Strengths," Sun Tzu praised those who modified their tactics based on the enemy's situation, moving like water, responding to attacks in an infinite variety of ways. I've watched how Augustin moves. The school will do anything to protect its traditions, its image. There's gonna be a clapback. But what're they gonna do? Put me on a longer probation for writing the truth? I'm not on the newspaper, all I did was submit an Op-Ed. No probation violated. The most they can tell me to do is stop writing.

"I just can't stand some people," Janeil says, her voice almost seething. She runs her fingers through her hair, which is pulled back into a single puff, the movement more unsure than usual. I still haven't asked her exactly how she felt about what happened with Lydia. She refuses to come back to the STEM Lab or join the team no matter how many times me or CJ brings it up. She stops to cross her arms, deciding whether to continue or not. "It's like they think they still have ownership of our bodies."

"Aye," Saleem says, kissing Janeil's cheek. Now that they're officially a couple, Saleem has been nonstop with the PDA the past week. "You good?"

She pushes him off, not forcefully, but definitely not affectionately. "You're a dude, you don't get it."

"It's America," Saleem says, taking a breath to get serious. "We all knew the deal when we came to Augustin. We're not here to beat racism. I do my football thing, do my school thing, keep it moving."

"That doesn't mean you don't fight," Janeil says to Saleem. "Like what you been sayin about bein passed up for captain."

Saleem's head snaps sideways with disapproval, as if she said something she shouldn't have. "Y'all doin too much." He regains his composure, the sudden scowl gone. "We can protest around the world and nothing will change," he says. "I mean *that* happened. And we still got Karens calling the cops on us and cops just shooting us."

"Can't expect you to speak up," Janeil says.

"What's that supposed to mean?" Saleem asks. His eyes pinch and he takes a step back. I've never seen him off his game.

"You're in a sport that leads to concussions," Janeil says. "That NFL doesn't care about its Black players and protects players that abuse and rape women."

"What's that even got to do with anything?" Saleem rolls his eyes. "You can't turn everything into a cause and something to protest. Look, I gotcha back. Whatever you decide to do, Ima be down for you. But don't make this situation about me."

"Whatever," Janeil mumbles, walking away. "Ima go to the newspaper office."

Saleem throws up his hands and looks at me for answers. I got nothing. He sighs, then follows after her in a half run.

"What was that about?" Tammy asks, walking up beside me.

"I got no idea," I reply. "But I'm pretty sure Saleem gotta apologize."

"Hope he didn't say anything to upset my girl."

I shrug, wondering if and when me and Tammy will be official. After Rej came over, I was fully out of it. Me and Tammy worked a little, then I walked her to the train. We hugged. No kiss goodbye. Then it's kinda just been back to business.

She grabs hold of my shoulder, excited. "Everywhere I go people are talking. Students. Faculty. There's a lot of shock. It's been decades since articles like this have been written at Augustin. And there's never been anything specifically calling out issues of racism here. I think a lot of people are still processing that, but the conversations are being had." Her grip tightens on me with each word. And I want to put my hands around her hips, bring her in close so I can feel her heart beat against mine. "When I was leaving Pre-Calc, I even heard Jill complain to her friends that the *PAW* is becoming like the *Washington Post* and the *New York Times*." She snorts and then hides it. "This is what I've wanted for the newspaper. For us."

Us. That's what I want. I know she's referring to the collective BCC. But me and Tammy, we're a team. Working, fighting, sharing stories together.

"You know, it's always felt like there's a weight on me at

Augustine," she continues. "Constantly being judged no matter how many things I accomplish." Her lip curls anxiously to the side. "I know the administration will probably have something to say about the piece. But that's a conversation. One I'm ready to have. I want the *PAW* to have the chance to grow, become the paper it should be."

I latch on to the tension in her eyes. "You said it best," I say. "This is the start of something different. Every Black student here's got a story. And all of them have trigger points. We keep writing and we'll have a chance to finally turn Augustin into the school it should be."

"Stinks it took three years to get here," she says. "My attention's been split between school and working on my Early Action application to Yale." I still haven't decided on my top schools yet. "Then I can breathe again."

We head down to the newspaper to see Janeil facing off with the dean and Ms. Flemming. Standing next to them is Jill. I still remember that tiny pocketbook from my first day. But something else about her looks familiar. The way she stands. Her eyes. My spine tingles. She looks like a younger version of Julia. The leader from parent-teacher night.

"Everything okay?" Tammy asks, looking as confused as I feel.

The dean adjusts his tie, drawing in air as if to bellow. "I've just met with both the president and headmaster," he says. "And I want to say that it saddens us all that you would publish something so divisive." He holds up the paper. "Augustin champions both full inclusivity and diversity. And yet this article is the opposite. It's one-sided, unbalanced, unfair . . . and accusatory, I might add."

Tammy was hoping for dialogue. A chance to talk about improving the *PAW.* This isn't that.

"The article only brings to light systemic problems with Augustin's approach to Black students," Tammy says.

"Then why not bring your concerns to me before printing this?" the dean asks. *So she needs permission to do her job?* It's like he's taken a lesson from Julia. Using the nice-helpless-victim voice to talk down to Tammy. "I have an open-door policy. Not to mention the Parents' Committee. After all they do for you students. What are our alumni supposed to think of this poor picture you've painted of everyone?"

Something's off. I wrote the article. But he's solely going after Tammy.

"That we're students with opinions that can analyze facts," Tammy says firmly.

"The facts as I see them are Mr. Powell is on probation and shouldn't have been writing for the newspaper. Obviously, he wants to put his scholarship at risk." Before I have a chance to respond to the threat, he holds up his hand to shush me. "And you. Your fourth year here. You've performed exceptionally well in your classes, excelled in your activities, represented us as one of our top Tigers, been invited to numerous alumni events. Not a single blemish during your time here, until now." He tosses all her accomplishments back at her as if her achievements were gifts. "And yet you say there are 'systemic problems' here. You're a front-runner for valedictorian, Ms. Washington. The truest mark of a Tiger. But you have to understand that your actions have consequences."

"'Consequences.'" Tammy tries to make sense of the word. "There can't be consequences for writing an Op-Ed. That's the purpose of an Op-Ed."

"Think about it from Martin Luther King's perspective," Dean Bradley says. My teeth grind waiting for the typical conservative's distortion of Martin Luther King Jr.'s words. "He'd want to uplift everyone. Keep us united."

I barely hear the words *are you serious* hiss through Tammy's lips. Her face is tense, her jaw trembling, forcing herself to hold back.

"This is our anniversary year," the dean says. "A chance to highlight accomplishments, grow our endowment so students like you can have an education like this." He sighs as if he's about to drop a bomb on us after some hefty soul-searching. "I've talked it over with Headmaster DeSantis. And we both think it best that someone on the faculty more closely supervises the paper. So Ms. Flemming will supervise the *PAW* to provide a more moderate approach."

"The newspaper has always been student run," Tammy says.

"And it will still be," the dean says with the assurance of a lawyer who has hidden the truth in fine print. "That's why there will also be a new editor to ensure that *all* of our students' voices are equally heard."

"You can't be serious," Tammy says, ready to burst. "You're replacing me? There's no student who's put as many hours as I have into this paper."

"Well, we've already solved that. We picked a student who is equally involved in the school's activities and is really in touch with the student body. You'll still be able to write; this merely ensures that the direction of the newspaper continues to serve Augustin."

Mr. Bradley doesn't need to say her name for us to know who it is. And I don't turn to see the smug expression on her face.

"Jill," the dean says.

I can almost feel Tammy's heart collapse. And I know I'm the reason.

PART III
Employment of Secret Agents

What is called "foreknowledge" cannot be elicited from spirits, nor from gods . . . It must be obtained from those who know the enemy situation.

SUN TZU: *THE ART OF WAR*

24

The BCC is ready to throw down. If you're Black, you're here on the fifth floor. There must be over forty students packing the tiered lecture room. At desks, sitting on the floor like it's the stoop, standing. Sharing stories. The clamor is furious, loud enough to break through the closed door I'm leaning on. It's what Tammy wanted. *But not like this.*

Word spread quickly. To everyone in this room, Tammy isn't just the newspaper editor or just the BCC president. She's touched all their lives in some way. Friend. Tutor. The person with a word of encouragement when things got rough. The person who steps in front of an enemy. Like she did for me when we first met. She always has their back. Like Rej and Stretch have mine. Like I have theirs. *Had theirs.* Rej hasn't responded to any of my texts. And on our group chat with Stretch, it's mostly one-word replies. I need to talk to him, like really talk, face-to-face, clear the tension between us.

But I'm fixated on Tammy. Her hands are on the podium. She stares out the windows as rain beats violently on the glass, obscuring the view of Central Park. I don't know what's going through her head. Her chin is up, shoulders back, expression a stolid mask.

In "The Nine Variables," Sun Tzu said it is a doctrine of war to not assume the enemy will not come, but rather to rely on one's readiness to meet him. To be reckless, cowardly, quick-tempered, delicate, or compassionate are faults that lead to calamity.

I can't help but blame myself for what happened. My article, my need for this war, ended up hurting Tammy. Did Sun Tzu have personal relationships that were hurt by his actions? Did he have compassion for them when sending them to war or if they were casualties? What my article did to Tammy. *I have to make this right.* But I also can't give in to the administration now. Not with the energy in this room so high.

"Parker Hall . . ." I say the words to no one in particular. Somehow it cuts through the conversations, calling attention to the front of the room. There's a question that's been lingering in my head for the past two weeks. "Is it a coincidence that it's the same as Terry's last name?"

"Nah," Saleem says. Even he cut out of football practice to be here. Janeil's next to him. Quieter than usual. Maybe he's here more for her. "Terry's grandfather paid for that. He always be talking about his family and they legacy." There's some bitterness in his voice that I've never heard before.

"And that woman Julia, from parent-teacher night." I direct the question toward Tammy. We haven't spoken since she lost her position. She stormed away not saying a word. I called after her, but she put up her hand and walked out the front doors. "That's Jill's mom, isn't it?"

She nods a slow yes. "The people on the committee tend to be the school's biggest donors."

Money. That's what runs this school. Money and nepotism. And the dean said it, the only thing they fear is a threat to any of that.

"That article was a start," I say. I try to keep my voice controlled, not be reckless, but decisive. That's how Tammy leads. "We gotta keep moving forward."

"Wuddyoumean?" Janeil asks. She's leaning back in her chair, arms crossed. Mouth a straight line. "There's no newspaper. Jill ain't gonna publish anything we write. That joint is censored and dead."

"The administration needs to know it can't take away our voices," I say.

Tammy moves from behind the podium. "Dean Bradley threatened me and made it sound as though I owed the school for everything I worked to achieve. As if being named editor didn't come from working my butt off for three years, taking all the microaggressions. He could snap his fingers and take away my shot at valedictorian." Her voice trails off. Her head sinks. It's brief, but I catch it. "It's like all my work means nothing and I have no power."

"But we do," I say. "It's like you always said. Our stories are our power. It's who we are." Everyone is quiet, listening to me, waiting for a solution. The one I have, I don't know if it's the right one, but it's all I got.

In "Employment of Secret Agents," Sun Tzu says that those who are worthy or enlightened use the most intelligent people as agents and they're certain to achieve great things. It may not have been by choice, but from the moment each Black student entered Augustin, they became an agent. Gritting their teeth through all the aggressions, hiding their feelings, they've lived in Augustin, inside a territory that's been hostile to them. And it's their knowledge the world needs.

"Forget the school," I say. I think about that contact Mr. Neckles has at *The Root*. She's an Augustin alum. "The school cares so much about its image. So we create our own platform. Our own newspaper on social, for stories. Enough so that we get the Black alum involved, till Augustin has no choice but to pay attention."

The reaction is mixed, half seem to feel it, the other half shrug it off like it's the silliest idea they've ever heard. We're a community divided.

"The hardest thing for me when I went on probation was that I was criminalized. Felt like everyone had already made up their mind about me. That I was the one in the wrong. If it wasn't for the BCC, hearing about Tammy's experiences, feeling like I had people I could confide in . . . I dunno." I search the room, hoping that someone will say they understand what I'm saying. And I'm met with uncertainty, confusion.

I get it. Talking about what's going on, not just what they're doing to us, but the feelings we have about it. It's hard.

Saleem rests his hand on Janeil's shoulder, just letting her know that he's there.

"When something happens to any of us . . ." I say. "Especially something racist. It can take place in just a second, but feel like forever." My words are for me, Janeil, everyone here. "Attacks may be physical, like what happened to me. But the aggressions we play down and call small . . . The words people use, how we're seen and treated . . . Those small things are big, and they get bigger, especially if we don't have anyone to talk to. Or we keep replaying the memory, without confronting it. This is how we fight back."

"We shouldn't only focus on conservative encounters," Chijoke says. His family is from Nigeria. He probably speaks better English than most of the students in Augustin. "There are white students who always claim they're *woke*. Then they try to tell me what it means to be Black because they listened to a rap album or heard a few speeches from some Black activists. Don't try to take away my experience."

"I'm wit it," Janeil says. "It's like when that girl grabbed my hair. If you have a question, ask me. Don't make me feel like I'm the one that's crazy for having feelings. I don't care where your politics are, nobody has the right to touch my body."

"Mmmhmm."

"Right."

"Word."

A few hushed voices chime in to co-sign.

"I can describe the two times players on the football team groped me like it was no big deal," another girl, I think her name is Leylah, says. She's fully changed out of the dress code and is in full fashionista mode. "And when I went to the dean, he blamed it on my skirt hem being too high. Saying I chose for that to happen."

"You was talking about Parker Hall before," Saleem says a little reluctantly. "Well, there's definitely favoritism there that comes from those donations. And being one of the only three Black players on the team isn't easy. Coach may give me game time but he doesn't do anything to stop the side comments I get. And well . . ." He bites his lip, looking at Janeil as if for approval to continue on, but then slumps into his chair quiet.

"So we define who we are," Tammy says hesitantly. "Not just with the sad stories, but the joyful ones too. Saleem's successes on the field. Gil in robotics. Give everyone a full picture of every Black student here." The nods of approval grow. People are on board. "And we keep the circle tight," she says. "So that we have time to build. Make sure everyone in this room has had a chance to put something up."

"The account is public, right?" Chijoke asks.

"Something like this, if it's private, it'll be too hard to grow the following," I say. "And we need that if we really want people outside of this school to see our stories and listen to what's happening here." I think again of Mr. Neckles's friend. I'd love for a site like *The Root* to cover it.

"Then what if the administration sees it?" Chijoke says. "The dean already took away Tammy's position. I'm a junior. I've never been in trouble once since I've been here." His statements are more rational than nervous. "I'm not saying that I don't believe in this. But if anyone's name is out there, they would have to expect repercussions similar to Tammy's."

He's right. I can see everyone considering his words. There's fear spreading, especially in the freshmen and sophomores. We've been conditioned to not speak up because of the consequences. "Then we give people the choice to be anonymous or not," I say. "After Tammy edits the pieces, I'll handle posting them."

"So my name would be on it?" Tammy says.

"We don't have to put any of our names on it right now," I say. I can't tell if I'm losing them. But I need everyone united, or this plan to reach the media will fail. "We don't even have to write a description or publish a contact email." I can feel myself pleading. "If you don't want your name on your piece, we won't put it. But if you do have your name on it, there's going to be power in that."

"As well as a target," Chijoke adds. He's so sensible it's annoying. But, again, he isn't wrong.

"I could always make artwork for any anonymous posts," Janeil says. "Something that captures the emotion of the write-up. People see a cool pic, they'll want to read."

"Put a target on me," Leylah says. "My social accounts have always been public because of what I'm doing in fashion. And it's not like the school doesn't already have it out for us. I'm not afraid to have my name on anything I write." True, true. That's what I needed. Her words are so self-assured, she sways the room.

"Great," Tammy says. But her lips squeeze together like she's still deciding whether or not this is a good idea. She says to me,

"Then we can bring it to alum. Like your neighbor's friend at *The Root*." It's like she read my mind.

"What do we call it?" Janeil asks. "Gotta be something hashtagable."

"Call it who we are," I say. "BlackAugustin."

25

Six weeks after getting suspended, I'm a free man. Off Augustin's probation. It's just after 4:00 p.m. I'm downstairs in the Fabrication Center making a few adjustments to our robot's code. No more sneaking around. I can come and go without worrying about Mr. Abato finding out and telling the dean. I've managed to keep the probation quiet from my family this whole time. So no added stress on Granma, who I have no doubt would've come right back to the Upper West Side to tell off Dean Bradley.

I'm not the only one free. CJ's cast is off. He's on the floor setting up an indoor practice field. The Fabrication Center has more room than the STEM Lab, so we can move around machine parts without bumping into anything. There's a lab table, a couple computers, then space for the lathe and CNC router.

I should be happy. But since BlackAugustin started last

week, that's the only thing me and Tammy speak about. When we talk to students and collect their stories, there's always a unifying theme. Black students feel isolated, like they got no one to turn to when something happens because the administration and faculty downplay reports to make us feel invisible. And some students don't want to come off like they're snitching. But when they're ready, we got an outlet for them to be heard. I just got no one to talk to about what's happening with me and Tammy. At school, we're always in a crowd, so no testing the intimacy there. After school, she heads straight home to work on her college apps. And weekends I'm in the lab since we got the competition at Freedom Academy in ten days. So I guess me and her are on hold before we ever really started. I wonder if she's upset at me. Blames me for losing her position. 'Cause I blame myself.

"These stories are real?" CJ asks, while looking at his phone.

"What're you talking about?" I respond.

He walks over and sits on the stool next to me, showing me the BlackAugustin account, thumbing through the stories. I try not to react. Not let him know I'm behind it. "Janeil showed me what you've been working on," he says. I guess our tight circle includes CJ. The posts have been flowing—the good . . . and the bad. Tammy edits them, Janeil handles any art, I set up the post on social. So far we've published six stories that've all been anonymous. They're good, but they're missing a personal touch. I just hope Leylah does what she said and uses her name. Other Black students see her face with her story, it'd empower them. "First that article you wrote, now this, you really going for it. I wish I had the guts to put out my experiences. I got a whole

Instagram and TikTok following, but I stay off anything political. Just travel, parties, jokes, keep it light."

"Do people really mess with you like that?" I say. "You're the influencer who travels to New Zealand to ski."

"C'mon, Gil," he says. "You can't seriously think money protects me from bigotry. I'm queer. Asian. I live my life. And if I have to cry, I don't let them see it."

"My fault," I apologize. I stand to give him a pound that turns into a full hug. "I wasn't thinking." There really is no safety zone from all the things we gotta deal with. "I am surprised Janeil told you though."

"We been friends since freshman year," CJ says.

"Hey guys," Lydia says brightly, entering the room. "Can't wait. In a little over a week we'll be able to show these schools what Augustin can do." Her eyes light up when she spots the mini-soccer field CJ designed. "That's so awesome," she says. "Now we just need to agree on our robot's name."

"I've got targets set up at different heights so we can test our robot's launcher," CJ says, delighted about the response to his work. He gets up to do a walkthrough of his creation. Lydia plops down next to me on the stool he was just on. "I'm still working on it, but in a few days, we'll be ready to give our robot a real run-through."

"What's this?" Lydia says, looking down at CJ's phone. "BlackAugustin?"

CJ moves so fast, it's like he wasn't even in a cast a week ago. He grabs the phone and tucks it in his pocket. "Oh, nothing, just lost in a social media wormhole, trying to hunt down these new sneakers I been hungry for, when I should be working." He says it so coolly, I almost buy the cover story. It's not like we're trying to hide the account, but we're also not promoting it beyond our close friends. Me and Tammy agreed we needed to make sure the account had enough momentum behind it before we bring it to Mr. Neckles's reporter friend. So we build a repository of stories, and hit friends of friends, recent alumni Tammy and the other seniors know and so on. "Anyway, you were saying, robot name, right?"

"I got it! AI or Die," Heath proclaims, walking into the room, in a eureka moment. "That's the name."

His twin groans. "How many times do I have to tell you, no death names," Lydia says.

"Why don't we stick to something simple, like TigerBot," CJ says. "It's our mascot, it's a robot." He holds out his hands weighing the two words like a scale.

"How 'bout MechaTiger," I say, getting into it. "Give it a lil anime flair."

"Oh, I like that." Lydia perks up. "Big *Evangelion* fan."

"I'm down with it," CJ says.

Heath shrugs a yes.

"MechaTiger it is," Lydia proclaims.

The other six members of the team arrive. I say hello to them for the first time. Mr. Abato is the last to show up, wearing his usual dusty boots and lab coat. He strokes back his beard proudly when he greets me. "Good to have you back, Gil," he says. "You've missed a lot, but at least you'll be able to help with the testing phase."

He has no idea I've been working this whole time, burning up my nights and weekends getting MechaTiger working. Part of me wants to yell, *That's my code, I put this together.* But I hold it in. Keep my emotion in check.

"Since we'll be heading to Freedom next weekend, I expect everyone to be present this weekend and after school over the next week so we can finalize tests," Mr. Abato continues. "Everybody okay with that schedule?"

"I have an event this Saturday," I say. It's the last martial arts tournament of the season. I have to go. I've already let too much time slip by since folding on Rej. Going to the tourney will force us into the same room. "I'll be here Sunday and after school."

The move is subtle. But I can see the disappointment in the way Mr. Abato tilts his head. I've let him down. He's not the only one.

"I've had a chance to look at the new error-logging system that's been added, it's pretty remarkable," Mr. Abato says. The system that I designed. I look away, trying not to show the frustration on my face. My code is there, but it's like I've been erased. "So we're going to be in good shape come January."

He makes a motion toward Heath, as if Heath did the code. The other students pat him on the back. I guess I never thought he'd be the one to take credit for my work. Is that what I agreed to? CJ shrugs at me. Lydia looks away.

"We still should discuss who is going to be the driver at the Freedom competition," Mr. Abato continues. My eyes pop. If I could drive MechaTiger in the competition for Granma to see—that would mean everything. It'd be some consolation.

I did beat Heath in our own matchup last month. "I was thinking of giving everyone a test. Something that covers all aspects of robotics. However, considering all the work Heath's put into revamping the code, if everyone's okay with it, I think he should be our driver."

"How's that fair?" I say.

"Fair?" Mr. Abato asks.

"We should do the test," I say. "At least that would give everyone a chance."

"At our last meeting, neither CJ nor Lydia wanted to drive, and most of the other students are new." Another meeting I couldn't attend because of the probation. I'm not really free of it, am I?

"But what about me?" I blurt out.

"You're new as well," Mr. Abato says, not understanding. "I don't doubt that you're capable, but this is basically your first meeting. And a little while ago you said you won't even be able to come in on Saturday to support your team." He shifts his focus back to the group, addressing everyone, but it still feels like he's talking directly to me. "I want everyone here to develop a solid work ethic. There's no shortcuts. No quick rewards. Engineering is all about building at a steady pace. Not rushing for a quick payoff."

"That's right," Heath says. His red eyebrows are lifted high over a devious smirk. "Plenty of time to put in the work." It's like he's daring me to tell the truth. Tell Mr. Abato that I've been breaking probation. Then what . . . not be allowed to be at the competition at all. Heath wants me to get in trouble. Expose myself. Either way, he wins. "You, or anyone here, can always be the driver in the spring."

That's months away. With the way Granma is, who knows how she'll be come spring. I want to tell Mr. Abato. Let him know that the reason the team can even compete is because of the upgrades I programmed. But I know Augustin. I know how the school retaliates if you step out of line. Writing the Op-Ed was one thing. What would Augustin do if they knew this whole time I had been going against their ruling? And what would my family think if they found out I failed them again?

26

There's no rush, no excitement for me, as I walk into the East Coast Fall Classic in Long Island. It's always been one of my favorite tournaments, closing out the competition season like a block party for martial artists. This is also the first tournament where I took home a trophy in sparring and double medaled in weapons. Dad was there, holding the Jamaican flag up, jumping out of his seat, his accent triumphantly rising over the crowd.

It's Saturday morning. The sun is just rising. And I know I don't belong here. I should be at Augustin. A few hours from now, the RoboAugs will be meeting up in the city without me, testing out a robot with my code. It's like I can't let it go. I can't just be content, knowing it's my work that I'm not getting credit for. But it was also my choice.

The basketball court has been repurposed for the tournament. Two rows of blue mats line the sides. Each row has four square stages, for fighting or demos, and a safety border surrounding it. Judging tables are laid out in the middle from hoop to hoop. There are bleachers on either side that would usually host people cheering for the home or away basketball team. Today, they'll be cheering for weapons, forms, and kumite.

I'm only here for the kumite. Haven't had time to practice weapons. Clear strikes to the head, face, neck, stomach, side, and back are scored on technique, accuracy, power, distance, timing, and sportsmanship.

Sportsmanship. A concept that doesn't exist in war.

My pocket buzzes. Maybe it's Tammy. She and Janeil said they'd come out today.

DAD

morning Gil. mek sure yuh mash up dem ras

I close my eyes and try to imagine him saying the words. Nothing.

Why'd he have to remind me that he's not here? *Stop. I'm being childish.* But what happens if his new business does well? Does he get the visa or green card to return to the States only to head right back? I guess when I go off to college it'd be the same thing. Distance. I stick my phone so roughly into my pocket it might rip through. What's the point of responding. To say thanks? That'd be as hollow as his well wishes.

At least Tammy will be here. It'll be good to see her away from Augustin. Have a chance to talk.

Competitors and spectators start to fill the gym. There are familiar faces from dojos I've met at tournaments in the city and Queens. Then there are others from the tristate area and beyond who made the trip just to be a part of the Classic. I need to get my mind right. I'm the only one who doesn't want to be here.

The sea of karate gis and colored belts swells. Rivals exchange head nods. My pocket goes off again.

TAMMY

Gil! Sorry! I'm struggling with this Yale essay and it's due Nov 1. Plus I have to proof all these BlackAugustin articles and match them with some of the artwork Janeil made. Good luck at the tournament 🙌

Great. It's like a birthday party where everyone I want to come cancels at the last minute.

I pull up the @BlackAugustin account. The latest post features three pictures of Leylah, the first of her sitting on a bench in Central Park facing the camera. She's dressed stylishly, showing off her love of fashion. In the second pic, she's smiling with friends at lunch, and the third is a wide shot of her in the Augustin dress code. She didn't want her write-up to be anonymous. The first line reads: "(1/5) My clothes shouldn't make me a target." Leylah goes on to recount the first time she attended the Harvest Ball as a freshman. Two football players, one a senior and another a freshman at the time, groped her from behind. The next four parts to the story will be released throughout the day. One of those posts indirectly implicates the administration who she reported the situation to. She doesn't mention any names, but I know she's talking about the dean.

And the freshman involved in the first incident, I have an idea who that might be as well.

This is big. We did a few posts over the past week, but they've felt more like general posts about racism, probably because they were anonymous. Leylah putting her face on this, making it personal, her words hit immediately. Maybe I should feel some excitement, seeing our fight come to life like this. But all I feel is numb. She's been holding on to this for so long. Having to see the people every day who assaulted her, and the dean who did nothing.

Two of the younger students from my dojo show up with their parents. We bow and salute. Then Kenya shows up with Nakia and her dad . . . wait, that's not her dad.

"Hey," I say to Nakia. I almost go for the hug, but I'm stuck studying the dude standing next to her. He looks like he's got at least two years on me. He's got a groomed goatee and a bald fade that eases into the curls that crown his head. It connects so well, it'd make Stretch jealous.

"Hey," she replies. "This is Darius."

"Sup." His high yellow hand grabs mine into a dap, making sure to flex his college muscles as he does.

"Ready for your weapons routine?" I ask Kenya. I try not to look at Nakia and Darius. But I'm wondering if this dude . . . is Nakia's dude. 'Cause I'm definitely getting that vibe.

Kenya's already dressed in her gi, with her purple belt on. Her hair is pulled back into two puffs.

And Nakia. She's looking good. The sun is creeping in just enough to cause the jeweled undertones in her dark skin to glow. It's perfect fall weather and she's not afraid to let her curves show.

"Nah," Kenya replies. "Only fighting today."

"Really?" I say. Kenya is great at sparring, but she really excels in nunchucks. People expect that she'll be slow because of her frame, but Kenya moves like lightning. She just needs to believe in herself. "You sure? You could still register."

"I'm good," she says a little dismissively. "I better check in." Her actual dad walks over. Maybe I read that wrong, but her mood seemed different.

"I'll go get us seats," Darius says, holding Nakia's hand much longer than necessary. He gives her a wink, then turns a sly grin on me as he walks away, marking his territory.

"What?" Nakia says, probably in response to my blank expression.

"Nah, it's just that I haven't seen you," I say. "So who's Darius?"

"You haven't seen me and all you ask about is who's Darius?" She shakes her head. "It's been weeks, Gil."

"I'm sorry, there's been a lot going on. Granma. School."

"Excuses. Excuses. That's all I'm hearing." She's not letting up. "Life is always gonna be a lot goin on, that's life. You expect me to hang around, wait for you to call? I gotta live my life too."

"I'm not saying you don't," I respond. She made it so easy to talk about Dad during the summer. Never judging my feelings. And with me and Rej the way we've been, all my feelings toward Dad have been shifting too. More upset. More angry. Like I got no one to turn to except a book with some guiding principles on how to wage a war that I didn't start but have to finish. "I just miss talking to you is all."

"Boys always want to miss you when they see you with someone else," she says. "If you need a friend, you can hit me up. But you gotta pick up the phone to do that. I can't be the one."

She heads off to join her fam, and I go to register. Mom and Granma join me a few minutes later. They dropped me off in Mr. Neckles's car and got breakfast while I prepped mentally for the day.

"We gon whoop all a deh butts today," Granma says. I laugh.

"Facts, Granma," Stretch says, rolling up behind Granma to give her a hug, followed by Rej. "Pure beatings gettin handed out today."

"Wussup." We exchange daps, not really making eye contact.

"How you holdin up?" Rej asks Granma, standing in front of me as if I'm not even there.

"Me all right yuh know," Granma says. "Thankful fi every day di Lawd give me. And me haff some news me wann share with unnu. But it'll haffi come later."

"Everything okay?" Rej asks. "Don't tell me Gil got suspended again?"

"No, no." She laughs. "Leave GC alone. More a celebration. An mi wan all a mi grandkids deh. But lata all right, me need fi sit down."

"You okay?" I ask, jumping to her side, worried she's about to have another episode.

"No need to fuss," she says. "Me juss need some watah and a chair."

"I got her," Mom says.

The neurologist hasn't had anything new to report on Granma's condition. But that hasn't calmed our stress levels, especially since the fire. Not all doctors give the same care to all people, especially Black people. If only we could afford home care. Maybe I'm the reason we can't.

Mom and Granma head to the gym to find seats, leaving me with Stretch and Rej. Stretch senses the awkwardness coming from me and Rej.

He lunges between us, throwing his arms over our shoulders, dragging us toward the locker rooms. "Look at this, my prodigal sons back together." Stretch gives an extra squeeze to my neck. "I know Kenya happy big bro is here. She didn't even want to enter weapons 'cause that's you and her thing."

"Yeah, I just saw her and she said she was only doing kumite," I say.

"I mean, you helped her get good with nunchucks," Stretch says plainly. "Not getting to practice with you over the past month probably affected her confidence."

"You putting more of your time into that prep school than your real school." Rej lands the surprise attack. "You only got one year at Augustin, you been with the dojo your whole life."

"Not sure what you tryin to accuse me of," I say. "My whole life isn't the dojo." I've been waiting to apologize to him, but instead my voice jumps a few decibels and I'm starting a whole new argument. Martial arts was never the endgame for me. "What happens when I leave Augustin and go to college? Especially if I go outta state?" Dad's not here. Tammy's been ducking me. Nakia just friend zoned me. Everything is temporary. It's like Sun Tzu said in "Weaknesses and Strengths," nothing lasts forever. We have to change, adapt to the territory and situation. "Why you making this an issue?"

"That's the whole point," Rej says. There's a bitterness coming from his words that makes me think he's wildin over something else and taking it out on me. "We build for when we aren't there. So the school continues on. Just like we train to fight on the worst day. That's what Sensei taught us."

"I hear you, but you making a lot outta nothing," I say.

"Damn," Rej says. "So I'm nothing now."

"You gettin it twisted," I say.

"Gil." A strong voice from a short girl with a baldie, cool brown skin, and thin eyebrows calls out to me.

"Janeil?" I ask, more trying to register the change in hair.

"Have you seen this?" She doesn't waste time with pleasantries. With Rej and Stretch looking on, she cues up a video on her phone so that we can all see. It's from an account called AugustinNowDnI. There's only one post, but it's been viewed over ten thousand times. There's a caption over the video that says *Perils of Diversity and Inclusion*. She lets it play.

It's me. Punching one of Terry's goons in the groin, then kicking the other into him. That's the video. On loop. Not what happened before. Not what happened after. Just me. Attacking.

"Whoa," Stretch says. Even he's at a loss for words. Seeing it, making my situation real for him.

I feel Rej's hand on my back. "You good?" he asks.

I can't stop watching it.

"Whose account is this?" I finally ask.

"I dunno," Janeil says. "I been following that RNY podcast

through a VPN CJ set up for me so I don't get tracked. They shared the video on their page. Killian's doing all the press with the election coming up. Talking 'bout he's the keynote speaker at the gala next month."

"Hey," Renee says, her short green hair lighting up the hall. "Tournament's starting, y'all need to change and get out there."

"C'mon, Gil," Stretch says.

So the day of the fight, when my vision blurred, there was a fourth person. Not just watching. Filming. And that person knows the truth. And has the video to prove it.

THE MORNING EVENTS are mostly forms and weapons. I watch from the sidelines, my padded gear at my side. My mind—thirty-five miles away on the Upper West Side, wondering who's out for me now.

Stretch does his bo routine for the competition. He spins his staff like a helicopter blade, holding side kicks in the air to show strength and precision for the judges and audience to see. When Stretch does his routine, he's hyperfocused, it's just him and the staff out there. Each ki shout is stronger than the last, eight directional staff strikes followed by shows of balance. We've always debated which is the best weapon. I'd say nunchucks were the best since they're the most dangerous to learn. He'd just say I liked Michelangelo from *Teenage Mutant Ninja Turtles* too much. Stretch earns second place, while Rej comes up empty. Just like me, Rej is best at fighting. Last year I took first while he took third. I cheered him on, but his heart wasn't in it with his dad gone.

After lunch the kumite event starts. The younger divisions go first, while the adult divisions are on Sunday.

"You got this, Kenya," I say to her. She dips her head in a way I haven't seen her do since she was a white belt. Like she's already defeated. I know the feeling. "You good?"

"Yes, Joshu," she says. She heads to the center of the mat to start her match. The referee bows to each competitor. Then Kenya bows to her opponent.

There are seven other fights going on at the same time. I only see the one. And it's not a physical fight, it's one going on inside the head of my lil sis. There's doubt in every block. Dwindling conviction in each punch. Her steps are unsure. She doesn't want to be here.

The fight is over after a few quick exchanges. Kenya doesn't walk off the mat so much as charges off.

"Kenya," I say, hurrying after her. "What's wrong? That didn't seem like you out there."

"Why do you care?" she snaps. "Not like you're around anymore. You don't even come to demo practice when you said you'd show me some new techniques." The words sting like a slap to the face. She doesn't give me another look, marching away.

"Hey Gil," her dad says. "I think you're up."

"Thanks, sir," I say. I hang around to watch Nakia chase after Kenya, and then head back to the tournament stage.

My first opponent is Javier. Last year at the Classic, it was me and him in the finals and I won. He's from a dojo in Queens. He's slow. His kicks are weak. He fights like a character in *Street Fighter* or some anime cartoon. He always keeps his defense down, his stance wide, as if he's taunting his opponent into an attack.

I check my headgear and mouthpiece. Bow to the referee. *I hope Kenya's okay.* She's not the only one on my mind. I'm thinking of Granma in the bleachers. Dad in Jamaica. Mom, I can't hear her over the roaring crowd, but I know she's yelling out my name. For her, everything I do is that big. And I'm wondering why I didn't respond to Dad's text. *Is he thinking about me right now?* Who is the AugustinNowDnI account? It has to be a student.

I bow to Javier.

"Hajime." The referee throws down his hand, starting the match.

Javier's got the same wide stance as last year, but this time he's bouncing more on his toes, energized, ready to fight. Two cross punches are launched at my face, then a back kick. They're telegraphed. I block in time, but the blows still connect. His knee comes up, feigning an attack, then backpedals.

I rush into the opening. A hook kick greets my face, sending my spine into a twist. He earns the point. I wait for the referee to give us the word. But my mind is still on Kenya. The referee begins again. I come back in with two punches. He quickly adjusts, switching his stance. A side kick slices through the center to my chest.

"Ki!" Javier yells.

My punch knocks out Javier's mouthpiece. The clock is running down. I hate point matches. *Intentionality* earns points in this scoring format. And everything's pulling my mental away from where it needs to be. He's hitting faster, connecting more cleanly.

Soon the three minutes are up and the points are in.

I've lost.

Renee meets me when I get off the mat. "What was going on with you out there?"

"A lot on my mind." It's true, but it's an excuse. That was my event to win. And I got knocked out in a preliminary.

"I could tell," she says. "Them wild punches you was hurling. You weren't focused."

"I shouldn't've come."

"Cuz, I know you got a lot going on," she says. "But if the fights you're fighting at school are as unfocused as what I just saw, you won't win any of them."

27

'm back home. Sitting at the dinner table with Granma, Mom, and Renee. The barely touched takeout container of jerk chicken from Peppa's lets my family know that I'm not doing well.

When it comes to Jamaican food, there isn't one restaurant that does all the dishes to perfection. The sit-down restaurants cater to Americanized tastes, so the food is less spicy and more fusion. The spot on Linden may do escovitch fish well, but uses canned ackee with the salt fish. Another restaurant may make some nice curry chicken, but the goat is tough. And don't get the roti there either, go to the Trinidadian spot on Nostrand. Some places cook the rice and peas with the gungo peas and not the red beans. It's as upsetting as it sounds.

As for jerk chicken, there are two places that cook the flavor into the chicken without letting everything hang on the sauce.

My favorite is Peppa's on Flatbush. I can nyam a large order and still want more. Today is not that day.

"Yuh wann me to rewarm yuh food?" Granma asks.

"I'm good," I say. I'm picking at the jerked skin in the round container while staring at my notebook. "I'll be right back, gotta check on something for school." I take my journal to my room and drop on my bed with a thud.

Rej and Kenya hit me harder than Javier. The video Janeil played—that was the knockout blow. All this time, I been thinking about how the dean didn't believe me, when someone had evidence of what started this war. Would things at Augustin be different if the truth was out? Maybe the Black students wouldn't be sharing as many stories. We wouldn't know first-hand how much influence the white parents had over decisions at the school. But Tammy would still be editor. And maybe we'd still be talking.

Stop. She's just busy. College applications. Sifting through all the stories and helping people write their truths. That's who Tammy is. Always giving of her time.

I was texting her on the drive back around 6:00 p.m.

ME

Hope the essays are going well.

TAMMY

Meh. Starting. Stopping. Starting over again.

I decided I'm not going to go on the Ivy Tour. Don't want to be a part of it. So I'm also working with my mom to plan a few school visits.

> Respect. Still not sure what school
> I really want to go to. But maybe
> I can set up a visit to Howard.

> Yo Janeil cut her hair

Yeah, helping her write the story now

> Oh word? Dope.

> Can we catch up?
> Maybe after school?

Sure. Monday I'll be around for a bit.

Sun Tzu always talks about resources and troops getting divided, but my problem isn't an army. It's time. Can't be with my friends in BK. Can't be with the robotics team in the city. Choose one and get punished by the other. Sun Tzu doesn't get high school. Doesn't get that in some fights, the only person you have is yourself.

My family thinks I'm pissed about the tournament loss. And hell yeah, I am, but I'm trying to rework everything that's happening. The model I diagrammed for the next few years seemed pretty straightforward. Outside of the scuff-ups at Augustin, my path was linear. Ignore the noise, do well in robotics, college, internship, then "Sky's the Limit," like B.I.G.'s song on *Life After Death*.

But mapping out my life is like figuring out the best way to design a program. Focus only on one function and the rest suffers. Botched apologizing to Rej. Failed Kenya. And I can't pull back on robotics. Not when I could have the opportunity to work with Dr. Gunther.

My phone buzzes, alerting me to the new post from Black-Augustin. Tammy just made the fifth part to Leylah's write-up live. I read it before. But reading it, published like this, hits hard. Leylah's last line reads, "Phew. Writing this has been a journey. It doesn't define me. But it's a reminder that I am not invisible."

I look over at the painting on my wall. This really is for us.

Since Tammy's busy with college apps, I volunteered to help Chijoke and Saleem. I don't want to lose momentum, give up on these battles I been pushing for. It's also an excuse to hit up Tammy without pressing her to hang out again. It's been weeks since we last kissed. It's like I been emotionally ghosted.

I push the thought aside and open up the AugustinNowDnI account on my phone. If we made BlackAugustin for us, then is AugustinNowDnI a direct response to what we're doing? It's not like we're tagging people in posts or adding hashtags. We decided to build up the repository of posts before taking it to Mr. Neckles's friend. CJ knew. But he's cool. Has anyone else been sharing the page? I can't say I know everyone in the BCC. So it's possible. But they wouldn't make that account. So who did?

I feel a sinking pain in my head. A migraine is trying to creep in from thinking about this. And the squeaking sound from my stomach reminds me that I didn't eat.

I head out of my room.

I can feel Renee, Granma, and Mom examining me as I return. One of them is going to try to solve me like solving for x. Come up with a solution to a problem they don't really understand. They want to help. My phone buzzes. It's not Tammy. There's a WhatsApp alert on my phone. I don't need to read it to know it's

Dad trying to reach out and be a part of the heal-Gil tour. I close out the alert and flip the phone facedown on the table.

I don't need solutions.

I need time.

"Gil, you can't beat up on yourself, you've been taking on a lot more responsibility," Mom says. She thinks she can tell me how I should feel and everything will be better. "But you also need to enjoy being in high school."

"It's really okay," I say. She doesn't get it. It's not only about the tournament. Renee said it a while back. No matter where I go, I'll be in these white spaces. I stop fighting now, that just means that'll be who I'll be for the rest of my life. Always looking back, thinking about why I didn't stand up for myself. Mr. Neckles chose his path. I gotta choose mine. That means go harder. "It's one tournament."

"Uhm, this was our last one of the season, so not just any tournament," Renee adds, taking off the filter. "You could've practiced more. At least come to a sparring session or two." If there is one thing Renee knows how to do, it's land a punch. "Showing up the way you did." Her nose twitches like she smelled a fart. "Losing is one thing. Goin out on the mat, throwing them weak a—" She censors herself, remembering that Granma is here. "Throwing those weak punches . . . ain't you."

"Javier's good," I say in my defense. "He obviously got better since the last time."

"Um, he was o-kay," Renee says. "At best, o-kay," she repeats for effect. "He got knocked out the next round."

"You don't gotta tell me that," I say.

"And we got a demo in two weeks," Renee says. "You've missed multiple practices. Kenya been asking for you. Something about you teaching her a new move. And I don't know what's going on with you and Rej. Why's he so upset?"

"I just have a lot of things happening at school," I say. I don't mean it to come out as a growl, but it does.

"Did somebody else say something?" Mom says, concerned. "They're fighting with you again?" She grabs my face, checking it for any new bruises. But all I have is the lingering scar from the Friday after Labor Day.

"No. No fighting," I say. Not physical at least. "Sorry. Thinking about the robotics competition next week. I came up with the new logic design for our robot. It's called MechaTiger." I change the subject, hoping they get the hint.

"Yuh nah haffi apologize," Granma says. "Mi know yuh still bex about what happen at school, but yuh haffi let it go. Udda wise yuh neva gon move on. Some tings juss not worth it."

She can read me. She has always been able to reach past the barbed wire and find the soft spot I keep hidden.

"I will," I say.

"But dis article ere," she says, taking out the edition of the Augustin *PAW* from her bag, my Op-Ed folded to the front. I left the copy in her room last week. Didn't realize she read it. "'Parents Condemn Blackness as Political.'" She holds it up like a trophy. One that today she remembers. "An look at dis byline. 'Gil Powell.' My granson!" My heart swells. "But hol on, mi have some more good news." Her face is so bright as she makes her way to her room.

Minutes later she's back with a floral dress with a wide collar. It's on a hanger, covered in plastic like it came back from the dry cleaners.

"This di dress dat Pauline made fi me." She stretches it across her body, and shifts from left to right. Her cheeks lift with each turn, brightening the room more than any light.

"Okay, Granma," Renee says, snapping her fingers like she's at a poetry jam.

I grab my phone, opening the camera app. "Over-the-shoulder pose." I turn into paparazzi, doing a photo shoot. Granma gets into it, modeling Pauline's latest design for us.

"Yuh beta put dem photos pon di intanet. What dem know 'bout fashion!" Granma proclaims.

She catches her breath, pausing to lean on a chair for balance. For a moment I wonder if she's okay. Then I see that glimmer, her face gushing brilliantly. She's just making sure everyone's giving her their full attention. "Granma," she says, talking in third person like Caesar, "is gettin an award."

We all pop up at the news.

"Dat's right," she says, the whole kitchen her stage. "Di Caribbean Teachers' Association is gonna be honoring me at di annual fundraiser. And me expect all of unnu to be dere." She points toward me. "Including mi udda grandchildren," she adds, referring to Rej and Stretch.

"That's great," I say, pulling myself out of my funk. Granma's been helping them with their annual fundraiser for as long as I can remember. But with the dementia, she can't manage numbers the way she used to. It's good to hear she's getting recognition. She and my parents would always come home late from those events, dancing the night away. This is the first time Dad won't be here for one.

"You deserve it," Renee adds. "I don't know a better teacher. You helped me figure out who I was when I didn't know if I was ready to put it into words," Renee says, referring to her sexuality.

"They gon give me di lifetime achievement award fi service," she says. "Mi wasn't really inta it at first. Lifetime award sound like yuh dead, and me haff a whole lotta livin fi do."

"Damn right," I say. Mom immediately checks me for the word *damn* and I throw up my hands. Of all the words, that one's gotta get a pass at seventeen.

"An I'm gonna wear dis pretty new dress dat Pauline mek fi me," Granma says gleefully.

"Aye, we celebrating right now," I say.

I go to the living room. Next to the TV is one of Dad's Gemini turntables hooked up to the speaker system. He stopped DJ'ing ages ago. And I'd never tell him this, but my aunt, Mom's sister, was always better. I search out and grab Rita Marley's "One Draw" single. The green cardboard sleeve with Rita's face on it is dog-eared with age, but the record is still in pristine condition, except for a tiny scratch I added when I was a kid. I crack a smile, thinking of all the times Dad would bring up how I scratched his record before I was old enough to even have memories. I cue up the needle, let the soft popping hiss take hold with that old-school sound.

The bass drops.

"Yes, yes, yes," Granma says gleefully.

She and I begin to dance the two-step every Jamaican knows when culture tunes come on. Lifting our knees, arms moving to the rhythm.

Mom moves her hips, joining us. Her eyes are closed. "I still remember the first time your dad danced with me. It was to this song."

When Rita cuts through the tune, singing about getting high, we each lift one hand in the air, heads down, swaying, enjoying culture. By the time the main verse drops, Renee is up too, joining in on the dance party. I'm not thinking about school or competitions. There's only the now, being here, being present, enjoying my family as it is. I love them so much. And I want them to be proud of me.

I grab Granma's hand and spin her. Our two-step is vicious. Our family forms a circle as we add in some of the newer dances. Granma knows them all.

This cut of "One Draw" is the extended version. The only one we ever play. When the bridge comes on and the *teacher* begins roll call, we each take on one of the characters. Granma is teacher welcoming the class. I go first as Smokie, putting all the gravel I can into my voice, channeling Rej. Renee is next as Herbie, and Mom is Mila. When Mom comes in to do Mila's verse, I remember how lovely her voice is and how hearing her sing uplifted me when I was younger.

This is joy, and I let it cover me.

28

I bite into a burger that gets more unsatisfying as I chew. It's Monday. I'm in the cafeteria with Leylah, Chijoke, and a few underclassmen from the BCC. I'm exhausted. I spent all of yesterday working in the Fabrication Center with the RoboAugs. Didn't even take a break 'cause I didn't want Mr. Abato to question my *work ethic*. Lydia invited me and CJ out to eat with her brother, but by 6:30 p.m. I had a migraine and was ready to pass out. So I'm forcing myself to eat today. Finally getting up with Tammy after school, so I don't want to look like I'm tired *and* starving.

"So how long've you been doing martial arts?" one of the freshmen asks.

"Ten years, I guess," I respond. It's been an odd day. Practically everyone in school must've seen that video. Some people have started staring at me with a kind of cult admiration. It's weird.

And this is at least the fourth time someone's asked me about martial arts. On the other hand, Jill and her friends walked by me this morning and glared at me with pure disgust. That might've just been them being them.

"I've always wanted to do it," another student says.

I'm half paying attention. Met with the college counselor last period. I was psyched that he believed I had a shot at MIT and Columbia. But every time I brought up Howard, he kind of glossed over it and started talking about another school. Even when I brought up their robotics program and my specific interest in attending an HBCU, he'd say something like "I understand why someone like you would want to go, but you should keep your options open." Out of curiosity I asked him about Morehouse, and he had to get on Google just to read up on the school. It's like the HBCUs are as invisible to him as the Black students are to Augustin. But that's going to change.

My phone buzzes. It's a text from Tammy.

TAMMY

Sorry Gil. I should've texted you yesterday, but my mom and I were able to work out a last minute day trip to visit Princeton University. So I have to run home after school. Thursday?

ME

All good. Thursday works.

I put my phone on silent and dive back into the conversation, trying not to think about Tammy's message.

"You thought about your story, Chijoke?" I ask him. I've been thinking about my own story. I've been wanting to write about my probation. But I just keep scrapping every draft.

He lets out a long sigh. "I am still deciding what situation to write about," he says. He fixes his tie. I've noticed he does that every time he's about to talk for a while. "I was initially thinking about the time I was working on a group project in AP Bio, and a student in my group tried to make a joke about me by 'speaking' in what he considered a Nigerian accent." His eyes widen as he relives the moment. "And everyone in the group laughed and I smiled. I didn't want to but I did. And I hated it. I thought about it every day. I still think about it." His voice fades, unsure of what to say next. He clenches his palms together as if in prayer. Leylah rests her hands on top, offering him support. "I have a lot of white friends here, or I think I do. But I never feel like I can fully open up to them because I always think about that time. Even now, maybe I'm overthinking it and I'm being too sensitive."

"Don't ever think that," Leylah says. "Your feelings are always valid."

"So I thought I'd write about the time Mr. Jacobs singled me and another Black student out for talking in class, when other people were clearly talking," he continues.

"That's so jacked up," Leylah groans. "Literally, everyone talks in Mr. Jacobs's class. That's the only reason people want to have him for French."

"I have so much schoolwork right now," he says. I can already hear him giving up. "Maybe the right story will come to me in a few weeks."

"We don't want to lose this momentum," I say to him. "You read Leylah's post, right?" He nods his head. "She didn't just write about an isolated incident. She put herself down on that page. All her vulnerabilities." I don't push this when I talk to freshmen or sophomores about writing. But getting a junior like Chijoke to not write anonymously would be huge. He's as respected and known in his year as Tammy is in ours.

"It was harder than I thought it would be," Leylah says. "Tammy really got me through it."

"I respect what you did," Chijoke says. "Putting your face with the story. You have so much courage." Everyone nods in agreement, looking at Leylah with admiration for her bravery. "I don't think that's me."

"It is if you want it to be," I say. "I didn't come here seeking a fight. Leylah was just living her life, dressing how she wanted to." The cafeteria is noisy from the lunch crowd. I've been trying to keep my voice down so the neighboring tables can't hear us, but I feel myself getting louder. "They took the paper away from us because they were afraid of exactly what we're doing. Telling our truths. They want us to hide." I think about Mr. Neckles and the reason he changed his name. "Do that now, and you'll just go on livin your life like that." Maybe I'm pushing too much.

"Whatever you decide, we got you," Leylah says to Chijoke.

I feel a breath on my shoulder and notice everyone's eyes look at me. No, they're looking behind me. When I turn, I see the buzz cut before I see his face. It's Brandon, Terry's boy who I punched in the groin. He's much shorter than me, but easily three times my width, and that's all football strength.

"Why'd you mention me in this?" he asks, but not to me. He's holding up his phone, looking at Leylah. He's on the Black-Augustin account.

So it's out.

I stand up, putting my body between him and Leylah.

"Look, I'm not trying to fight you again," he says. "That day was all Terry. He's my boy, so I was there for him. I only want to speak to her." He points at Leylah.

"What do you got to say?" Leylah asks from her seat.

"Suppose my parents saw this or the school?" he asks. "You ever think about that?"

"So you're not here to apologize," Leylah says. She gives the briefest laugh that is full of disgust. "You're worried about how you feel? How this makes you look?"

"It was a party," he says. "Everybody was drunk that night. How are you going around saying I was sexually harassing you and grabbing you inappropriately?"

"I wasn't drunk and you did," she says. Her voice spikes and I see her gripping her leg to maintain control. "Saying 'c'mon, you know you like to twerk,' then grabbing me. You wouldn't have done what you did or said what you said to one of the white girls. But if you're worried about the school, I didn't mention your name. And if you're feeling guilty, then you should."

"You described me though," he says defensively. "Somebody read this and told me 'cause they knew it was about me."

"Who?" I ask. People at the neighboring tables are turning, starting to pay attention. I think Brandon notices too.

"Don't try that," he says in a low voice. He turns up his lip at me with a snarl. "I'm not telling you who." He steps closer so that his shoulder is touching me and he can almost cast a shadow on Leylah. "Look, just take this down, okay. Stop trying to make this into some kind of race thing. It was a party. That's it."

He gives us both one last look and turns away.

Leylah's silent. Her arms are crossed almost like she's shivering. I rest my hand on her shoulder.

After a moment I ask, "You good?"

"I'll be fine," she says, a little unsure of herself. "He's not going to intimidate me."

"I'm here, we all are if you need us," I say. She mouths a *thank you*.

"I'll do it," Chijoke says. We turn to face him. "I'm going to sign my name to my piece. But I may need your help putting it together."

29

The next day has been a blur of classes and robotics. Now I'm at Rej's place because Stretch pitched an impromptu meetup. I know Stretch is doing his peacemaker thing, trying to get the group back in sync. Mom has the day off and is with Granma, so my evening is clear and homework is light.

It's after 7:00 p.m. Rej and Stretch were already watching a movie on Crunchyroll by the time I arrived. Put anime on in a room full of Black teen martial artists and we're quiet as ever, locked into the action, which is good and bad because we don't have to talk—or bring up feelings.

We're in a two-bedroom apartment on Clarendon. Rej used to have the second bedroom, but he gave it up to his sisters. They all share the same mom, but the sisters' dad passed away two years ago. Now the living room is the family room, his bedroom, and his studio, where he built a floating booth with eggshell cushion to record artists.

The decorations are minimal. There are family photos on the wall. But the desk with his studio monitors are the centerpiece, more so than the TV. He's also got some foam on the walls to help with the acoustics when he's mixing. Rej helps look after the sisters so much, while his mom is working, that she doesn't mind that the family room is now his studio.

I get a text.

RENEE

Cuz, what happened to you Sunday? We moved demo practice so you could spend Saturdays with granma.

how you not gonna show? This was the last one before our performance.

ME

Had to work at school. Robotics joint is this Saturday

She responds with the side-eye emoji.

RENEE

Aight cuz. Just don't fold on the demo team.

"Yo!" Rej backslaps me three times on my arm without breaking eye contact with the TV. My phone bobbles out of my hand, but I catch it before it hits the ground.

I don't know what the movie title is, but it's like *Demon Slayer* or *Attack on Titan*. Some character who has been pushed to the side digs deep, uses some unheard-of special technique, and saves the day. Rej is amped because it's about to happen. The lead character is on the brink of death and just said *enough is enough*. Now light is shining out of her eyes and her hands are on fire, like a ball of energy is about to burst out.

"Reggggie, we're hungry," Rej's youngest sister, Anne, says. She's lighter than Rej, coral skinned. Her pleading four-year-old eyes expand like an anime chibi character. It's heartbreaking.

"It's almost eight o'clock," Francesca says, slamming her head into the couch's armrest to show the desperation. She's older than Anne by almost three years and better at playing up their hunger plight. My stomach growls in solidarity.

"The movie's gonna be over in like . . . twenty minutes," Rej whimpers.

"Awwww," they groan in harmony, looking up to the ceiling for divine intervention.

"Fran, al pran manjé pou li," Rej says, sucking his teeth, not wanting to be bothered. He pauses the movie.

"It's Francesca!" She holds up her fingers. "I'm six and a half. Stop calling me Fran."

"That's right. You're grown," Rej says, doing his best impersonation of someone trying to be firm. "So get your sister some yogurt or something." She crosses her arms, not budging, letting him know who runs this house.

My phone buzzes again.

CHIJOKE

I wanted to start my piece "What is blackness." Thoughts?

Chijoke is the definition of studious. Trick is to get him to reach into his emotion to make his post hit.

ME

Try to make it more personal, less analytical. Think about the freshmen and sophomores reading it. They need to get to know you.

Do you have a suggestion?

Maybe "Don't define my blackness." It'll be like you're talking directly to someone, having that conversation. Then go from there. Walk us through who you are, what people said, how that made you feel.

Thank you

"Whachu got in the fridge?" I ask Rej.

"You know how to open it." Rej waves me off.

I get up. This movie's not continuing. And I don't even think I drank water today. I kept trying to show Mr. Abato how much I knew about the code without saying directly that it's mine. Would he even care? He's always seemed cool, but at Augustin I can never tell. It's like Lydia grabbing Janeil's hair. She's dope to work with but then got too comfortable and crossed that line.

"Thanks, Uncle Gil," Francesca says, grabbing my hand as we

go to the kitchen while sticking her tongue out at her brother. She's not one for smiles. Her mouth is always a straight line. It's the subtle way her eyebrows and smooth bronze-tinted cheeks move that tells you how she's feeling. Right now, just her presence is lifting my mood. "Can you be our big brother?" she asks. Francesca may only be six, but she's easily going on sixteen.

"Mezanmi!" Rej rolls his eyes. "Let me go help y'all beforc Fran has a fit."

"Francesca," she enunciates.

"Yeah, yeah," he says. He sticks his head in the fridge, scouring for food. "We got some some fish, espagéti . . ."

The sisters exchange glances and say, "McDonald's," in unison. A synchronized attack.

"Nobody here's got McDonald's money," Rej says. "We got leftovers. I can put this fish on bread, reheat these plaintains—they'll be like french fries—and if you get your crayons—you got a happy meal. Boom, better than McDonald's."

"We'll have cereal," Francesca utters, defeated.

"For dinner?" Rej shrugs his shoulders. "Y'all don't know what you're missing," Rej says. "That McDonald's gonna give you the bubble guts in a few years."

"Shoot, let me get some of that banan ak poule," Stretch says. He's already grabbing saucepans from the cabinet to heat up the chicken with some diri kolé as if this were his home.

"Put on some for me too," I whisper to Stretch.

Rej sucks his teeth in an endless hiss. "Don't think I didn't hear that," he says.

My phone vibrates. It's CJ.

CJ

Hey, didn't want to bring it up while we were working earlier, but I never asked you about that video. How you feeling?

ME

I'm good. Crazy thing is I felt there was someone watching the whole time. Between the blood and glass, I couldn't keep up.

I know you're tied in more than me. So if you hear anything . . . about who it may be . . . let me know. I want that full video.

I got you Gil.

But for real, that was an amazing kick. Didn't know you did martial arts. And Brandon, the guy you punched in the balls, hopefully he won't be having any kids after that hit. Which is probably a good thing 😭

Even to CJ it's just a fight. He doesn't have the context. Didn't see the way Terry and his friends looked at me. Didn't hear him say *that word*.

A single light bulb faintly illuminates the table where Rej's sisters eat their cereal, reading the box as if it contains precious secrets. Rej kisses each of them on the head and they hug him. Then he claims the couch for himself, the plastic covering making a sound like a bag exhaling air as he plops down, legs resting over the sofa's armrest. Stretch hands me a plate of food, then takes a seat on the living room floor. I go to the rolling chair at the desk. CJ texts again.

Sorry dude. I know I shouldn't make fun.
People are already posting reaction vids
on TikTok.

Still sucks about the suspension and
probation. I know it's got to hurt that you
can't be the driver when you put all that work
into redesigning the code. The team would
have a robot spinning out of control again
like last year if it wasn't for you. Anyway. I'm
going to talk to Lydia when her brother's not
around. See what we can do.

ME

It's all good. don't worry about it.
I don't want to beg for anything

this ain't that . . .

"Everything cool, son?" Stretch asks.

"He probably got a text from that girl he checkin," Rej says. "The one he bailed on me for."

"You seriously can't think that's what happened," I say to Rej. I stand up. I may be taller than him, but the way he's looking at me, he's the one casting a shadow.

"Ah, c'mon, dudes," Stretch groans. "Can we just put this behind us already. Y'all gotta learn to ease up and relax."

"You know if I could, I would've went," I say to Rej. "I want my dad back here as much as you want yours back." Rej barely shifts, deciding if he wants to respond. Stretch begins twisting the blond tips on his head. Then, he takes out his phone to swipe through social, avoiding the conversation altogether.

"You know, I used to always think of our situations as similar," Rej says. His tone is so calm it sends a chill through the room. "That we shared something 'cause of it. Both our dads undocumented." He gets out of his chair so fast his dreads thrash around his face. The expression he's giving me—it's not anger. It's disappointment. "The way you was looking out for me last year after they grabbed my dad up." He pauses. Has me sit in the discomfort of knowing where he's going with this. "But I'm not a citizen here yet. You are. And your dad can come back."

"I shoulda been with you, I know that," I say. "But that night, at the parent-teacher meeting, I learned that it wasn't just the administration who put me on probation, but the parents who pushed for it too. You gotta understand why I had to be there. Whenever you need me next, Ima be there."

"I played this conversation over in my head, how it would go," Rej says. "At first I was angry at you." He sighs like he's already given up on me. "Fam, you didn't text. Didn't call. Just said 'my fault.' Like you was apologizing for bumping a stranger on the street."

"You know that's not what I meant by it," I say. It's hard to meet Rej's face. Because I see the empty expression. It's like looking into my failures.

"I realized a while ago my dad's not coming back," Rej says. He tilts his face to make sure that I can see him and not focus on anything else. "No time soon at least. Me finding a pro bono immigration lawyer. That was never about me. It was about your situation. My way of saying thanks to you and your dad for being there for me during all that." His eyes widen, he leans in closer.

He drags out the next words as slow as possible. So that I never forget. "And you dusted it to the side like it was nothing."

Awkward silence settles like a fog. I have no response that can solve this. I'm wondering if Sun Tzu has any tactics that help mend friendships. But if Sun Tzu had friends and family, he probably looked at them as soldiers, allies to be used in war.

Moments pass before Francesca breaks the tension. "Are y'all fighting?" she asks. Her lack of filter rivals Granma's.

"No," Rej grunts from the couch. "Don't talk while you're eating or you'll get indigestion."

"What's indji—indig—what's that?" Francesca asks.

"In-di-ges-tion," Rej clarifies. "It's a tummyache."

"Okay," she calls back. "But you should hug if you're upset. Hugs make me happy."

Rej lays his head on a pillow, being overdramatic. "So what's good with the robotics competition?" he finally asks. "That's Saturday, right? You gonna get ya butt handed to you like at the Classic?"

"Wait, is that possible?" Stretch tags in. Pleased with the change in mood. "The way Javier took you out though, oooo . . ." He grabs his chest, wincing in pain like he's been kicked. "Still feelin the bruises."

"Whatever, yo." I suck my teeth, making sure they hear it. "Calm all that down," I say. "There other things going on at school. I mean, you seen the fight video. I gotta figure out who shot it." I catch them up on the probation, me doing all the code, then being skipped over for driver. Then go into BlackAugustin.

"You really can't catch a break, can you," Rej says.

"I still want to get you to visit Augustin," I say. "Actually get you in the lab. May not be anytime soon though." I wonder if our situation is resolved. If we're cool again. Like old times. Neither of us really apologized, but at least we said everything we needed to say.

"Say less," Rej says. "Worry about yourself." The way he says that last line. It's like he's cast me off.

It makes me think about Tammy. What will she say on Thursday when we meet? I want to text her. See how her visit to Princeton was. But I don't.

30

It's Thursday after school. Tammy cancelled our meetup on Monday over text. I replied *no problem*. But it kind of is. I spent the last few days thinking every single person at school is an enemy. One of them has a video that can show everybody the truth about my first week here. And that person sent the video in to the RNY podcast. Who was it? Tammy knows what it means to observe. She's been reporting on the school since freshman year.

Tammy said she had to help Janeil write her article, then put the final touches on her Early Action application. What was I supposed to say? *Forget your friend, forget your future, what about me?* Pretty sure that wouldn'ta went down well.

But we're meeting up today, 3:15. So I'm killing time in the STEM Lab. It's just me and CJ in here. I'm adjusting Chijoke's write-up into a six-part post. He really opened up. Maybe he took the cue from Leylah. He wrote about what it means to be from a family that emigrated from Nigeria. The perceptions from both Black and white students. Then went into situations with the white students at Augustin.

Chijoke even mentioned a recent incident at another student's house in Long Island. The other student went to the bathroom and left Chijoke alone in the family room with his parents. They were watching election coverage on the TV. The parents then started lecturing him on how racism doesn't exist and that Chijoke's family being immigrants and him attending Augustin was proof of that. He began to argue their perspective, but they spoke over him like they were shouting him down. His voice was silenced. He felt trapped.

Chijoke gave us pictures of him with his family to use in the post. One portrait shows his mom and dad, two brothers, and three sisters. There are so many shades of Black in his family. His story will go live next week. Tammy said there might be another big essay that should be published before his.

Reading these stories reignites my own trauma. There's so much unease inside me that my whole body shivers, like it's being besieged. I'm second-guessing every conversation. Wondering if the smirks, the side-eyes in the hallway are about me. The only time I feel remotely safe is when I'm around at least two people of color. I latch on to them, walk between them like they're a force field against the doublespeak being hurled my way.

If I could talk to Tammy about it . . . It's just that—

I miss the way her lip curls to one side like she knows a secret that no one else does. The way her touch fills me with confidence. When she talks to me, her eyes radiate from those blue frames, making me feel like I matter.

I've seen her in school every day. But other students are always around and the only thing we talk about is BlackAugustin. Which is what I wanted. *Right?* Students are speaking up. This post from Chijoke—it's a shot fired. And Ima keep doing what I'm doing. Another result of that video going viral, more Black students are coming to me, especially underclassmen, asking me about my experience. So I get them thinking about what stories they want to share.

"Yo, I'll be back around four," I say to CJ. That forty-five minutes isn't going to change Mr. Abato's opinion about me controlling MechaTiger this Saturday.

"Cool," he says. "I'll be in Fabrication."

Tammy's waiting at the front desk. A loose checkered beige cardigan is draped over her shoulders. During the day, she's on straight autopilot. Right now, it's the most relaxed I've seen her since she lost the editor position. "I like that hoodie," she says, referring to my pullover with the word *Melanin* on it.

"Thanks," I say. Finally, it's just me and her. "That sweater looks right on you," I say as we walk through the double doors. She gives me a pleased head nod. Like the one a sister or brother gives. Not a partner. I bite my lip, figuring out what I need to say. Tell her how much it means to me to have someone like her to talk to. Be around. No. I should get right to it. I want her to be my girlfriend. Nah. I can't do that. I don't know where her head is at. I'd look so stupid after three weeks of not even talking like that.

The fall breeze hits my face. The rain has died down to barely a drizzle, the remnants of a tropical storm that had passed through Jamaica. I wonder what Dad is doing right now. Sitting out on the veranda, enjoying the sun, Brooklyn a distant memory? Nah, that's not him. He's always grinding. It just feels like his work is more important. But I guess that's what Rej was saying about me too.

That's when I spot Janeil, waiting for us. And all of a sudden we're a crowd. We say whatup, but I can't help but be disappointed. *Did Tammy invite Janeil to avoid talking to me one-on-one?*

We head to a pizza spot halfway between Augustin and Central Park. Everything looks like somebody's artistic rendering of what pizza should be. Either they splatter some white cheese on top or they got a big-old leaf on it and say, "Five dollars, pay up." On Nostrand, I can still get a couple slices and a soda and still have change.

We each grab a slice. There are no seats, so we check the coffee spot. Also packed. "The sun's out," I say. "Why don't we just post up in the park."

"It's such a relief," Janeil says to Tammy. "To finally get that out. I feel like I've taken back my power. And that's 'cause of you two."

"I'm glad I was able to help," Tammy says. "So many new stories coming in. Getting harder to juggle my time." I'm trying to follow the conversation, but all I can think is that I'm not going to have the chance to talk to Tammy about us.

"You was there for me that night," Janeil says, making sure Tammy hears the *you*. "Both of you, yeah, but Tam, you got me through it. I was so self-conscious about my hair. Anyway, I'm past it now."

As long as I've known Janeil, she's always seemed to be about her hairstyle, constantly checking it on her phone. I thought it looked cool. But she's not doing that anymore. She walks with her chin up, a confidence about her that I've never seen before.

"I know you been handling the posting," Janeil says to me. "But I went ahead and published the first part of my piece myself. Felt I needed to be the one."

"I was just on the account," I say, confused.

"Hit the button when you and Tam were at the switchboard," Janeil says. "Happy it's out. Not with me as everyone wants me to be. But me as I want to be."

I reach for my phone and pull up the BlackAugustin account. On it is a new post with a side profile self-portrait Janeil must've drew of herself, spotlighting her new baldie.

What I read is not a story about Janeil's interaction with Lydia. It's a story about a Black girl struggling with what the world deems is acceptable for Black hair. Trapped under the white gaze, fetishized, while dealing with the sudden loss of her hair. It started off with a few strands of hair, then patches. A student saying something behind her in Math class one day. Then touching her head. Her dad took her to the doctor, where she was diagnosed with alopecia areata, a genetic condition that usually happens later in life. That's when she started wearing wigs. Then code switching. Anything to distract people from commenting on the way she looked, talked.

The things these comments do to us as Black people. Strip us down to nothing. Force us to hide who we are. I never had to think about any of this at Union. Being ourselves was a given. But in these white spaces . . .

Trees line the park entrance in a brilliant array of red, brown, and gold leaves. Drops of rain shimmer on each one. Tammy grabs our arms before we enter, pulling us into a scheme only she knows. "Let's jump it," she says.

She must be joking.

The stone wall that separates the sidewalk from the park grounds is about four feet high, but looks even taller in my khakis. I ain't trying to bust up another pair of school pants like I did that first week.

"The entrance is literally right over there," I say, pointing. "And there's mud."

"Come on, Brooklyn," she says in a way that puts my Brooklynness under question. "It's been nothing but work for me these past few weeks. I'm finally done with my Yale application." I haven't seen her like this, filled with so much energy, since last month. I'm almost tempted to do it.

"Oh, you should totally jump it," Janeil says seriously. "Imagine the dean's face on the other side of it. And when you land. Splat. Right on Bradley's head."

"I think he's worried about getting his khakis dirty," Tammy says.

"Mm-hmm," Janeil cosigns. "Your boy fancy."

"Whatever, yo," I say. "Y'all acting like y'all gonna jump?" Tammy raises her eyebrow at me as if I just dared her. She walks up to the wall, presses herself up with arm muscles she's been hiding under her blazer. Next her right foot goes up and she's over.

Harlem got some hops. I'm impressed.

"Come on, Brooklyn," she says.

I toss my paper plate and the last bit of crust in a green trash can and jump over. I land crouched, mud splashing onto my shoes and just above the ankle on my khakis. Glad I didn't switch to my sneakers 'cause I'd be heated.

"Y'all fools," Janeil says, walking around and using the entrance, not a blemish of mud on her.

"Yo, you didn't jump," I say.

"Um, no," Janeil says. "Y'all wildin. I ain't doing extra laundry 'cause y'all tryna be cool." She busts out laughing. It's contagious.

"You want to know what's crazy?" Tammy asks, her voice electrified with joy. "First the newspaper, now BlackAugustin. It feels like the start of something different. People are talking. Showing up." We pull up on a bench that seems to be out of the pigeon-dropping zone, she takes out a paper towel from her bag to wipe the rain, and we sit down.

"We are up to two hundred followers," I say. A fraction of that number is current students. But we been getting Black alumni following, liking posts. Meanwhile, the fan base on the Augustin-NowDnI account is growing exponentially. I went down the wormhole. Watched some of the reaction videos. There's a lot of negative. But there have been a few people asking what led to this. I want Mr. Neckles's friend Rashida to take a look at these stories, maybe cover it. But I dunno how many stories is enough for someone at her level to pay attention. "Have y'all thought about who might have filmed that video?"

"Does it matter?" Tammy asks. "What would you do if you knew?"

"I don't know," I reply. "But at least I'd know who I couldn't trust."

She sighs. "One thing I learned with reporting. Some questions you don't get answers to. And you have to be okay with that."

"Maybe I can't be."

"At all?" Tammy asks. It's like my response let her down. "That's an impossible space to put yourself in." She sighs. "From the moment I came here, I always faced the same question. Do I respond or don't I?" I see the tension in her neck, the consequence of a seemingly endless struggle. "And once I make that decision, I have to be okay with it and move on." Is it really that easy for her? Why can't it be the same for me? "But everyone's situation is different."

"Word," Janeil says. "Like a whole notha class. Saleem's always been at predominately white schools. This was all new for me. I been on guard since I got here."

"I read what you wrote," I say to Janeil. "I had no idea you were going through all that. When Lydia—"

"See, that's the thing," Janeil says, her voice rising. "White people want my story to be about them. It's not. 'Oh, she did this to me and I reacted.' And truth is, that's what I almost wrote. That Lydia grabbed my hair, tried to gaslight me. I was so hot." Janeil pulls back. Gives her nerves a chance to ease up. "But Tammy helped me take control. Write me."

I feel like trash. I been wondering if Tammy was dodging me all this time, when she was doing the work. Helping her friend. Being there for Janeil. The way Rej has been looking out for me. The way I used to look out for him.

"My life started before I got here, and everything being everything, it'll continue after I leave," Janeil continues. "See right here. These moments with y'all, my fam, these are the times that really make me. This is what I'm about."

"True, true," I say. She's right. I been giving so much energy to thinking about what they've been doing to me. This war. I haven't been paying attention to the things that matter.

"That speech I'm giving at the gala next month," Tammy says, frowning. "I'm basically introducing Killian as the keynote speaker." She hears me groan. "I know. Maybe I can add something. Talk about what inclusion really means. I haven't decided yet. Finishing off these college apps has been my priority."

"Whoa, y'all seen this." Janeil shows her phone to us. Her post has over five hundred likes. "Some account named TheR1 just shared it."

That's Rej's account. All the way in Brooklyn. He always has my back. Looking out.

I'm WALKING TAMMY to the train before I head to Augustin to prep MechaTiger for transportation to Freedom Academy. We left Janeil a few minutes ago at 72nd Street. She takes the C train downtown to 50th to transfer to the E line to Queens. I remember that first BCC meeting, hearing her speak. Thought she was from the Bronx. She is, but lives in Queens now with her dad.

"Are we good?" I ask after an otherwise silent walk west to Broadway.

"What do you mean?" Tammy says. She doesn't turn to look at me, doesn't stop, just keeps moving forward.

"We haven't really talked, talked, you know," I say. My hands are fumbling around, as if they can help my brain figure out what to ask or how to phrase it so I don't sound like an idiot. "Things between us were a little different. Before . . . before October." I don't bring up what the dean did because it might make real that it was my actions, my words, that led to it. "Us being there for each other that night in the Legacy Wing. Then at my place." Kissing. I want to say kissing. But I don't. "I don't know, I get the feeling like you're pushing me away."

She finally stops walking, and looks at me. Like really looks. And I'm reminded of all those times we talked, a flood of emotion surging through my veins. "I don't want to push you away, Gil," she says. It's almost forced, like she's reluctant to even give me that one line. "I feel like we rushed into things, and with college, BlackAugustin, I need time to figure some things out."

"So it's not me," I say.

She shakes her head with a subtle eye roll. "I need space for me." Her lips purse and her eyes drop. The rest of her body slumps as if fatigued. "Newspaper was my everything. Don't get me wrong. I love what we're doing with BlackAugustin. I only wish it could've been done through the *PAW*. That was my dream. To have it taken away. That's years of work. Like what was it for?"

"For this," I say. Pulling up the BlackAugustin account. I thumb through the articles. "All of these people, anonymous or not, are empowered because of you." She nods her head wearily. "If not for you and the paper, none a this woulda happened."

"I just wonder if there was another way," she says. "And I wonder what you really want."

You. That's what I want to say. But I don't. "I want people to hear us. The same thing you said that first BCC meeting."

She examines me, maybe only half accepting my answer. "I like you a lot," she says.

"I like you too," I say.

"But I'm not sure I know you enough to commit."

"I mean, what do you need to know?"

She rests her palm on my cheek and I nearly melt inside the touch. "All answers aren't that simple," she says, her lip curling. "Can I get some time?"

"Of course," I say. "And I get that."

"I will be at your robotics competition Saturday," she says. Like she was supposed to be at the martial arts tournament last week. "This isn't me saying no. Just give me a couple weeks."

It's like I have no one to talk to anymore. Dad. Tammy. Everyone needs space to do their own thing. Get their own mind right. I guess I should too.

PART IV
Energy

Order or disorder depends on organization;
courage or cowardice on circumstances;
strength or weakness on dispositions.

SUN TZU: *THE ART OF WAR*

31

Our bus pulls into Freedom Academy's parking lot at quarter to nine on Saturday morning. It's not the usual cheese bus we'd get at Union, but a charter bus with a bathroom, lots of space, and reclining seats with no duct tape.

I got my earbuds in, tuning out the chatter of the team, listening to the Carnival mix Rej made over the summer, back when the only things I had to worry about were Granma and Dad. I should be enjoying the music. I try to think about J'ouvert, the last time I partied with Rej and Stretch. My head's nodding, I'm quoting the lyrics, humming to the beat. But I'm not hyped. I feel the muscles in my forehead twisting into the tightest knot.

This is my first robotics competition with the team. And only three people know that I even contributed. Mr. Abato sees me as some brand-new slacker who wants all the payoff but doesn't want to do any of the work. Lydia's been checking me the whole time, staring over her shoulder, trying to make eye contact. Meanwhile, the other students flock around Heath like he's some kind of coding guru.

If I tell the truth, I get a third strike. Dean Bradley suggested, more like threatened, that I'd be removed from the team permanently if that happened. Then what'd happen with my second semester bill? Would they take away my scholarship too? Make us pay the balance? Medicare and Medicaid ain't enough to cover all Granma's health expenses.

"All right, everyone," Mr. Abato says. "Let's unload all the equipment. Find our station inside and get set up."

I don't say much as we clear out the bus, lifting MechaTiger's base off first, then grabbing the rails, the storage bins. Heath grabs the driver station, a Pelican Case with the laptop and game controller. The part that I should be holding. Maybe I'm being entitled, but this ain't right.

In "Marches," Sun Tzu says to fight downhill, to never ascend into attack. But isn't that all I've been doing? There is no way to fight when Augustin has all the power. All the control.

I turn off the music on my phone and see messages from Janeil and Dad. I look at Janeil's note first.

JANEIL

hey, not gonna make it today

Saleem is all kinds a pissed, nothin to do with u. but Ima spend the day with him. good luck!

> thanks. hope everything is aight wit Saleem.

I switch over to Dad's text.

> You alright Gil? Haven't heard from you.
> Good luck today. Proud of you.

> thanks

I give the most basic reply, as if I'm texting with someone I barely know.

"Okay, RoboAugs," Mr. Abato says, pointing at the logo on the new team T-shirts he made for us. "While I register us, start putting MechaTiger together." He takes a deep breath filled with anxiety. "And I know I told you this is just a friendly pre-season event, but the world is always watching." It's true. But the words mean something different if you're Black. We're always under a microscope. What we do. What we say. Our clothes. Our hair. All open game for criticism. "And there's a slight, very slight chance that Dr. Gunther will also be here. So if Augustin is going to land any of the internship spots she has open, today's the day to shine." He walks up to me, rests his hand on my shoulder like a father talking to a son. But he's not my dad. "You may not be the driver, but you're still a member of the team. So cheer them on. You don't have to be in the limelight to be a leader. When the time's right, I know you're going to do great things."

Was that supposed to be a motivational talk or a way to remind me of my place in the background?

Sun Tzu's closing message in "Attack by Fire" is that a general cannot attack out of rage or resentment. So what do I do with these flames bubbling inside me?

"Understood," I say to Mr. Abato.

There it goes. Like Tammy said. *Do I respond or don't I.* I just chose the latter. And I hate myself.

"Good, then get your T-shirt on," he adds, referring to the black-and-green team shirt tucked away in my bag that everyone else wore to school.

The gym inside Freedom Academy High School has been transformed into a mini–ninja-warrior playing field for our robots. There are padded walls with three levels of holes that we'll need to fire a ball through, which they call a power cell. The matted floor is a little different from what we've practiced on. We've just tested the wheels over the smooth hallway floors, which have less friction. There are also different obstacles and ramps to go over, lots of room for the robot to topple over. Hopefully, the adjustments we made hold up. CJ and Lydia did their thing with the remodeled launcher.

The team gets to work assembling the moving parts onto the car. There are only five other teams here. We'll be playing three rounds in parallel, then do some alliance matches.

By the time we're done, the gym has begun to seriously fill up. I've seen videos online, remember the one Dad and I went to, but seeing the crowd come out for a robotics competition that I'm actually in has my adrenaline in overdrive. I start looking at the other teams. Each team has like twenty to thirty members while we barely got a third of that.

"Wow, they came with whole armies," CJ says, nudging me. "How do you think we're going to do?" Just off the numbers we're at a disadvantage. More developers, more builders, testers, more people to spread the workload and idea creation.

"Hopefully everything we did holds up," I say. It comes out more dismissive than I meant. I got no reason to be curt to CJ. It's just the situation. *Focus, Gil. Keep it about the work.* "We have an edge, everyone considers us a meme after last season. So we take advantage of their unpreparedness. The terrain may be fixed, but there are always variables that can change." It's something Sun Tzu said. There's never one approach. "If Heath plays a steady game, doesn't rush any of the shots. Then we got a chance."

"You really should be the driver," CJ says, flicking back his hair. He shakes his head when he sees Heath grab the control box and head to the staging area, followed by Lydia. "It isn't right."

"Whatever," I say, almost snapping. I take a breath, trying to push my feelings aside. "The other teams are already set up and practicing." I need to be a leader for my team. "We put in too much time. Gotta make sure MechaTiger is running right. Let's go." He nods and gets to work.

"GC!"

I look up and see Granma, Mom, Renee, and her girlfriend Nicole in the bleachers, along with Mr. Neckles. I make my way through the crowd and up the stairs to welcome them. Granma wraps me up in the biggest hug, easing some of the tension twisting inside me.

"Oh, this like *American Ninja Warrior* for real," Renee says.

"Ha, that's exactly what I thought," I say.

Last night Renee told me she had to cut down my part in the dojo's demo tomorrow. I missed four practices. So I couldn't really argue. She also let me know Kenya was still upset because I promised lil sis she'd get to do a new piece. One that included a move I never got around to teaching her. No matter how much I try to do it all, there just hasn't been enough time to focus on getting a head start on the career of my dreams and the demo. I made my choice. I just wish I didn't have to. But there'll be other demos.

"So how does this work?" Mom asks. "You don't have to fight the robots, do you?"

"Nah, nothing like that," I say. "Each round is two and a half minutes. The first fifteen seconds, our robots run auton." I see the puzzled look on their faces. "Autonomously. So MechaTiger, that's the name of our robot—"

"Shoulda named it MechaTygra," Renee says. "Woulda got bonus points for the cartoon reference. Unc woulda got a kick out of that." I feel my eyes roll at the mention of Dad. "He used to make me watch all those eighties cartoons."

"Well, maybe next year," I say. "If he comes back."

"He's coming back, Gil," Mom says, a little shocked at my remark. I dunno where it came from or why. But I said it. And the way she's looking at me, maybe she thinks the same. "You can't think like that." Is she saying that for her or for me?

I nod my head, let her know I heard, then get back to it,

trying to keep my mind clear. "So in the first fifteen seconds, the robots sensors have to spot the ball, pick it up, and launch it. Then the next two minutes and fifteen seconds are driver controlled."

"You the driver, cuz?" Renee asks. "Don't tell me you got your license before me."

"Nah." I grit my teeth. "This other kid, Heath, is." I try to hide the eye roll, but I know she caught it. So I get right into the rest of the rules before she has a chance to blow up my spot. "We score between two and six points depending on which scoring zone the ball lands in. Then there's a precision test, where the robot has to press a glowing button that comes on intermittently for additional points."

"So which one is dis MechaTiger?" Granma asks, looking down at the field.

"The one with the green bumpers."

"Oof. Some a di udda ones look pretty pretty, what happen to yours?" she asks.

I scratch my head, looking down at all the robots. She ain't lying.

"Hey, Gil," says a sweetly familiar voice. It's Tammy. She showed up. I'm so excited I want to hug her. But I hold back, thinking of our last conversation, even though I want to rest my head in her neck, feel her body against mine.

"Mm-hmm," Renee says. She nudges Nicole with a smirk. "So this is Harlem? Granma told me about you since Gil didn't."

I may not have gotten a hug, but Tammy wastes no time giving Granma one. Granma has that effect. She gives me a wink. "I tell yuh, me like dis one," Granma says.

"Ahem." Mom clears her throat.

"Oh, Mom, Renee, Nicole, this is Tammy," I say. "Tammy, this is Moms and everyone."

"Hi, Ms. Powell," Tammy says.

"Sit down next to me," Granma says to Tammy. "We have lots to talk about."

"Hold up," Rej says, walking in with Stretch. "Sorry, Granma, this one's sitting next to me." He throws his arm around Tammy, while Stretch daps me up.

"Don't get fresh now, Reggie," Granma says. "And me better see both of unnu at me award ceremony." Rej and Stretch quickly nod to let her know that they'll be there. "Me have a new dress and everyting. So we gon party well into di night." She leans into Tammy. "And yuh should come too. It's two Thursdays from now."

"I'd love to," Tammy starts to say. "But our school's gala is that evening. And I give the opening welcome speech."

"Well, if anyting change, yuh know seh yuh invited," Granma says. "Then yuh can see me shake my leg on di dance floor."

My lips part. It's a smile. The thrill in Granma's voice, me surrounded by my friends from BK, my team, and Tammy. This is dope.

"Gil, Tammy," Mr. Neckles says as he arrives. "I wanted you to meet Rashida James. She's the writer and Augustin alum at *The Root* I told you about."

"Hi, Gil, Tammy," she says, shaking each of our hands. "It's a pleasure to meet you. Shareef's told me a lot about you and what you're doing." Hearing her call Mr. Neckles by his first name makes me do a double take. But I guess at Howard University there wasn't any need for him to be anything but his authentic self.

"A pleasure to meet you as well, Ms. James," I say.

"I can't say that we had anything like this when I was at Augustin," she says. "Robots were just for movies. But we did have the Black Culture Club. Glad to see you're still meeting, supporting each other."

"It's helped me a lot," I say. "Transferring in my senior year, dealing with the adjustment, the people."

"I read that article you wrote, Gil," she says. "And when Shareef mentioned the BlackAugustin page, I took a look at that too. The stories felt too familiar. But I was surprised I didn't see any stories from you there. I been following a lot of what the conservative news has been saying about you. The fight video."

"I didn't think it had reached that far," I say.

"Well, I really only got around to reading yesterday. One of my friends follow a local music producer that shared the post on Black hair." I look over at Rej. From the grin he's giving me, he realizes too that the producer she's referring to is him. "That story hit."

"Tammy's the one behind it all," I say. "She helped Janeil with that piece. All the pieces really."

I throw it to Tammy and step away as the announcer gets on the PA system.

"Welcome, ladies and gentlemen, to some off-season robo fun!"

"Hey, I better get down to my team," I say. "Ms. James, great meeting you." I shake her hand again. "Hopefully we get to talk more." Everyone wishes me good luck and I hustle down the bleachers to join the RoboAugs.

The team forms a circle while Mr. Abato gives us some words of wisdom. "Okay, there's no need to rush. We're still a new team. What we want to do is finish and finish strong. Let's have a deterministic approach. Finish. Then do it again in the next round. And so on. Take it slow. Let's show them the RoboAugs have come to play, and they better watch out come spring." He turns to me. "Gil, looks like you'll be our driver."

"What?" My voice breaks over the huddle so everyone nearby can hear my confusion. Why is he playing with me?

"Heath said he doesn't want to drive anymore," Mr. Abato says. "And Lydia suggested you should run the controller. Since she's the other captain, I'm trusting her decision."

Why did Heath back out? And why is Lydia choosing me? Heath is staring off to the side. The redness in his cheeks matches his hair. And Lydia, she's looking at me too eagerly. Whatever happened, it wasn't Heath's choice.

"Y'all sure?" I make eye contact with Mr. Abato and everyone on the team. I want this so bad. Granma's here. All my friends are watching. But something ain't sitting right about this last-minute change.

"Of course," CJ says. "Just make sure you represent."

I'm ready.

"The first round will be the team of the RoboAugs versus Academic Armory," the announcer growls as if he's watched a lot of MMA and boxing matches and can't decide if he's Michael or Bruce Buffer.

We stand behind our line. The controller is on the table two feet away from me. The first fifteen seconds, MechaTiger just relies on its autonomous programming and sensors. I look across at the driver for Academic Armory, Freedom Academy's team name. He returns a smug look.

"Three," the announcer begins the countdown. "Two, one. POWER UP!"

And the game begins. The crowd starts cheering with the energy of a sports competition. That's exactly what this is. MechaTiger launches its three preloaded balls at the round target, which is kind of like a basketball hoop except it's positioned horizontally. Two balls go through the hole, while the other bounces back. The buzzer goes off. Auton is over. I pick up the controller.

The field is covered with several balls. I drive MechaTiger over the closest ones. It sucks in three out of the five. Each target is at a different height. The highest hoop earns the most points, six, versus two for the lowest one. It's also the most difficult to hit, like shooting from the three-point line versus taking a layup. But I got confidence in the robot we built. So that's the one I aim for to grab the early lead.

All three balls bounce off the surrounding wall.

Heath, Lydia, and CJ let out a collective groan.

"Aww, c'mon," CJ yells.

There are six balls spaced about a foot away from each other. MechaTiger is only able to pick up one. I fire it at the top target. I miss. Again.

"Go for the lower target," Lydia says, her voice like electricity, charging me up. "We need points. Watch the angle."

"Target the cluster of balls instead of the ones that are spaced far apart," CJ says. "I think the friction material isn't strong enough when it's one."

I go for the cluster. This time getting four balls.

"Yes," CJ yells.

I aim for the middle target. This time, all four balls score. I drive MechaTiger back, pushing the balls close to each other in reverse, then turning around to go over them. The robot tilts on a ramp. No. No. No. It's going to topple.

"Aargh!" CJ cries out.

MechaTiger teeters on its side and then falls back on its wheels. We all release the pressure out of our lungs.

I repeat the process. Push the balls together, then roll over them. The time is running out. I calculate the tangent line in my head, and fire at the highest target. Nailed it. No time to celebrate. *Deterministic*, Mr. Abato said.

Twenty seconds are left.

"Get the light," CJ says, tapping me on the shoulder frantically.

I see the power button illuminated. If I get MechaTiger to press it, we get an extra fifteen points. I position our robot in front of the button as precisely as I can while trying to not move too fast and have it flip on the ramp again. MechaTiger's machine finger edges toward the button.

"*Tiiiime!*" the announcer growls as the buzzer sounds.

"Did it count?" Lydia asks. We look up at the score. We're a full one hundred points behind. All the cheering has died down. It's not just us, everyone in the auditorium is waiting, anxious to hear the announcer call the official win. Two months of Augustin. Two months to get here.

The button press counted!

"Winner of the first round is the Academic Armory of Freedom Academy," the announcer booms over the speakers.

This may be a loss, but my team is all smiles, patting me on the back. This is only the team's second round of competitive play. And last year, they didn't even finish the first round. Now we have a chance to continue on and prove that we belong here just like anyone else.

"What you did just now was nothing less than excellent," Mr. Abato says proudly. "Consistency, that's one of the most important things in any scientific trial. Plus, with Heath's added logging system, we'll be able to use all the data we collected when the season begins." And just like that, the victory feels hollow. I may have held the controller, but I'm getting none of the credit. "They're going to have something to be afraid of." He looks each of us in the eye. "All right, RoboAugs, on three." Everyone puts their hand in the circle. I join reluctantly. "One, two, three—"

"TIGERS."

I'm the only one who says nothing.

"Excuse me." A woman with fading reddish hair walks up. She's vaguely familiar. "What just happened?"

"Pardon me?" Mr. Abato says, confused.

"My son"—she points at Heath—"was supposed to be the driver." She says it with such authority. Like . . .

It's the woman from parent-teacher night. The one who carried herself like a lawyer, who always backed up Jill's mom, Julia. The one who wanted to call me a thug. She's Heath and Lydia's mom?

"You gave that role to someone on probation," she continues.

"Well, his probation ended a few weeks ago," Mr. Abato says.

"Mom," Lydia says. She pulls her mom off to the side.

I'm trying to process what just happened when another woman walks up to greet Mr. Abato.

"RoboAugs, this is Dr. Gunther," Mr. Abato says. It's the scientist who works with robot-assisted neurosurgery. She has tan skin and is probably mixed, but I can't tell with what. There are craters underneath her eyes wanting for sleep. And her skin clings to her like she lives off water and nothing else. But her energy feels like she's ramped up on caffeine.

"Dr. Gunther," I say, extending my hand to introduce myself. "I'm a huge fan of your work."

"Thank you," she replies. "You know, when I saw you down there, I thought you looked very familiar."

Great. Does she know me from the video too? I step back, unsure of what to say next.

"I only got to see the end of the match," Dr. Gunther continues. "But wow, did that make me excited to be a Tiger. To go up against teams of close to thirty students. That's a victory. Numbers are important. But they're not everything. Execution, delivery, consistency, that's what people remember." She looks over at me. "And you didn't break. Another driver would have given up after missing those first shots, but you knew your robot. Stayed consistent. That's a smart approach. Coding is the same. Who was your lead architect?"

"That's our Heath," Mr. Abato says. "Also founded the team with his sister."

"Well, we should talk," Dr. Gunther says to Heath. "I'd love to bring on an intern from Augustin. Does that sound like something that would be of interest?"

"That would be great," Heath says without hesitation.

And I nearly die on the spot.

32

It should feel good to be back with the Always Persevere team. But after a month of not showing up and that *L* at the Fall Classic, I'm feeling like a stranger. Doesn't help that yesterday's robotics competition left me sick. I barely closed my eyes last night, knowing someone else got rewarded for my work.

It's Sunday afternoon. We're at the YMCA in a dance rehearsal room. The hardwood floor is cool beneath my bare feet. I watch Stretch and Kenya doing their nunchuck warm-up drills in front of a wall lined with floor-to-ceiling mirrors. Rej and Renee are going over their combinations. Outside of a few small changes from year to year, our demonstrations are pretty much locked, like a Broadway show. We do an intro, synchronized moves, a choreographed fight sequence, weapons, then wrap it up.

So why does my stomach feel like it's got a pair of nunchucks doing wrist rolls inside it trying to break out?

Outside of the whatup greetings, nobody's chatting me up or saying anything about my absences. Maybe I'm overthinking it, but the air here is definitely cold. Everyone's probably expecting me to fail.

I look over the texts Tammy sent earlier.

TAMMY

Sorry I couldn't hang out after the competition yesterday.

ME

Np. Cool you came out and got to chill with the fam. Know granma was happy to see you.

Ha. Your granma is great. She was leading your cheering section.

My parents and I just got to New Haven. Visiting Yale so I'll be back in school on Wednesday.

Dope! Have a fun trip.

I feel like it's a matter of time before she sends the "let's just be friends" text. All our exchanges are just general convo. Nothing about us. I want to talk to her about what happened with Dr. Gunther. Maybe she can give me some advice on what to do. But it's been a month since we talked like that.

I tighten the black belt around my tournament gi. I've done this routine countless times, at the dojo, exhibitions, summer recruitment drives. I know each turn by heart. I don't get nervous in front of strangers. But it's been four weeks since I practiced the routine. If it was another student, they probably woulda been pulled off the team already. But I know I'm getting the unspoken pass from Renee, Rej, and Stretch.

I examine my chucks. Can't remember the last time I held these. I start practicing my behind-the-back passes, then my horizontal wrist rolls. I move on to more advanced techniques. Stretch is acting like he's not watching me out the corner of his eye, but I peep him in the mirror's reflection.

"I was hoping you were going to teach me that before today's demo," Kenya says. I meet her eyes, which are filled with heartbreak.

"Kenya," I say, stumbling for the words that need to follow. "I just been caught up with school." The same school that has turned my whole existence into a debate in the conservative media and a talking point in an election. "I didn't expect this demo to come up so soon. But I'll definitely teach you some moves for next time."

"Like when you said you'd be at the test, or come to demo practice," she says. The sarcasm stings.

"I'm sorry," I say because there's nothing else I can say. I'm out of excuses. "Robotics team is done for now. So Ima be at the dojo every Saturday." I bite my lip immediately. Every Saturday is a lie, 'cause I still have to be at home if Mr. Neckles or someone else isn't there to be with Granma while Mom's at work. And then what happens when the full robotics season begins in January? New game rules, a new robot to construct. I'll have to go into the city. And even if I put in twice as many hours in

January, Mr. Abato will probably still think that I'm just working off the code Heath wrote, which he didn't.

"It's whatever," she says with a jab. "You don't keep your promises. You like your new school more than me." The combo crushes me. *Was that the choice I made?*

"Aye." Stretch jumps in the convo to bring peace. "Joshu Powell isn't the only one good with the chucks," he says smoothly. "I can teach you some new techniques. We're all here for you."

"First my mom and dad split up," she says. Her eyes tighten, holding the tears inside. "Then you leave us."

"What?" I ask, confused. She rubs her eyes and walks out the door. This time I don't just feel it, I see everyone gaping at me, a single accusation on their minds.

You left us.

I drop my chucks and run after her. The hallway is empty. As I walk down the corridor, I hear the low rumble of sobs from behind the bathroom door. I knock. "Kenya," I say. She doesn't answer. "Kenya, I'm really sorry I haven't been there." I don't really know what to say or how to say it. Truth is, I haven't been thinking about her or the dojo. She calls me big bro, and I've been anything but that. Dad's face pops into my head. What would he say to Kenya? I haven't even done a video call with him recently. *Is this how I feel about Dad?* That he left us. That it was a choice and not something he had to do. "Kenya, can we talk?"

I sit down with my back to the wall, waiting for her to come out. She eventually exits, wiping her eyes. I need to fix this, but I don't think I can.

"When did you find out?" I ask. "About your parents?"

"Before the Fall Classic." She sniffles. She takes a seat next to me on the floor. I didn't even notice her mom wasn't with Kenya the day of the tournament. She's always there at Kenya's matches. That's how Dad used to be in my corner.

"Hey," I say, resting my hand on her shoulder. "My parents are kinda separated too. My dad's been in Jamaica for months. So I may be experiencing a bit of what you're feeling. And if you wanna talk . . ."

She shrugs off my hand. "How're we s'posed to talk if you're not there?"

"You can always message me, call me," I say. It feels shallow. Messages are fine. *But actually being there in the room is what matters. That's sacrifice.* That's something I can't give her if I gotta keep going hard with robotics. *It's what Dad can't give me.*

There's just not enough time.

"Gil, Kenya," Renee says. "We gotta start soon." I look at my cousin. Her time is stretched between NYU, hanging out with Granma, work, dating, and the dojo. But here she is. "You good to go?" She stares right into me.

I turn to Kenya. "I know that calling and text messages don't sound like enough," I say. "Not when I always been there. But I'll find a way. And maybe you can help, work with me to figure out how to balance all this." I reach out my hand. "Deal, lil sis? 'Cause we're fam, and I want to be there for you."

She crashes into me, wrapping her arms around my neck. "Okay, big bro," she says.

I nod to Renee that we're ready to start.

"What's going on," Nakia says, approaching from down the

hall, sensing her sister was upset. "What'd you do?" she asks me pointedly. Her thighs are right in my face.

Pushing myself off the ground, I rise to meet her eyes, so round and full of spirit, waiting for an answer. I stopped talking to her when Tammy entered my world. Sure, it was only friendly flirting, but I miss those conversations. And now I feel like I can't talk to either of them. I peek briefly over Nakia's shoulder, wondering if her dude is somewhere behind her. "I think we're good," I say. "Right, Kenya?"

"Right," Kenya says with a bright nod.

We head back to the prep room as the demo team lines up. Everyone's doing last-minute stretches: hips, calves, quads, shoulders. They've been practicing. They're ready to go.

I'm not.

I can feel it in the tingles in my spine, the offbeat murmur in my chest. There's a fog in my head. Instead of the fight choreography, I see Terry, Heath and Lydia's mom, the faces of Dean Bradley and Headmaster DeSantis. I see Dr. Gunther and Mr. Abato congratulating Heath. He looks at me with that smug expression. When I picture the front flip that I'd do to transition, I end up slamming into the floor, my bones cracking from the fall. The audience bursts with laughter.

"You good?" Stretch asks as I step into line.

"Yeah," I lie.

"You may want to get your chucks," Rej says. The way he says it, I can hear that he's still holding a grudge. I jump out of line, rushing to where I left my set of nunchucks. On the way back, I hear Rej whisper to Stretch, "I wonder if he even remembers the routine."

I take my time getting into formation so I can listen in.

"Sonnn, can yaaa'll just chiiill already," Stretch replies. His voice is so even toned, he could be lounging. "He got this. And if he don't . . ." Stretch shakes his head with the cool smile only he can manage. "It is what it is." At least there's one person I haven't let down. "Just let the beef go already."

I take my position as the music comes on. It's Rej's mix. The bass is amping everyone up—except me.

The twelve of us run out into the performance space, clapping to the music, getting the audience's energy up for the show. The room is a little longer than the length of the dojo and twice as wide. Students break off, two to a corner, while me, Renee, Stretch, and Rej begin the intro. My muscles are a little stiff. But we're in sync. Renee and Rej do backflips, flanking me and Stretch to give the audience a teaser of our nunchuck performance, mixing figure eights and wrist rolls. The team keeps the audience hyped, adding in sound effects, yelling in awe at the backflips and movements. We switch out so each student gets to be a part of the opening.

The team breaks into four groups of three, positioned at each corner of our stage area. The groups alternate, one student rushing the center at a time to perform their technique. When I take the center, my kicks are clean, my form is smooth. Each student is in perfect symmetry. I got this.

Me and Stretch are at opposite corners. He gives his ki yell, and I follow it up with an equally powerful yell. It's time for our choreographed fight sequence. It begins with me doing a flying side kick that he'll parry. We've done this over a hundred times easily.

He does a three-kick combo into the center of the stage, then gives a ki yell, calling me out like a challenge. I take my cue. Running to the center of the invisible box, I plant my front leg to jump off it. I don't know if I ran too fast or if my left leg twisted too much. But my right heel drives directly into Stretch's forearm, which collides into his head with a loud clap.

No!

"Whoa," our team yells. "Did you see that?!"

"Maybe he needs backup?" Renee says, addressing the audience.

They're working fast, trying to cover up what I just did as if it's part of the show. Rej lets out a ki yell and runs into the center of the stage in front of Stretch, who backs away, holding his head.

Rej begins a combo. His movements are slower than usual. He's directing me, letting me know he's finishing out Stretch's routine.

The crowd cheers. Thanks to my team, they didn't notice the error.

I finish out the fight sequence and head back to the corner to join Renee while the next duo goes up. The way she's grillin me lets me know everything she's going to say before she says it.

"You're off weapons," she says. "That's the end of your demo."

I nod. She's right. I'm not just off my game, I'm also hurting people. My family. I look over at Stretch. That relaxed smile he always has is gone. He's glowering at me the same way everyone else from Brooklyn has been since I transferred.

It's like I'm hurting everyone except the people who hurt me.

33

I don't care if it's my third strike. I need Mr. Abato to know that it was my code. Forget the scholarship and next semester, I'll go back to Union. I just can't let all my work be taken.

All this time I been thinking that using *The Art of War* would help me navigate my time here. Find a better way to fight back. The truth is, Augustin has been using *The Art of War* long before I was even born. Every tactic is ingrained into each drop of cement that makes up the school's foundation.

"I'm almost finished reading Chijoke's story," CJ says.

Chijoke's post went live over the weekend and Janeil made a reel to go with it today. It's the Monday before Election Day. We're walking out of Philosophy class with Janeil. Between Janeil's post and Rej's sharing, BlackAugustin's followers have more than doubled.

"It's heavy," CJ continues. "I've had that same feeling of being trapped when I'm in a room full of straight people who want to comment on queer issues." He taps my arm, noticing that I'm distracted. "You good?" CJ asks me. He's been asking me the same question since Saturday. At the competition, over text, now back in school. "You seemed real quiet in class."

I want to tell him what I'm going to do.

"Lot on my mind, that's all," I say.

"Taking that 'unexamined life is not worth living' concept from Philosophy a little too seriously," CJ says.

"Speaking of serious, we only got three days to finish off that video for the gala," Janeil says to CJ.

"The RoboAugs will have a booth at the gala," CJ tells me. "You should ask Mr. Abato to come. Me and Janeil been working on a cool one-hundred-fifty-year retrospective for it in Video Production Club. Should be some other engineering alum there too. Dr. Gunther isn't the only game in town."

I'm only half paying attention to him. Down the hall I spot the familiar lab coat. "Hey, Mr. Abato," I call out. He doesn't hear me over the noise of students switching classes. "Be right back," I say to CJ and Janeil. I weave through green blazers on a mission. He turns when I catch up to him.

"Mr. Powell, everything okay?"

"Would you have a second to talk?" I ask. "In private."

He scratches his beard, a little surprised. "Well, sure. If you have a free period now, I'll be in the STEM Lab in about fifteen minutes. Just have to do an errand in the faculty lounge first."

"That works," I say.

As he walks off, CJ and Janeil catch up to me. The look on Janeil's face is total disgust. She shows me a text from Leylah on her phone.

LEYLAH

We need to meet. Augustin Lounge. Now.
Check this . . .

Below the text is a screenshot from the RNY Podcast's Instagram account that reads, "BlackAugustin or BlackHoax? New episode today. #ElectKillian."

"It's ELECTION DAY tomorrow, so I hope everyone has either sent in their early ballot or is ready to line up and elect Hugh Killian for mayor. He's an independent candidate, someone who is truly bipartisan, a successful businessman, and a person who actually understands what New York needs."

Me, Chijoke, Leylah, Janeil, and Saleem are gathered around the table in the Augustin Lounge. We're listening to the host of the RNY Podcast. He's mentioned a special guest who will be offering insight into BlackAugustin, but so far it's been mostly stuff about tomorrow's election. We've been skipping forward through the episode, trying to find the right section.

It's already eight minutes into the period, and I'm supposed to meet with Mr. Abato.

"That's why I started the Parents of Augustin Facebook page," a woman says. She has a calming voice, like someone directing a Yoga class or a meditation, but it sends a shiver up my spine

because I recognize it. *"It's only been two weeks, and we already have a few thousand followers. Both parents and alumni are really passionate about what's going on right now at our school."*

I can never forget that voice or the face of the person it belongs to. Julia. She was so condescending on parent-teacher night. She said having an HBCU tour sponsored by the school was the opposite of inclusion, then she accused us of reverse racism.

"Stop," I say to Leylah. "Go back."

She finds the start of the section.

"I'd like to welcome Julia Davenport, respected entrepreneur, an alumnus of Augustin Prep, and parent of a current student," the host says.

"That's Jill's mom," I say. "She's the head of the Parents' Committee, the one who talked down to me and Tammy before I wrote the article."

Julia and the host exchange brief pleasantries, before the host focuses on BlackAugustin.

"One of the parents had learned about this Instagram account that spreads propaganda about Augustin's Black students," Julia says. *"We initially brought it to the attention of the school, only because we were worried about the students. All of them. What impact these disparaging stories would have on the whole student body. But the account didn't have a huge following, there were no names attached to it, and the administration couldn't really do anything about an independently run account."*

"So they been following us this whole time?" Janeil says.

"And it sounds like they was trying to shut it down," Saleem says.

"Makes sense," Leylah says to them. "I told y'all how Brandon came up to us in the cafeteria." She motions to me and Chijoke. "He was basically ordering me to pull my article down."

"Are some of these stories cause for concern?" the host asks.

"Again, our parents care about ALL of the students. That's why I organized the Facebook page. But what we have to pay attention to are stories that can be harmful to another student or to the educational process, when the person telling the story is embellishing or lying purely to get publicity or promote themselves."

Janeil almost jumps out of her chair. "She can't be serious right now."

"I want to call attention to three stories by three students. One student who accused a football player of sexual assault at a party. Now if two people dance at a party, is that assault? No. But that's what she tried to make it out to be so that she could ruin an innocent person's future. And if you look at her own social profile, this is a girl who is obviously working on building a fashion line and dresses to call attention to her body and promote herself."

Leylah trembles. Her right hand grips her left so tightly I can almost see the blood being pushed away.

"Another student is an immigrant whose family is obviously struggling with infidelity. Did they come into the country legally? Who's to say. But you can tell from the picture that some of his siblings aren't from the same parents, and that has to weigh on him. He's a good student from what I've heard. But those kinds of people obviously have issues at home. He doesn't want to approach his parents about it and chooses instead to lash out against his fellow students."

"Why is she going after my family like this?" Chijoke asks.

He's looking right at me, filled with so much doubt. "Why'd you tell me to use my name," he says accusingly. "I should've never written that piece."

I don't know what to say to him. I want to tell him this just means what we're doing has worked for them to respond like this. But to go after his family and Leylah's character is low. We need to strike back because Julia can't get away with this.

"C'mon, don't blame Gil," Saleem says to Chijoke.

"That is easy for you to say," Chijoke says. "Did you even write an article?"

"I did," Saleem says. "The one about being on the football team. That was me."

"You didn't put your face with it," Chijoke says. His voice cracks, trying to hold back a yell. "You stayed anonymous. Your family isn't getting attacked."

"And this other girl. Smokes weed and probably does other drugs. You can see it in the artwork on her social profiles. But the real issue is that she is violent. Have you seen the video on the AugustinNowDnI account?"

"Oh, we have," the host replies. *"And we'll be sharing a link on our show page."*

"Just like the other student who started the fight at the beginning of September. Students like this do a disservice to themselves and hurt other students who are working their hardest to take advantage of the great education Augustin has to offer."

Janeil's eyes are wide and her mouth can't decide if it wants to yell or just grunt out whatever it is she's got to say. She's looking at her phone and has already pulled up the AugustinNowDnI account. Saleem wraps his arm around her. Leylah turns off the podcast.

We all look at an edited video of the day Lydia pulled Janeil's hair. Except it's only showing the thirteen seconds when Janeil reacts. Making it out like she's crazy, going off on a scared innocent white girl. And there's only one person who was in the room at that time, who had that angle to shoot the video.

I think back on the fight. That reddish blur in the corner. The fourth person, watching in the cut as I was jumped. There was never blood clouding my eyes. It was red hair, belonging to the same person I've been working with for the past several weeks. The same person who wanted to prove that I wasn't able to compete with him. Then had no problem taking credit for my work.

Heath.

"This doesn't end here," I say to everyone. But if there's another move, I don't know what it is.

THERE'S ONLY FIVE minutes left in the period. I'm sweating from running up the stairs. Hopefully Mr. Abato is still here. Walking into the STEM Lab used to be one of the few joys I had at Augustin. Now this room feels tainted along with the rest of the school. Julia went after us and Heath is behind the AugustinNowDnI account. He knew the truth about the fight, had the video of it the whole time, and chose to share it to a media outlet he knew would go after me. To him . . . me, Janeil, we're just entertainment. And now Janeil, Chijoke, and Leylah are getting dragged through the conservative news.

Is Lydia involved? She is Heath's sister. I actually liked her. There wasn't a moment she didn't have me hyped to be here.

She's the one that got Heath to back off on being the driver at the competition. I thought that meant she had my back. Lydia was talking to her mother when Dr. Gunther offered Heath the internship, but she obviously has to know by now that her brother got the job. But she hasn't spoken up yet. Is she like one of Sun Tzu's double agents, playing both sides, only pretending to have my back? I feel betrayed.

"Gil," Mr. Abato says. "You're late. I was just about to leave." He's not saying it dismissively, only stating a fact. I was already upset when I got to school today, but this whole thing with Julia has me heated in a way I've never felt before because Chijoke blames me. Maybe Janeil and Leylah blame me too.

"What can I do you for?" Mr. Abato asks. "By the way, great work at the tournament the other week. I've been meaning to say that directly, but with the gala this Thursday, I've been stuck on calls with alumni, making sure we have a strong attendance. Dr. Gunther will be there, along with an alum from Boston Dynamics, from—"

"I wrote the code," I say, cutting him off. "All of it. I started the week my probation began. Redesigned it from the ground up. All the pseudo-code you'd see on the walls, that was my writing. Not Heath's. He doesn't deserve that internship. You need to tell Dr. Gunther that." I don't care if I don't get it. But there's no way I'm letting Heath come off on my grind.

Mr. Abato's blank expression says it all. He doesn't believe me. "I'm not sure what to say." He clasps his hands together, undecided about how these next few minutes will go. "These are some heavy accusations," he says. "And the implication . . . You have to understand why I can't believe you without proof."

Because I'm not white. *The dean never believed me. Why should you?*

"Heath founded the team," he continues, listing out the reasons he can't trust me. When I can't trust anyone here. "Helps with recruitment. Whereas I've never seen you in the lab until recently. And if I did . . ."

"You can ask CJ," I say.

"Why come to me now?" he asks. "Why not say anything before the competition? It sounds like you're . . . upset Heath got the internship and not you."

"I don't care about the job," I say. Sun Tzu outlined five ways to attack by fire and the result is always the same—everything gets burned. "Ask me anything about the functions that were written. I can tell you because I designed it."

"Which would also mean you broke probation."

"To help the team. To do what I came here to do."

"This is a lot, Mr. Powell. Give me some time to think on it. I'll also have to talk to CJ."

I'm not expecting much. But I said my piece. Now there's one more person I need to see.

34

Lydia's always down in Fabrication after her lunch period. I don't know how she has so many frees, but hang out with someone enough and you learn their whole schedule . . . even if they've been deceiving you this whole time.

I cut AP Lit and head to the sublevel. I'm sure Ms. Column will have something to say tomorrow.

Sure enough, I see Lydia's red hair through the square window in the metal door, tinkering with MechaTiger.

I don't open the door so much as I shove through it. "I thought we were cool," I say.

Her face flushes. "Gil . . . I was looking for you earlier. After your Philosophy class."

"Why? To touch my hair?" I feel my voice rising. "See how I'd react so you and your brother can film it, share it? It's not enough that he got the internship that I deserved."

"No, that's not it." She looks sick to the verge of throwing up.

"I've been following the BlackAugustin page since that time I saw it on CJ's phone." So the twins made the AugustinNowDnI account in direct response to BlackAugustin. They used the video of me to go viral. I guess that means they were also the ones who shared it with Brandon. And their mom knows Julia from the Parents' Committee. "I read Janeil's story. I tried to apologize to her." She jabs her finger in her chest. "I really did. I want her to know that I understand."

"So you trolled her." If she expects me to fall back now, it's not happening. "You went after me, fine. Everyone's already doin that. But after reading about her condition, you go after her. And you want me to what? Feel sorry for you? As if it's not enough that we gotta always watch what we say, what we do, or get penalized in this school. We have to worry about our own teammates. And you wanna claim to be an ally."

"It wasn't me," she all but screams.

"You just said you been following the page," I say. "It was definitely Heath filming that video with Janeil."

"That night, I was reading the posts at home," she says. Her hands go up to plead her explanation. "He must have seen it when I set my phone down. I didn't know he started following BlackAugustin too. I had no idea he made the AugustinNowDnI account or that he had the video of the fight with Terry until after it was already shared. I'm really sorry."

"So all of October, when we were working together, as a team, you knew Heath had the video and posted it." I feel my body go rigid. She looks like she's on the border of tearing up. But it all seems fake to me. I don't feel any sympathy for her. I can't.

"I told him to stop posting on the account," she says. "And he did . . . for a while. But he'd already shared the video with our uncle, Hugh Killian. And it was out."

"Uncle?" I ask. "The same Killian running for mayor?"

"Uncle Hugh is my mom's brother," she says. "He was a Tiger too."

So that's why my situation has been so personal for Killian and his campaign. He's an Augustin alumnus. I wish Tammy were here. I need someone to talk to. But she's out of town today visiting the University of Pennsylvania.

"I made Heath give up being the driver at the Freedom competition. So your family could see all the work you did."

She thinks that a consolation prize makes up for two months of suffering.

"But why not speak up when it came to the internship?" I'm ready to blow. "Why not tell Mr. Abato that the code was mine?"

"You don't understand," she says. "He's not just my brother, we're twins. No matter how much I disagree with him, we have a bond. Would you snitch on your family?"

"It's like you read the BlackAugustin articles but haven't paid attention to any of the effects of everything we have to live with, every day." I'm pacing around the room. I can't contain myself. "In September, your mom called me a thug. Do you have any idea what that means? Do you have any idea how much it ate me up, knowing I had to keep quiet about my work on the team or possibly lose my scholarship? Your brother has been right next to you stealing credit for my work without an ounce of regret. What does your apology mean if you're not ready to confront him, or your mom, or your uncle? Your silence makes you as guilty as them."

I need to get out of here. Not just this room. This school. But can I really escape these white spaces? Renee made it sound like it's not possible. Is this what I came here to learn? That there is no escape? I make my way to the door. I need to go back to Brooklyn.

Dad, why aren't you here?

"Wait," Lydia says as I grab the doorknob. My jaw is tense. A migraine is chewing away at me; even the light in this room hurts. I see my rage reflected in her eyes. "I got the full videos off my brother's phone. You should have them."

A few seconds later, both videos are on my phone. I watch them. Uncut. Unedited. Lydia doesn't say a word. And I don't either. Then I walk out the door and text Janeil.

ME

> You said you and CJ was working on a video for the gala right?

JANEIL

> Yeah. But I don't even know if I feel like goin anymore. I don't wanna be in the same room as Jill's mom or any of them.

> I hear that. But meet me after school. I got an idea how to strike back at everyone. The parents, the school. We can catch Tammy up when she's back.

35

Two days have passed since we listened to Julia's attack on BlackAugustin. CJ doctored up a Facebook account just so we could read the comments being left on Julia's parents group. There are actually people calling her brave for what she did, while making personal attacks on each of us. The comments have started to flood the BlackAugustin page too.

This is why quotas aren't good.

You should feel privileged to go to a school like Augustin.

You're a teenager, don't dress like a prostitute.

You know how people from those countries are.

In my day . . .

That's when the comments started getting real bad, but I've been deleting those.

This has to stop. I've got a plan. Leylah, Janeil, Saleem, and CJ are on board. It was harder to sell to Chijoke. The negative comments against his family and Black immigrants were sickening. Rej went off over text after he read some of them. Chijoke wanted to take the post down completely. But I asked him to give me until the gala. See if we can get BlackAugustin featured. Now I just got to tell Tammy.

It's sixth period on Wednesday. Me and her are sitting in the far corner of the library. It's like the architect designed this area so that students could have a place to talk outta earshot.

I already sent her the RNY Podcast last night to listen to, but felt it best to discuss the plan in person. Now she's watching both videos that Lydia gave me. Tammy's expression is full-on disgust.

"They're trying to bully us out of BlackAugustin," I say, my voice slightly above a whisper. "We need to use these videos to get everyone's attention."

"You mean share them on our account?" she asks.

"Eventually," I say. "But we need to make sure everyone sees it. The RNY Podcast already had an audience, that's why AugustinNowDnI took off so quickly. Rej's been sharing BlackAugustin posts but it's not enough. We have to go big now." She looks at me with a mix of curiosity and eagerness. There are a few other people in the library, but it feels like it's just me and her. We haven't been alone together since that afternoon when we were leaving Central Park. I want to talk about us. But nothing is more important than striking back against all these negative comments. Leylah, Janeil, and Chijoke sacrificed their anonymity to help BlackAugustin. I gotta make what they did count. "Look at some of these comments." I show her the Facebook group.

"I don't need to see it," she says. "I heard what Jill's mom had to say. And I agree." There's so much conviction in her voice. I've missed this. "I got Ms. James's card at your robotics competition. I'll contact her, ask her to really go through our stories and see if there's a chance to cover it. We shouldn't have to live like we're under siege."

"That's not enough," I say. My voice comes out too loudly and the librarian walks over to shush me. I wait for him to walk away. I try to talk as low as I can, but the anger still seethes out. "We do it at the gala. CJ and Janeil are editing together some of the BlackAugustin stories. We're going to play it there along with the unedited videos Lydia gave me."

"How?" Tammy asks. "The school isn't going to just play something like that."

"CJ and Janeil are handling the anniversary video," I say. "It's supposed to play right before you go on. So they're going to switch it. And CJ is doing a reaction video for TikTok and the gram. He's got more followers than Rej. So he'll publish that simultaneously to his accounts."

"What happened to choice and anonymity?" she asks. "If Janeil plays those videos and I go up, the school will come down on me. What do you think they're going to do?" I hesitate a moment too long. "Have you even thought that far ahead?"

"I'll speak instead," I say. "Let me be the target. Killian, the podcast, Julia, they've all been going after me. I'll take the blame for whatever happens. But this is the way. With Ms. James in the room seeing everyone's reaction, it'll give her an instant story."

"You have your granma's fundraiser to go to," she says. "The gala starts at six. You'll never make it."

"The video plays at six. I'll be out by 6:15, home by 7:20 or 7:30. The Caribbean Teachers' fundraiser doesn't start until 8:00 p.m."

"That schedule is too tight," she argues. "You're giving it fifteen minutes, that's only if everything starts on time. Have you even talked to Mr. Abato yet about coming?"

I shake my head, *no*. I don't think I can stomach being in the RoboAugs booth with Heath and Lydia.

Tammy lets out a deep sigh, then pushes her blue frames up the bridge of her nose. "You need to go to your granma's event," she says. "I know how important she is to you. I'll do it. I've been wanting to say something in my welcome speech. This is my chance."

When I came up with this plan, I just pictured the school putting the fault on me. And I was good with that. Janeil was also down to take any punishment for switching the video. We worked together over the past day to get testimonials, add in other footage. The video is looking strong so far. Janeil just had to make a few tweaks. I already blame myself for losing Tammy's editor position, which put space between us. She can't be the one to go up.

"I dunno if I can let you take the fall like that," I say. "Not again."

"*Let me?* Do you think you get to dictate what I choose to do or not do?"

"That's not what I meant," I say.

"You're not my protector," she says firmly. "I don't think we should show the video of the fight. That redirects the attention from BlackAugustin." She's wrong. Everyone needs to see how this all started. It's important. And there are other parts to the new video too, not just the fight.

"The school needs to hear Terry say that word." I want to tell her more, but I feel like I'm sinking, pushing us farther apart.

"And they will . . . after the gala," she says. "You're angry now, I get it, but you're lashing out." Her face is heavy in thought. "What if Janeil isn't able to play the video?" she continues.

"She'll be in the production box."

"BlackAugustin." She stops and I know the conversation is over. "That's what we need to focus on. That's what I'll make my speech about."

In Sun Tzu's chapter "Attack by Fire," he closes it by saying: "The enlightened ruler is prudent and the good general is warned against rash action . . . Thus the state is kept secure and the army preserved."

So maybe Tammy's right. Maybe what I want to do is a little too rash, not prudent. I just don't think words are enough. The entire system is already broken, and exposing it is the only way we'll ever feel secure.

36

It's almost 9:30 p.m. I'm sitting at the bottom of Granma's bed, talking to her about the podcast, the plan I had, the video CJ and Janeil made that we're no longer going to show.

Mom just sent me a text from work.

MOM

Gil, Ordered a special bouquet for your Granma. Want to surprise her. So if you can get Granma ready tomorrow night, I'll pick it up and meet you at the venue.

ME

No problem

There's also a text from Janeil.

The video came out dope. Wish we were still showing it.

By this time tomorrow night, Tammy will have given her speech and Granma will have received her award. I spent the last hour rereading BlackAugustin posts, deleting comments that are getting more and more vulgar. Some of them are probably not even coming from alum or parents. They could be students, or random internet trolls emboldened by people like Killian and the RNY Podcast. At least it looks like Killian lost the election.

"I need to be there tomorrow," I say to Granma. Tammy doesn't understand what I went through these past two months. She's listened, but she doesn't get how it's affected me. "I can't let Tammy do this alone."

"Den yuh should go," she says. Her face is stern but encouraging.

"I'll be back by 7:30," I say. Even if I leave the gala by 6:30, the walk to the train and ride is only fifty minutes, maybe an hour. And a cab from the apartment to the venue is only five minutes.

"Don't worry about me," she says. "I'll be all right. Juss make sure yuh handle your ting."

37

My fingers shake as I read Dad's text.

DAD

Sad I'm going to miss di party. Big night for di family. Make sure you take a lot of pictures

He's referring to the Caribbean Teachers' Association fundraiser later tonight, but I feel like he's watching and sending me a message to not do what I'm about to do. Mom expects me to be home by seven, but I got the go from Granma to get home a little later.

Most of the senior volunteers got to the Ziegfeld event space between 4:00 and 4:30 p.m., enough time to get settled in, eat pizza in the back, chop it up before tonight's festivities. I didn't volunteer and didn't ask Mr. Abato's permission to be at the

RoboAugs booth. I simply crashed. The location is on Fifty-Fourth Street in Midtown, perfectly situated for businesspeople to hit right after work. The digital banner over the entrance proudly proclaims:

CELEBRATING 150 YEARS OF AUGUSTIN
WELCOME HOME, TIGERS

Tonight's a celebration for some.

There's a red carpet at the entrance like it's a Hollywood movie premiere. Alumni and corporate sponsors alike will be guided two floors up to the mezzanine for cocktail hour. The school wants them to get loose on liquor so they're ready to donate to Augustin's growing legacy. Some of the athletes, like Terry and Saleem, are up there, acting as greeters.

Janeil and CJ were here before noon. They watched the production team set up, run tests, do the video run-through, and sound check. Janeil is in the production box right now; it's a small space, practically invisible, nestled beneath the mezzanine and above the back bar.

The door to the main ballroom is all about opulence, an Emerald City in the heart of Midtown. The school colors shimmer from streamers strung from the high ceiling. Instead of hosting a gala, they could have just used the money they put into booking this space for the endowment, but that wouldn't be as good a show, would it?

That's what they're going to get tonight.

The ballroom is divided into two sections. A third of the space at the back has booths highlighting student organizations.

The other two-thirds include the stage and a field of tables for dining. CJ told me this morning that Heath and Lydia won't be at the booth since their uncle is the guest speaker. So I'm posting up with him. They'll arrive later and sit at a table close to the stage with the rest of their family. Important donors, the headmaster, president, and dean will be seated at tables to either side of them.

They'll be right under Tammy as she gives her speech. I just wish I could be up front and see their expressions.

Five o'clock comes around, but not soon enough.

"Janeil's pretty bummed she's not going to debut the video in front of everyone," CJ says. He's disappointed too. I can hear it in his voice. They both helped with it.

"People will see it on the BlackAugustin account after Tammy gives her speech," I say without any enthusiasm. I adjust my green blazer and tie, which are both feeling extra uncomfortable tonight. I haven't seen Tammy yet. She must be in back preparing. Didn't tell her I was coming either. Granma's approval was enough.

"Well, I still made the TikTok reaction video for what it's worth," CJ says. "It's got everything Terry says at the top. Hopefully that raises the signal."

The mezzanine fills up with people getting their drink on after a long day, having mini-reunions with old friends, while a few people start to wander around the booths, asking students questions about their activities. A couple stops by our booth, looking me and CJ up and down.

"The RoboAugs." A late-forties-looking man reads our sign. "Didn't have that when I was there."

"Wasn't too progressive either, from what you've told me," his husband says.

"It was a different time," the man replies as they walk off.

Most of the conversations go like this, people talking, but not really asking questions. It's dizzying.

Maybe thirty minutes pass by, and then I see her. It's Julia. She's wearing a floor-length evening dress with partial lace sleeves and a low neck. The lights seem to be drawn to her, reflecting the venue's green decorations off her silverish dress. Julia's talking to Headmaster DeSantis, praising him, going overboard on the compliments on how well Augustin is running.

"This evening is so perfect," she says. Julia comes to a full stop in front of the RoboAugs booth. I can almost feel her looking at me through the side of her eye. "All the decorations look lovely." She lets out a sigh that's as fake as her smile. "But it feels like so much. Can we talk to the Ziegfield manager?" She panders to the headmaster. "I'd love to donate any food that we don't use to a food bank, or the homeless."

That smug expression she has causes me to look away and mask the anger that wants to burst out.

"I'm sure we can arrange something," Mr. DeSantis replies jovially. "And we're grateful to you and all the parents who helped with planning the night."

"Augustin has always been such a beacon to the students and the community," Julia says. She motions to our booth, but doesn't turn for a moment to look at us. "We have a robotics team now. We couldn't have dreamed of this kind of progress when I was a student, much less my father. And I know we can do more," she says. "The way *some of the students* have been . . . belittling my alma mater, it's a little disgraceful. I don't know if they value what we're giving them. In my dad's time, they weren't even allowed to have certain hairstyles."

Some of the students? Certain hairstyles? She talking about my fro? CJ gives me a slight elbow. He heard it too. Jill's mom could've stood anywhere to have this conversation, but she chose to be right in front of me. And I know she's seen me. She wants me to get angry, explode so that I can prove the point that she, Lydia's mom, Killian, and the dean have all thought but don't want to say directly—that I'm some angry thug who doesn't belong here.

They continue talking, but I only replay everything they've said to me these past months, the way they manipulate the phrase "diversity and inclusion," the hate the RNY Podcast spews, and all the biases the dean and Julia have used against me, the Black Culture Club, and Tammy. Undercover racism like this has left an invisible scar on each one of us. It can't go on like this.

"We need Augustin to get back to its core values, and that centers on how we build our community," she adds.

I look at my phone. It's almost a quarter to six. The program's gonna begin soon.

I text Janeil.

ME

u bring that video?

JANEIL

I did . . . Whyyy wussup??

> Can we switch it still?

> Uhh . . . maybe. Engineer just went to the bathroom. Can you cover the door.

The mezzanine is clearing out, quickly packing in the ballroom floor as if it's rush hour in the city. I press through the wave of guests still mingling or searching for their assigned table, then shuffle past the bar area and up to the production box.

Janeil sits at the control table. There are multiple monitors, a large mixing board, and other devices Rej would probably know better than me.

"How's it going?" My lungs heave from the adrenaline.

"Trying to download it off Google Drive now," she says. Her voice is as frantic as I feel. "Couldn't give me any more warning? You're lucky Dave didn't lock the computer." She must be referring to the engineer.

"Julia was at the RoboAugs booth," I say. "You should've heard her."

"Stop, I don't need to hear anything that comes outta her mouth." She flashes me an urgent look. "Aye, go cover the door."

"Gotchu," I say.

I could text Tammy, let her know we're making the switch, but after our conversation yesterday, I'm sure she'll try to talk me down. I head to the bottom of the stairs and quickly spot someone who may be in his late twenties, dressed in blue jeans, a black shirt, and a brown baseball cap that's covering up scraggly blond hair. He's got a headset on. Definitely not a guest.

"Hey, are you Dave?" I ask.

"Yeah," he says awkwardly. He tries to go around me to the stairs.

"I had a quick question," I say, while trying to come up with a lie. "Do you do internships?"

"Internships? What? Look, I have to get upstairs."

"It's just that I've always wanted to work in production," I say. "And I was told you were very knowledgeable."

"Well, maybe I can help you later, but the program is about to start," he says. "Maybe you can stop by the production box toward the end of the program."

"Hey, Dave, show's about to start," Janeil says. "Where you been?"

"Sorry," he says to me as he bounds upstairs. "See me later."

Janeil gives me the thumbs-up as he goes inside. It's done.

I search the room, moving toward the stage, looking for Tammy. I need to let her know.

"Gil." Ms. James stops me.

"Ms. James." I greet her with a handshake. "Glad you came out," I say. "Tonight's gonna be a big night."

She tilts her head at me. "The way you said that," she says, "like the anniversary isn't the big thing."

"Have you been keeping up with BlackAugustin?" I ask.

"Sadly, no," she replies. "It's on my plate, but it's been a busy news cycle. Hoping to dive deeper over Thanksgiving."

The ballroom lights start flashing.

"Please take your seats." Dave's voice comes over the speaker. "The program will begin in five minutes."

"Make sure you're facing the stage," I say. "The first video will be a little different."

"Okay, you've got me interested," she says. "And I would love to talk to you and the other members of the BCC about BlackAugustin after the holiday."

"That'd be great," I say. "I'm sure we'll have a lot to discuss after tonight. And keep an eye on table 5. That's where the administration is sitting." I shrug. "In case you have any questions."

As Ms. James walks away, I spot Dr. Gunther.

"Gil, right?" Dr. Gunther asks. I nod yes. She says, "I have to take my seat, but we should talk when there's a break in the program."

"Sure thing," I say. But I doubt I'll be staying that long. Who knows what she'll think after the video drops.

I text CJ.

ME:

Janeil's gonna run the video. Get ya phone ready to get everyone's reaction

CJ:

Serious?? Got u!

The crowd settles as the music cuts off, the lights dim. Tammy is at the corner of the stage with Killian. She's supposed to introduce him, but instead will give a speech on BlackAugustin. Neither of them know the original footage has been replaced.

Wine glasses stop clinking and everyone turns toward the screen. The video should start off with the president and the headmaster, then a mix of teachers, alumni, and business leaders talking about how great Augustin is, intercut with shots of student life and sports at Augustin.

That's what's supposed to be shown.

But instead, the *150 Years of Augustin* image fades. And a vertical video plays.

"Did I say you could talk?" Terry's voice comes out of the surround-sound speakers. The video of us that Heath took, my trauma projected onto a movie screen for all to see. "This is our school. I didn't give you permission."

Everything plays. Nothing is bleeped or edited. The audience hears the N-word and gasps. My eyes have adjusted to the dim light. I see Killian back away from the stage. Tammy searching . . . probably for me.

As the fight video comes to an end, the BlackAugustin art Janeil made is revealed. Snippets of articles are displayed, with me and Janeil alternating the narration. There's even a clip from Saleem, who wrote a new story with his face and name attached to the article. *"There's no safe space in the locker room,"* he says. *"Not when being Black is the punchline to every joke. It taints everything I do on the field."*

Everyone's asking questions. Wondering what's happening. Knowing that this isn't the video that's supposed to be playing. I look at my phone. Janeil's texting.

JANEIL

turns out Dave's a G. He's letting the video play.

That's an ally fareal fareal.

The last time I stepped in front of the Augustin parents, it was an accident. This time, I'm ready to walk onstage fully aware of what I'm about to do. But still unsure of what I'll say.

Someone jerks back my arm. I turn to see Dean Bradley gripping me tightly. His eyes cold.

"Let him go," a voice says so powerfully even I shiver. It's Ms. Willis, Augustin's only Black teacher. Standing next to her is Mr. Abato. The dean immediately releases his hold. I can't tell if Ms. Willis and Mr. Abato know what I'm about to do, but they're not stopping me. Tammy's at the opposite end. When I move toward the center, she walks away.

There are so many tables, filled with people. With the spotlight on me, I can't even see how far back they go from here. I tap the mic and the sound reverberates through the room. I look right at Julia. Her lips tighten.

"Over the past two months, this school has done everything to make me feel like I don't exist. Or that I shouldn't." My throat grows dry. I try to swallow but it feels like there's a rock lodged inside. "I remember when my dad took me to my first robotics tournament. I was still a kid. But seeing teens working together, building these amazing creations, it made me dream about doing the same.

"So when I got accepted to Augustin, to transfer here, I was so excited." My words are slow, evenly paced, but my voice cracks and my chest shudders, thinking of all the hopes I had. "I just wanted to learn. But I had to spend all my time fighting. And I'm not the only one. You've seen just a fraction of the stories. Aggressions. Microaggressions. Constant attempts to steal our humanity as Black students. As Black people."

I look from the dean to the parents and alumni. A few people avert their eyes. I don't know if it's shame or if they just don't care what I have to say. But I have to go on.

"Outside there's a sign that celebrates one hundred and fifty years of Augustin and says 'Welcome Home Tigers.' You talk of Diversity and Inclusion. You use our faces on your marketing and promotional materials. But do you really want us to feel at home here? Can you really say that when there's never a thought to the ongoing trauma or the lasting effect that these interactions have?" I point toward the screen, the BlackAugustin image still displayed. "Why is it so easy to look at us as if we don't exist or to make us feel invisible? And some of you see these racist actions. You hear your colleagues, peers, and family members spewing the hate but you only silently admonish them." I know Lydia's eyes are on me, but my words aren't only for her. These are feelings that I've been holding on to for too long. "Don't come to me and tell me how much they're wrong. I know. We all know. Call them out. And do it in public, let everyone know where you stand. 'Cause I don't care if you're a teacher, a parent, or a student, you can't sit back and say nothing. I mean, can you truly say you have remorse when you do? When it's so frequent? I just want to know."

It's so quiet in here. Are they waiting for me to say something else? Have I said enough?

"And don't worry," I add. "That full video is online now. Unedited. Augustin's truth." I back away. And walk off the stage.

Headmaster DeSantis takes my place in front of the podium. "Apologies, everyone," he says. "We're going to take a brief intermission and proceed with the dinner portion of our program."

I feel like I'm navigating through a dream. Ms. James has her phone in President Keene's face, using it as a camera, asking him questions. There's a man that must be Terry's father, yelling at him, maybe for calling me the N-word, or maybe for getting caught. Everyone's standing up talking. It's as loud as if I were standing in the middle of a waterfall. I see CJ running around, capturing the fallout. But I don't stop. I'm moving out of instinct toward the rear of the ballroom.

"Gil." Tammy's voice grabs me. "Why? We talked about this."

"A speech wasn't enough," I say.

"You didn't even warn me," she snaps. "Instead you leave me up onstage so that I look like a fool."

"That wasn't my intent," I say. "There just wasn't enough time. You didn't hear Julia."

"But there was enough time to switch the videos." It's not a question. Her arms are crossed. The way she's looking at me. She's hurt. "It must be that you didn't trust me because you didn't even tell me that you were coming."

"I dunno," I say. "Everything's been different between us. You've been pushing me away."

"You're not serious," she says. "Do you know how busy I've been this past month, not just college applications, but BlackAugustin?" She points at me so directly her hand could slice through me. "You might read the articles, help post them, or maybe you even encourage students to share their stories. But who do you think they come to when they need to figure it all out? Who do you think has to listen to all their trauma, take it all on, and help them work through it? Leylah, Janeil, Chijoke, and so many others, none of them were writing in a vacuum."

I never thought about it. That night when Lydia touched Janeil's hair, Tammy was there. I helped Chijoke with his first line, but when his story came back, it was so personal, he must've gone to Tammy for help. And how many other students did Tammy help to find their voice?

She helped me find mine.

"I give my time and myself to everyone, the same with you," she says. "Because that's who I am. But you're so wrapped up in whatever war's inside you, you couldn't even come to me with the truth. You made tonight all about you." The disappointment in her eyes, it stings. "I was wrong about you."

She turns her back to me and disappears inside the crowd.

38

grab my book bag and coat, then bust through the doors of the
Ziegfeld. Fifty-Fourth Street is lined with bumper-to-bumper
traffic. Cabs are fighting to overtake each other even though this
is a one-lane street.

It's over between me and Tammy. I shoulda said goodbye to
the others at least. But I can't be in there right now. *Is Tammy
right? Did I make this all about me?* I wasn't the only one involved.
But it was my plan. My push.

Right now, I just want to get back to Brooklyn, be with my
family. Celebrate Granma. She'll understand. It's like I just ran
a mile, my chest is so heavy.

This damn tie! I tug at it, trying to rip it off, but it fights back,
choking me. I take the loop from around my neck and stuff it
and the blazer in my bag, letting the evening chill hit me, soaking it in deeply.

"Aye, you good, son?" a familiar voice asks.

I meet Stretch with a vacant expression. "Whatchu doin here?" I ask.

"Damn, not even a wussup?" he asks. I check myself and give him a dap. The fading blue bruise around the corner of his eye shines too much on his light brown skin. I haven't seen him since the demo. I apologized after our show for the mistimed kick, but now I'm stuck looking at the consequences of my actions.

"My fault," I say. I walk so fast to Seventh Avenue, I might as well be running.

"I was over at Macy's in Herald tryna find a gift for Granma that wasn't just flowers, when I got the alert the full fight video dropped on BlackAugustin," he says, shaking his head with surprise. "Knew you was up here, so figured I'd meet you to make sure everything's good."

"I dunno," I say. We turn south toward the bright lights of Times Square. The streets are packed. We have to maneuver through the maze of tourists who either look lost or are snapping photos with their camera phones. "Tammy . . . was pissed."

"Phew." He sighs. "Y'all gonna be good?" That's Stretch— even though I wounded him, he's already moved on, worrying about me.

I shrug my shoulders and try not to look at the black eye on his face that looks like it's glaring at me.

"It's whatever, yo. Tonight's about Granma. What'd you end up getting her?"

"Nothing," Stretch moans as we get enter the 1-train station at Fiftieth Street. "I'll just get flowers. Can't say I didn't try, but picking out gifts puts my brain on overload."

The after-work crowd is pushing to get through the turn-stile and on the train. It's perfect since Stretch probably used his three swipes for the day. I swipe my MetroCard and Stretch follows right behind me on the same swipe.

We head to the platform, where the train is waiting. Then we switch at Forty-Second Street to the 2 train. It's also there. This never happens. But if the trains are running smoothly, I'll take the win. People jam inside. There's barely standing room left, but we manage to find some bar space to hold on to overhead.

"Please keep your belongings in sight," the subway recording starts.

"So you really not gonna talk about what happened, son?" Stretch asks over the announcement. I'm not sure if he means his eye or Augustin.

"I'm sorry," I say. "I shouldn't have done the demo that day. My mind wasn't in it."

He smiles without any hint of anger or resentment. "C'mon, I know it wasn't on purpose. I've taken worse in sparring." He tilts his head and says with a smirk, "And, aye, it's also been a conversation starter with the girls, so I should thank you." He laughs. I can't stand it. I almost wish he was mad and would yell at me. I'd take anything right now over this easygoing, grass-is-always-green perspective he has. When most people say "I'm good," they don't mean it. *I know I don't.* But Stretch is always fine. He's always walking around with a smile, without a single worry. "I'm talking about the gala."

"Why, so you can say 'stop stressin' or I need to relax and enjoy life?" The words come out like I'm upset with him. And I'm not. If there's one person I can't stand right now, it's me.

"C'mon, you know it's not even like that," Stretch says. He starts fidgeting. Gazing at the subway ads. "Stress is just not healthy," he says. "My dad's got heart disease, the doctor said stress was a big factor. I don't want it for him and I don't want it for us. So I try to just be as chill as I can so I don't break."

It takes a moment for the words to hit. And for the first time in a while, I really see Stretch. Has his smile been a mask all this time? How did I not notice? Rej couldn't have known either. We always thought Stretch's life was perfect compared to our situations. "I didn't know," I say. "Is he gonna be all right?"

Stretch's cool composure breaks. "We don't know if he has to get surgery yet." He wipes his brow, then drags his hand through his dyed curls. "Right now, it's just a lot of lifestyle changes," he says. "He has to adjust his work and sleep habits. His diet's been a big adjustment. It's why I always be eating by you and Rej's. Dad's basically vegan now. When a Caribbean can't have full-flavored food, it's rough."

Even now, Stretch can find the lighter side.

"I wish you told me," I say.

"You know how us Caribbeans be," Stretch says. "Secretive like our parents."

I shake my head as the train speeds downtown. At each stop, more people squeeze in, forcing their way inside a train that would burst from the overflow if it weren't made of metal. Trying to manage everything at school, I haven't been paying attention to my fam. It's like everything's a job. School. Family. Relationships.

The train screeches to a stop between Clark Street and Borough Hall. It jumps forward two paces, then stops again.

Then repeats the process three more times over what feels like ten minutes. Everyone starts to groan and hiss. They just want to get home.

The lights go out, the train's motor stops, and the cursing begins.

"Due to a police investigation at Atlantic Avenue—" the conductor begins to say. I can't hear what's said next, but I know the story. We're screwed. This train isn't going to move for at least another ten minutes. I'm gonna be late to help Granma get ready.

Ten minutes turns into twenty before the train resumes its crawl. Nothing's gone right today. Or maybe it has. I did what I set out to do. No. *We did*. It wasn't just me.

The train enters the Beverly Road stop. Me and Stretch dap into a hug.

"Ima see you over there," Stretch says, getting off.

"Aight, yo," I reply.

I start running the moment the doors open at Newkirk, rushing through the turnstile, taking two steps at a time till I hit the street. The artificial lights of pizzerias, smoke shops, and corner stores light up Little Haiti as I make my way to my building.

I don't even try the elevator when I get inside. It may have worked this morning, but I don't wait to see if it's out of service again. Leaping up four flights of stairs, my hamstrings tight, I'm reminded I need to get back to stretching. I open the door after fiddling with my key.

Granma is standing at the door when I enter.

"Weh yuh been, GC?" she asks. "I don't like being late." It's almost 8:00 p.m. Granma paces around on her bare feet, wearing the new embroidered floral dress that Ms. Pauline designed with a matching jacket that has a wide collar. She starts rummaging through the closet with the jitters she gets when she's confused. "Mi cyaan find mi hat, mi wrap."

"Granma, what is it?" I hold her by the shoulders, getting her to focus on me, and bring her over to the living room so that she can sit down. "Which head wrap do you want? I'll find it."

"Di plain white one with di gold trim. Nothing too fancy. I don't want it to distract from mi dress."

"All right, I'll go find it."

"And get mi a glass a watah," she says. "Mi tirsty bad."

I go into the kitchen and bring her the water first. Then head into her room to search for the head wrap. I check the second drawer of her dresser first. This isn't the first time I've had to help her get ready. And I can help her wrap her head if she needs it. I see every head wrap but the one she wants.

A tremor ripples down my leg. I reach for my phone and see Janeil calling. I tap ignore. My phone starts up again. I go to shut it off and see it's my mom.

"Hey," I answer.

"Gil!" Mom replies. I already know what she's going to say. "Where are you? The banquet is starting soon."

"We about to head out," I reply. "We'll just get a cab over to Bedford and Church."

Terrific. If this were any reggae concert, we'd still be two hours early. I shouldn't have tried to do both events. Maybe Tammy was right. Maybe I made tonight all about me. *But to see their faces.* I did it. I finally put them on blast. And Ms. James was there to see it. "You telling me it's actually starting on time?" I feel the tension in my voice. My sarcasm comes out as anger.

"Yes, Gil," Mom says. "I asked you to do one thing."

Here comes the guilt trip. "Yo, we gonna be right out. Just trying to find Granma's head wrap."

"It's in my room," she replies. "I left a message on your phone."

"Aight, I'm on it. Let me get off the phone so I can get outta here. I'll see you there." I hear her voice about to say something as I hang up. I look at my messages and notice I got multiple from Janeil and Mom. Nothing from Tammy.

The head wrap is folded neatly on my mom's bed. The tremor goes off again like an aftershock.

It's Janeil.

"Yo, I can't really talk now," I say.

"Gil," Janeil says, ignoring me. "You shoulda stuck around. The administration tried to play it off, but the video, your speech, they HIT. You shoulda seen them scrambling. They was strugglin tryna adjust the program. Couldn't do nothin to big up Augustin after we blew 'em up. Killian didn't even speak." Janeil busts out laughing. "CJ was capturing all of it on his phone. The reel's gonna kill."

"Oh word," I say. I wish I could enjoy this moment more. "Good." But what I'm feeling isn't joy. It isn't even a release. It's like a task that had to be done that may have cost me my relationship. *Maybe it was over already and this was the push it needed.*

"That reporter," Janeil says, trying to remember Ms. James's name. She keeps talking before I can answer. "What's her name? Anyway, she was lookin for you. Asked me some questions about what I wrote. It's gonna take em another hundred fifty years to forget this anniversary."

"What'd Tammy say?" I ask, sitting down on the bed, taking it all in.

The silence answers before she does. "Aye." She stumbles . . . "Don't worry. She gonna get over it. Like this couldn'ta went down better." She's trying to pick up my spirits, but the way Tammy spoke I don't think there's any going back. "Ms. Rashida," Janeil says, remembering her name. "That's her name. She was saying she gonna write this piece up."

We got what we wanted. But will Tammy forgive me for how I did it?

"Gil, you there?" Janeil asks.

"Yeah, I'm here."

"Look, this had to be done."

"Ima have to get the story from you tomorrow or something," I say. "I got this thing with my granma right now and I'm mad late already."

"Aight, aight, do ya thing."

I hang up and bring the wrap out. "Granma, got it."

The living room is empty.

"Granma?"

I check the kitchen, the bathroom, Mom's room, mine, crying out her name. My heart is ready to shatter along with every nerve in my body.

rush to the door. It's open. I dip my head over the banister, nothing. The elevator screeches behind me. I turn, hoping to see Granma.

A delivery person walks out.

"Did you see a woman when you came in?" I ask.

He looks at me like I'm crazy. "Who?"

"A woman, in a floral dress and jacket?"

"Four G," the person says, holding up a plastic bag with take-out, not understanding me.

I hear the buzzer go off back in my apartment. Maybe she went downstairs and got locked out. I run inside and press the intercom. "Granma?" I ask.

Static and the muffled voice of Rej comes back. "It's me, Gil. You looking for Granma?"

"Yeah, is she down there?" I ask back.

"Nah, man." I buzz him in. He sprints up the stairs, sensing the fear in my voice.

"What happened?" he asks, entering through the open door.

"I was getting her ready, and, and I dunno, she musta left."

"You tried calling her?" he asks.

I dial Granma's number and I hear her ringtone go off from her handbag on the sofa.

"Aye, she couldn't have gone far," Rej says.

"It's the dementia," I say. "She's not supposed to travel by herself. She gets confused."

"I gotchu. Lemme check the street."

I slam the door closed, dashing down the stairs, her pocketbook in hand, right behind Rej as if I'm escaping a burning building. We bust out the lobby door. I signal to the left. Rej takes the hint and storms away in that direction to search for Granma. I hurry to the opposite corner. The late-evening blasts of music and sirens overload my senses.

I don't see her anywhere.

I dart back to the front door. Rej is there. "She has no ID, no money, she couldn't have taken a cab," I say. I'm spitting out theories trying to figure out what to do, holding on to her head wrap and pocketbook, all I have of Granma.

"Calm down," Rej says. "We gonna find her. She probably went to the venue."

"Call Stretch," I say. "He was goin straight there. Maybe he can walk up Bedford to see if he sees her, I'll go up Nostrand."

"Got you, fam," he says.

"Stay here in case she comes back," I say.

"Done," he says without hesitation. "I'll call some folks, see if they can help out."

"I swear. If something happens."

"G." He looks me in the eye, steadying my quivering body. "We gonna find her. Push all that fear out ya head. Right here. This where you are. We got you. Let's go."

I give him the nod and take off, making the right on Nostrand, looking around like mad.

I pick up the phone and call Renee. "Renee, I need ya help," I say before she has a chance to speak.

"What is it, cuz?" she asks. "You supposed to be here."

"It's Granma," I say. "She left. I dunno where she is."

"Whaaa?" The question comes in a shout. I can hear my mom talking to her in the background as Renee relays the information. This is no time for secrets. I hear the *Lawd Jesus* cry from my mom.

I bypass the talking-to I know is coming. "Look, Rej is at the house, he callin Stretch to check Bedford. I'm going up Nostrand."

"I'll go down Rogers," Renee says. "And see if anyone else can help."

Other than storefront lighting, it's dark out. The streets aren't packed like Times Square. The only people out are those picking up takeout, getting last-minute groceries, or posting up outside the smoke shop. I check each store to see if Granma may have stopped inside.

Across the street, I see a floral dress between a bunch of dudes. The light is red, but there's a break in traffic, and the panic inside says go for it. I make my way through the cars like I'm a frog in one of those old video games my dad liked. A bus slams to a halt just in time to not hit me. I barely make eye contact with the driver to wave a weak apology. Curses fly at me from all directions.

I press into the middle of the group and an arm pulls me back. I come face-to-face with the person in the floral dress who is not wearing a floral dress at all but a shimmering outfit designed for a night of clubbing that's been reflecting the streetlights.

"Wuss ya problem, kid?" a man says. He's wearing a fedora, flashing a golden grill at me.

"Sorry," I say, panting. "I thought she was my granma."

"Granma?!" The woman in the shimmering dress steps back like I just picked a fight.

"No—no disrespect." I start stammering. "I lost my granma and—and—"

"Whadayu," another man, with wide studded sunglasses and a Grenadian accent, says. "Breath nuh bai."

"It's my granma," I say, inhaling deeply. "She has dementia and she wandered off. She was wearing a dress with flowers on it. The lights. Her outfit. I just thought . . ."

"It's good," the man with the fedora says. I'm immediately grateful that these were some OGs and not people my age. This woulda played out totally different.

"Wait deh," the man with the sunglasses says. "Ain't yuh Miss Bailey's chile?"

Ms. Bailey is Granma's maiden name. I perk up, hoping.

"Have you seen her?"

"No, but me auntie Pauline mek her dress," he says. "So me know who you talkin bout. Known her long time."

"If you see her—" I hesitate. I don't know this guy. Under

normal circumstances I wouldn't give out my number, but he says he's Pauline's nephew. He's Caribbean and an old head. I get enough spam calls these days that I figure everyone basically has it anyway, so might as well. "Could you please call me?"

"Of caarse," he says.

I give him my number. We slap palms and I keep it moving. By the time I get to Church Avenue, I figure she couldn't have gone this far. I've been moving at a fast pace. I open the group chat with Renee, Rej, and Stretch. No one's seen her. I text:

ME

at Church n Nostrand. Ima double back and
see if she went up a side street

I start going back down each block looking for any sign of Granma. Stopping at each cluster, hustlers on the corner or people just kicking it on a stoop, I ask if anyone's seen her, flashing the picture I have on my cell. The night chill doesn't do much to stop the sweat stinging my eyes. My cell gives me the 10 percent battery warning.

Several ambulances speed past me east on Tilden toward Holy Cross Cemetery. My heart drops. I follow the flashing lights like I'm in a trance. Then I chase after them. They pull over on the corner of New York Avenue. There's been an accident. A car must have run off the road. The police are pushing people back. I stop at the outskirts of the crowd and force my way forward, knowing that there is no forgiveness for me. No salvation. Two months lost to these battles at Augustin that's just cost me everything. I can feel the tears struggling to break free.

It looks like there is a body on the ground. My heart pounds so hard it feels like I'm being punched. I see a bike mangled in the distance with a food delivery satchel in the opposite direction.

I can finally make out the body. A deliveryman lies on the street, his body contorted and broken.

Wiping my eyes, I fall back, fighting, always fighting, prying myself free from the crowd. A cold hand grips my palm.

"Ahmad," a friendly voice says.

I can't believe it. I see the floral dress, the loose strands of gray hair, and that full face that's always been there to comfort me my whole life.

"Granma." I break down, burying my head into her shoulder, wrapping my arms around her, never letting go.

40

The night's a disaster," Mom says on the phone. "I received her award and will see you at home soon."

The shade strikes hard. I deserve it. Granma's resting on the couch, still wearing the dress she had custom-made just for tonight. Rej and Stretch sit next to her. All those years working in education led to this evening that was supposed to be about her, not me. This was *her evening* to take the stage, shine at the fundraiser, be recognized by her community and her family. She should've had the chance to enjoy it all while her mind is still present, even though her son isn't. And I ruined it.

"Hey, bighead," Renee says, entering the apartment, seeing the worry scrawled on my face. "Tighten up. Granma's safe. Everything's gonna be okay."

"But what if she wasn't?"

"Don't think like that," she says.

"Why not?" I reply, not able to hold back. "Everyone else is thinking it."

"Can't concern yourself with everyone else," she says. "You gonna age yourself way quick if you keep doing that. Life's short. Gotta keep moving."

She's trying to do the big-sis thing she always does. I'm not feeling it. All I can think about is the worst. That moment with the ambulances. "She could have died." My inside voice leaks out. "There was an accident. This delivery dude and some cars." My lips shiver. "It wasn't Granma in the street, but that's who I saw. Her lying there. Mangled. And it woulda been my fault."

Renee wraps her arm around my back. "What's going on with Granma, that ain't ya fault."

But what could have happened is. I don't need any positive spin or pep talk. All this focus on school and Augustin. I shoulda been home with my family. Renee leaves me be in the kitchen, staring at the stove where Granma had set a fire just weeks after I started school.

This stove. This was the sign. I should've been home more. Not diving deeper into this war with Augustin. What'd that gain me?

Tammy was right. Maybe I did expose the truth just for my sake. I showed them up, only to ignore everyone else. Her. My family. Rej and Stretch always been there, gas'n me up, even if I haven't been there for them recently. One day my family's all together, the next Granma's fading, Dad's gone. And I don't know what's happened to me. It's only been a short time. But I really did leave Brooklyn behind. From now on, I just want to hold on to every moment and make them count.

I feel a hand rest on my shoulder.

"Gilbert Clifford Powell," Mom says. "You had one responsibility tonight. One thing you needed to do." Her eyes aren't filled with anger, only disappointment. Maybe it's a good thing Dad's not here right now. It would crush me to see them both look at me like this.

"I know," I say, defeated.

"If you're not able to help out 'cause you had things that were more important, you needed to let me know," she says. There's nothing more important than my family. But I lost track of that. "I could've checked with Mr. and Mrs. Neckles, seen if they were able to help out. Renee could've helped."

Nothing I say can make up for what might've happened. Maybe I should argue and blame it on the train delay. But I didn't need to be at the gala tonight. I knew I'd be cutting it close by trying to do both events, juggling my life in the city and in Brooklyn. Why didn't I let Tammy handle it her way? I keep redrawing the day, the week, replaying every outcome, and at each turn it comes back to the choices I made. I wanted to get in front of everyone. Terry. The dean. The parents. Lydia. Mr. Abato. I needed to be in the room that Augustin built and watch their expressions as the lie they had been telling themselves was revealed for what it was. Maybe I even needed to be the reason that the media covered BlackAugustin. It was a victory—that could've cost me everything.

I GO TO my room after everyone leaves. I didn't say much to anyone. There wasn't much to say. The night's ruin is on me. I stare at Sensei's copy of Sun Tzu. So many ways to look at war. So many variables. All of which can end in defeat. All I see is that mangled bike now. Granma's body.

Tap. Tap. Tap.

"Come in," I say softly.

Granma enters the room and takes a seat on my bed. I sit up, resting my back against the wall. The tension inside me ready to snap. I hold it back. My body trembles.

"I know dese past few years haven't been easy," Granma says. "An everyting at di new school. I juss want yuh to know dat Granma will always be dere fi yuh."

And that could've ended tonight because of me. *Say that. Just say it.* "I was supposed to be there for you," I mutter. "You been there for me my whole life. Everything I am is because of you. And I almost lost you today." My teeth chatter, the tidal wave building inside for months ready to burst past the levee I've built up.

"But you cyaan juss live fi me," she says. "Yuh haffi live your life. Dat, yuh see, is my award." She emphasizes each word. "That yuh have di chances dat I didn't. Dat yuh father didn't."

"What chances?" I say. "I been pushing hard for no reason at this school. Obsessed with keeping my scholarship when they're not gonna change. Racism isn't going away. What's the point? I don't wanna be like Mr. Neckles. Switching up who I am just to fit in. Just to be accepted. I don't got it in me to censor myself and play that game of respectability politics.

"And I tried to play by their rules. Use strategy. But they been at it for so long, nothing I can do could battle it." I look at her. Waiting for her to offer an answer. Solve the unsolvable. But she just looks at me. Listening. No answer. No quick fix. Just Granma.

"I put it all out there tonight," I continue. Each word comes out more feverish than the last. I tell Granma that Tammy said showing the video would pull the attention off of Black Augustin and the BCC and put it solely on me. I wish me and Tammy had found a middle ground. I don't know if I'm explaining it to Granma or myself. But I can't stop. Because she hears me. She's always heard me and seen me. "I don't want to look back and have regrets."

I think of that conversation with Dad the night of the fire. He was so happy to finally be recognized for his talent in coding and get paid what he's worth. That's part of what I wanted, right? I felt like I lost my worth coming to Augustin. I was fighting for people to believe me, people who because of their biases may never believe me, just like that family Chijoke talked about in his piece.

"Dad said he doesn't have regrets, but that's why he really left, isn't it? The regrets? Not being able to live up to his potential because of the way America is? Working every day and still not be considered American 'cause of some papers." Is this about me or about Dad? Granma clenches my hand tightly.

"I don't know how to deal with this," I say. It's all a jumble. So many conflicting thoughts, struggling to be heard. "There's times when you're right in front of me, looking me right in my eyes, but I know you're not there. When I couldn't find you . . . saw the ambulances . . . the body that got hit . . . everything ended." It pours out through gulping breaths. Every thought that I've had since I started the new school breaking free. "I've been trying to figure out who I am. And I can't always go to you 'cause I know that's more stress. I have to go through every day, knowing that you're not going to get better. You call me by Uncle Ahmad's name sometimes and I know there's gonna be a point when you forget my name completely. Nobody has my back like you."

She locks eyes with me. I know she's here, present. But at any moment, her mind could wander off. Even now, she should be resting. But she's here, sacrificing sleep and her health, to sit with me. My shoulders collapse. She draws me in. The tears finally flow.

I don't know how much time passes. But I feel the release. Like I'm not holding anything back.

Granma embraces me. "Yuh need to talk to yuh father," she says. "Di struggle yuh face is juss like him." She shakes her head. "Mi neva wanted it fi unnu. But it deh. Dis kinda ting. Battles. Racism. All a di ting that come from bigotry. It's not unnu fault." But sometimes that's how I feel. "It exist long before you or I even born. An while we haffi fight, yuh cyaan mek yuhself suffa. Yuh need balance. Me see yuh read di Sun Tzu, but dis kinda balance yuh cyaan find inna no book." She sticks her finger into my chest, right at my heart space. "Yuh haffi find it right deh suh."

"I really messed up tonight," I say. "Should've been here with you."

"Stop dat," she says. "Don't mek it about me. Dis is your life. Don't get me wrong. I hate coming out a one a dese spells I have, not knowing where I am. Or not knowing a name. It's like my thoughts, my memories, everyting I love juss fading away. Like mi body betrayin me." She pauses, rests her hand on my cheek, her thumb brushing away a tear. "But di only thing that gives mi joy is knowin dat even though my memories may disappear, your memories won't fade of me. Dat you are still fighting every fight, gives me reason to fight. Don't eva back down. From any ting. And I promise yuh, I will do whateva I can to not back down from dis disease. But yuh muss be true to yuh self. And I pray Lawd Jesus give me the strength to fight dis ting as long as I can so I can see all di great tings you do. Yuh understand?"

"Yeah, Granma," I say. "I think I finally do." I wrap my arms around her and let the day fade away.

41

G il, check on the turkey and baste it."

"Aight, Mom," I say. It's just after 1:00 p.m. on Saturday. We're prepping food for the Always Persevere Dojo's annual Thanksgiving get-together, which starts in a few hours. Sensei is out of town next week, so the dojo moved it to a week earlier. It'll be good to give Sensei back his copy of Sun Tzu.

Thankfully, Augustin was closed Friday for Veterans Day, so I didn't have to be around any of the students or faculty. But I did get an email from the dean's assistant asking me to come in for a meeting with the president and Board of Trustees first period Monday. I don't know how that'll go, but I'm ready for whatever they throw at me. Then, between Janeil blowin up my text messages and Ms. James calling for a quote, I decided to silence all alerts on my phone. I just needed to unplug. Get back to what matters.

Family.

We spent Friday night baking sweet potato pies and watching *The Matrix*. It just felt right. Afterward, I went through Dad's record collection playing different reggae albums so that Granma could dance. She didn't get the tribute she wanted, that she deserved, but she doesn't stop finding moments to celebrate.

"Why didn't we make oxtail or curry goat?" I groan. "We don't even like eating the turkey on *actual* Thanksgiving. All we ever do is put the gravy from the curry goat on top of a piece a turkey and wonder why we cluttered up the plate with the turkey in the first place."

"Gil, do you know how much oxtail costs now that white people like it?" Renee says. It's a lot. Anytime there's a conversation about inflation, two things come up in this neighborhood: gas and oxtail.

"All I'm saying is oxtail beats turkey," I say.

"Oh hush," Mom says. "Your friends will be able to take some home and make turkey sandwiches."

"Better be careful what you say, Auntie," Renee says. "Gil may find a stage to get up on and tell everybody that we the only Jamaicans that actually like turkey on Thanksgiving. It'll be all over the news." This is Renee's way of keeping the mood light and off of what happened with Granma.

"Well, me happy yuh stand up fi yuhself, GC," Granma says.

I didn't know what to expect after the gala. But the reel CJ put together captured it all, especially the administration's panic. Ms. James wrote an article for *The Root* on private school education, highlighting Augustin, sharing the gram page and all the other social sites. Last I checked, we had over ten thousand followers. Then the *New York Times* messaged the BlackAugustin account, followed by *The Atlantic* and the *Washington Post*. I should be excited. But of all the fears I had, the one fear I didn't realize was losing the friendships I made at Augustin. And everyone's trying to hit me except the one person I want.

Tammy.

She hasn't responded to my texts or voice messages. I should've stopped after the first try, but I rambled on so long that the voice mail got cut off and was sent. So I called back and tried to clean it up with another message. Both were probably bad choices.

"What time are the Neckles coming over?" I ask Mom.

"Should be in an hour," she replies. "I told them three. Everything should be ready soon so we'll have time to pack up and get to the dojo by five."

So I got an hour before the convo turns into a tell-all on my time at Augustin. "Ima go call Dad before everyone arrives," I say. I give Mom a hug before I leave the kitchen and kiss her on the cheek. I've missed her hugs, there haven't been many over the past year.

I head to my room and sit at my desk. My notebook is open to a story I've been working on for BlackAugustin about my probation. I close it, then hit Dad on WhatsApp.

"Gil." He answers on the first ring.

"Hey, Dad," I say. I've been practicing this conversation several times in my head over the past month. But I can't push it off any longer.

"How you holdin up?" he asks.

"Just waiting to see if I get suspended again or booted from Augustin," I say, forgetting any preplanned script I had in mind.

We don't really talk about what's going on inside. He may quote something from a song or poem, but rarely how he's feeling. I'm probably the same. But after everything, I think that's the one thing I can't hold back. "I'm supposed to have a meeting at school on Monday. I'm sure Granma or Mom told you about Tammy 'cause there's no secrets around here, but pretty sure me and her are done done. Not that we was a couple. But there was a time when I thought we was getting there. But, hey, the *New York Times* is trying to talk to me. So you know. Same ol.'"

"So yuh sayin, yuh been busy," he says.

"Pretty much," I respond. I point over at the dresser, angling the camera so he can see my first robot. "You know, I still remember when we put that together. That excitement of building. You coaching me along the way. I missed that these past months." Getting caught up in Augustin, I never realized that the last time my whole family might be together is already in my rearview. "You was always talking about the future, projects you were working on, but never the future here. Felt like you didn't want to come back."

The sigh he lets out makes me think that's exactly what it is. Did it change while he was there or was that always his plan? "That's not it," he says. "The way I came into di country . . . I was only a teenager. It was so hard to see opportunity anywhere. I watched my brother die. Then I didn't have a visa, so I wasn't able to attend a college like Shareef . . . or work in di same capacity." He lets go the filter, finally showing his struggle. "Yuh know I felt lost. If it wasn't for your mother . . ." He shakes his head, searching for a lost puzzle piece. "And then you. I don't know where I would be."

"Then why has it taken you so long to come back?" I say, more as an accusation.

"When I was coming back to Jamaica, di only ting on my mind was getting di visa and returning straight to you. But then I started meeting people and getting actual opportunities." He sucks his teeth, upset at whatever it is he's about to say next. "Doing dem pickup jobs in di States, I couldn't make any real money that could help your mother with di tuition. I always wanted you to have di opportunities I didn't. Sending money home made me feel like I was doing my part, contributing to your future." He bites his lip before continuing as if he's trying to build up the courage to say a truth he's been hiding inside. "But I also wanted you to be proud of me too. In America, I was never able to succeed at one of my projects. So I always felt that you might look at me as a failure. I wanted you to believe in me."

"I've always believed in you." My face is so tense, I don't know if the words actually came out. I rub my eye. He's never talked to me like this. I lean back in my chair, my palms pressing into my tapered fro.

"Yuh don't know how much it pained me to be away from you. There was never a moment where I haven't wanted to come right back to my family. I just needed you to know that I could do it. That I can succeed. Something I could never do there."

My eyes squeeze shut. When they open, I say, "I wish we talked more like this. Not knowing how you felt, or what was going on with you. I just felt so alone."

"I'm sorry, son," he says. "Yuh haffi know that wasn't my intention."

"You know I tried to do it all," I say. "Family, school, work in robotics. But I couldn't keep up. I wanted to be there for everybody, for myself."

"You have choices. That is what your mother and I wanted for you. But yuh cyaan control it all and some tings yuh juss haffi ease up on. If robotics is yuh ting, yuh may juss haffi take a break from martial arts. Yuh friends will understand. But you have to tell dem that. Juss like I should've told you all a dat."

Hearing him say all this lifts the rock that's been pressing against my chest these past months. Always feeling like I have to do everything at a thousand percent. Like there's no room for error. Even picking up Sun Tzu. Everything became binary, life and death. "What do I do if they kick me out?" I ask.

"Yuh find another path," he says. "There's never just one way. I never gave up on my dream, but I knew I couldn't do it then. My priority was my family. And you have to decide on what your priority is. Everyting cyaan be top of the list all di time. And sometimes yuh haffi step away juss fi come back and analyze di problem from a different angle. Juss don't hold on to di stress. It won't stop eat at yuh."

"And Tammy?" I ask.

"Well, dat's not an option." He laughs. "From what yuh Granma tell me di gyal real nice eee. So yuh betta go an check her."

It's the first time I've laughed with Dad on the phone in I don't know how long.

"Thanks, Dad."

42

I got no expectations.

For the first time I'm walking through Augustin's entrance and I'm not anxious. I'm not worried about who my friends are or thinking that this is my only chance. If robotics doesn't happen for me here, I'll find another way. I already proved what I can do at the competition. And I posted my piece about the probation on BlackAugustin. The truth is out there.

When Sun Tzu talked of terrains for battle, I only thought about what that meant inside these walls. But being Black in Augustin or Black in America are both the same. Dad went back to Jamaica when New York wasn't working out for him because companies wouldn't give him a shot as an undocumented immigrant. So he changed the terrain. He never quit. I won't either.

Heath walks by. He doesn't say anything to me. I don't say nothing to him. So it goes.

"What's up, Gil," Janeil and CJ greet me on the way to my locker.

"Sup yo," I respond. "Just saw Heath." I shrug.

"Whatever with him," Janeil says. "You know how good I been feeling after Thursday? They talking 'bout the dean might be replaced. I ain't even code switching round these fools no more. Three years avoiding bein myself around everybody. Pssht. Was killin me."

"How you doin though?" CJ asks. "Know you got that meeting with the president."

"Yeah," I say. "Just me and a bunch of people who want to decide on my future." I didn't really think too much about it when I got the email Friday. But it's not just the president I'm supposed to meet with, it's the Board of Trustees as well. Guess they're taking time off from their workdays to give me the business. Maybe they want to boot me in person before I have a chance to do anything else to the school. At least it's just me. Nobody else has to go down. I'll take the blame for it all. "First period like I'm going on trial."

"Let me know if you want me to go with you," Janeil says.

"Nah, it's good," I say. "I got this."

"Aye, I forgot to tell you," Janeil says. "Lydia apologized at the gala after you left. Like really apologized for her ignorance." She crosses her heart. "Her words not mine."

"Oh word?" I say.

"Yeah, it felt . . . I dunno . . . honest," Janeil says. "She even went off on her moms and Killian. It was kinda dope."

"Maybe she is a real one," I say. "I better go."

"Aight," Janeil says. "We'll walk you over there."

We head toward the school's business offices through the Legacy Wing. The dim lighting even in the daytime adds to the hallway's moodiness. All those portraits from Augustin's Hall of Fame still glaring at us. It's the same place me and Tammy stood when we first kissed. I try to remember the taste of her lips. But the memory fails me.

When we make the turn toward the business offices, the hallway opens up. The light is bright and instead of old wooden doors, there are glass-walled rooms. No real personality, just white and shades of gray with the occasional art piece or accent furniture that some designer added in to make it appear less businesslike. I haven't been over here since that meeting where I was put on probation.

Tammy's sitting outside. Did they call her in too?

"Aye, CJ, let's go," Janeil says, reading the situation. They wave to Tammy, then say bye to me.

"Hey, Tam," I say, sitting down.

"Hey," she replies. From the moment we first met, it was always so natural to talk to her. The energy she had, pulling me out of Terry's path, clowning me in the cafeteria. Even writing that article, I poured so much of myself into that first piece just because she was the editor. Probably wouldn't have done that for anyone else. If I'm being honest, I also wanted to impress her. This silence is sour to my whole system.

I turn around to look in the conference room. It's a mix of corporate casual and full suits. Most of the faces I don't recognize, but I see Ms. Willis inside and President Keene in mid-conversation. No dean. No headmaster.

"When I first got here, you pulled me away from Terry 'cause you knew what would happen," I say. "You'd been here. Doin the work. Seen how things played out. You created spaces so that people like me could have the option to write how we felt. I got caught up in that. The need to be heard. Me alone."

The uncertain look she gives me lets me know just how broken things are between us. "BlackAugustin. A big part of it was about trust," she says. "And despite our conversation about your plan, that night at the gala, it felt like you went behind my back, chose to do what you wanted to do anyway. It was like you were lying to me."

"And Ima have to live with that," I say.

"You were probably right," Tammy says. She considers her words and maybe for a moment I sense the wall she's put up coming down. "The commotion that video caused, it did get everyone's attention."

"None of that matters," I say. "I just want you to know that I'm sorry. I'll take the blame for anything that happens in there. I know that doesn't fix anything. But know that this, you and me, losing what we coulda been, even if I get kicked out, that's been the biggest loss. Because school, robotics, BlackAugustin, nothing matters more than relationships."

The door to the conference room opens up and Ms. Willis steps out. "Come inside," she says.

President Keene motions for us to take a seat. Outside of the gala, I think this is the closest I've ever been to him. These are the specters behind all the academics and politics at Augustin, directing the school's finances and image from afar. Me and Tammy look at the open chairs, then at each other.

"We'll stand," she says.

I can't read President Keene's expression. His hands are folded together on the conference table. His thumbs are tapping away at each other.

"As you can imagine, we've had a lot to discuss since the stunt you pulled at our anniversary gala," President Keene says. "We've been flooded with calls from the media, parents, alum . . ."

"It wasn't a stunt," I say plainly. "You still don't get it. That coded language you use. It was the only way to be heard. To show that the opportunities given to the white students here don't apply to the students of color. But now you're listening because the media is listening and the public is talking. I just want you to know that it was me and me alone who was responsible for the video. Tammy, the other Black students, don't put any of this on them."

Tammy rests her hand on mine. It's the first time I've felt her touch since . . . I don't know. Outside the glass wall, I see CJ and Janeil. I'm not sure when they came back, but they're skipping first period and they've brought Saleem and Leylah.

"There's nothing for you to put on us that this school hasn't done already," she says to the board. "The problem here is that these stories were never heard before . . . never listened to." Her grip tightens around my hand. "There was a time I worried about the repercussions. Not saying things bluntly because it might hurt my chances to get into college. This administration made that clear when you stole my position as editor. That's what you did. You stole my dignity and my work. And you did this every day to every one of us because you were okay with it happening. The dean gaslit me and made me think that I had done something wrong by giving a student a platform to share objective opinions . . ."

"We aren't just a cause," I say. I grip Tammy's hand tighter, feeling the warmth, her strength. "For you to use in your public relations push."

"I understand where you're coming from—" President Keene starts to say.

"No you don't," I say, not as a snap, but just as a fact.

"And that's the point," Tammy tags in. "Whenever you respond to any student of color, whether it's to a question or in a disciplinary situation, you base that response off of assumptions. You never have a conversation with us and try to understand our perspective. By doing that we're silenced."

Is this what Tammy was going to say in her speech? Maybe I'll never know.

There are more members of the BCC outside now, including Chijoke. And they're not alone. Members of the AAPI Club and Latinx Club are with them. They're watching us, their presence giving us strength.

"The dean represents Augustin in its interactions with students. But if you talk to any student of color who has interacted with him, they will have a story of his conscious or implicit biases. The Parents' Committee, which has less than five percent representation of people of color, has a huge say in student affairs. That group also represents Augustin. But when the head of that committee, Ms. Davenport, went to the media to slander students . . . what did the school do? Nothing."

Tammy points out the glass wall. The hallway is packed now. I can't count how many students are outside, but they've all cut class, including Lydia, to be here. Tammy organized this. "Whatever happens to Gil, happens to me, happens to all of us."

President Keene leans in as if to speak, but is cut off by a member of the board wearing a gray suit. Judging by the way Keene closed his mouth and backed off, she's someone important on this board. "I don't think any of us really understand where you're coming from," she says. "But I think our goal moving forward is to try. We've appointed Ms. Willis as the acting dean. That's just one of the steps we're taking as we move forward. We want a clear and open dialogue with all of our students of color. And we know we have a long way to go. This meeting wasn't called to reprimand you." She says the words, but I wonder if the media didn't pick up this story, if we didn't go big, if this would be their same tune. I doubt it. "It was called to let you know that we want to work with you to improve Augustin."

"Appreciate the words," I say. "But I'll wait to see the action."

"The BlackAugustin stories will continue to be shared," Tammy adds.

Tammy lets go of my hand as we walk out.

"This doesn't mean I've forgiven you," she says just for me to hear.

Students swarm around us before I have the chance to respond, breaking us apart. I lose sight of her in the barrage of questions.

What happened?

Did you get suspended again?

This protest doesn't need to stop here.

I give out quick answers, only half paying attention. I'm standing on my toes, looking left, looking right, trying to peek over the multitude of students. I'm still surprised so many cut class. That's when I see her blue frames turning toward the staircase. Janeil and a few others are around her.

I cut through the pack as quickly as I can, saying "my fault" each time I step on someone's foot. I push through the doors to see Tammy and my friends, waiting for me.

"Aight, let's give them their space . . . again," Janeil jokes. "We'll stand on the other side of the door, so you can talk."

We're alone. She measures me as I cautiously step closer, neither of us certain of what to do or say. The silence doesn't feel uncomfortable, but actually feels right, like the moment when you first open your eyes after a much-needed sleep.

"I wonder how many students or alum can say they told off the Board of Trustees," she says.

I'm close enough that I can smell the coconut wash from her hair. She hasn't backed away. I reach out for her right hand first, feeling the smooth skin in my hand. Our eyes meet. Then I hold onto her left hand.

The slightest fraction of her lip curls up. "So you gonna kiss me, Brooklyn?" She asks.

I press my lips against hers, and let everything else fade away.

43

It's a little after 1:00 a.m. on a Friday, and I'm strolling along the Brooklyn Bridge walkway with Stretch and Rej. It's the holiday break and we just spent the night partying with my cousin and her college friends by NYU. Then we went to some private after spot that wasn't carding on Reade Street in the Financial District. Artists be knowing all the hidden joints. Plus, it was a way to celebrate my birthday.

I'm eighteen.

It's cold. Not like fully zipped-up, scarf-, hat-, and gloves-on cold, but I got the hoodie on under my jacket and some fingerless gloves Renee's girlfriend gave me. The 4 train wasn't running, so Stretch had the idea to walk across the bridge. And we listened.

A knitted tapestry of suspension cables, peppered with Ben Franklin–esque streetlamps, guide us across. One World Trade

Center shines brightly. Across the water is the Manhattan Bridge, illuminated like an arc of Christmas tree lights strung in the air.

There is no one out on the bridge tonight. It's just us as we look out toward Brooklyn. The lights from high-rises that have popped up from Tillary to Atlantic Avenue pale in comparison to the city. They don't capture the culture, the people that made Brooklyn Brooklyn. The real light of my borough.

"So you really a full-on Tiger now?" Stretch asks.

"Whatever yo," I say in my defense. "I'm just me. Call me a Tiger, call me Brooklyn. I'm just me. The terrain may change, but Ima still be about one thing. My people."

"Cool about those internships though," Stretch says.

"Yeah, still haven't decided between Boston Dynamics and working with Dr. Gunther," I say. "Just kinda happy Mr. Abato made things right."

"I mean . . ." Rej gets ready to pontificate, massaging his palms together with the squinted eye. "Gil did give Augustin more notoriety. He's in the news. Basically a celebrity now, more followers than me," Rej says. "How could they not put you on."

We post up on a bench.

"It's kinda cool to see things start to change over there. I know they just replaced the dean, but it feels like a shift. And without this battle it wouldn'ta happened."

"I feel that," Rej says.

"I don't know what to expect next semester. How things are gonna play out with the students. I know Ms. Willis is only one person and the school is still the school. They can flip everything at any second. I just want to be honest with myself about my time. I can't be everywhere for everyone. And I have to be upfront and tell people that."

"Say less," Rej says. "You know we got ya back."

"That goes for all of us," I say. "We been friends for so long, we got to be upfront with each other." I tap Stretch. We've had a lot of conversations since he told me about his dad's heart condition. "I know you smile and laugh off everything, but let us in, especially when it has to do with your fam."

"Understood," he says.

"I know things went sideways," Rej says. "But we here, even if it's just to talk." We look out at the East River. "Don't stop fighting though," Rej says to me.

"Never," I say.

And I won't. Going to Augustin wasn't just about being in a robotics program. It was a reminder. The world is bigger than Augustin. And there's always gonna be another fight. A new terrain. New players. And obstacles lurking in every corner. I just want to be a part of the shift and not get lost in it.

But for now, I got my friends and a girlfriend in Harlem. And they got me.

True. True.

Acknowledgments

There's a part of me in this book. The most important part is the love I have for my family and friends, my heritage, the neighborhood that raised me, and the culture that inspires me every day. So I have a lot of appreciation for the people—some of whom are no longer with me except in spirit—who have been there to keep me breathing and smiling through the pitfalls.

First, I have to thank my parents. Thank you for all your sacrifice and love. They made books the center of my life. If my library didn't have a book, my dad would find one that did. My mom shared my love of stories, and we'd sit down and talk about our favorite characters. Helen, Rich, and Jonathan, the mighty three, thank you for your guidance, support, and strength.

Granma Iris, Granma Claris, Aunt Lena, Aunt Thelma, and Aunt Daisy, I always feel your presence shining down on me.

Big up to Uncle Jeff and Dianah for leading the way, and to

Lori-Ann for putting me on to my first operetta, which made me think, *Maybe I like the arts more than science.* And Aunt Elaine, your wisdom and perspective were always welcomed and needed.

To my nieces and nephews: Aiden, Anni, and Avery, you can't read this book for many years, but know that I love you. And Bree, your calls and FaceTimes throughout the time writing this book kept me in high spirits when I was in a rough place.

Thank you to every person and instructor I trained in martial arts with since third grade. Special thanks to NY Budo, which taught me that perseverance works.

Doc Caesar and the African American Culture Club, y'all know I'd be lost without you. Special love to my big brothers in HS: Geoff, Malik, Kwame, Brian, and Jose. You gave me more than a key to an office, you showed me what work and discipline meant. And thank you to Mr. Foley, my philosophy teacher extraordinaire.

Much thanks to Stacey Barney, a brilliant editor and amazing person, who saw potential in this writer and signed me to Penguin. I still remember your enthusiasm on our first call. I'm so grateful for all your input and direction in helping this book come together. I couldn't have done it without you. Your encouragement and motivation kept me going through those tight turnarounds. Whether it was at 10:00 p.m. or you were across the ocean, you always carved out time to help me grow as a writer.

Thank you to Lanie Davis and Joelle Hobeika, who read my zombie satire and said, "Hey, Don needs to write a book." Thanks for pushing me throughout the publishing process and for your guidance. Thank you to Josh, Sara, and the Alloy team for championing this book.

Thank you to Nancy Paulsen and everyone at Penguin Teen and Nancy Paulsen Books. Caitlin Tutterow, thank you for educating this confused soul in the ways of the PDF and the first pass. Big thanks to Cindy Howle and Ariela Rudy Zaltzman for all your excellent notes during the copyediting and proofreading process. Thank you to Lathea Mondesir, Chandra Wohleber, and Ronni Davis for your help throughout the production and promotion of this book.

Big up and respect to Billie J for this cover—it's straight fire. Thank you to Theresa Evangelista for the wonderful design. And thanks to Felicity Vallence and Shannon Spann for helping with the cover reveal.

Much love to Danielle Paige for all your encouragement and phone calls. You've helped me so much and I'm eternally grateful. Thank you to Cristine Chambers for being the voice of reason when I'm in panic mode. Thank you to Chris Huggins, my first friend in life, who always picks up the phone to listen to my stories.

Thank you to Syndia and Oseye for helping me with the language passes.

All love to the Wingz crew: so many adventures behind us and so many ahead, your families are my family. Larry, thanks for making sure I didn't get hit by the bus that day I walked out the bookstore with a marble notebook after the CSE 261 test. That day would change my life. Dan, thanks for never doubting me.

Much love to Tarik Davis, LeMar McLean, Amy Archibeque, Eddie Shieh, and Eric Hutchison. Thanks for letting me lean on you. Gotcha back.

Thank you to Rashida Olayiwola for always checking in on me and making sure I took a moment to give myself grace while I was writing. We got stories to tell. Thank you to Sean Bell, you already know: team bfocus for life.

Thank you to my cousin Sean, who made sure I not only didn't quit but that I couldn't. Big up to my cousin Carrie-Ann for always listening to me and hooking me up with resources when I left corporate.

And to all my aunts, uncles, cousins, and extended family and friends, I am so blessed to have had you in my life.

Thank you to Mark Guest, and big up to the Master's Club Martial Arts. Special thanks to Lewis Lashley and Eric Smith.

Big up to Kwame Mbalia and the *Black Boy Joy* fam. Love y'all.

Much love to all the teens who find themselves in difficult situations and struggle to find a voice. You are seen and you deserve to be heard.

Thank you to all those who embrace empathy and take time to listen.

Finally, to Brooklyn . . . to Jamaica . . . to every Caribbean at home and abroad . . . to the ancestors . . . much love. My village is strong.